THE BLOOD CURSE

SPELL WEAVER: BOOK 3

ANNETTE MARIE

dark owl
fantasy

Dark Owl Fantasy Inc.
PO Box 88106, Rabbit Hill Post Office
Edmonton, AB, Canada T6R 0M5
www.darkowlfantasy.com

Cover Copyright © 2018 by Annette Ahner
Cover and Book Interior by Midnight Whimsy Designs
www.midnightwhimsydesigns.com

Editing by Elizabeth Darkley
arrowheadediting.wordpress.com

ISBN 978-1-988153-20-9

BOOKS BY ANNETTE MARIE

STEEL & STONE UNIVERSE

Steel & Stone Series
Chase the Dark
Bind the Soul
Yield the Night
Feed the Flames
Reap the Shadows
Unleash the Storm
Steel & Stone

Spell Weaver Trilogy
The Night Realm
The Shadow Weave
The Blood Curse

OTHER WORKS

Red Winter Trilogy
Red Winter
Dark Tempest
Immortal Fire

THE
BLOOD
CURSE

ONE

FIVE, *four, three …*

Lyre watched the clock's second hand tick, the exposed gears turning. The weaves aligning. The magic thrumming with power and purpose.

… two, one, zero.

With a click, the second hand snapped into place. The weaves flashed gold, the magic pulsed, and then … nothing.

Snarling, Lyre slammed his fist down on the steel desktop. The clock jumped from the impact and he was tempted to smash the stupid thing into pieces. How many cycles had he wasted on this?

He dropped onto his stool, growling profanity under his breath. A nearby wooden box overflowed with gems, arrowheads, metal discs, and more junk, all contaminated with failed weavings. With this new spell, he'd be able to clear them instantaneously so he could easily start over.

Ignoring the half-finished commissions heaped on the other side of the desk, he scooped up a handful of his notes and flipped through the diagrams. The weaves were perfect. The theory was sound. He'd accounted for everything.

He tossed the papers down and folded his arms, contemplating the clock. The gems set in the gears sparkled back at him. It should work but it didn't. Something was missing.

He spun the stool in a slow circle, his eyes going out of focus. Something was missing. But what? He spun around again, the sofa and bookshelves and desk passing by. A spell that could clear lodestones.

The room blurred as he spun. A spell that could erase magic.

He dug his heels into the floor, bringing the stool to an abrupt stop. His head roiled dizzily but he scarcely noticed as he stared wide-eyed at the clock. Of course something was missing. A weave to erase magic needed more than magic. But would it work? Was it even possible?

Nerves tightened his stomach, but his excitement was stronger than his apprehension. Grinning, he reached for the device.

With a grinding click, the second hand started to move, twitching down the clock face. Lyre's hand hovered above it, his brow furrowed. The key to wind it sat on the desk, untouched.

The second hand ticked past the halfway point and up the other side of the face, the weaves priming, the power building. Unexpected panic bloomed in his chest. He wanted to grab the clock and physically stop it, but he couldn't move.

Tick, tick, tick. The second hand struck twelve and stopped. The weaves flashed bright gold, then darkened until they were pitch black.

Ebony power oozed out of the gems and pooled across the desktop. It bubbled upward like a gelatinous liquid, sucking the light into it, and Lyre backpedaled. His stool crashed to the floor.

The rippling darkness expanded in every direction, absorbing his desk and reaching for more. Lyre stumbled back another step.

The power exploded outward. It hit him like a punch to the chest and sucked him into the screaming oblivion within it. The world disappeared, darkness swallowing everything.

He writhed in the nothingness, unable to breathe as it consumed his magic, his life. Somehow, he could feel the power racing outward, spreading and spreading as it devoured Chrysalis. Devoured Asphodel.

Devoured the Underworld and every living thing in the realm.

LYRE'S EYES flew open.

He jerked upright and a threadbare blanket slid into his lap. He gasped for air as he stared wildly around the unfamiliar bachelor apartment. Beside him on the narrow, sagging bed, Clio was curled in a ball on her side, hair matted with dried blood and a bandage taped to her cheek.

As his heart rate slowed, he raked a hand through his hair, shaking off the dream so he could focus. Where the hell was he?

He surveyed the room a second time. Dingy walls, a tiny kitchen with barren cupboards, and a pair of mismatched chairs. Two closed doors and a window with nothing but darkness and a few scattered lights beyond the glass.

Lyre's bow leaned in a corner, and nearby was another set of weapons—a huge sword in a black sheath, two shorter blades, and an assortment of daggers.

The back of his neck prickled. He snapped his head around and spotted a pair of golden eyes staring at him from atop the kitchen cupboards before the small creature ducked deeper into the shadows.

One of the two doors swung open. A daemon walked out of a small bathroom, a ragged towel in his hand. His hair was damp, dark strands that shimmered with wine-red iridescence clinging to his face. He wore dark pants and a black t-shirt, the red tie that was normally braided into his hair hanging from one pocket.

Without his combat gear, Ash almost looked like a normal guy.

Cool storm-gray eyes turned to Lyre as Ash flipped the towel over the back of a chair and dropped into it. "You're awake."

Lyre suppressed a shiver. Even with glamour disguising his dragon-like form, Ash's deep, sepulchral voice didn't sound quite human.

"Surprisingly," Lyre replied cautiously. "I expected to be dead."

He watched the draconian lace up his boots, struggling to piece together how he'd gotten here. He remembered the abandoned park where Bastian had taken him, and Clio arriving to fight her half-brother. He remembered getting hit yet again by the shadow weave, his magic devoured and his body left too weak to move. And then …

"Reapers," Lyre muttered. "What happened to the reapers?"

There had been two of them. Their arrival had spooked Bastian into fleeing with the KLOC, but the reapers had overheard what it could do. They'd planned to take Lyre and Clio back to Asphodel. Then Ash had joined his reaper handlers, and that was the last thing Lyre remembered.

"The reapers are dead," the draconian replied.

Surprise flickered through Lyre, followed by relief. He contemplated that simple statement, sifting through what hadn't been said. "You killed them."

"And destroyed the evidence." Ash leaned back in his chair. "You fucked up, incubus."

"Can't argue there, but what specifically are you referring to?"

"Creating that spell, first off. Then letting it out of your control. What the hell were you thinking?" He didn't pause to let Lyre respond. "What the nymph said about it wiping out daemon armies and destroying ley lines—is that true?"

Lyre nodded.

"You're an idiot."

"Thanks for that keen observation," Lyre said dryly. "Can we skip the part where I explain how the shadow weave was a huge mistake and get on with the important stuff?"

Ash stretched his legs out. "Samael doesn't know your spell exists, and it needs to be destroyed before he finds out."

Samael, the warlord of Hades and ultimate owner of Chrysalis, wasn't just the most politically powerful daemon in the Underworld. He was also the daemon who controlled Ash's life, though by what means, Lyre didn't know.

"Is that why you saved us?" he asked, glancing at Clio, still dead to the world.

"Why else?"

Lyre drew in a deep breath, forcing himself to think before he made a smart-ass retort. Only days ago they had battled to the near-death in the alleys of downtown Brinford, Ash forced to obey Samael's command and Lyre desperately defending himself.

"You're under orders to kill me."

"And I will. Just not yet."

Not *yet*. A quiet chuckle that was part bitterness, part amusement escaped Lyre. "Better than nothing, I guess."

"Orders are orders." Ash shrugged dismissively. "If you don't want me to kill you, don't let me catch you next time."

"I'll work on that." He shifted backward to slouch against the wall. "The nymph prince Bastian has my spell. He's nursing a grudge against Ra, and depending on how much his ambition outweighs his brains, he might try to incite a war. We have to get it back before he gets that far."

"We?"

"Were you planning to destroy a weave that could annihilate the realms all by yourself?"

"Who said I was planning to help at all? If I'm seen with you, it'll be my neck on the line."

"How convenient you're so good at getting around unseen, then." Lyre let his head fall back against the wall, watching the draconian with half-closed eyes. "You dragged me and Clio here so we could deal with this together, before the worst happens. After that, we can go back to killing each other guilt-free."

Ash propped an arm on the back of his chair. "Will you be able to keep up with me, incubus?"

Lyre smirked, the memory of leaping across Asphodel's rooftops on Ash's heels flashing through his mind. "Maybe if I put an arrow in your leg first."

Humor fading, Lyre gave the room another slow assessment, his gaze lingering on Clio. "You're right, Ash. I messed up, and if Bastian unleashes the shadow weave near a ley line, it'll be bad. I don't know how bad, but bad." He exhaled. "I can't find Bastian on my own. Not in time to stop him."

"You need my help."

Ash had said those words to him once before, and Lyre gave the same simple answer. "Yes."

Ash measured him with a glance. "Wake the girl and let's get started. I need to know everything you know."

Back in that abandoned park, faced with the pair of reapers while too weak and exhausted to move, defeat had weighed on Lyre like frigid ocean waves. But now, as he reached for Clio to gently shake her awake, he felt the first spark of hope. Ash's power. Lyre's weaving. Clio's magic.

Maybe, together, they stood a chance to fix this before his worst nightmare became a reality.

TWO

CLIO HELD perfectly still, trying not to blush.

Lyre gently held her jaw as he examined her cheek, fingers pressed to the shallow scratch, courtesy of Eryx's dagger. Heat washed across her skin as he applied faint touches of healing magic.

She sat on the bathroom counter, Lyre standing in front of her. Ash had left hours ago to hunt for Bastian, and the dingy room outside was empty.

She still couldn't quite believe it. After nearly killing Lyre—and attempting to crack his skull after that—Ash had *saved* them. Keeping the shadow weave out of Samael's hands was more important to him than following orders, and now the draconian was risking everything to help.

While she hesitated to trust Ash, Lyre didn't seem to have any reservations. How he could just forget about the damage Ash had inflicted on him, she didn't know. *She* definitely hadn't forgotten, considering she'd spent hours healing his injuries.

Lyre's fingers lifted from her face and he straightened. "That's all I can do for now. I need to charge some lodestones, though that'll only help so much. I'm no good at healing."

He grimaced at the last part, but the expression did nothing to diminish the mouthwatering perfection of his face. Like her, he hadn't returned to his glamour form yet, saving every drop of magic while he recovered.

Exhaustion ached through her body and she felt hollow inside, as though all her innards had been scraped out. She'd never been hit by the shadow weave before, and she never wanted to experience it again. Not even a long shower had relieved the fatigue, so deep and overwhelming she couldn't think about anything else.

Well, anything except Lyre so close, his spicy cherry scent distracting her from her weariness.

"Thank you," she said, not sure where to look. He was standing almost on top of her, though it wasn't on purpose. The bathroom was just that tiny.

His fingers brushed her face again, this time tracing the edge of her jaw. She looked up in surprise, unable to suppress her blush this time.

"Are you okay, Clio?" he asked softly. He must have been waiting until Ash was gone to see how she was holding up—not from her physical injuries, but the wounds that had cut far deeper.

She opened her mouth to tell him she was fine, but instead memories of Bastian rushed through her. First, realizing he had been lying to her for years, then facing him again on Earth where he'd ordered Eryx to slit her throat if Lyre didn't cooperate.

Her half-brother had nearly killed her, and he hadn't shown the slightest hint of hesitation or remorse over it. Since her mother's death, Clio had depended on him for everything, from her livelihood to her sense of self-worth, but that support had been torn away. If she wasn't Bastian's loyal half-sister, devoted to helping him and earning her place in his family, then who was she?

She lifted her head. "We're going to stop him."

Lyre didn't have to ask what she meant. "We will."

Her heart beat faster at the intensity in his amber eyes. Even with almost no magic to fuel his supernatural allure, he was mesmerizing. She wanted to touch his cheek where the dark tattoo revealed his bloodline. She wanted to trace the points of his ears, pierced with tiny gold hoops and a diamond stud. She wanted to run her hands in his short, tousled hair, a fine braid hanging beside his face with a ruby at the end.

"Thank you," she said again, her voice hoarsening with emotion. "For everything, Lyre."

A crooked smile pulled at his lips. "I don't know what you're thanking me for. I haven't been particularly useful."

She rolled her eyes. "Instead of arguing, could you just accept it?"

"Accept what, exactly?"

"That I would never have made it through any of this without you."

His teasing smile faded into a serious stare. "You would have found a way. You're tougher than you think, Clio."

She twisted her mouth doubtfully—and Lyre's gaze drifted to her lips.

She had only a moment to realize the shift in his thoughts before his fingers slid across her cheek and sank into her hair. Her heart stuttered as he guided her head back.

His lips brushed softly across hers and she closed her eyes, instantly lost in the rising heat in her center. He melded their mouths together, deepening the kiss. Winding her arms around his neck, she parted her lips in invitation.

A loud trill broke the silence.

Clio jerked back from Lyre and banged her head on the cracked mirror behind her. Clinging to the doorway with wings half-spread was a small dragon, her golden eyes glaring admonishingly. The small creature chattered, the sound stern and disapproving, then she sprang off the doorframe back into the main room.

Clio had first seen the small creature—called a dragonet—in Asphodel. She'd since learned that wherever Ash went, his dragonet was never far away—except in this case. Maybe he'd left the creature behind to supervise his houseguests?

Lyre scowled at the empty threshold, then turned back to her. Before she could guess his intentions, he kissed her again, hands sliding into her hair, still damp from her shower. She pressed against him, warmth spiraling through her.

Another furious burst of trills and chitters erupted from the doorway.

He pulled back again, leaving Clio breathless, and smirked at the growling dragonet. "You aren't the boss of me, little dragon, and neither is your master."

Clio sighed. Lyre and Ash working together would either be a dangerously perfect partnership—or a complete disaster.

LYRE RAN his fingers across the chain around his neck, mentally tallying each gemstone and the spell it contained. Thanks to Bastian's thievery, he was down from three chains to two. At least he hadn't lost his bow. In his current circumstances, he'd never be able to replace it with a weapon of comparable quality and craftsmanship.

His fingers stopped on a gem containing the weave for his best dome shield—the same one Ash had blasted through when they'd fought on the bridge. That fight had been close. So many times, either of them could have died.

And now they were working together again.

Pulling one leg onto the chair, he propped his chin on his hand and stared out the apartment window. Behind him, Clio was sleeping on the mattress. She'd slept most of the past twenty-four hours, her body exhausted by the shadow weave.

Lyre's hand drifted from his chain to his pocket, where a pouch of lodestones brimmed with power.

Having suffered the aftereffects of the KLOC before, he hadn't wasted any time this round. Just before dark, he'd ventured out of the hideaway apartment. It had been a risk when his magic reserves were critically low—and a risk leaving Clio alone—but he hadn't wanted any company for that mission.

With the sun setting and the bustle of the workday winding down, he had gone on the hunt. Twelve human women, helpless against his power, had provided enough emotional energy to charge most of his lodestones. Within a few hours, he'd recovered his magic entirely, and now all he had to deal with was the lingering physical fatigue. Unfortunately, his lodestones were attuned to him and useless to Clio.

When he'd returned, revitalized and recharged, she hadn't commented. She must have guessed that charging lodestones at a dance club hadn't been an option this time, but she didn't ask how he'd charged them.

He glanced back at her, sleeping peacefully. She probably assumed he'd bedded a bunch of women to charge those stones, but if she'd just ask, he could assure her he'd ... he'd what? That he'd been faithful to her?

Seriously? He was worrying about *that*? He was *an incubus*. He wasn't ashamed to seduce or sleep with as many women as he damn well pleased. Incubi didn't do monogamy. They *couldn't*. It was impossible.

He scrubbed a hand through his hair, then let his head fall back with a sigh. Before he could sink even further into the confusing quagmire of his thoughts, an icy chill ran down his spine. He stiffened, gaze flashing around the room then back to the window.

A huge black shadow dropped out of nowhere and landed on the windowsill.

Lyre lurched away from the glass, toppling his chair. He hit the floor on his back as the nightmarish shadow on the sill pulled the window open and squeezed through the gap.

In the moment it took his feet to touch the floor, Ash shimmered into glamour, his wings and tail vanishing. He gave Lyre, sprawled on the overturned chair, a disparaging look before closing the window.

"Holy shit," Lyre groaned as he righted the chair and checked that he hadn't woken Clio. "I think you scared a few years off my life."

"Don't sit in front of the window, then."

Lyre dropped back into his seat and scanned the draconian. His casual look hadn't lasted long. He was in full gear again, strapped head to toe in weapons with that huge sword slung across his back—a blade that had tasted quite a bit of Lyre's blood.

Perched on the kitchen cabinets, the dragonet—her name was Zwi, Ash had revealed—grumbled loudly at her master. Was she tattling on Lyre for earlier? Watching Ash unbuckle his weapons, Lyre waited for the jitters in his limbs to fade. The draconian's sudden appearance would have startled him no matter what, but that wasn't the main reason for Lyre's bout of panic.

"Do you think you could cut back on the fear thing?" he asked, massaging his chest.

"No."

"Is it really necessary to terrify me every time you have your wings out?"

Ash pulled his large sword off his back and set it down with a thud. "It's inherent to my magic. I can't 'cut back.'"

Lyre opened his mouth, then closed it. The draconian ability to panic everyone in the vicinity was involuntary? Damn. He tried to imagine what life would be like if he had no control over his aphrodesia.

Ash finished unloading his weapons and headed for the kitchen. Heaving off the chair, Lyre followed him. The draconian pulled a can of pork and beans out of the cupboard.

"How did it go tonight?" Lyre asked, reaching over Ash's shoulder to get a second can. Ash had been gone for over twenty-four hours. Did the guy ever sleep?

"Probably found them."

Lyre paused with his hand in the cupboard to stare incredulously at the draconian. "You found Bastian? Already?"

"I haven't seen the nymph prince yet." Ash pulled a battered knife from the drawer and cut the top of the can open. "Abandoned building about three blocks from the Ra embassy, right by the river. Pairs of blond and redheaded men coming and going."

Lyre slowly set the second can on the counter. A solid lead, that fast. No wonder Lyre hadn't been able to evade the draconian. "Coming and going where?"

"Several locations, but mainly scoping out the Ra embassy."

"I don't like the sound of that."

Ash passed the knife to Lyre. "So far, they've only been active at night, and they're moving carefully. I don't know how many men the prince has brought in."

As Lyre cut his can open, Ash fished in a drawer for a spoon. Lyre plucked the can out of his hand and set them both on the hot plate.

"Cold beans are disgusting," he declared as he turned it on. "We need to know what we're dealing with before we make our next move."

"I've tracked their scouting patterns. Tomorrow after dark, I'll capture one for questioning."

"*We'll* capture one," Lyre corrected. "Clio can identify castes with her asper, so she'll make sure we don't nab the wrong daemon. And I'll do the interrogating. Aphrodesia works a lot faster than torture, plus I can guarantee truthful answers."

Ash stiffened at the mention of aphrodesia, his eyes darkening. "These daemons are all male."

"Not surprising. That just means I'll have to work harder at it, not that I can't do it."

Ash's expression hardened further. Reaching around Lyre, he pulled a can off the hot plate, shoved his spoon into the unappetizing mixture, and started to eat.

Lyre reached for his can and felt the heat a moment before touching the metal. Hissing, he snatched his hand back and gave Ash a flinty look. Exactly how fireproof was the draconian? Wadding up the only dishcloth for insulation, he picked up the can and unenthusiastically stirred its contents.

"So," he continued, "the three of us will interrogate one of Bastian's nymphs, find out what we're dealing with, and figure out how to intercept Bastian. I'd rather avoid another free-for-all brawl."

Ash grunted in agreement. "Assuming the prince hasn't amassed an army, this can be over by sunrise tomorrow."

"I'm not that lucky." Lyre poked at his beans. "Whatever luck I might've had ran out back in Asphodel."

Ash leaned against the counter beside Lyre. "What do you plan to do about the bounty?"

"What *can* I do?" Lyre stared at his meager meal, his mouth too dry to even consider eating now. "Destroying the KLOC doesn't fix anything as far as my death sentence goes. Hades and Chrysalis won't stop hunting me."

"Whining about it won't help."

Lyre snarled. "There's nothing I can do except keep running."

"If you were the type to run away like a beaten dog," Ash said, "you wouldn't have fought me to your last breath."

"What other option do I have?" Lyre's voice rose before he remembered Clio was sleeping.

Ash set his empty can in the sink. "As long as you're alive, they'll keep hunting you." He stepped out of the kitchen and glanced back, his dark eyes gleaming. "There's more than one way to disappear."

Leaving Lyre in the kitchen, Ash crossed to the far corner and sank down, leaning against the wall and closing his eyes. His dragonet slunk out of the shadows and climbed into his lap, her golden eyes alert while her master rested.

Lyre stood at the counter, watching the draconian. The sick dread that had taken up residence in his gut quieted and he absently resumed eating, scarcely noticing the taste as he mulled over what Ash had said.

If he wanted to survive long enough to enjoy his new freedom, then he needed a plan. And it was past time he figured one out.

THREE

"IS THIS IT?" Lyre whispered.

Clio crouched on one side of him, and on his other side, Ash had just pulled his black wrap over his lower face. It was an ominous gesture.

The dark alley where they lingered looked like every other reeking back street in downtown Brinford, but visible above the surrounding two- and three-story buildings were the glowing windows of a skyscraper. The Ra embassy.

Ash nodded in the opposite direction. "They're holed up in a warehouse another two blocks that way, but pairs have come this way multiple times."

"Probably a nymph and a chimera," Clio murmured. "They make a dangerous partnership. We'll have to be careful the nymphs don't see our auras."

"I wonder what they're planning with the embassy," Lyre murmured, squinting toward the scattered lights shining from the embassy windows. "Bastian has to realize that attacking it would be suicide."

"I've been wondering about that too." Clio chewed on a fingernail. "He can't be planning to use the KLOC on them, can he?"

Lyre shifted his weight, legs aching from crouching for so long. As usual, Ash didn't seem bothered by the physical demand. "Bastian knows the shadow weave is a chain reaction. If he unleashes it on the embassy, there's no way he and his men could get far enough away to avoid getting caught in it too."

"How far are we talking?" Ash asked.

"Depends on how many daemons are in the embassy and how much stored magic they have." Lyre glanced around. "I would guess that, if triggered in the embassy, the shadow weave would cover at least the entire downtown core. If the prince is stupid enough to use it ..."

"Bastian isn't stupid." Clio brushed her hair out of her eyes. A faint line marked her cheek, the cut mostly healed after a lot of painstaking effort on his part. "He won't put himself at risk like that."

Lyre silently agreed. Generally speaking, he was a firm believer in strategic cowardice, but Bastian wasn't merely averse to personal danger. He was also happy to manipulate others into risking their lives in his place.

With that in mind, Lyre wasn't feeling all too great about the nymph and chimera soldiers they would soon have to deal with. The daemons were loyal to their prince, not bad people. Probably. Maybe they were all pieces of walking garbage like Eryx was. He could hope, right?

Ash canted his head as though listening to something. "A pair is on the move, heading this way. We can get in position."

The draconian was up and heading farther down the alley before Lyre or Clio could respond.

She glanced around with a frown. "I thought we *were* in position."

"Apparently not." Lyre waved at her to follow as he hastened after Ash. "What I really want to know is how he can hear them at this distance."

He trotted a few yards to catch up, the draconian's long stride carrying him swiftly away. Ash moved with purpose, and it was obvious he'd already scouted this area and knew exactly where he wanted to go. Wheeling around the corner of a two-story brick building, he took three running steps and leaped, grabbing the bottom of a rusting fire escape.

Lyre swallowed back a groan as Ash easily pulled himself up, the muscles in his arms and shoulders flexing impressively. The draconian didn't wait—or even glance back—as he climbed the rickety metal structure that looked like it might break free from the wall at any moment.

"Um," Clio whispered.

Lyre rolled his shoulders. First the desert-trekking jinn Sabir, now Ash. All these assholes making him look out of shape.

Puffing out a breath, he stepped closer to the fire escape, turned, and cupped his hands together. Clio looked at the fire escape six feet above his head and let out her own heavy sigh. Backing up a few steps, she ran at him.

Her foot landed in his hands and he launched her upward. She caught the metal rail and hopped over it, landing neatly. Ash was out-muscling him, and Clio—aside from her epic clumsy moments—was impressively agile. Damn it.

As she climbed, he rubbed his hands together, then took a running leap at the fire escape. He caught the bottom bar and hauled himself up with a muffled grunt. Ash had already reached the roof, and Lyre and Clio swiftly joined him.

The draconian crouched near the rooftop edge, peering into the alley below. Lyre squinted through the darkness. At well past midnight, the downtown core was almost devoid of light.

"I see them," Clio whispered. "A nymph and a chimera."

"How far?" Lyre asked.

"Twenty-five yards," Ash answered before she could. "Get down so the nymph doesn't see your auras."

Lyre lay down on the rooftop and Clio flattened herself too, giving Lyre another "what the hell" look. Without asper, how could Ash see their targets when Lyre couldn't make out a damn thing?

In the silence, the soft sounds of cautious footsteps grew audible. Lyre peeked over the edge and, after a moment of squinting, picked them out of the darkness. The short, slim nymph moved with quick steps, his blond hair gleaming. His chimera partner had a steadier pace, his head swiveling as he checked the shadows all around them.

Ash didn't budge, watching as the pair passed beneath their position on the rooftop. Lyre bit the inside of his cheek, unable to ask what Ash was waiting for. Any noise would be a risk.

The draconian rose to his feet and put one foot on the ledge, but he didn't make his move. Down the alley, something clattered. The sound echoed off the buildings and the two soldiers froze.

Ash's fingers curled. Dark magic swirled in his hand as he prepped a binding spell, then with a flick of his wrist, he flung it downward. It struck the nymph in the back and the daemon fell.

Ash sprang off the rooftop. Not bothering with his wings, he hit the ground in a roll and came out of it with a sword in each hand. Lyre lurched up, eyes wide, as the draconian caught the hapless chimera in the middle of dropping glamour.

It was over in a heartbeat. A swift, clean execution.

As Ash pulled his sword out of the fallen daemon, Clio gasped in alarm. Lyre jerked his attention to the nymph soldier. He'd freed himself from the binding spell and was scrambling to his feet.

"Shit," Lyre growled, grabbing the rooftop's edge. "Wait here."

He jumped. Two stories was not a fun drop. Doable for a daemon, but not fun. He hit the pavement hard and rolled. In the time it took him to launch back to his feet, the nymph had bolted in the opposite direction—and he was *fast*. Ash turned, flicking the blood off his sword, and watched his quarry flee without making the slightest effort to give chase.

"What are you—" Lyre began angrily.

Skidding footsteps. Almost invisible in a patch of heavy shadows farther down the alley, the nymph had stopped. He backed up, hands outstretched as though warding off evil. As the nymph retreated, something else appeared in the darkness.

Something solid. Something *big*.

A black dragon stalked out of the shadows, its teeth bared and golden eyes glowing. The size of a horse with enormous wings blotting out the alley's exit, it advanced on the nymph with prowling steps, its curved talons clicking on the pavement.

Lyre didn't move. He didn't even breathe.

Ash sheathed his swords and headed for the distracted nymph. Grabbing the daemon by the neck, Ash hauled him backward.

The huge black dragon, only a few paces away, growled softly. Dark fire erupted over its body, engulfing its form so suddenly that Lyre jumped. The flames leaped upward, then died away as fast as they had appeared. With a final poof, they were gone.

And in the black dragon's place, the little dragonet Zwi stood.

Chattering cheerfully, she jumped onto Ash's back and climbed up to his shoulder. The draconian dragged the unresisting nymph back toward Lyre, and he blinked stupidly when he saw Ash had cast a sleep spell on the daemon.

"Um." Lyre cleared his throat. "Your dragonet can … shapeshift?"

"Clearly."

"You didn't bring her into *our* fight."

Ash gave him a cold stare. "This nymph isn't a master weaver."

Lyre looked again at the little dragonet. What defense did a dragon, even a big one with lots of sharp, pointy teeth, have against a master weaver's magic?

He glanced up. Two stories above, Clio's pale face peered over the rooftop's edge.

"Why don't you stay there?" he called in a low voice. "Keep watch while we question this guy."

"All right."

He suppressed a smile at her reluctant agreement. He and Ash, with the unconscious nymph in tow, retreated into a narrow gap between buildings. Ash dumped the daemon against the wall.

"Your turn," he muttered.

"Yeah," Lyre agreed. "Feel free to stand back."

Ash stiffened but didn't move away. Crouching, Lyre took hold of the nymph's jaw. Letting his aphrodesia loose was always so easy, like relaxing tense muscles. As power flowed from him, he dropped his glamour and Ash belatedly stepped back.

With a touch of magic, Lyre broke the sleep spell. The nymph's blue eyes opened, hazed and out of focus.

"What's your name?" Layered harmonics vibrated through Lyre's voice, and he kept his hand on the daemon's chin, their eyes locked.

"Ajax," the nymph whispered dreamily. "Who are you? You're beautiful."

Lyre's eyebrows rose. Well, this was unexpected. How convenient that Ajax happened to be more susceptible to his aphrodesia than most males.

"Let's talk about you," he suggested. "What brings you to Brinford?"

"Oh …" Ajax's vague expression saddened. "I can't tell you."

"You can tell me anything." He leaned closer, smiling his irresistible incubus smile. "Why are you here, Ajax?"

The nymph's eyes glazed over even more. "The prince asked me to come. A top-secret mission offered only to his best and most loyal soldiers." He puffed his chest with pride. "We're going to save Irida."

"What's Prince Bastian planning to do here?"

"The Ra embassy. We're going to wipe it out. That'll get the attention of those arrogant griffins, don't you think?"

"It'll definitely get their attention," Lyre agreed darkly. He pulled his sultry smile back into place. "Your courage is admirable, Ajax, but the embassy is well guarded. How will you attack it?"

"The prince has made all the arrangements. He'll brief us on our attack strategy soon."

Lyre grimaced. Smart of Bastian not to share too much with his underlings, but problematic for interrogators.

Ajax reached up with fumbling fingers and stroked Lyre's cheek. "I've never seen a daemon like you before."

Lyre allowed the touch, more interested in keeping Ajax cooperative. The poor guy was drowning in aphrodesia, but nymphs were so passive he wasn't even resisting. Most daemons would be attacking Lyre in blind lust at this point.

"You can't be the only trusted warrior the prince recruited," Lyre observed. "How many others have the honor of joining Bastian on this mission?"

"There are twenty of us."

"How many nymphs?"

"Only five."

Interesting that Bastian was relying more on chimera strength than nymph asper. Lyre hummed thoughtfully, wondering just how cooperative Ajax might be. With a less susceptible victim, he could ask only simple questions, but the nymph was surprisingly lucid while still completely under his sway.

"Ajax, I have to say, attacking the embassy seems like a big risk for little reward. Surely there are better ways to get Ra's attention?"

"The embassy is just the beginning," the nymph replied, squinting blearily at Lyre. "The prince called it a test. Plus, there's a prize we've been waiting for—the thing that will really get the Ra's attention."

"What's that?"

Ajax leaned forward, pressing against Lyre's hand curled around his jaw. "A member of the Ra royal family just arrived at the embassy."

Lyre's breath caught, and he dared to look away from Ajax to Ash, standing a healthy ten paces away. The draconian tilted his head in a "finish this" gesture.

"You seem tired, Ajax," Lyre purred. "Why don't you take a nap?"

"I can't. I need to get back." He blinked slowly and a faint spark of focus came into his eyes. "I was almost finished my last patrol and I can't be late …"

"Your *last* patrol?" Lyre prompted, adding more power to his voice. "What are you late for?"

"Bastian was waiting for the Ra royal to arrive." He twitched as though trying to throw off a drowsy lassitude. "We're ready to move out as soon as … who are you?"

Lyre pulled the nymph's face closer to his. "Ajax, *go to sleep.*"

Power thrummed through the command, and the nymph slumped down the wall, his eyes sliding closed and face going slack. Pulling his glamour into place, Lyre pushed to his feet.

"They're making their move tonight," he growled, turning to Ash. "We don't have much time."

Ash jerked his chin toward the nymph. "Aren't you going to finish him?"

"No." He reached for the daemon to add a sleep spell. "We'll be done before—"

Shoving Lyre aside, Ash planted his boot on the sleeping nymph's chest, grabbed the daemon by the hair, and wrenched his head sideways. Bone crunched as the daemon's neck broke.

"Holy fuck!" Lyre lurched backward in shock. "What the hell was *that*?"

Ash swept past him toward the alley. "He needed to die."

"He was *unconscious*," Lyre snarled, storming after the draconian. "Bastian tricked him into doing this. He wasn't—"

"*Why* he's an enemy doesn't matter." Ash pivoted, forcing Lyre to jerk to a stop. His dark eyes were as hard as his steel blade. "Leaving loose ends like that is how you end up dead."

Lyre bared his teeth furiously.

"*You* wanted my help, incubus. Regretting it?"

Drawing in a deep breath, Lyre forced his anger and guilt aside. He'd known what he was getting into when he teamed up with Ash—and he wouldn't regret it, because without the draconian, he and Clio would still be aimlessly searching for Bastian. But he would keep in mind that Ash's blanket policy was, "When in doubt, kill."

Once Clio had jumped down from the rooftop—without commenting on the nymph's death, though she must have witnessed it—they hastened through the maze of alleys with Ash leading the way. His dragonet was conspicuously absent, and Lyre wondered where the creature was. With the ability to turn into a huge winged monster at will, Zwi warranted a lot more attention than he'd been paying her.

Ash, stalking ahead of them with impatience bleeding into his movements, slowed to a cautious prowl as they came to a junction of streets. On the other side, a blank four-story façade, broken by a single metal door with a buzzing light bulb above it, blocked their way forward.

Ash hesitated, then walked boldly into the open. Swearing under his breath, Lyre followed, Clio hurrying on his heels.

"Shouldn't we be a little more careful?" he hissed at the draconian.

"Coast is clear." He glanced at Clio. "Unless you can detect something I can't."

She shook her head. "I don't see any magic or auras."

"That's because"—he put a hand on the metal door—"the place is empty."

He shoved the door open, revealing a cavernous interior filled with industrial storage racks that bore a few dozen dusty pallets. They walked inside, their light steps echoing.

"Isn't this their base?" Lyre asked, the emptiness magnifying his hushed words.

"It was. They were here only a few hours ago." Ash assessed the shadows, scarcely touched by the light leaking through the open door. "They might have moved closer to the embassy."

"This is already pretty damn close."

"Ajax said they were attacking the embassy tonight." Clio shifted her weight from foot to foot. "What if they've already begun?"

Ash canted his head as though signaling someone. His dragonet swept out of the darkness and glided out the threshold, vanishing into the alley.

"Zwi will check," he said. "But I set detection spells on all the plausible routes from here to the embassy, and none have been triggered."

"Maybe the nymphs spotted your spells," Clio suggested doubtfully. "Your magic is very difficult to see in the dark, though."

"Well," Lyre said with a sigh, "let's check this place out, see what we can learn."

They split up, scouting through the warehouse's huge main space and several floors of offices and storage rooms. They found signs of recent occupation but the place was abandoned and it didn't look like anyone planned to return.

"Damn," Lyre muttered as they reconvened in a top-floor office with a window that overlooked the warehouse interior. "Should we head toward the embassy?"

"Zwi has scouted all around it. There's no sign of them."

Lyre narrowed his eyes at Ash, but it was Clio who asked the obvious question. "How do you know that?"

Ash gazed stonily back at them, unwilling to divulge all his secrets.

Shaking his head, Lyre held his light spell a little higher, illuminating the ancient desks covered in an inch of dust. "Now what?

Ajax said Bastian was planning to make his move tonight, yet he and all his men have vanished."

"Maybe he reconsidered his plan," Ash rumbled. "Assassinating a Ra will get a stronger reaction than he thinks. Or, more likely, he panicked when the nymph and chimera pair didn't report on time."

"Shit," Lyre muttered.

"What do we do now?" Clio asked nervously. "Should we scout farther out from the Ra embassy?"

"For now, we should …" Ash trailed off, his expression tightening as he turned his head—listening. Lyre focused on the sounds within the warehouse, then realized he could hear a low pitched roar from outside. What the hell was that? An airplane? Not exactly common these days.

Without a word, Ash pivoted on one heel and sprinted out of the room.

Lyre exchanged an alarmed glance with Clio, then raced after him. The draconian hit the staircase and shot upward. Slamming through the door at the top, he ran onto the warehouse rooftop, the gravel crunching under his feet.

The pulsating roar quadrupled the instant Lyre got outside. The Ra embassy was a few blocks away and, lit from beneath by the tower lights, two stocky black helicopters hovered above its roof.

"Helicopters?" Clio gasped.

"Helicopters," Lyre growled. Damn that nymph prince. How much had it cost him to hire two of the rarest machines in the modern world? And not just any helicopters, but thick-bodied military beasts that could probably hold ten men each.

"How strong is your strongest arrow?" Ash demanded.

Lyre's explosive blood arrow could take out both helicopters, along with the top floor of the tower—if he could make the shot across the distance. He'd never shot a helicopter before and he had no idea how the wind from the blades might disrupt an arrow's flight.

As one helicopter descended, almost low enough to land on the embassy, Lyre released his glamour and reached over his shoulder.

"They just dropped something onto the roof!" No sooner were the words out of Clio's mouth than both helicopters shot into the dark sky.

"They dropped the KLOC on the building?" Lyre yelped, disbelief freezing him.

"They've already triggered it!" Clio grabbed his arm. "It was a big glowing bundle of magic. He must have wrapped the clock in a bunch of lodestones to make sure it would—"

Lyre whirled around, his eyes scouring the streets. Where exactly were they? "We have to get to water! Where's the river?"

Ash grabbed Lyre's and Clio's arms and ran for the edge of the warehouse rooftop. Lyre's heart crammed into his throat. Two stories he could safely jump, but not four. Ash either didn't know that or didn't care as he pulled them straight for the ledge and leaped.

Lyre caught a glimpse of the street far below—and the black river on the other side. Of course. Bastian had deliberately chosen a staging area close to water.

They plummeted ten feet before shimmers rippled over Ash and his wings snapped wide. Terror slammed into Lyre so hard he almost lost control of his stomach.

Ash didn't try to fly. Instead, he locked his wings as they half fell, half glided toward the river. Panic pounded through Lyre and he counted in his head, but he didn't know if Bastian had dropped the KLOC immediately after winding it.

The shadow weave was going to activate, wrapped in magic and released on top of a daemon embassy. He didn't know how bad it would be, but whatever happened was his fault—because he had created it, he had let it fall into Bastian's hands, and he had failed to get it back in time.

As they fell, he felt it coming—the drop in pressure, the approaching shock wave of expanding power racing away from the Ra embassy.

Ash snapped his wings tight to his back and they plunged into the icy water.

FOUR

LYRE'S HEAD burst out of the water and he gasped in a lungful of air. Clio surfaced beside him, and a few feet away, Ash shook the water from his eyes.

"You two okay?" Lyre asked. They'd escaped the shadow weave—but how many other daemons hadn't been as lucky? No one in the embassy would have been spared—and if Bastian proceeded to slaughter the helpless griffins and a Ra royal, the consequences for Irida could be catastrophic.

As they swam for shore, the roar of the helicopters grew louder. Spotlights pointed downward and rotor blades a blur, they descended toward the embassy again and vanished from Lyre's line of sight—meaning they had landed on the building.

He scrambled onto the gravel bank with Clio and Ash behind him.

"We need to get to the embassy and stop Bastian before he can do any more damage," Lyre said urgently. "And we take the KLOC back for good this time."

Ash scanned the horizon where the embassy lights glowed. "I'm going ahead. I'll start from the rooftop and head down. You two go in at ground level. We'll trap him in the middle."

He didn't wait for agreement before shimmers rippled over him. His wings reappeared and he took a few running steps before launching into the air. Wings thundering, he swept upward. Shadows coalesced around him and he faded from sight.

Fighting the terror the draconian had triggered, Lyre grabbed Clio's hand. Together, they sprinted up the riverbank and into the streets toward the embassy.

A high wall surrounded the grounds, the thick stone topped with sharp wrought-iron spikes. Lyre blasted the gates open and they dashed between statues carved into the shapes of the griffins' mythical namesakes—a pair of winged, eagle-headed lions. At least he and Clio didn't have to worry about the magical traps or defenses that the shadow weave had no doubt consumed.

Lyre gave the double doors the same treatment as the gates and they rushed inside. An elegant foyer greeted them, with shiny marble floors, leather furniture, and a two-story water feature behind the curved reception desk. The entire building was hollow, and the atrium rose fifteen stories to a glass ceiling. Balconies circled the cavity at each floor, lit by rows of soft yellow pot lights.

Their footsteps echoed as they slowed to a wary halt. After peering at the glass ceiling over two hundred feet above, Clio trotted to the reception desk and leaned over it.

"There's an unconscious griffin here," she told Lyre, straightening. "Her aura is so faint it's almost invisible, so it'll be difficult for me to spot—"

She suddenly ducked behind the desk. Lyre jumped to her side and crouched, no idea what she'd seen but knowing better than to just stand there like an idiot.

A moment later, rumbling voices broke the silence, their words distorted by the echo. Clio silently pointed and Lyre glimpsed at least two daemons walking near the balcony on the sixth floor. They moved away from the glass railing, disappearing from sight, but their voices continued in a low, rapid conversation.

"Two chimeras and a nymph," Clio whispered.

"Let's go." He raced across the foyer and into a plain stairwell. On the sixth floor, he pushed the door open. As Clio went ahead of him, he paused to drop glamour and pull his bow and quiver off. Slipping back into glamour, he buckled his quiver on again.

Bow in hand, he followed Clio down a tiled corridor with the steel-and-glass railing that bordered the atrium on one side. They passed a few doorways, some open to reveal dark offices or cubicle banks—boring office spaces at odds with the imposing foyer and griffin statues outside. At least they were empty.

Lyre drew two arrows and nocked one, squinting around. "Do you see their auras?"

"No," Clio whispered back. "I'm not sure where—"

The air crackled in warning.

An orange band of magic blasted out from an open door and slammed into Lyre and Clio. He flew into the balcony railing, crunching against the metal post—and Clio hit the center of a glass panel. It shattered and her scream rang out as she pitched backward, falling out of sight.

His heart lurched into his throat. He shot his arrow through the doorway and the spell exploded in a starburst of golden spears that launched in every direction. Ignoring the strangled cries erupting from the room, he spun around, expecting to find Clio crumpled on the marble floor six stories down.

When he leaned over the edge, his heart started beating again. One floor down, she clung haphazardly to the bottom of a steel post, her face white and jaw clenched.

"Clio," he gasped.

She dragged herself up and rolled over the handrail. As she disappeared, he ducked into the room where he'd fired his arrow, but their three attackers were already dead. The chimeras with their reddish skin, goat-like horns, and scaled tails looked like brutes next to the petite blond nymph.

Lyre returned to the railing and Clio leaned out to look up at him.

She pointed. "Ninth floor. I just saw five or six auras run by. Go ahead, and I'll catch up with you."

His heart rate hadn't slowed since she'd fallen. "I can wait."

"I, uh, need a minute. I'm bleeding a bit."

"Do you need healing?" he asked in alarm, his attention torn between her and the atrium balconies where enemies could appear at any moment. They were too exposed.

"I'll be right behind you. Go!" Her head disappeared, then popped out again. "Be careful."

He gritted his teeth, debating whether to go get her, but maybe it wouldn't be a terrible thing if she stayed out of the fight for a few minutes. "I'll head for the ninth floor. If you can't keep going, get out. Ash and I can hunt down the KLOC."

"I'll catch up to you soon."

Pulling two more arrows to make a trio of weavings, he raced back along the balcony to the stairs. Three stories up, he came out on the ninth floor.

This level didn't have the look of an office building. He sped past a stylish sitting area, his feet silent on the carpet. Scanning the atrium, he couldn't see anyone on the balconies. Where had the troop of daemons gone? Had they left this floor?

He paused, holding his breath so he could listen.

The floor vibrated, then a muffled boom. Lyre's head snapped up and he darted down a wide corridor, following the crackling energy—almost like battle magic. But who would the daemons need to fight when the shadow weave had devoured the griffins' magic?

Another sizzling hiss as a spell went off. Ahead, double doors hung open and Lyre skidded to a stop to peek inside. His gaze skipped across the luxury suite—floor-to-ceiling windows and a grand fireplace framed by plush leather sofas—to the far corner where five chimeras and a nymph had formed a loose half circle.

Trapped in the corner was a griffin—and somehow, he was on his feet. Barely. He held a long-handled halberd, using it half as defense and half as a support to lean on. His eagle-like wings with rich golden-brown feathers swept wide.

Something about the way the griffin stood made Lyre look again. Behind him, crumpled in the corner and feathered wings folded tight, was another griffin. A much smaller one.

A child.

Oh, shit. Even Bastian's men should have balked at slaughtering a child—unless it wasn't just any child. Was this the Ra royal Bastian intended to capture or kill?

Apparently, the chimeras thought so, because two of them were advancing on the half-collapsed griffin. Judging by the blood drenching his side, this wasn't the first attack he'd warded off while protecting the child.

Lyre dropped two arrows back in his quiver and selected a different pair. Working fast, he pressed his fingers to the doorframe and wove a spell across the opening. He triggered the defensive weaves embedded in his spell chain, then he set the first arrow on his bow and activated its shield-piercing weave.

Inside the room, weapons met in a deafening clang. Lyre stepped into the threshold as the griffin, despite his obvious exhaustion, whirled his halberd in a deadly spin that forced the chimeras away.

Lyre pulled the string back and loosed his arrow.

The nymph didn't even know he was in danger until the bolt struck the base of his skull. He was dead before he hit the ground. Although most nymphs weren't as dangerous as the rare mimics like Clio and Bastian, Lyre still needed to neutralize the daemon's astral perception before anything else.

The chimeras retreated from the griffin and turned to find the new threat. The griffin braced the butt of his pike on the floor, breathing hard.

Lyre fired his other two arrows in quick succession. The first missed when a chimera ducked, but the second struck his comrade in the eye. The daemon collapsed with a whimper. Wheeling around the corner out of sight, Lyre slung his bow over his shoulder and pulled two short daggers. Activating the spells embedded in the cross guards, he waited.

The two chimeras leading the attack ran right into his weaving across the threshold. Golden light sizzled over them and they froze where they stood, paralyzed.

Lyre sprang out and his daggers flashed. Blood spilled down their fronts. The paralysis spell faded as its power was expended and the two daemons dropped to the floor.

Lyre leaped over the bodies and into the room. The last two chimeras lunged to meet him, swords in hand. His defensive shields saved his life yet again against the experienced warriors—faster and stronger than him, but unable to get their weapons through his barrier. His daggers found openings in their guards, and nothing could stop his weave-coated blades from sinking into their flesh.

When the last one fell, he let out a long, tired breath. Six against one were not odds he liked in close quarters. He was lucky they hadn't been able to attack him together.

Sheathing his daggers, he turned to the griffin and his ward. The guy looked ready to keel over, but neither his fatigue nor his injuries could take away from his magnificence. Those huge wings arched gracefully off his back, and his long lion-like tail ended in a fan of matching feathers. His waist-length hair, woven into a thick plait, was a rich yellow that gleamed in the light, and his eyes, even dulled by weariness, were a vibrant yellow-green.

Wary stare unblinking, the daemon didn't relax as Lyre cautiously approached. Lyre glanced over him, unsure how to read his clothing—fine garments, to be sure, but with a military cut that suggested a soldier. A bodyguard for the child?

Said child hadn't moved, slumped in the corner. Having no experience with kids, Lyre wasn't sure how old she was—not teeny tiny, but not close to adult-sized either. Fine blond hair spilled around her like curtains of silk, and her clothes—a ruby-red skirt and top decorated with gold chains and jewels—were rumpled and splattered with blood. Her bodyguard's blood, it looked like.

"Um," Lyre said. "So, this is kind of awkward, but the girl is in danger."

"I noticed," the griffin said, not shifting from his defensive stance. "Who are you?"

To Lyre's surprise, the griffin's voice was deep and beautifully melodic. Almost as pleasing to the ear as an incubus's harmonic tones.

"I'm … well, an ally. Temporarily. The princess—she is a princess, right?—is their target." He glanced over his shoulder. "And there are more of them coming."

The griffin's eyes narrowed suspiciously and he opened his mouth to speak—then his legs gave out. He hit the floor on his knees and Lyre jumped to his side, ignoring the deadly halberd. That the daemon had fought at all was a shock.

Lyre could only assume the griffin had been carrying lodestones under his glamour. The shadow weave consumed all magic as it spread outward like a breaking wave, but glamour twisted the laws of nature. Magic carried beneath glamour didn't fully exist until the daemon shifted forms, and as Lyre had experienced, the moment of delay between the shadow weave hitting him and his loss of glamour was enough to spare whatever power he carried in his other form.

This griffin got lucky—he must have been in glamour when the KLOC struck, while at the same time carrying fully charged lodestones under his glamour that he could draw on to fight after the rest of his magic was consumed.

"Is there somewhere we can hide the girl?" Lyre asked.

The daemon squinted, his stamina near its end. "Do you intend her any harm?"

"No, not at all. Is there somewhere for—"

"Say it," the griffin ordered breathlessly, his green eyes darkening. "Say you intend her no harm."

"What?" Lyre shook his head but did as asked. "I swear I intend her no harm."

Something flickered in the daemon's eyes, then he nodded as though accepting Lyre's promise. "There's a hidden panic room in there, but the protective spells are gone."

Leaving the griffin, Lyre swept into the bedroom and found a wall panel already open to reveal a small, windowless room with thick steel walls. The spells protecting it had probably been the best the Ra family could make or commission, but the shadow weave devoured weavings indiscriminately—powerful or weak, they were all consumed.

He returned to the sitting room and picked up the girl. The griffin's face tightened but he seemed unable to stand. Careful of the girl's drooping wings, Lyre carried her to the panic room, then went back and pulled the griffin's arm over his shoulders. He helped the daemon across the suite and lowered him to the floor beside the girl.

"Are you going to bleed out or anything?" Lyre asked.

"Probably not," the griffin replied breathlessly, slumping against the wall.

Lyre put his hand on the door. "I'm going to seal you in. I'll either come back and let you out, or the spells will deactivate on their own in six hours. Don't try to get through them yourself."

He pushed the door shut and it blended almost seamlessly into the paneled wall. Laying his fingertips against the wood, he sent magic spinning into the steel on the other side. He wove swiftly, layering the wards—one to hide the presence of people within, one to seal the door shut, one to kill anyone who touched it, one to deflect magic attacks, one to explode upon impact if someone tried to use brute force to break in.

Not perfect, but it would have to be enough. A nymph would be able to see the wards—and a mimic would be able to disarm them—but the spells would stop any other daemon.

Giving his work a final glance, he closed the bedroom door and hastened out of the suite, stepping over bodies on his way. With the girl safe, he could focus on his main objective: getting his damn clock back from Bastian.

As he jogged down the corridor toward the atrium, he wondered if Clio had retreated outside. Otherwise, she would have caught up with him by now. He hoped—

An earsplitting detonation rocked the building. As the floor shook and something crashed loudly, Lyre grabbed a wall for balance. How much did he want to bet that Clio was somehow involved in that explosion?

Swearing, he sprinted toward the magic's source.

FIVE

ONCE LYRE had continued without her, Clio allowed herself to whimper. Just one whimper. It made her feel slightly better about the three pointy glass shards sticking out of her arm.

The blast had thrown her backward and her forearm had gone through the glass panel first, followed by the rest of her body. She supposed she should be glad the glass was stuck in her arm and not her back.

Retreating into a shadowy doorway, she ripped a few strips of fabric off the bottom of her shirt. Then she pinched the largest shard, took a deep breath, and yanked it out.

Ugh. She allowed another whimper, blinking away the tears before they could fall. She pulled out the other two shards, gave the puncture wounds a quick examination, then bound them tightly with the makeshift bandage. They weren't bleeding too badly.

Exhaling shakily, she rose to her feet. The balconies formed stacked rings around the atrium and she imagined that during the day, with sunlight streaming in through the glass ceiling, it was spectacular. But right now, it just made her feel exposed.

She located the stairs, counting until she reached the ninth floor. Lyre couldn't be far ahead of her. She would catch up to him and they would—

She paused with her hand on the door. Was that a glowing light leaking down the stairwell?

She hesitated, then rushed up the next flight. Better to check it out real quick. At the twelfth floor, she found a simple tripwire in green nymph magic—a spell that would alert the caster when someone opened the door. Reaching out, she hovered her fingers above the neat green weave. This was Bastian's magic. She was sure of it.

What should she do? Go get Lyre from the floor below? But if that took too long, Bastian could move to a different level.

They needed to know how well protected he was. Now that she had an idea where to find him, she could sneakily scope out the situation before going back for Lyre.

It took only a moment to dissolve Bastian's trip ward without triggering it. She slipped onto a new balcony, huge executive offices with tall windows and polished desks lining one side. As she crept past them, scanning for any auras or magic, she saw blood sprayed across a glass wall. On the floor beside a wide oak desk, a griffin with bronze wings and blond hair was sprawled in a puddle, his throat slit.

She swallowed and continued on. Passing three more offices with dead griffins and a boardroom with four murdered daemons, she had to fight down nausea. Even if Ra had been poised to invade Irida, this would have sickened her.

She slunk past another fancy office with its occupant slain. Ra might not have been planning an invasion before, but after this, retaliation was inevitable. How could Bastian put their homeland in so much danger? This wasn't demonstrating Irida's strength. This was a cowardly, unprovoked attack that would enrage Ra.

Ahead, she finally spotted auras. Voices murmured and she ducked behind a reception desk in front of the last executive office.

"... not reported back," someone was saying in a low tone.

"Have *any* of the teams reported back?"

"No, Your Highness."

Clio's hands clenched at the sound of Bastian's irritated voice. She peeked out from behind the desk to see Bastian and six burly chimeras exiting another office—probably having just murdered a helpless daemon.

"The other teams have no reason to take this long," Bastian snapped, brushing his fine blond hair out of his face. Out of glamour, he wore simple but fine nymph clothes—a green tunic and fitted pants.

"Our information about which floors to check for royals could be wrong," a chimera suggested. "They might be searching other levels."

"They should have reported back first."

The chimera pressed his fist to his chest in a salute. "What are your orders?"

Clio's spine prickled. She whirled around—and discovered a sword blade inches from her face. The two chimeras behind her glowered stonily.

"Your Highness," one called.

Clio ground her teeth, furious at herself. The chimera twitched his sword and she cautiously rose, her hands held up in surrender.

Bastian stopped a dozen feet away, his guards arrayed behind him.

"Well, you just won't quit, will you?" His mouth thinned. "You weren't worth the effort to hunt down, but now you've presented yourself for execution."

"And what is your justification for executing me, Bastian?" she demanded coldly. "Is refusing to help with your insane plan a crime?"

"You're a traitor to our kingdom, Clio. You don't seem to grasp that, but if it's simpler for you to understand, then I will execute you for allying with a known enemy and killing loyal Iridian soldiers."

"You weren't calling the Chrysalis weavers enemies when you wanted to steal from them."

Bastian gestured to his guard, who pushed Clio down onto her knees. The other chimera laid his sword against the back of her neck— the position for an actual execution. Her whole body went cold.

"Should I thank the master weaver for my missing teams?" Bastian asked. "He will face the same punishment for his interference."

She lifted her chin to glare into his eyes until the last moment, but a flicker of movement behind him caught her attention: a gray dragonet, perched on the steel handrail, watching Clio with sharp golden eyes.

She jerked her gaze back to her brother and smiled tauntingly. "Actually, *Lyre* isn't the one you should thank for your missing men."

"What—"

In a silent rush, Ash swept down from the level above. He landed on the handrail and, wings snapping open, launched off it directly into the six chimeras. Terror caught every daemon in its icy grip, and two chimeras died before anyone could react to the draconian's sudden appearance.

Fear nearly petrified her too, but Clio dove away from the sword at her neck. She rolled and came up on her knees, spells forming in her hands. She threw them over her shoulders without looking, then sprang up and whipped around.

The nearer chimera snapped his sword at her and she cast a shield. As his sword bounced off, she grabbed his wrist. A quick paralysis weave sent him crumpling to the floor.

The second chimera slashed at her, forcing her backward. Baring his teeth, he raised his other hand—and she raised hers. As he cast, she mimicked it, and their spells collided in an explosion of green and orange magic.

Someone howled in agony and her opponent glanced past her, his face going white. She risked a quick glance in the same direction.

Ash had a short sword in each hand, and he spun through the remaining three chimeras with eerie grace. He was back in glamour, his wings unneeded for this fight, but it didn't make him any less terrifying. Black fire coated his blades, and when a chimera tried to block a strike with his sword, Ash's weapon cut right through the steel—and the daemon's ribcage.

Bastian was pressed against the wall, his eyes black with fear as the draconian cut down his men. Either he was too shocked or too cowardly to join the fight. He just stood there while his soldiers died one by one.

Coating her hands and forearms in a shield spell, Clio catapulted toward her opponent. When the chimera brought his sword down, she caught the blade in her hands and sent another paralysis weave rushing through the steel and into his body. He fell too.

As Ash ran his sword through the second-last chimera, Clio flung two binding spells at Bastian.

He snapped out of his horrified daze and jumped clear—then sprang at her. She backpedaled but he grabbed her wrists, magic crackling over his hands. She expected to feel the chill of a lethal spell, but instead, Bastian threw her with a blast of raw magic—right over the balcony railing.

Dropping one sword, Ash snatched Clio's arm, yanking her out of the air. Without missing a beat, he pointed his other sword at the last chimera. Black flames twisted down his blade and a spear of power tore through the chimera's shield. The daemon crashed to the floor.

And that left Bastian alone in the corridor, surrounded by fallen soldiers he hadn't tried to save.

His lips pulled back in a sneer. "I'm curious how you can afford a draconian. Is the incubus funding your new attack dog?"

Clio shot to her feet beside Ash, who watched Bastian with dark eyes, his lower face covered and blood dripping off his sword.

"Give me the KLOC, Bastian," she ordered. "This is over."

"It's only just begun, Clio."

"You've already put Irida in enough danger."

He arched one delicate eyebrow. "You can't destroy the clock. Without it, Ra will attack Irida. Would you take away our most powerful weapon?"

"You're insane. Ra is far too powerful for Irida to fight. They outnumber nymphs by—"

"Numbers mean nothing. Just ask your hired mongrel." He smiled icily. "I will teach Ra to respect us."

"You'll be solely responsible for Irida's annihilation! Give me the KLOC. I can see it in your left pocket. Hand it over *now*."

"I already told you, if you take it, you'll be—" Bastian broke off when Ash shifted his weight, the subtle movement radiating impending violence. "Fine, Clio. But the consequences will fall on *your* shoulders."

He slipped his hand into his pocket, where the golden light of Lyre's magic glowed through the fabric. He withdrew his hand—and a green spark flashed among the gold.

Clio flung her hands up, casting a master-weaver shield as Bastian hurled a gemstone. It hit her shield and exploded. The blast, ten times more powerful than anything Bastian could conjure, ripped through her barrier and hurled her and Ash backward.

She slammed into the floor, little bolts of electric power running across her limbs. Gasping, she shoved herself up. Ash was even faster, already launching to his feet with black fire igniting over his hands.

A flicker of golden light—another gemstone glowing with Lyre's magic—hit the carpet between her and Ash. A circle of runes whooshed out from the gem, covering the floor with spinning symbols, then hissing electricity surged over them. She and Ash fell to their knees.

Bastian walked over to the two chimeras Clio had paralyzed and broke the spells. The daemons clambered to their feet, their expressions bleak and angry.

"The master weaver's spells are good." Bastian pulled a third gem from his pocket. "This one is particularly nasty. I certainly wouldn't want to die like this."

Green light flashed as he triggered the spell—then a feathered arrow sprouted from his wrist.

He cried out and the gem flew from his hand, landing on the carpet in front of the binding spell trapping Clio and Ash. The gem blinked warningly.

Bastian dove out of the way as a second arrow whipped past his head. The chimeras hurled orange magic at the unseen attacker as Bastian scrambled up. With a furious glare, he bolted in the opposite direction, and the two chimeras retreated after him.

Footsteps thudded, approaching from behind Clio and Ash.

"Shit, shit, shit," Lyre chanted breathlessly as he sprinted past the binding spell and dove for the gem on the floor. He grabbed it, golden power racing over his fingers. "Disarm, disarm, *disarm!*"

The gem flashed one more time, then the weaving darkened. Lyre sat back on his heels, exhaling heavily. "Holy crap, that was close."

Pocketing the gem, he drummed his fingers across one edge of the binding circle. The paralyzing electricity vanished with a pop, and Clio collapsed on her face.

"Are you okay?" Lyre's warm hands closed on her shoulders and he pulled her upright. "I almost forgot that bastard stole my spell chain last time we met."

"He's making good use of your work," Ash growled irritably, retrieving his swords and sheathing them.

Lyre grunted unhappily.

"He's escaping." Ash stepped over to the railing. "I'm going down the fast way."

"No," Lyre said. "We stick together. He's not that far ahead, and once he gets out of the building, we'll have more space for a proper fight."

Ash glanced at Lyre's bow, then nodded. "Let's go."

The two guys ran toward the stairwell and Clio followed a step behind, her heart thudding painfully. She should have done better against Bastian. She should have been able to immobilize him instead of the other way around.

They charged down flight after flight of stairs, and far below, she heard the echo of Bastian and his guards' footsteps. She, Lyre, and Ash were passing the third-floor landing when a door below slammed. Bastian had reached ground level.

Pulling ahead, Ash jumped the last twelve steps and reached for the door handle.

"Stop!" she yelled.

He jerked back an instant before touching the metal. Lyre moved aside and she raced down to the landing. A web of green light spanned the door. The lethal spell was sloppy—Bastian must have woven it in mere seconds—but it could still kill.

Tapping a knot of runes, she dissolved the spell and yanked the door open. Ash pushed in front of her again but didn't rush ahead. Clio gave the front entrance a quick examination, but it was trap free.

"Let me check first," she told the other two.

She grabbed the handle, cracked one of the double doors open, and poked her head out. The grounds were dark and silent, the mangled front gates hanging off their hinges. The wall around the property blocked most of her view, but straight ahead a green aura and two orange ones headed down the street, already two blocks away and fleeing fast.

She opened her mouth to tell Ash and Lyre the coast was clear.

A daemon stepped from the shelter of the wall and into the open space between the broken gates. His aura shone bright gold, his pale hair tousled, and for an instant, Clio's stunned brain couldn't understand how Lyre had gotten outside when he'd been standing right behind her.

Except he was still standing behind her.

The incubus outside flashed a smile, then pulled an arrow from the quiver on his shoulder and flipped it into place on his bow. Another incubus with a bright golden aura stepped into view as the first one lifted his weapon and drew the string back.

She slammed the door shut. Force exploded on the other side, and Lyre and Ash threw themselves into the doors, holding them shut. Golden light flashed as Lyre wove a lock spell over the heavy wood.

"What the hell was that?" Ash demanded.

"Clio, what did you see?" Lyre spoke without looking up from his weaving, his face white.

"Incubi," she gasped, scrambling up with every bone aching. "Two of them."

"We're getting out." Lyre shot a look at Ash. "You need to disappear. Right now. If they see you—"

Ash didn't even wait for Lyre to finish. He ran three steps and sprang into the air. His body shimmered, wings snapping out, and he shot toward the atrium's glass ceiling. Gulping back the terror triggered by the draconian's true form, Clio grabbed Lyre's hand. Together, they bolted back across the lobby and into the stairwell.

"Lyre, how are *we* going to escape?"

He swore, his complexion almost as pale as hers and his eyes black. "I don't know but we can't hang around the door. My magic won't stop them for long."

"No, but we can slow them down." She skidded to a halt, crouched, and wove a swift replica of Bastian's lethal spell from the door. They raced up another floor and she cast it again, and two steps up from that, Lyre wedged a gemstone in a corner, the spell waiting for someone to get too close.

They reached the fourth floor and stopped to listen. Breathing hard, Lyre rubbed a hand over his face.

"Bloody hell," he whispered hoarsely. "What shit luck that they were close enough to sense the shadow weave and trace it, but far enough away that they didn't get caught in it. Did you recognize who it was?"

She squinted, bringing the archer's grin into her mind's eye. Her stomach lurched sickeningly. "Madrigal."

"And the other one?"

"I don't know. I didn't get a good look at him."

"Damn. Once they're in here, they'll no doubt—" He broke off, his eyes widening. "Oh shit."

"What?" she demanded, her senses straining. Somewhere below, the two incubi were probably breaking down Lyre's traps on the door—or they were already inside.

"If they search the building, they'll find—" He grabbed Clio's hand and started up the stairs again, forcing her to sprint to keep pace. "The Ra royal. If they find the Ra princess in here, they'll kill her—and Irida will take the blame for it."

Cold rushed through her. "*Princess*? What princess?"

"The one I sealed in a room on the ninth floor," he said grimly. "And let's hope she knows a way out of here that doesn't involve a Rysalis family reunion."

SIX

CLIO'S LUNGS burned as she and Lyre ran into a sitting room littered with dead bodies. Their breakneck charge up to this floor had left her legs aching but she didn't slow down—not with the two incubi somewhere below. She'd thought she'd left the Rysalis master weavers behind forever, and she felt more terrified now than she had with an executioner's sword at her neck.

Not so much as glancing at the corpses, Lyre strode into a bedroom. Inside, his wards glowed brightly in her asper, spanning one section of the wall. He slid his fingers over the wood, dissolving the spells, then yanked the panel open.

Light glinted off the swinging blade of a dagger.

He leaped back with a yelp, the tip of the weapon catching his shirt and tearing a line across it. Half crouched inside the hidden room, a young girl brandished the dagger with her teeth bared. Golden-feathered wings quivered against her back.

"Hold up!" Lyre held his hands out placatingly. "I won't hurt you."

Her eyes narrowed. "Who are you? How did you find us?"

"I'm the one who put you in there and set up the wards."

She bit her lip, then lowered her weapon. A ruby sparkled in the center of her forehead, hanging from a delicate gold chain that disappeared into her long blond hair. Her scarlet skirt fluttered as she straightened. Several layers of fabric had been roughly cut away.

"We're going to get you out of here," Lyre promised, a soothing croon in his hypnotic voice. "There are enemies in the building. We don't have much time."

The girl drew in a shuddering breath and leaned against the doorframe, the heavy dagger trembling in her hand. Clio knew what the bone-deep fatigue of the shadow weave felt like and she was impressed the girl could stand at all.

Lyre extended his hand, fingers spread invitingly. "Come on, princess. You'll be safe with us."

"I'm not leaving without him," the girl said, looking over her shoulder. A second griffin was slumped against the wall behind her. Strips of red fabric from her skirt were bound around his middle in a makeshift bandage.

Lyre also glanced into the room. "He's unconscious. We'll have to leave him, but I'm sure he'll be okay until—"

"*No.* You said there are enemies here." The girl's voice quavered. "I'm not leaving without him."

Clio and Lyre exchanged unhappy looks. Should they immobilize the girl with a spell?

Seeing their hesitation—or perhaps sensing the direction of Clio's thoughts—the girl lifted her chin imperially. "I know how to get through the embassy without being seen. All you have to do is carry him."

"All right," Lyre said heavily. "But let's hurry."

He dragged the male griffin out of the safe room while the girl ran into the massive walk-in closet and returned with a red shawl. She and Clio used it to bind the griffin's wings against his back so they wouldn't drag. Then Lyre heaved the daemon over his shoulder, grunting from the effort.

"Holy crap." He struggled with the weight of the taller, heavier daemon, then shook his head. "Sorry, I've gotta drop glamour for this."

Shimmers rippled over his body, and when they faded, his jaw relaxed and he straightened properly under the heavy burden.

"Wow," the girl breathed.

Clio silently agreed. Lyre's bronze eyes, darkened by urgency, flicked toward the girl and he flashed her a smile that weakened Clio's knees.

"Lead the way, princess."

After one more wide-eyed, ogling look at him, the girl raced out of the room with Clio on her heels and Lyre trailing after them with the unconscious griffin.

"There's a hidden stairway," the girl said breathlessly as they entered a corridor lined with windows that offered a sweeping view of the city lights. "It will take us to a back exit. There's a car there. Can you drive?"

"I can," Lyre grunted.

The girl glanced at her limp companion, then increased her pace, her breath growing more labored. By the time they reached the stairs, hidden behind another concealed panel, she was staggering so badly that Clio had the girl climb onto her back. They raced down, down, down, then entered a barren concrete tunnel with water-streaked walls. At the end, a metal door opened into a spacious garage with four sleek black cars.

Irida was a wealthy territory, but Clio wondered just how much wealth Ra was hoarding. Vehicles on Earth were already hard to come by, but a small fleet of matching cars? The vehicles were worth a fortune all on their own.

"That one," the girl whispered, pointing weakly.

Clio tried the back door handle and found it unlocked. Pulling it open, she helped the girl inside, then raced around to assist Lyre with unloading the male griffin. They stuffed him into the backseat, slammed the doors, and Clio jumped into the passenger seat. By the time Lyre circled to the driver's side, he was back in glamour but still panting for air, his forehead shining with perspiration.

He found the keys in the ignition and started the engine. As he fumbled with a set of buttons—triggering the large garage door to slide upward—Clio's skin prickled warningly. She glanced around the garage as light from the streetlamps flooded in.

"Go, Lyre," she whispered. "Hurry."

He shifted the drive stick in a mysterious pattern, then hit the gas. The engine revved and the car tore out of the garage.

Red light flashed in her peripheral vision.

Two reapers had appeared beside the open garage door, and standing between them was an incubus with a glowing golden aura. As their car sped away, the incubus's icy stare bored into hers. He raised his hand toward the fleeing car and light danced over his fingers.

Lyre jerked the wheel and, tires squealing, the car skidded around a corner. The incubus vanished from view. Lyre steered through the streets at dangerous speeds but Clio didn't watch the road. She stayed twisted in her seat, staring back at the shadow-swathed avenues.

Fear skittered along her nerves, and it wasn't until they'd left the downtown core behind and were bumping across a crumbling freeway that she finally settled into her seat properly.

The first incubus, the archer she'd seen through the embassy's front doors ... Madrigal. But the cold incubus who'd almost caught them in the garage, almost stopped their escape at the very last moment ...

Lyceus, the head of Chrysalis and Lyre's father.

CLIO LEANED against the armrest as Lyre brought the vehicle to a stop. He braced his elbows on the steering wheel, then dropped his head onto his arms.

In the backseat, the young princess had fallen asleep, curled against her unconscious guardian's side. The male griffin's age was difficult to read but he was younger than Clio would have expected for a professional bodyguard. His clothes, scarlet with silver accents, had a military look to them, and an insignia marked his left shoulder.

The bandages around his middle were stained with blood. During the drive out of the city, Clio had checked his injuries and done a quick healing to stop the worst of the bleeding, but he needed proper care. With his magic drained by the shadow weave, he probably wouldn't wake up anytime soon.

Lyre let out a long, exhausted sigh. He'd parked off the highway in a clump of bushes and she could sense the nearby ley line. Peering at her with one tired amber eye, he mumbled, "Well, overall, that was a huge bust."

She nodded glumly.

"Bastian attacked the embassy just like he planned. We did shit all to stop it." He rocked his head back and forth. "And he got away with the KLOC on top of that."

"But thanks to you, he didn't accomplish his main goal," she said bracingly. "We saved the princess."

"Yeah, if she'd died …" He pushed himself up and slumped back in his seat, the overhead light in the car casting sharp shadows across his face. "It's still bad though, Clio. Bad for Irida. Ra won't shrug this off just because their princess survived. I'm not well versed in inter-kingdom political decorum, but I'm fairly certain attacking an embassy is considered an act of war."

"I think so too," she agreed quietly. "And the nymph soldier you interrogated said this was just the beginning—just a 'test.'"

"Now that Bastian's attack on the embassy was mostly a success, he'll probably pick a larger target for his next assault."

"What's a larger target than Brinford's Ra embassy?"

"Maybe Ra's holdings in Habinal City," he mused, referring to the human capital, "but for a truly impressive target, I don't think there is one … on Earth."

An ominous chill washed over her.

Lyre turned in his seat to face her, his expression bleak. "How much does your father know about Bastian's anti-Ra campaign?"

"I didn't have a chance to explain anything before I ran off to find you." She rubbed her forehead. "All the king knows is that Bastian left Irida with a few guards."

"Then he has no idea what his son is up to. That's a problem."

Clio nodded. If King Rouvin didn't know Bastian was recruiting soldiers and leading them in attacks against Ra, he couldn't stop it.

"Bastian is frustratingly clever. Using helicopters—a *human* technology—to hit the embassy with the shadow weave … I'd counted on the KLOC's restrictions to hold him back." Lyre ran his fingers through his hair, an unhappy expression pulling at his features. "Clio … your king needs to know what happened at the embassy tonight."

"Yeah," she sighed. "I'll have to get a message to him or—"

"No, I mean, he needs to know *now*," he cut in. "Before the Ra family finds out. If he's going to have any chance of preventing war, he needs to act immediately."

"But … how will we …"

He closed his eyes. When they opened again, the amber gleamed with hard resolution. "*You* need to tell him."

"Me?"

"Who else can? I can't. Bastian won't. The Ras will inform him with a declaration of war, and by then it'll be too late for diplomacy."

She let out a shaky breath. "Right. I guess it has to be me. But you could …" She trailed off hopelessly. "You can't come with me, can you?"

"It would just complicate matters. Besides"—he tilted his head toward the backseat—"someone needs to take care of the little princess. I'll figure out how to get her back with the griffins."

"That's too dangerous. Griffins aren't friendly toward Underworlders and if they figure out who you are …"

"There's no way they'll guess who I am."

She pursed her lips. He had a point. Few daemons knew that Chrysalis's top-ranking master weavers were incubi, and the bounty on Lyre's head, if by some unlikely chance Ra had heard about it, didn't actually tie him to Chrysalis. Samael was too smart to reveal that one of his dangerous and highly valuable weavers was on the loose.

"Once you get the girl back to the Ras, what will you do?" she asked worriedly.

"I'll catch up with Ash and we'll start tracking Bastian again—see if we can figure out where he's gone to ground this time."

"Once I've filled the king in, I'll join you. Do you have any more of those signal spells so I can find you again?"

He nodded and opened his door. Outside the car, he shimmered out of glamour and dug into his pouch of spells. Waiting in her seat, she kept her eyes closed as soft but irresistible longing washed over her. When the feeling faded, she opened her eyes to find him safely back in glamour. He pulled her door open and she got out.

He passed her an azure gem. "Don't use it until you're back on Earth. And if I trigger mine, maybe barge in with a *bit* more caution than last time."

"I'll try to remember that." Her rueful smile faded and she lightly touched his cheek where, under his glamour, an intricate family mark was tattooed on his skin. "Lyre, what about Madrigal and ... your father?"

The ghosts of fear lingering in his eyes sharpened. "I'll stay well out of their way. Ash is good at hiding and he won't want any encounters with them either. He'll know how to steer clear."

"Will Ash help? He's supposed to kill you."

"He'll help ... probably. Until we get the KLOC back." Humor chased the phantoms from his eyes. "When we meet up again, I imagine he'll have a few words for me—angry words with a lot of foul language."

"He won't be impressed that Bastian escaped right out from under us, will he?"

"Not one bit." Lyre chuckled. "I wonder how much I can irritate him? For an emotionless killing machine, it's surprisingly easy to rile him up."

"Um, maybe *don't* antagonize the assassin." Realizing she was still touching his cheek, she started to pull her hand back.

He caught it, holding her palm in place. "You should go now."

The words were soft, unhappy. She bit her lip, fighting back a wave of rising emotion. She wanted to tell him this felt wrong, that they should stay together. Being apart was ... wrong.

The words stuck in her throat. Saying it ... *we belong together* ... would change something between them. She opened her mouth, then closed it, caught in indecision. Squeezing her eyes shut, she rose onto her tiptoes.

His warm mouth met hers without hesitation. She slid her arms around his neck and he pulled her against him. He kissed her with slowly building urgency until she was gasping for air, her head spinning and molten heat gathering in her center.

With a final brush of his lips, he stepped back. His eyes, darkened to bronze, were hot and hungry as they slid across her face.

"Be careful in Irida," he said huskily. "You don't know who might be loyal to Bastian."

"You be careful too—with the princess *and* with Ash. Don't tick him off or he might change his mind."

"He's the definition of bullheaded. He won't change his mind." When she gave him a hard stare, he laughed quietly. "But I'll be careful."

"Good." It took an effort of will to pry her arms off him. Her hands fell to her sides, cold and empty. "I'll be back soon."

"I'll be waiting."

Her chest tightened until it hurt. Why was this so difficult? Giving in, she reached for one last kiss. His lips caught hers, equally as passionate, and renewed heat dove through her. She reluctantly pulled away. His dark, intense eyes followed her as she turned and broke into a swift jog, racing into the trees. Racing *away* from him.

She didn't want to leave him behind again. Last time, Bastian had captured, tortured, and nearly killed him. This time, she was leaving him in even more uncertain circumstances. But she didn't have a choice. She would just have to return as quickly as she could.

She was so determined to keep moving that by the time she looked back, only the glare of the car's headlights was visible through the scraggly pine trees. Her heart lurched but she forced herself to keep going.

The ley line danced over the leafy ground, its warm power rushing across her senses. With effort, she put Lyre out of her mind and focused on the task before her. Return to Irida. See the king. Tell him … tell him his son had betrayed their homeland and put their people in terrible danger. Would the king believe her?

She stretched a hand toward the shimmering power, tasting its essence as she focused on the White Rock ley line a few miles north of the palace. Her other hand slipped into her pocket, closing around the tracking spell.

With a deep breath, she stepped into the ley line and cast herself into the Void between worlds.

SEVEN

LYRE SAT on the sleek black car's hood, elbows braced on his knees, chin resting on his hand. He stared at the spot where Clio had disappeared into the trees, wondering why he felt so damn cold.

She hadn't looked back. Should that bother him? It kind of bothered him.

He rubbed his face, pulling himself together. Since the moment his father and brother had appeared, he'd felt like he was cracking apart at the seams, his emotions churning in a sickening mess of fear, dread, loathing, and shame.

The last one surprised him. Was he ashamed of his fear? Or was he ashamed for … betraying his family?

It never ended, did it? No matter how much he tried to convince himself he didn't care, that he hadn't cared for years, part of him still wanted to make his father proud. But even before developing a defiant streak in his youth, he'd never earned a single word of praise from Lyceus. As a child, he'd been the slowest learner of his siblings. Dulcet, younger by two seasons, had surpassed Lyre quickly.

He squinted at the black sky. His sluggish progression through the apprenticeship curriculum hadn't been entirely due to a lack of talent.

He'd just wanted to learn different things. Before his third apprenticeship season, he'd already been an expert in illusion weaving. That, however, had not impressed his father. Nothing had.

He pushed off the car. Impressing his father was a desire he'd thought he'd crushed out of his psyche years ago, but here it was, still lingering. A lifetime of indoctrination took a lifetime to overcome, he supposed.

Circling to the back of the car, he pulled the door open to study his new charges. The girl was curled up against her guardian's side, hugging his arm the way a child might hold a parent. How close was their relationship? No wonder she'd been unwilling to leave the guy behind.

What a strange twist of fate that Lyre was now the guardian of a Ra princess. From the moment Clio had shown up at Chrysalis, his life had grown more unpredictable with each passing day.

"Princess?" He gave her thin shoulder a gentle squeeze. "Wake up."

Her forehead wrinkled, then bright yellow-green eyes popped open. Fear flashed across her face.

"It's okay," he soothed, using a touch of aphrodesia to calm her. It didn't work on children the way it did on adults, for which he was eternally grateful. "You're safe—for the moment, at least."

Her gaze flashed around, taking in their new location, then she touched the griffin's bandaged side, her fingers trembling when wet blood stained them. "He's still bleeding."

"He won't die. My friend did a little work on his injuries, though we'll need to get him to a healer soon." Lyre crouched beside the open door, putting his head lower than the girl's. "We're outside Brinford, but we don't want to hang around. Where should I take you?"

"Take me?" she repeated blankly.

"You don't want to stay here, do you?" he asked teasingly, flashing her a warm smile. Her fear-stricken expression softened. "The embassy was attacked, so where's the next best place for you to go?"

"Home."

"Back to the Overworld, you mean?" When she nodded, he sighed. He'd been afraid of that. "Do you know how to travel ley lines?"

"I've never done it by myself," she said, "but I can travel the lines with someone else. I know lots of ley lines in my kingdom."

"If I carry your friend, I can shield you both across the line, but you'll have to guide us. Can you do that?"

She nodded again, and he hoped her confidence was appropriate to her skill level.

"The ley line we go to," he clarified, "needs to be a place where you can get help easily, but also somewhere that will be safe for me."

"For you?"

He arched an eyebrow. "I'm an Underworlder."

"Oh."

"You're a smart kid, princess," he told her. "I'm sure you understand that if an Underworlder waltzes into Ra territory with their princess as his 'prisoner,' it won't go well for them."

Her eyes widened. "Am I your prisoner?"

"Not at all, but I can't let you out of my sight until you're safe with your people. Can you think of a ley line where I can drop you off and also leave again without getting in trouble? Somewhere that isn't guarded."

Her eyebrows scrunched in thought. "You want to drop us off then leave?"

"Yep. Like I said, I'm an Underworlder. I need to get back to, you know, Underworld things."

"Why did you save us, then?"

"It's a long story, but the short version is that I don't want to see a child murdered for political gain, and I don't want to see a lot more people get hurt in retaliation."

"You're not what I expected Underworlders to be like."

He grinned. "I'm not like most Underworlders."

Her lips twitched in a small smile. "I know a good ley line."

"Excellent. Let's get you back home, and your pal here can get some healing."

He helped her out of the car, then circled to the other side. Dragging the unconscious griffin from the backseat, he heaved the daemon over his shoulder again. The girl following, he trekked through the bushes.

The ley line came into view, the wall of green and blue light rippling sedately.

Holding the griffin with one arm, Lyre extended his other hand to the girl. "Ready?"

She hesitated, her lower lip between her teeth. "You saved our lives."

"You're welcome," he replied in amusement, wiggling his fingers in invitation. "Now let me take you home."

She cautiously placed her small hand in his. Pulling her forward, he stepped into the line and its soft power rushed over them, a warm current he could feel inside his body.

"Once I shield us, you can go ahead. I'll follow your lead."

She nodded, her young face tightening with concentration. Closing his eyes, he enveloped the three of them in the magical protection required for crossing the Void—the emptiness between worlds. Taking three people across would exhaust him, but he'd have enough power reserved to return.

Opening his eyes, he glanced down the line once more, wondering if this was the same spot where Clio had gone through. How long until she returned? *Would* she return?

The Ra princess tightened her grip on his hand. She stepped forward and, following her guiding touch, he plunged into the howling oblivion.

THE PRINCESS'S small hand guided him from the ley line and blazing sunlight blinded him. He stumbled, sand shifting beneath his feet. Hot wind whipped across his skin and he squinted painfully.

Then voices erupted and shadows blocked the light—daemons surging toward him.

They grabbed him as others wrenched the girl away. They ripped the unconscious griffin from his hold and the butt of a weapon slammed into his stomach. He doubled over, unable to breathe as he was shoved roughly into the sand.

"Don't hurt him!"

The princess's command rang out but the daemons pinning him down didn't gentle. They yanked his arms behind his back and bound them with a spell. A jumble of male voices sounded and the princess's high, pleading tones rose above them. The chaos reigned for another minute, then quieted.

Lyre spat out a mouthful of sand. Eyes watering from the sunlight's intensity, he caught a sideways view of the walled compound that enclosed the short ley line. Six tall, muscular griffins with golden-brown wings surrounded him. Their loose, flowing garments and shining armor matched, down to the laces on their boots. That, combined with their long halberds topped with curved blades, could only mean they were soldiers.

Fancy soldiers, by the look of it. Important soldiers.

Another three griffins surrounded the princess's unconscious bodyguard, two propping him up while a third checked his injuries. The princess stood halfway between the two groups and an older griffin kneeled respectfully before her while she spoke.

Lyre slumped in the hot sand. He wouldn't be fighting his way out of this one. Bloody hell, had this backfired. Trusting a Ra, even a young one, had been a mistake.

The soldier kneeling before the princess nodded and rose to his feet. She turned, her hands twisted together, and stepped closer to Lyre.

"Um," she began in a hesitant whisper.

The older soldier cleared his throat pointedly and the princess straightened her spine as though he'd poked her.

"Underworlder." This time, her high voice rang with imperial command. "We owe you a life debt, and upon my family's honor, I swear it will be repaid."

His mouth twisted angrily. "How about letting me go, seeing as you didn't choose an *unguarded* ley line like we agreed?"

She flinched, tears filming her eyes, but she lifted her chin higher as though to deny them. "This is my family's emergency ley line. It's the safest one."

"Let me go, then."

"I can't do that." She glanced at the older soldier for support. "It's not—not my place to make that decision. My brother will decide what to do with you."

Despite the blazing suns in the clear sky, Lyre went cold with apprehension. Being turned over to a Ra prince did not bode well for him.

"Once he wakes up," she added, glancing over her shoulder.

"Once he … oh, hell." He jerked his head toward the unconscious griffin. "That guy is your *brother*?"

The princess clasped her hands together. "Eldest prince and first general of the royal guard, Miysis Ra."

A prince and a *general*. That explained the militaristic outfit. And his fighting ability. And why he was solid muscle that weighed a damn ton.

Lyre hadn't saved one Ra royal. He'd saved *two*. And it was the deadly prince, not the young princess, who would decide Lyre's fate.

EIGHT

CLIO LET the cool water from the fountain trickle over her fingertips. It was almost as refreshing as the sweet breeze that whispered through the courtyard, carrying the scents of leaves, flowers, and sun-warmed rock. The scents of home.

Beams of amber light streaked across the valley that the Iridian city, clinging to the mountainside, overlooked. Beyond the quiet courtyard where she stood, soft sounds of life filled the palace—guards on patrol, servants going about their duties, nobles and advisors murmuring to one another.

She brushed her wet fingertips across the blossom of a floating plant in the fountain's basin. Gems inlaid in the carved edge sparkled brilliantly in the dying sunlight. Elegant trees, twice her height, surrounded the fountain, their branches intertwined above her head. Just within the circle of trunks, two carved benches faced each other, the fountain between them.

She turned toward the nearest bench.

Rouvin Nereid, king of Irida and ruler of the nymphs, sat with his elbows braced on his knees and face in his hands. Pain clung to him like invisible chains dragging at his limbs.

Throat tightening, she crossed the polished stone tiles and sank down beside him. Rouvin had been sitting in silence, with his head bowed, for nearly ten minutes. He hadn't moved since she'd finished explaining.

She had told him everything. Maybe that would prove to be a mistake, but omitting Lyre's involvement would have left huge gaps in the tale. If her father turned against Lyre later, she would find a way to protect him.

Rouvin finally raised his head. His pale blue eyes were haunted as he tipped his gaze toward the stars appearing in the darkening sky. "Part of me has feared this day for many years."

"What do you mean?" she asked. "Did you know Bastian was planning something like this?"

"I never could have imagined *this*, but I have feared the day he would cross an unforgivable line." He turned his hands over as though he held invisible secrets upon his palms. "In what way did I fail him? Did I push him down this path? Could I have stopped him, redirected him?"

She hesitated, unsure if she should say anything. "It's not your fault."

"I am his father and his king. Who else can I blame?" He folded his hands together and rested his chin on them. "As a child, his mother and I marveled at his quick mind—how he could trick sweets from the maids or preferential treatment from his tutors. It seemed harmless."

He closed his eyes as though blocking out the memories. "I'm not sure anyone but my wiliest advisors recognized his manipulations for what they were. His mother certainly didn't."

"I didn't either," Clio whispered. "I never suspected he wasn't being sincere. Kassia knew, though. And Lyre too."

"I encouraged Bastian to rely on honest communication instead of deception, but ..." His jaw clenched. "Never did I imagine he would construct such an elaborate and destructive deceit as the one he inflicted on you."

"I was just a pawn." She looked down at her lap. "All those little jobs spying on Ra agents were just to train me for the important one— stealing from Chrysalis."

As the last of the suns' glow faded, the shadows deepened. Clio straightened her skirt, the fabric torn and stained from recent battles. She shook off the ghostly feeling of Eryx's blade on her throat and the sound of Bastian's cold, unfamiliar voice.

"What now?" she asked.

His lined face tight and weariness dimming his eyes, Rouvin steepled his fingers—a gesture Bastian favored as well. "I don't know."

Her stomach turned over.

He glanced at her, a sad smile on his lips. "A king should never admit such a thing, but this … this is beyond anything I could have anticipated." He exhaled, the rise and fall of his chest slow and methodical. "Clio, please locate a royal advisor and instruct him to gather the council for an emergency meeting."

She started to rise but hesitated, wishing she knew what to say. Instead of getting up, she slid closer and touched the back of his hand.

"Father," she whispered, her voice cracking on the unfamiliar address—a name she had never called him before. "This isn't your fault. What Bastian did isn't your fault."

He placed his other hand atop hers, clasping her fingers between his warm palms. "Perhaps not, but it is my responsibility."

"There isn't much I can do, but I want to help if I can."

"You have a kind soul, Clio. Perhaps if Bastian had grown up with you at his side, things would be different." He withdrew his touch. "Please alert the council. I need … time to think."

Nodding, she crossed to the arched doorway that led back into the palace. Four guards stood at attention, out of earshot but close enough to jump to their king's defense. She glanced back to where Rouvin sat on the bench, staring sightlessly at the fountain.

Bastian had inflicted a terrible wound on her heart with his lies, his threats, his attempts on her life. But that was nothing compared to the damage he had callously dealt his father, and that more than anything underscored the prince's true cruelty.

That he could hurt the bastard sister he'd never cared about was one thing. That he could shatter his father's heart with such a deep betrayal was a whole different evil. Was his vendetta against Ra worth tearing his family apart and putting all of Irida at risk?

CLIO SAT cross-legged in the cool grass, her face tilted toward the stars. A refreshing night breeze washed over her, but her mind was far from the palace where she was waiting for the council meeting to conclude.

Where was Lyre? Was he looking at Earth's stars? Were the night skies in the two realms the same, just viewed from different parts of space's vast expanse?

More likely, he had already reunited with Ash and the two were busy tracking down Bastian and his men. If Bastian was on Earth, Ash would eventually locate him. She just hoped that didn't happen while she was gone, because she knew what the draconian assassin planned to do if he caught the prince.

Fireflies and glowing bell moths fluttered from flower to flower, filling the garden with enchanting spots of luminescence. Lyre hadn't seen the palace gardens at night and she wished she could show him.

She watched the dancing insects, unable to shake Lyre from her thoughts. Fretting about where he was, if he was safe, what he was doing. Aching to see him again. No matter how many times she told herself it was ridiculous to think about him constantly, it made no difference.

We belong together. How she'd wanted to say those words, but she had no idea how *he* felt. He cared about her, of that much she was certain, but he was an incubus. Incubi never fell in love. Everyone who'd ever heard or told a story about the caste said the same thing.

She plucked a blade of grass and methodically shredded it. She hadn't learned about aphrodesia until after meeting Lyre, but she'd heard all sorts of stories about incubi's bedroom prowess and influence over women. Was she just another foolish girl who thought she could tame an incubus?

Quiet footsteps broke into her thoughts. Two nymph guards, each with a sword sheathed at her side, walked into the garden with their charge between them.

Hands clasped together, the young princess of Irida stood in a white dress made of lightweight fabric, the edges decorated with delicate lace and sparkling diamond chips. Her long blond hair was loosely braided, and she had the same pale blue eyes as her father and brother. In the two years since Clio had seen Petrina, the girl had grown from a child to an adolescent with glimmers of the woman she would eventually become.

As her guards retreated to the garden's edge, Petrina stood with stiff shoulders, her hands folded regally in front of her but her fingers twisted together so tightly it looked painful.

"Petrina?" Clio asked softly.

Tears filled the girl's eyes. Prying her hands apart, she padded across the grass, dropped down, and leaned against Clio's side.

Clio drew in a silent breath. What did Petrina know? Had Rouvin talked to her or had she overheard something? The girl leaned against Clio, sniffling quietly. Even as a young child, she'd never been the type to ask for help or comfort outright, but that didn't mean she wasn't in need of it.

Closing her eyes before her own tears escaped, Clio wrapped her arm around Petrina's narrow shoulders. Her thoughts tumbled through the three years she had spent in the palace, with countless afternoons and evenings spent with the princess, playing silly games, digging in the gardens, and practicing curtsies—even at six years old, Petrina had been an etiquette pro. Those carefree days seemed like a dream now.

She held the princess close, grieving silently for what her half-sister had lost. Life for the Nereid family would never return to the way it had been. Whether Bastian gave up his plans and returned peacefully, or he continued his campaign of lies and violence to incite a war, he would never again walk the palace halls as the revered crown prince.

What was he thinking? How could he have sacrificed all he had for this insane, prideful scheme?

A nymph in the green livery of a royal messenger squeezed past Petrina's guards and entered the garden. He bowed deeply to the princess, then offered Clio a respectful nod.

"Lady Clio, His Majesty has summoned you."

Clio gave Petrina a comforting squeeze, then rose to her feet. The princess, hugging her legs, watched Clio leave.

The messenger led her through the stone and marble halls and into a tall spire. They climbed endless circular stairs, the walls embellished with a tile mosaic of curling vines that climbed with them, until they reached a landing where four royal guards waited outside a heavy wooden door.

A guard pulled the handle, swinging the door open as she approached. Inside, a spelled crystal in the center of a heavy wooden table illuminated the circular room. Seated around it were the twelve members of the royal council, and at the head of the table, the king looked up at her entrance.

"Clio." He waved her in as the guard shut the door. "Please sit."

He gestured at the empty seat beside him—the only unoccupied chair in the room. The silence pressed in on her. The elder nymphs of the council watched with judgments in their eyes—though whether favorable or hostile, she had no idea.

As she stopped beside the empty chair, positioned by the king's left hand, she realized whose seat it was. Bastian's seat. Her chest constricted, and with stiff movements, she lowered herself into the chair.

"Thank you for coming, Clio." The king adjusted the stack of papers in front of him. "I just received an initial report from the investigative team on Earth, confirming there was an attack on the Ra embassy, as well as the presence of nymph and chimera magic."

She nodded, unsurprised Rouvin would verify her story before deciding on a plan of action.

"The situation is grave," an advisor said. "Ra could declare war."

"Would they risk the trade agreement that easily?" another asked doubtfully.

"The agreement is already at risk. We have not completed negotiations."

"If we knew what Prince Bastian is planning, we would have a better idea how to act. He is no fool. His plans must involve—"

"He is no fool?" Rouvin repeated, his voice as bitterly cold as the north winds that blew down from the mountains in winter. "He has endangered our kingdom for no more than reckless arrogance. The safety of our people must always supersede pride."

"The trade agreement puts us in a subordinate position to Ra, financially and politically," a younger advisor murmured. "Ending it and asserting our independence would benefit Irida in the long run."

"The *trade agreement* isn't what puts us in a subordinate position," the oldest nymph corrected firmly. "It's the simple fact that we are a tiny kingdom with a small population and an insignificant military."

"But without it, we could sell our exports at higher prices. Increasing our wealth would—"

"Would make us an even more appealing target for any who wish to encroach on our borders—not just Ra."

"The trade agreement is mutually beneficial," Rouvin proclaimed with finality. "As it has for centuries, it serves our kingdom by ensuring our most powerful neighbor imports the majority of our expensive gems and metals at fair prices—not the highest prices, but fair ones. And it ensures no other kingdom views us as a weak or isolated target."

He looked around the table, his pale eyes stern. "What my son has failed to grasp is that our subordinate relationship with one powerful territory protects us from *many* territories. It is not ideal, but it is our best reality." When none of the advisors argued, Rouvin slid his stack of papers to Clio. "These were uncovered in a concealed compartment in Bastian's library."

She hesitantly flipped through the complex notes, all pertaining to Ra territory—populations, military assessments, trade routes, economy, even their climate. At the bottom of the pile were several large, folded sheets that she opened to reveal detailed maps of three Ra cities and a human city. On the Brinford map, the Ra embassy was marked in red. The warehouse where Bastian had set up his base before the attack was also marked.

She looked at the other maps. Ilvanad, Aldrendahar, and Shalla'isa. The three Ra cities closest to Irida.

"From these, we can assume Bastian intends to expand his targets to the Ra territory in the Overworld," Rouvin said. "Once he attacks on Ra soil, Irida will be doomed. Regardless of this ultimate weapon Bastian has acquired from Chrysalis, Ra will crush us."

"I don't understand why Bastian would do this," Clio mumbled. "How does he not realize that Irida can't defeat Ra?"

The elderly advisor cleared his throat. "I do not think Prince Bastian intends to allow a war. I believe his intention is to commit a series of atrocities against Ra, then force them to sign a peace treaty to prevent further loss of life. It is a gamble most would never consider. Regardless of how effective—or abhorrent—his attacks may be, the Ra matriarch could refuse to treat with him."

"She may not have a choice." A nymph tapped two fingers on the tabletop. "If he unleashes this clock weaving on a city, he could slaughter every resident with only a small force. Never has a magic existed that can eradicate all defenses in one unstoppable sweep."

"If it's too close to a ley line, it could eradicate all magic across the realm," Clio cut in, not liking the hint of awe in the daemon's tone. "It must be destroyed."

"Our most urgent priority is Ra," Rouvin said. "If Bastian attacks again before we make contact, it will be too late to reverse the damage."

"Make contact?" Clio repeated.

"I must meet with the Ra royals." Sudden anguish tightened his features before he composed himself. "And before them, I will disown Bastian Nereid as my son, my heir, and a citizen of Irida. I will depose him as crown prince and brand him a traitor."

Painful silence rang through the room.

"Further," Rouvin continued, his voice empty of emotion, "I will decree to all of Irida that Bastian has committed crimes against the kingdom and the crown. He is wanted for treason, along with all those who have aided him. We have already begun an investigation into missing soldiers."

"Ra will demand Prince Bastian's execution," an advisor said.

"What of succession?" Another nymph pressed both hands to the tabletop. "Petrina is ..."

He trailed off under Rouvin's icy stare.

"My daughter is what?" the king asked quietly.

"Her education hasn't been tailored to this role," the advisor answered hastily. "She has no experience and ... perhaps not a firm enough temperament to rule?"

THE BLOOD CURSE 69

"She will be eligible to take the throne by her twenty-first year. She has plenty of time to learn." Rouvin's expression hardened. "She is now the heir apparent and she *will* rule as Irida's queen."

Clio pressed a hand to her stomach, feeling sick. Irida's fate was irrevocably changed, and she had played a role in its titanic shift.

"Clio," Rouvin said, turning to her. "I cannot ride into Ra without sending word ahead, and it must be quick—before Ra can organize a response to the embassy attack."

She nodded, unsure why he was explaining this to her.

His pale eyes, lined with hidden grief, met hers. "Will you ride to Aldrendahar as my emissary?"

The floor tilted precariously under her chair. "M-me?"

"It must be you. I cannot trust anyone else. Aside from this council, you are the only nymph in the palace who knows what Bastian has done."

She stared at him, speechless.

"And lastly, you alone witnessed Bastian's attack and heard his declarations of intent. Only you can share this firsthand truth directly with Ra." He exhaled. "It will be dangerous. You will have to cross the desert to Aldrendahar first, then travel onward, wherever they direct you. They may turn you away or try to kill you."

She swallowed back a bitter laugh. Neither crossing the desert nor defending against violent griffins would be a first for her.

Rouvin pressed his lips together. When he spoke again, his voice was soft, almost inaudible. "I do not want to lose my daughter as I have lost my son, but I must give you this task regardless. There is no other option."

Strange pain washed through her at his words, and she couldn't look at the twelve other nymphs at the table. The royal council knew she was Rouvin's bastard child but the secret had never been acknowledged, even in private.

"I will go," she answered. "I will take your message to Ra." Lyre's face flashed through her mind, but she pushed thoughts of him aside. This was just as important as joining Lyre to search for Bastian on Earth. But how long would this extend their separation?

Aldrendahar. In her mind's eye, she could see the distant towers surrounded by a high wall, nestled amid endless sand dunes. She had glimpsed the city while crossing the desert with the jinn Sabir.

A sad smile pulled at Rouvin's lips. "Thank you, Clio. Thank you."

She looked up at her father, frowning. "What did you mean when you said only I could speak the … firsthand truth about Bastian?"

Rouvin leaned back in his chair and steepled his fingers. "Are you not familiar with the griffins' unique caste ability? It is deceptively simple and harmless, but it may be the most powerful ability of all."

Eyes wide with alarm, she shook her head.

"They are truth-seers," he told her. "And to lie to a griffin is to invite death."

NINE

AS FAR AS prison cells went, this one wasn't so bad. Lyre really couldn't complain.

He stretched his arms over his head and arched his back, then slumped into the silk cushions. Beside the daybed, a round table held a platter of fruit and a pitcher of water that had been full of ice when it had arrived, the outside covered in condensation.

Lips pursed, he considered his accommodations. The spacious suite boasted a comfortable sitting area with the daybed where he currently lounged, a table with two chairs, and a bookshelf and desk on one wall. On the other side of the room, heavy drapes hid a ridiculously comfortable bed. Everything was exceptionally fine—rich fabric, intricate tile work, expensive ceramics, and potted plants.

In the room's center, a sunken pool was filled with scented water. At first, he'd been baffled by the bathtub in the middle of a sitting room, but when the afternoon heat had surpassed "baking oven" intensity, he'd figured it out.

It was a luxury suite intended for a rich businessman or an important diplomat. Lyre would have happily enjoyed this impromptu vacation if not for the fact he wasn't allowed outside the room.

He grabbed a handful of grape-like red fruits and popped them into his mouth, savoring the sweet juices. Who was he kidding? He was a prisoner in a foreign realm, his only two allies were unaware he was missing, and his fate depended on the whim of a prince he'd exchanged all of ten words with ... but he was still enjoying himself.

He flopped back on the pillows again. Why not enjoy it? No one was trying to kill him, so it was a big step up from last week. And this was a hell of a lot more luxurious than his house back in Asphodel.

Occasionally grabbing more fruit from the platter, he resumed flipping through the books he'd pulled off the nearby shelves. He couldn't read the language but instead perused illustrations of foreign landscapes and drawings of pottery, fascinated by the glimpses into another culture.

Eventually, he rolled off the daybed, stretched lazily, then walked past the sunken bath toward the room's farthest end. The wall, if it could be called a wall, featured arched windows that started at the floor and rose to the ceiling, a thick stone railing all that separated the suite from the open air.

Lyre propped his elbows on the top rail and leaned out, letting the hot sunlight warm his face.

Beyond the railing was a straight drop of at least five stories, and below that stretched the city. Orange stone buildings, some short with flat roofs, some tall with rounded peaks, were tumbled together with little rhyme or reason. A high wall enclosed everything, and shining water filled a wide canal that cut through the city's center.

Unfamiliar palm trees interspersed the buildings and clusters of rich plant life bloomed in every nook and cranny, but green wasn't the only color that graced the city. Red fabrics, shining gold embellishments, bright paint accenting carved decorations on the buildings—there were bright hues everywhere.

Daemons moved about the city with lazy purpose, dressed in layers of flowing garments. From his lofty perch, Lyre observed a nearby bazaar, the wooden stalls shaded by vibrant fabric roofs, hundreds of daemons—some winged griffins, some not—wandering among the merchants. A flock of birds that resembled pheasants, their dark plumage marked with turquoise patterns, fluttered across the rooftops, waiting for scraps to steal.

Beyond the encircling wall, however, all colors besides burnt orange disappeared. Sand stretched in endless dunes as far as the eye could see, not a single landmark to interrupt the horizon.

When the heat grew unbearable, Lyre retreated into the shade and grabbed the heavy drapes, pulling them partway across the windows to keep the room cool. He stopped on the patterned tiles that edged the tub, watching flower petals float on the water.

Relaxing was all well and good, but he was growing restless. How long would he be stuck here, comfortable but imprisoned? With nothing else to do, he returned to the daybed and drifted into a restless sleep, but his nap was cut short when a ping of magic went off in his head. Someone had triggered the hidden ward he'd put on the door.

He was on his feet, still blinking groggily, when the door swung open. He expected guards delivering his evening meal, but it wasn't a soldier who walked into the suite.

If the guy had looked like *this* last time, Lyre would never have mistaken him for anything but royalty.

Miysis Ra, eldest prince and first general of the royal guard. His waist-length hair, rich golden-yellow, hung over his shoulder in a thick braid woven through with fine chains and chips of topaz. Similar jewelry looped around his neck, just over his top garment—a piece of clothing Lyre had no name for. It was like a hooded cloak that fell only to elbow-length, woven of fine silk and weighted with heavy tassels on either side to hold it down.

It was bizarre, but on a griffin, the design made perfect sense. The garment covered his shoulders and upper arms but didn't interfere with the golden-brown wings tucked against his back. A tail swished idly behind him, ending in a fan of matching feathers.

The cut of the top left the prince's lower torso bare. His musculature was impressive enough, but in the style of this place, an extra splash of color had been added: turquoise designs were painted over his abs and around his forearms.

Lyre realized he was gawking and pulled himself together. Lucky for him, Miysis probably hadn't noticed—he was too busy giving Lyre an equally thorough once-over.

Lyre suspected he looked just as exotic and fascinating to the prince. And it probably helped that Lyre wore a very similar—though less bejeweled—version of Miysis's outfit. The cloak-ish top garment didn't make much sense on him, but he liked the pants—loose, flowing layers that kept him wonderfully cool, bound in place with a wide tie wound several times around his hips.

Miysis completed his appraisal and a slow smile pulled at his lips. His jewel-bright eyes, their color somewhere between yellow and green, were accented with a turquoise line traced beneath each lower lid.

"The clothes suit you," he observed, the melodic richness of his voice taking Lyre by surprise all over again.

"Everything suits me," he replied with a sharp smile.

"I must apologize for keeping you waiting so long. I imagine you'd like to stretch your legs."

He had no idea what to think when Miysis walked right out of the room again, waving at Lyre to join him. Half expecting an ambush, he cautiously followed the prince out. Four guards with halberds and gold-accented armor stood twenty paces away. Miysis waited alone in the hall, weaponless and apparently unconcerned that Lyre might attack him.

Lyre scanned the tile floors, carved pillars, and gold wall sconces holding light-spelled crystals, searching the corridor for danger.

"This isn't a trap," Miysis murmured, starting forward at an unhurried pace. "If I wanted to kill you, you would be dead."

Unable to disagree with that, Lyre fell into step beside the prince. "After two days of confinement, I might be a little paranoid."

"Again, I apologize. Between my injuries, our urgent preparations, and the side effects of that … spell, this was the earliest I could meet with you."

Lyre kept his expression neutral, wondering if he could pinpoint the change in his accommodations to when the prince had first woken from his healing. Lyre's initial imprisonment hadn't been nearly as

THE BLOOD CURSE   75

comfortable as the luxury suite, which he'd only enjoyed for the past day.

"Preparations?" he questioned, not liking the sound of that.

Miysis paused near the end of the hall. "Would you mind pulling up your hood? I'd rather not advertise your presence. It could prompt awkward questions."

Bemused, Lyre drew his hood over his head. With the guards trailing behind them, Miysis led Lyre into a maze of wide corridors.

"Let me be clear," he went on in a low voice. "You are not a prisoner. If you want to leave, I'll take you to a ley line. First, however, I need to understand what happened at the embassy two nights ago."

Lyre studied Miysis out of the corner of his eye. Interesting. If Bastian, the other prince he'd dealt with recently, had promised him freedom upon request, Lyre wouldn't have believed a word of it. But his gut said Miysis was being honest.

Of course, just because his instincts believed Miysis's sincerity didn't mean Lyre would be a trusting fool.

They entered an open plaza bordered by twin staircases that folded down into an even larger foyer with a gold fountain in the center. Two twenty-foot statues towered on either side—winged women in flowing robes—and busy griffins crisscrossed the space.

"Glad to hear it," Lyre replied as they headed down the stairs, "but I'm not sure I can answer your questions about the embassy."

Miysis's mouth quirked down, his bright eyes flicking over Lyre as though reassessing him. "I need to know whatever you know. You're involved somehow."

"How do you know I wasn't a random passerby who stopped to help out of the goodness of my heart?"

"Then surely the gods have blessed me that a daemon with lethal combat skills and rarely seen weaving ability would come *randomly* to my aid."

Lyre didn't bother to hide his sigh. So, the prince had gotten a good look at his wards before losing consciousness in the panic room. That complicated things. Spell weavers were uncommon, exceptionally skilled ones were rarer, and master weavers were a thing of legend. But the chances were infinitesimally slim that an Overworld daemon, even the prince of a powerful caste, would know anything about Chrysalis or the Hades bounty on an incubus.

"Blessed by the gods," he repeated, casually steering the conversation off topic. "Do griffins have gods?"

"You want to discuss theology?" Miysis replied in amusement. As they crossed the foyer, daemons stopped to bow but the prince didn't acknowledge them. "We respect the powers of nature, but we don't worship them the way some castes worship their gods."

"That's a relief."

Miysis slanted a look at Lyre. "Do incubi worship gods?"

He gave the prince his most seductive smile and purred, "We worship pleasure in all its forms."

Miysis blinked, surprised—but not repulsed like most men on the receiving end of that tone. "I thought incubi preferred women."

"Preferring one thing doesn't mean eschewing the other."

"Is that so?"

"Otherwise, who knows what carnal desires might go undiscovered … and unsatisfied?"

Miysis stopped, turning to Lyre with one blond eyebrow arched. "Are you seducing me?"

"Do you feel seduced?" Lyre mirrored the prince's arch look. "I'm always looking to tick something off my bucket list. 'Illicit royal lover' opportunities are few and far between."

Miysis stared at him, then shook his head. "I have no idea if you're being serious."

"I get that a lot."

Snorting in a very unprincelike fashion, Miysis swept into motion again and Lyre followed, smirking smugly. Good to know that he could keep even an aristocratic prince off-balance.

Ahead, huge double doors were open to a set of wide steps that descended to the city. Sunlight blasted Lyre the moment they walked outside, the heat powerful even late in the afternoon.

With guards in tow, Miysis cut diagonally across the stairs, heading for an arched doorway into another wing of the grounds. He had fallen into a thoughtful silence, so Lyre said nothing as they wound through covered pathways. With each cluster of armored griffin soldiers they passed, Lyre's nerves wound tighter, but Miysis merely nodded in response to their salutes.

They eventually came to one of the towers that graced the city skyline. Soldiers guarded the doors but they stepped aside before Miysis reached them. Inside, the building was plainer than anything Lyre had seen yet, but solid, clean, and impeccably cared for.

"I hope you don't mind," Miysis said as they started up a curving staircase. "I haven't had a chance to get out here in days."

"What is this place?" he asked as they passed a few wooden doors.

"The stable."

Lyre glanced around but decided not to ask how horses were supposed to climb all these stairs.

At the very top, Miysis pushed the last door open. The scents of fresh straw and musky fur wafted out. The prince strode inside, but Lyre stopped dead.

The top level was indeed a stable, but the creatures it housed had no need for stairs.

Six open stalls, carpeted in a thick layer of straw, formed a half circle around the center of the tower. On the other side, three huge arched openings revealed a dizzying view of the city and desert beyond.

Lounging in the stalls were six stunning beasts—lion-like bodies, elegant eagle heads, pointed ears like a cat's, long tails, and huge wings. Their heads and chests were covered in feathers that transitioned to smooth fur, and more plumage sprouted at their hocks and just above their giant paws. They ranged from snowy white to buttery tan to deep brown, with thick white and black bands on their feathers.

At Miysis's appearance, the six creatures stirred. The white one rose languidly and stretched, then prowled over to him and clicked its terrifying beak. The beast's head was level with the daemon's and it had to be four or five times his weight, but the prince showed no fear as he ran both hands affectionately over the creature's feathers before scratching under its chin. The beast closed its eyes contentedly.

The other five wandered over to receive a greeting. Once Miysis had given them all a head rub and murmured soft words, they drifted back to their cells as nonchalantly as they'd come over. Only the white one remained, waiting for another round of head scratches.

Miysis glanced over his shoulder. "Would you like to meet him?"

"What is it?" Lyre asked. It looked like the human-mythology version of a griffin, but since Miysis's caste was the *real* griffin form, he didn't know what to call the creature.

"He's an *opinari*." The prince rubbed behind one feathered ear. "Rushi here doesn't mind strangers. Come closer."

Lyre didn't move. "What about the others?"

"They won't attack unless I command them."

That wasn't particularly comforting. Reluctantly, Lyre ventured into the room, keeping a watchful eye on the opinaris. The other five were settling down to continue their naps, while Rushi stood patiently in the center.

Miysis waved Lyre closer, and when he took too long, the griffin grabbed his elbow and dragged him in front of the beast's hooked beak. It was even larger up close.

"Rushi, this is an incubus from the Underworld."

Rushi canted his head, then extended his beak toward Lyre, huffing a breath as he took in Lyre's scent. Jaw clenched, he held his ground.

"I'd tell you his name," Miysis continued, speaking to the opinari, "but I don't know it."

"Subtle," Lyre observed.

Miysis smirked.

Lyre hesitated, then gave a mental shrug. "Lyre."

"Welcome to Aldrendahar, Lyre."

"Wait, what? This is *Aldrendahar*?" He craned his neck to look out the archways and across the city. From this direction, he could see the distant mountains on the horizon. That meant Irida wasn't that far—though reaching the nymph kingdom would still require a trek across the sweltering desert.

"Sounds like you're familiar with the city."

"I've heard of it," he admitted, not adding that he'd seen it from a distance. "This isn't where I came through the ley line with the little princess, is it?"

"No, that was a different location. Once I was up again, I traveled here immediately and had you brought along so I could speak with you as soon as I had time." Miysis smiled briefly. "My sister wanted to come—she's fascinated by you, unsurprisingly—but I sent her home instead."

Ah, so the relocation from that other ley line to here would explain why Lyre had been bound, blindfolded, and spelled unconscious early yesterday. After that, he'd woken in the luxury suite.

"What was the big rush to come here?" he asked.

"Aldrendahar is our closest stronghold to Irida."

Lyre sucked in a silent breath. Miysis looked at him for a long moment, then crossed to a cupboard stacked with leather gear and other tools. He returned with a grooming brush and ran it over Rushi's furred haunch. Lyre backed up a few steps, breathing easier once he was clear of that beak.

"I didn't come up here just to tend to my opinaris," Miysis murmured as he worked. "Unlike at the citadel, there are no ears to overhear us."

That detail hadn't escaped Lyre's notice either.

"I'll tell you what I know of the embassy attack. I know a power like I've never seen before was unleashed against us, and it caused all magic in the building to disappear—everything from wards and locks to weapons to our own magic reserves. Many griffins passed out from shock and weakness." His hand paused in mid-motion, his grip on the brush tightening. "I know over fifty griffins were slaughtered while helpless or unconscious."

Damn. Bastian and his men hadn't held back.

"I know they were targeting my sister. They may have targeted me too, if they'd recognized me." Miysis resumed brushing with smooth, steady strokes. The opinari closed its eyes again. "I know I fought chimeras and nymphs, and that survivors reported seeing chimeras and nymphs as well, including one that the others called 'prince.'"

Lyre cringed.

"That's everything I know." Miysis patted Rushi's wing and the beast unfurled it, holding it out of the way. The prince began brushing Rushi's side. "And the only conclusion I can make is that Crown Prince

Bastian Nereid of Irida arranged an unprovoked attack on a Ra embassy, killed dozens, and attempted to abduct or assassinate our youngest princess. We are in Aldrendahar so I can prepare my forces to either defend against the next attack or invade Irida."

Silently swearing, Lyre wished he'd had the opportunity to beat some sense into that idiot nymph prince. "What do you plan to do?"

"At this point, I'm waiting, though not for much longer." Miysis faced Lyre, one hand resting on the opinari's shoulder. "The Iridian king hasn't issued a declaration of war or any other communication. My spies in Irida have reported signs of mobilization among the nymph forces, but their movements suggest defense, not offense."

Lyre blinked. Huh. So, there *were* Ra spies in Irida. He supposed he shouldn't be surprised.

"But the main reason I haven't acted yet is a mysterious incubus with even more mysterious skills saved me and my sister, and he was accompanied by a female nymph."

Miysis abruptly tossed the grooming brush to Lyre. He caught it automatically, then the griffin pulled him to the opinari's side.

"Brush him," Miysis ordered as he returned to the supply cupboard.

Lyre looked blankly at the brush. Rushi turned his head and clicked his beak expectantly, so Lyre hesitantly placed the brush against the creature. Miysis returned with a fancy comb, took up a spot beside Lyre, and began working on Rushi's feathered neck.

"I need to know what the hell is going on, Lyre," he said quietly. "I need to know before my people are drawn into war."

Lyre stroked the brush across the opinari's silky fur. The Nereid prince was desperate to incite a conflict so he could prove his strength, but despite having already been attacked, the Ra prince was desperately hoping to *avoid* war. Bastian of Irida could stand to learn a lot from Miysis of Ra.

"You've been more open and honest than I would have expected," Lyre said. "Are you always this forthcoming with strangers?"

"Not at all. However, honesty is something of a habit for griffins."

"Oh? Why is that?"

"Isn't it obvious?" Seeing Lyre's furrowed brow, Miysis halted his comb. "Don't you know?"

"Know what?"

"About our caste ability." When Lyre merely stared in confusion, Miysis's eyes widened. "I don't believe it. You were so evasive without lying that I thought you knew."

"Knew *what*?"

"Truth-seeing. That's our caste ability. I can tell when someone is lying to me."

Lyre's mouth fell open. Why had he never heard about that ability? "Wait. In the embassy, you asked me if I intended to hurt your sister, and you made me say it back to you. Were you checking if I was lying?"

"That's why I trusted you to help us."

"Well, shit." Lyre shook his head. "I had no idea. That's got to be handy."

"Extremely." Miysis resumed combing Rushi's feathers. "Are you just naturally evasive, then?"

"Old habits die hard. It's easier to avoid lying than to keep track of a bunch of fibs." Lyre ran the brush over the opinari's side, vaguely worried the beast might lower its wing down on his head. Miysis worked beside him, waiting while Lyre considered his next move. Sharing what he knew would be more to Irida's advantage than not, but it would put Lyre's secrets—and Clio's—at risk.

"Bastian has gone rogue," he said abruptly. "He's acting without the king's knowledge or approval."

Miysis absorbed that. "Are you certain?"

"As certain as I can be. I've never so much as spoken to the Iridian king, but the nymph who helped us escape the embassy has gone to Irida to report everything that happened."

The griffin prince stood quietly, eyes half closed, then let out a rough exhalation. "Maybe this won't mean outright war. Maybe." Guiding Rushi's head down, he combed the beast's crest. "Tell me everything you know."

Lyre pressed his lips together. "What if you don't like what I have to say? Will I still be free to leave?"

"You saved my sister from certain death. I do not take that debt lightly."

Lyre would rather leave it to Clio and her father to decide how much they wanted to share with the Ras, but he had a chance to undo some of the damage Bastian had inflicted.

"For me, I guess this all starts with Chrysalis," he began.

Wariness flickered across Miysis's features, confirming he was familiar with the name.

"The spell Bastian attacked the embassy with—that came from Chrysalis. So did I." Lyre grimaced. "From what I've learned, Bastian has been nursing a vendetta against Ra for years. He thinks you're oppressing Irida and that a demonstration of power will intimidate you into leaving the nymphs alone."

Miysis listened without expression, absently stroking Rushi's head.

"Bastian sent three of his people to Chrysalis under the guise of commissioning magic, but instead his man stole that spell and left the other two behind. One is dead but the other escaped with me."

"The female nymph my sister spoke of?" Miysis murmured.

"Yes. We tried to find Bastian and get the spell back before he could use it, but he attacked the embassy first. We were already tracking him, so we were able to stop some of his men, but Bastian escaped again with the spell." He shrugged. "That's it. The important stuff, anyway."

Miysis turned to him. "Everything you said is the truth as you believe it—except that last bit."

Lyre blinked, then swore under his breath. "There are some secrets I can't reveal—and not all are mine."

"How much do you know about the spell he stole from Chrysalis?"

Lyre was beginning to see patterns in Miysis's questioning— phrasing that helped him identify truthfulness in the responses he got.

"It's one of a kind," he replied instead of answering the question directly—which would have meant either revealing too much or lying. "Dangerous, volatile, and better off destroyed. That's my goal—the main reason I'm still involved in all this."

"Hmm," Miysis murmured, circling around to Rushi's other side. Lyre followed, and when the beast lifted a wing imperiously, he resumed brushing. "How does it work?"

"It consumes other nearby magic. Wipes out everything."

"A devastating weapon," Miysis observed. "I'm surprised Hades hasn't put it to use."

Lyre's hand clenched around the grooming brush. "Hades doesn't know it exists ... yet. That's something else I'm trying to prevent."

Miysis glanced at him, his green eyes darker than before. "What's your connection with that spell?"

Lyre said nothing, though his silence alone confirmed it was a smart question—too smart. Not much slipped past this prince.

After a moment, Miysis asked instead, "What is Bastian planning next? I can't imagine he intends to stop at one attack."

"I don't know. We've been one step behind him from the start."

Miysis took the grooming brush from Lyre and returned both tools to the cupboard. "I have a lot to do. I'll walk you back to your room."

"What if I'd rather go to a ley line?"

"Then I'll take you to a ley line."

No hesitation at all. Lyre rubbed his hand through his hair. What should he do? He was too far from Irida to get there easily, and even then his chances of making it through the territory weren't great. Should he return to Earth and join up with Ash to hunt down Bastian? He didn't even know if the nymph was still in Brinford.

He knew who *was* in Brinford though. His father. An icy shiver ran through him.

He didn't need to decide anything right this moment, did he? He could relax, eat, enjoy this reprieve from immediate danger for a while longer.

"Back to my room, then," he muttered. "For now."

The guards were waiting outside, and they preceded Miysis and Lyre down the stairs. When they exited the tower, the suns hung low in the sky and long shadows stretched over the city.

Miysis led him back into the citadel and up to his room. Lyre pushed the door open and took a step inside, glancing across the luxurious suite. He had no reason to linger here, yet leaving would mean going back to Earth ... where the hunter of his nightmares waited.

Returning to Brinford would be a fool's choice. He was completely unprepared to take on the deadliest master weaver in the three realms. He couldn't fight his father. He couldn't defeat the head of Chrysalis and caretaker of Rysalis's most lethal inventions spanning generations. He couldn't …

His eyes went out of focus. He couldn't defeat his father, but maybe …

"Lyre?"

He blinked, slamming back to the present. Miysis watched him with furrowed eyebrows.

"Miysis," he said abruptly. "I have a favor to ask."

"What do you need?"

"Tools." He glanced around the room. "Spell-weaving tools. Whatever you have."

"I'll see what I can find," Miysis replied, a note of caution in his voice. "Anything else?"

"One more thing, if you have it." Lyre swallowed against the sick feeling burrowing into his gut. "Quicksilver."

The prince's eyes widened. "Should I be concerned about this?"

"No … it's personal."

"I see. I'll do what I can."

Lyre nodded. Miysis gave him one more searching look, then quietly closed the door. Lyre listened to the light footsteps retreating, knowing that a guard or two would show up soon to supervise the Underworld guest. Miysis trusted Lyre's word—his truth-seeing ability saw to that—but he wasn't a fool.

Discarding thoughts of the griffin, Lyre strode to the desk where he opened a polished wood box to reveal neatly stacked paper and sharp charcoal pencils. Pulling out a few sheets of paper, he settled into the chair.

He couldn't do much without tools, but he could get started. He had a lot of work to do and precious little time to do it.

TEN

THE YOUNG WOMAN giggled flirtatiously. It wasn't a sound Lyre normally opposed, but right now, it set his teeth on edge.

"I know I've mentioned this about ten times already," he said, unable to keep the growling note from his voice, "but this *really* isn't necessary."

"*Shh*," the woman crooned. "Just *relax*."

"If you don't hold still," the other girl admonished, "I'll have to start again."

She brandished her paintbrush and he reluctantly sank back into the cushions of the daybed. Sunlight streamed across the floor, kissing the scented water of the sunken tub.

The griffin maiden reloaded her fine brush with black ink and, with a teasing smile, touched it to his abdomen. He glared at the ceiling, resisting—again—the urge to pull his arm out of the grasp of the other maiden, who was applying a complex pattern to his inner wrist in turquoise and black ink.

"We thought you would enjoy some pampering." The maiden working on his torso pouted. "*Most* men don't complain when we take care of them."

A dozen suggestive comebacks about how he wasn't like "most men" ran through his mind, but instead, he muttered, "I was busy when you two burst in and started preening me like a damn rooster."

It wasn't like him to be rude to women—especially beautiful women who were, all things considered, treating him very well—but his patience had run out at some point between the scented-water bath and being dressed like a helpless invalid who couldn't clothe himself.

"We know you were busy," the girl replied with a pretty roll of her green eyes. "That's exactly why Prince Miysis sent us to you."

"He said you didn't sleep at all last night." The other girl pointed her brush at his face, almost coloring his nose. "That is no way to take care of yourself."

"And you should definitely take care of yourself," the other added with an appreciative look over his bare torso. Not that they hadn't already seen more when they'd bullied him into the stupid tub. Good thing he wasn't shy.

"I slept last night," he protested.

Another threatening wave of the brush. "Don't lie!"

Damn it. Griffins and their truth-seeing.

"I slept for a few hours," he corrected. He didn't like stopping in the middle of his work. And how did Miysis know his sleep habits anyway?

"A few hours isn't much," the girl criticized. "It's past noon. Once we're finished, you should take a nice afternoon nap. Most of the city rests during the hottest hours."

"How am I supposed to sleep when I'm painted up like a noble peacock?"

The maiden giggled. "This ink isn't coming off without a sand-soap scrub."

Oh, lovely. He never should have let them touch him.

"Are you having trouble sleeping?" the other asked. Her fingers slid up his arm and kneaded his bicep. "I could give you a massage to help you fall asleep, if you'd like."

He chose not to acknowledge the unspoken offer for more than a massage. He didn't want massages or baths or female attention. He wanted to be left alone.

No incubus in his right mind would turn down that offer, let alone resent beautiful women pampering him with attention. Clearly, Lyre wasn't in his right mind. There were only two things he could focus on, and they had kept him up all night: weaving and Clio.

His night's weaving progress was hidden in the box on the bookshelf, out of sight from his visitors, but tools were scattered across the desk—a decent assortment but not as good as the collection he'd lost when he'd fled Asphodel.

As for Clio, she lingered stubbornly in his thoughts, overshadowing everything else. Was she safe? Was she in Irida? Was she looking for him in Brinford? Was she alone and in danger there? Not knowing was driving him insane. The worry kept scraping and scraping at his temper until he was so on edge he couldn't sleep.

"Relax," the maiden bending over his stomach commanded. "I'm almost done."

He snapped out of his internal monologue of anxiety and forced his abs—and his jaw—to relax. The wet brush glided across his skin as she completed the elaborate pattern that ran from his hipbones up to his ribs and around his sides. When she finally dropped the brush back into her paint kit, the other girl rose to her feet and leaned over Lyre.

"Look up," she instructed.

"Why?"

"I need to paint under your eyes."

"No, you don't."

"Yes, I do." She thrust out her lower lip. "You don't want me to get in trouble with the prince, do you?"

Guilt tripping him now? Grumbling, he rolled his eyes upward. The cool brush slid under one eye, then the other. She leaned back and smiled happily. "Perfect! You're all finished."

As she packed her supplies, the other girl handed him his *tapa*—the half-cloak thing griffins wore instead of a full shirt. He swung it into place and clasped it over his right shoulder.

The girls waved at him to stand. "Let's see! Come on, get up."

He swung his legs off the daybed and stood, tugging his pants a bit higher so they sat properly around his waist, the tie covering the bottom of the painted design. Suppressing his bad temper, he held his arms out to give them a better view of their hard work—made more difficult by his lack of cooperation.

"Ooh!" She beamed at her companion in a congratulatory way. "We're good, aren't we?"

"We are! Though, to be fair, it would be almost impossible to make him look *bad*."

"Very true."

He dropped his arms. "Are you done? Am I free?"

The pride and excitement slid off their faces, and the younger one dropped her gaze. "Are you not pleased?"

Damn it. These girls were just doing their jobs and he was being a miserable prick. He pulled himself together and offered them a smile. "Your patience with me is even more impressive than your skill and talent, which is really saying something. Thank you."

They brightened, and he kept his smile in place as they suggested repeatedly on their way out that he take a nap. He stood in the center of the room, waiting, until the door closed behind them. The latch clacked and his smile evaporated. Finally.

Shoulders slumping, he stretched his arms out to examine the painted designs. They were exotic and beautiful, the turquoise and black lines contrasting with his tanned skin. Add in his clothes, patterned in black, white, and a deeper shade of turquoise, and the overall effect was something to see. With his face covered, he might be able to catch as many stares as the Ra prince.

With his face *uncovered*, Lyre wouldn't have any competition. No man could compete with an incubus when it came to attracting female attention.

"It suits you."

Lyre started violently, then shot an irritated glower toward the door where Miysis leaned against the frame. Sneaky bastard. How had he gotten the door open without Lyre hearing?

"Why did you sic those beauticians on me?" he complained. "Is this punishment for hanging around your palace too long?"

"This isn't my palace," Miysis replied. Turquoise lines, probably matching the ones now painted under Lyre's eyes, drew attention to his yellow-green irises. "This is Aldrendahar's citadel, where the city council sits. The Ra palace is significantly more impressive than this, I promise."

"*Hmph.*" Lyre dropped onto the edge of the daybed.

"Did you not enjoy yourself? No one has ever complained about my body artists before."

"I'm surprised you would trust an incubus with two blushing maidens and no chaperone."

"I warned them." He shrugged. "They were perfectly willing. I suspect your good manners didn't live up to their expectations of a notorious sex god from the Underworld."

"Sex *god*? I like the sound of that."

Miysis ambled into the room, long braid swaying against his back between his folded wings, and picked up a pencil stub from the table. "How is your weaving going?"

"Not as well as I'd like." He'd made progress, but he was stuck on the implementation. He wished he could ask Reed for advice. "Any word from Irida?"

"Still nothing." The prince leaned against the table and stretched his wings to their full span, feathers spreading wide, before tucking them against his back. "My forces are ready and I can't delay much longer. Either I hear from the Iridian king today or I go to the queen for orders."

"Orders?"

"She'll decide how Ra responds to Irida's attack in Brinford." He folded his arms, gold bands around his wrists glinting. "So far, I've only given her the briefest overview and asked her to let me investigate. But she'll only wait so long."

Lyre straightened. "You're withholding details from her? Why?"

Miysis rubbed his hand over his mouth, his eyes distant. "It's easy to send soldiers to war when you don't know their names."

With that one statement, the prince revealed a great deal about himself and about his queen. Lyre looked the griffin prince over, seeing how young he was under his titles and confidence. He was Lyre's age, if that.

Young, idealistic, honorable, and perhaps a bit too trusting. Lyre wondered how the coming years as the prince and general of such a powerful caste would shape Miysis. His caste's reputation was ferocious enough that Lyre wondered if Miysis's idealism would last. How long before the ugly realities and tough lessons changed his outlook?

Lyre leaned against the daybed's backrest, relieved *he* ruled over his own fate and no one else's. Life was a hell of a lot simpler that way.

Miysis bounced one foot, betraying his uneasy tension. "What is Chrysalis like? I've only heard rumors."

"It's …" Lyre closed his eyes for a moment. "Cutthroat. Everyone is in competition with everyone else to be better, faster, smarter, more productive …"

"Sounds a lot like griffin nobility. Just add 'richer.'"

Lyre snorted in sympathetic amusement. "What's it like being a Ra prince?"

Miysis shrugged. "Difficult and demanding. Sometimes easy. Sometimes boring. This is a boring period."

"Interesting that you'd choose the Underworld stranger as your entertainment while bored," Lyre observed dryly.

The prince smirked. "Aldrendahar is on the outskirts of our territory. It's dull and backward and plebian. The highest-ranking daemons are minor nobles and city officials who constantly fawn over me, and I can only spend so much time with my soldiers before they get uncomfortable."

"So I'm the lucky recipient of your company?"

"You don't seem predisposed to fawning."

"Not at all."

"Did you never encounter any daemons of power in the Underworld? Have you ever met Samael Hades?"

Another one of those sneaky questions designed to catch Lyre in a lie. Miysis seemed so laidback and trusting that it was easy to forget he was also a royal practiced in maneuvering—and manipulating—other daemons. Lyre's mouth quirked down. Was he underestimating the prince?

"Samael Hades inspires cowering more than fawning," he evaded smoothly. "As does the Head of Chrysalis."

"What's he like?"

"Formidable. I don't know him well." That, at least, wasn't a lie. Lyre knew more about his father as the Head of Chrysalis than as a person. "What's the Ra queen like?"

"Formidable is a good word. 'Ruthless' also comes to mind."

That wasn't encouraging. If the Ra queen was a ruthless ruler, once she stepped in to take over from Miysis on the Irida issue, the chances of avoiding an outright conflict would dwindle significantly.

Rising from the sofa, Lyre brought his arms over his head, arching his back into the stretch. As he relaxed again, he caught Miysis's gaze flicking back up to his face. Oh? Had the prince been examining the body artists' work—or checking out his body beneath the art?

"I'd like to stretch my legs. How about I entertain you, sans fawning, while you take me somewhere besides this room?"

Miysis pursed his lips. "I'm not opposed, but I'd rather not showcase your presence."

"If you wanted to keep me a secret, you probably shouldn't have exposed me to a pair of gossipy women."

"Those two are my personal body artists. They won't gossip to anyone." Miysis pushed off the wall. "If you cover your face with the hood, I think—"

A sharp rap on the door interrupted him. Miysis flicked a glance at Lyre, and once he had pulled his hood up, the prince called a welcome. The door swung open and a griffin in red livery similar to a soldier's uniform but without the armor swept inside, his face shining with perspiration. Two guards from the hall followed him.

He dropped to one knee in front of Miysis. "Your Highness, an urgent message."

"Yes?"

"Twenty miles north, an entourage of nymphs approaches the city, bearing the flag of truce."

Lyre sucked in a breath, nervous but relieved. Finally. It had taken Rouvin long enough to get his ass in gear and do something. Hopefully, this meant the king had received Clio's news.

Miysis waved the messenger to his feet. "Excellent. Go straight to Captain Bakari and have him send a troop to escort them the rest of the way. As well, have the captain prepare a formal escort for me. I will meet the nymphs at the north gate."

The griffin saluted and rushed out again, the pair of guards returning to their posts in the hallway.

When the door closed behind them, Miysis glanced at Lyre. "Well? What do you say to a trip through the city instead? I wouldn't mind having you around for your insight on the nymphs."

Lyre's mouth curved up. "Can't promise I'll be useful, but if it means getting outside for a bit, I'll take it."

And he wasn't going to complain about the chance to hear firsthand what message King Rouvin had sent.

THE BAZAAR was more crowded than it had seemed from Lyre's elevated suite—or perhaps the people of the city were flocking to intercept the prince's escort.

Following a cluster of officials, Lyre ambled between a pair of soldiers—Miysis's personal guards, assigned to keep anyone from getting close enough to recognize him as an incubus. Miysis walked near the front of the procession. He may not have intended to start a parade, but that's what it had turned into.

First in line were the six soldiers clearing a path. Miysis came next, walking alone and flanked not by soldiers but a pair of opinaris. Rushi, the white one, and a tan one prowled alongside him, their heads and chests protected by glimmering golden armor.

Another six soldiers followed, then the babbling cluster of city officials. Lyre trailed after them, and even outside the group, he could see why the daemons annoyed Miysis. They would not shut up.

The procession ended with a troop of soldiers behind Lyre. He was the only one in the entire entourage that lacked wings, but with his face covered, he could pass for a griffin in glamour. An extra tan griffin.

His skin tone wasn't anywhere near the darkest in the market though. Griffins made up the majority of the population, but

Aldrendahar was clearly a trade city. Castes Lyre had never seen or heard of paused to watch the parade march by.

A male with skin a few shades darker than Lyre's with pointed horns, large animal ears and a thick tail that ended in sharp-looking spines. A female with mocha skin and curved antlers decorated with gold hoops, smoking a long pipe. A trio of younger males with golden skin, jet-black hair, tall jackal ears, and furred tails, shirtless under the blazing suns. A pair of unidentifiable daemons dressed head to toe in draping white fabric, faces covered with sheer silk, and snowy white wings tucked against their backs.

Almost all bustle drew to a halt as the armed escort crossed the bazaar, but the wildlife had no respect for royal comings and goings. Birds swooped across the rooftops, and a gang of strange reptiles — fox-shaped bodies covered in snakeskin with a lizard's head — lurked in the shadows. An oversized rodent with huge ears and a giant squirrel tail snatched a piece of fruit from a stall while no one was watching.

Lyre didn't get nearly as much time to study the market as he would have liked before they'd moved past it. They swept through wide streets of sand-dusted flagstone, the surrounding buildings draped in plants. The palm trees offered fleeting shade but the air shimmered from the rising heat. When they passed a canal of clear water, he had to swallow against his dry thirst.

They now approached the outermost wall — a barrier significantly more robust than the wall around the citadel grounds. The massive gates rose thirty feet at the highest point of the arch, and the wall was even higher and topped with an open parapet where winged soldiers stood at attention.

An empty plaza waited in front of the open gates, and the soldiers spread out in formation as Miysis moved to the center. There he stopped, flanked by opinaris, a troop of soldiers arranged across the flagstones behind him.

The griffin officials moved into the shadows of a building and Lyre followed, both eager for shade and unwilling to stand alone where he'd draw too much attention, but before he could make it out of the sunlight, Miysis gestured. Two officials hurriedly took up a spot on the prince's righthand side.

"You should stand with them," one of Lyre's guards murmured.

Obediently, Lyre moved to join the two older officials, standing a long pace back so he wasn't part of the greeting assembly.

Squinting against the suns, he peered through the gates. The endless dunes stretched toward the shadow of distant mountains, and a few miles out, a cloud of dust revealed the approaching party.

The suns hammered down as they waited in silence. The opinaris swished their tails, the only sign of their impatience. Lyre desperately wished for one of the colorful, handheld sunshades he'd seen daemons in the bazaar carrying, but Miysis didn't seem to notice the heat as he stared northward.

The minutes ticked by and the back of Lyre's neck prickled. Keeping the movement casual, he glanced around.

Miysis's escort through the city had been modest, but the prince wasn't taking chances. More soldiers had quietly filed in and now lined the plaza. The guards patrolling the parapet had doubled, and more warriors lurked on nearby rooftops. Apparently, Miysis wasn't as trusting as he'd led Lyre to believe. If this went badly, the Iridian entourage wouldn't leave alive.

The approaching party drew close enough that shapes appeared in the dust. First came the griffin escort—soldiers mounted on opinaris. Then came the nymphs, riding mounts of their own—heavy-bodied antelope-like creatures with tan- and black-patterned coats, flowing ebony manes, and a single horn arching up from their foreheads.

The opinari-mounted griffins swept over the wall and landed on nearby rooftops. Unescorted, the nymphs slowed their mounts to a loping trot. The thud of hooves on packed sand turned to a loud clatter as they passed through the gate and transitioned onto the flagstones. Of the seven nymphs, six wore green uniforms Lyre recognized from the palace guards in Irida, partly covered by lightweight cloaks and scarves to protect against the sand.

The seventh nymph wore something completely different, but it too was a familiar outfit.

They rode into the middle of the plaza and stopped. The lead nymph swung down, white fabric swirling, and handed the antelope's reins to a nymph soldier before walking forward.

The elaborate regalia fluttered with each step—white skirts with under layers of blue and green revealed by the long slit in the front. A wide band of green fabric wrapped around a slim waist, belted with a bejeweled chain. A short cloak had been added as protection from the suns, but beneath it was a high-collared shirt and draping sleeves bound in place around the nymph's upper arms.

A deep hood completed the costume, and a featureless white mask covered the upper half of the nymph's face. A jeweled tiara was fitted on the top, and long ribbons hung off the back, fluttering like streamers in the breeze.

Lyre had seen that clothing before, but even if he hadn't, he would have known. The way she held her arms, the sway of her hips, the stubborn lift to her familiar chin, the way those luscious lips were pressed nervously together—the messenger from Irida was Clio.

She walked unflinchingly toward Miysis, her face fixed on him and never turning toward Lyre or the officials. As she halted in front of the prince, Lyre became even more rigidly aware of the gathered soldiers and the watchful opinaris so close to her. Suddenly, he didn't trust a word Miysis had ever uttered.

Clio dropped into a smooth, deep curtsy, and the prince nodded in acknowledgment. She murmured something, then slipped her hand into her fabric belt. Withdrawing a sealed letter, she extended it toward Miysis.

As the Ra prince took the paper and broke the seal, Lyre mentally prepared himself. Depending on what that letter said, either Clio would be safe—or Lyre would die with her under the scorching Overworld suns.

ELEVEN

BY THE TIME the griffin city shimmered into view through the heat waves, Clio was ready to trade her soul for a drink of water. Her whole body felt like one giant bruise as she bounced in her saddle, jarred by the *tachy*'s rolling gait. The gentle herbivores lived mainly in the foothills but they were almost as comfortable in the desert.

She, however, couldn't have been more uncomfortable. Riding was only slightly less demanding than walking and she wasn't sure how much more she could tolerate. Her backside was on the verge of disintegration.

Relief swept through her at the sight of Aldrendahar on the horizon. It had been a long, trying two days. They'd set out the previous morning, traversing the full span of Irida to reach the southern border by nightfall. After only a few hours of rest, they'd headed through the foothills and into the desert before the first sun had even breached the horizon.

Once full daylight hit, travel had become an exercise in torture, but finally, the end was in sight. Or, at least, a break. King Rouvin had explained that, depending on what officials were or were not in the city, she might have to travel onward until she could present his message to someone of a high enough rank.

Dark spots hovering above the horizon took the shapes of flying opinaris. Her stomach turned over as light glinted off the beasts' plate armor, and soon she could make out their riders—equally armored griffins.

The captain in charge of her nymph escort called for a halt on the crest of a dune. Her tachy puffed for air, his sides heaving.

Six opinaris swept in and circled above her group. One peeled out of the formation and plunged down to land in a puff of sand. Her tachy jerked his head anxiously, his dark horn gleaming. She laid a calming hand on his neck, grateful for the stifling mask that hid her expression.

The opinari snapped its beak, wings flared. The soldier swung off and she forced herself to lift her chin as he approached. For years, she'd thought of griffins as her ultimate enemies. They were still dangerous, but her job now was to prevent them from becoming real enemies.

"You carry the flag of truce," the soldier declared, referring to the white flag with a black circle in its center held by one of her men. "Are you bound for Aldrendahar?"

"Yes," she replied, surprised to hear her voice was steady. "I bear an urgent message from King Rouvin of Irida."

"We will escort you to the city."

She nodded and the soldier returned to his mount. The opinari surged into the air again, and the troop glided ahead, leading the way. She nudged her tachy into motion.

The last few miles took forever but despite the endless hours of travel, she didn't feel ready to meet with important griffin officials. At least only minor nobles likely called the small outskirt city home.

For most of the journey, her thoughts had clung obsessively to an entirely different topic: Lyre. Where he was. What he was doing. Whether he was safe. Whether he was thinking of her as much as she was thinking of him. Pointless worries, considering she had no idea when she would see him again. Who knew how far she would have to travel? If she was lucky, the griffins would take her through a ley line instead of forcing her to continue across the desert.

The city walls loomed higher, spires rising behind them. The largest building, its thick tower topped with a round roof, sat in what had to be the city's center. The colossal gates were open, and two immense statues stood on either side of the entrance—twin opinaris carved from stone, their front limbs stretched out and paws touching to form an arch over the gateway. She swallowed, trying to work moisture into her mouth.

The suns glinted off a multitude of shiny surfaces just within the gate, but between the bright light and her vision-obscuring mask, she couldn't make out any details. The opinari escort swept over the wall and disappeared.

Alone with her guards, she straightened her shoulders and raised her chin. This was it.

Griffin soldiers lined the parapet, watching as she urged her tachy beneath the statues. The creature loped forward and the sudden clack of his hooves on stone after so long on soft sand startled her. As they came into an open plaza, a tall spire blocked the suns and in the sudden cessation of their glare, she finally saw what waited for her.

Her heart hit her rib cage like a sledgehammer.

A griffin, flanked by two opinaris, stood in the center of the plaza, with a few officials off to one side. *Those* were the minor functionaries she'd expected. The one in the center, however …

He was no minor noble.

Her gaze slid over him as she pulled her tachy to a stop. Long blond hair, braided. Half his torso bared, his sculpted abs painted with designs in the style of griffin nobles. Wings folded against his back, and a tail ending in a fan of feathers rested on the flagstones behind him.

She swung out of her saddle and handed the reins away, scarcely taking her eyes off the griffin. Who was he? Could he be a Ra? The family was large; along with the queen and her children, dozens of relatives both close and distant bore the Ra name.

Turquoise accents under his eyes drew her gaze to his yellow-green irises. With bold cheekbones, a strong jaw, full mouth, and those gleaming eyes, he was very handsome—young, though. Only a few years older than her.

Why did he seem familiar? She felt like she'd met him before but when had she gotten a good look at a griffin's face out of glamour? The only daemon she could think of was—

Her lungs seized with the realization.

She stopped in front of him, seconds left to decide how to react. Was he really the griffin from the embassy? She'd thought that daemon was a bodyguard to the princess. Yet, here he was, standing in noblemen dress. No one was introducing him, which meant they expected her to know who he was.

Gulping back her nerves, she dropped into a deep curtsy and hoped she hadn't guessed wrong. "Your Highness."

He nodded in acknowledgment but didn't speak, his eyes cool and unreadable. Since no one scoffed and corrected her, she must have gotten his title right.

"I bear a message from King Rouvin Nereid of Irida, to be delivered directly to the hands of Ra. May I present it to you?"

He dipped his chin in another nod, his stony silence unnerving. The weight of the mask hiding her expression was comforting. Slipping a hand into her fabric belt, she removed Rouvin's letter from the hidden pocket and offered it to the griffin.

He broke the royal seal and flipped it open. She didn't move—no one moved—as his eyes slid across the page.

Her skin prickled, a strange sort of restlessness shivering along her nerves. Despite her determination to stay focused on the Ra royal, her gaze darted away. It skittered across two nearby officials and jerked to a stop on the third one, standing a little farther back, his face shadowed by a deep hood.

For no reason she could determine, her stomach somersaulted with butterflies.

The Ra royal folded the letter again and she wrenched her attention back to him. He tucked it into an invisible pocket in his flowing pants.

"My lady, you must be tired from your journey," he said. "I would be happy to host you in the citadel while I consider King Rouvin's missive."

His deep, musical voice was so unexpectedly beautiful that she almost missed the honorific he'd used.

"I—I'm not a lady," she protested, her voice losing volume.

"My apologies. How shall I address you?"

"Just ... just Clio is fine."

His eyebrows rose and she inwardly cringed. She shouldn't have corrected him—at least not in public. Way to make things awkward.

"My people will tend to your animals and escort you to the citadel." He crooked a finger at the official beside him. "Lord Makin will see to your needs."

"Thank you, Your Highness," she managed.

"It is my pleasure." He bowed to her—a deeper bow than she would have expected—then walked away. His opinaris followed, tails snapping side to side. Lord Makin stayed beside her, but the other official scurried after the Ra royal.

The third one didn't move and her attention was inexorably drawn back to him. She couldn't stop herself from checking out his deliciously toned abs, ink spiraling across his golden skin. The white clothes, accented with black and turquoise, were striking against his tan. Unlike the others, he had no wings. Was he in glamour for some reason?

Realizing she was blatantly checking him out—thank goodness for her mask—she peered at the shadows beneath his hood, but she wasn't the only one who'd noticed that the daemon had lingered. Abruptly turning back, the Ra griffin snapped his fingers imperiously.

After a brief hesitation, the official hastened away. Clio bit her lip, feeling oddly guilty. Admiring another man felt like a betrayal, but she hadn't done anything besides look. And Lyre wasn't even here.

As Lyre and the mysterious daemon twisted together in her thoughts, she scrunched her nose. She had bigger things to worry about, like the fact she'd just handed her father's letter to a Ra *prince*. Assuming she wasn't mistaken, that was Miysis Ra.

And Miysis Ra was the unconscious daemon she'd left Lyre with two days ago. Suddenly, she was dying to finish here so she could return to Brinford, activate her tracking spell, and confirm with her own eyes that Lyre was safe and well.

She and her guards spent several long minutes getting organized—griffin attendants collecting their travel packs and leading the tachies away, others offering water and sunshades—before Lord Makin and a troop of soldiers guided her group away from the plaza. She clasped her hands together, too nervous to appreciate the city sights. Her thoughts lingered on Lyre—with occasional intrusions of the mysterious other daemon.

Damn it. Why was she so preoccupied with a stranger?

She finally started paying attention when they passed through another gateway and entered the citadel grounds. They climbed wide steps toward the citadel doors, set in an imposingly beautiful central tower. Inside was just as breathlessly overwhelming—polished marble floors, gold trim, another pair of huge statues. Two women this time, probably past Ra queens.

Lord Makin directed them up a wide staircase with a golden balustrade. They ascended several levels and entered a grand hallway, lined with pillars, ornamental wall sconces, and silk tapestries in vibrant colors.

Lord Makin approached a polished door, tapped on it, and when a muffled voice responded, he put his hand on the knob and glanced at her. "This suite is yours as long as you require. Your attendants may use the room opposite this one. His Highness awaits you to ensure all is to your satisfaction."

As her guards took up positions in the corridor, she tamped down her nerves. Lord Makin pushed the door open and a warm breeze smelling of flowers whispered from within. She stepped into the threshold, scarcely noticing the luxuriously appointed room. Her attention focused instead on its occupants.

Miysis Ra stood in the center of the room, his opinari guardians and armed escort nowhere in sight. Even at a glance, he looked more relaxed than he'd been in the plaza. He was speaking softly with the room's only other occupant: the mysterious official, his face still hidden by a hood.

She took a wary step into the room and dropped into another deep curtsy while Lord Makin closed the door behind her.

"There's no need for such formality, Clio," Miysis said. "Please, make yourself comfortable."

She straightened—and something yanked her backward. Arms flailing, she stumbled and fell over, landing on her butt in front of the door.

A moment of silence, in which Miysis stared and Clio's face erupted into a scorching blush. Before she could get up from the floor, laughter burst from the other daemon—a rich, husky laugh that was so familiar her heart twisted into a knot. Her brain fizzled into incoherency as the daemon started toward her.

"Stuck on a door *again*?" he observed in that deep voice that crooned to her all night in her dreams. "I'm getting déjà vu."

Pushing his hood back, Lyre grinned at her, his golden eyes bright with humor. She gaped at him, utterly speechless.

He reached over her head, cracked the door open, and pulled her ungainly sleeve out from the gap where it had been caught. Then he crouched beside her, eyebrows climbing.

"Not even a word? You had a lot to say after the last door incident."

Her mouth opened but no sound came out. Lyre reached for her mask and she grabbed his wrist, stopping him. His fingers were hooked under the mask's edge, skin brushing her cheek—just like last time. In Chrysalis, he'd tried to lift her mask up after she'd freed herself from the warded door.

This time, he didn't withdraw his hand. He lifted the mask up until her face was exposed and her vision clear of the obscuring fabric. She stared at him, her heart careening wildly.

"Hey," he said softly.

"Lyre?" she managed in a breathless squeak.

"That's me."

"But you—you—" Her gaze swung from him to the Ra prince and back again. "What are you *doing* here?"

His crooked smile returned. Sliding an arm around her, he scooped her up onto her feet. She wobbled, clutching his elbow for balance. Her stunned disbelief was wearing off and she had to fight back the crazed need to fling herself into his arms.

Lyre steered her past a sunken tub in the floor—what crazy architect would put a bathtub in the middle of a sitting room?—and pushed her down onto a cushioned lounge chair.

"Lyre, why are you *here*?" A little volume came back into her voice. "How—what—I mean, *when*—"

Miysis passed her a crystal goblet brimming with water and ice cubes, interrupting her stammered questions. She automatically took it, staring at the ice.

Lyre perched on the lounge chair beside her. "I'm here because the little princess walked us out of a ley line and straight into a gang of royal soldiers." He rolled his eyes with more amusement than resentment. "As for why I'm *still* here, ask the prince."

"I offered to let him stay," Miysis murmured. "He accepted."

Her gaze snapped between them, trying to read the undercurrents. Was Lyre a prisoner but unable to say as much?

"I regret it now," he groused at Miysis. "You're a damn bully, you know that?"

"I have no idea what you mean."

Clio hid her disbelief. How could Lyre talk to a Ra prince so casually? Didn't he realize Miysis was among the top dozen most powerful daemons in the Overworld? He commanded his family's personal militia and had partial control over Ra's main military, not to mention his influence among the highest-ranking nobles of not only his own kingdom, but all Overworld castes.

And why was the prince responding with equal nonchalance?

"Clio?" Lyre's voice softened again. "Are you okay?"

"You need cool, quiet, and water," Miysis told her. "Traveling in the desert during the day takes a heavy toll." He pulled a chair over from the nearby table and sat so he wasn't towering over them. "I need to review King Rouvin's letter again, but first, I wanted to ask—is there anything else you'd like to add?"

"Add?" she repeated cautiously.

"This began with you," he said. "Prince Bastian sent you to Chrysalis, and as a result, he has a weapon with which to attack my territory."

"The king wrote that in his letter?" she whispered in disbelief.

"Not explicitly." Miysis's gaze flicked to Lyre. "Your companion filled in the details. If not for the information he provided, the situation for Irida would be more dire than it is."

Her shocked stare returned to Lyre, who smiled sheepishly as though unsure whether she was about to yell at him.

Miysis frowned. "Clio, do you not know what King Rouvin's letter says?"

She shook her head. "It was for the Ras alone."

"I see." Miysis rose to his feet. "We will speak again at dinner—if you would be so kind as to dine with me?"

"Y-yes, of course. I would be honored."

"Excellent." He gave Lyre a sideways look. "You, however, are already the subject of enough rumors. I'll have dinner sent to your room."

Lyre sighed.

"Rest well, Lady Nereid," the prince said. As he stepped away, he gave Lyre an indecipherable look—and the incubus nodded in response.

She didn't remember she was supposed to return his farewell until after the door had closed behind him. Her brain felt like a pool of overcooked mush. Plucking the half-empty goblet out of her hand, Lyre refilled it from the brass pitcher.

"Drink it," he ordered, standing over her. "All of it."

Obediently, she brought the cup to her lips and drank. The cold water rushed down her throat to her middle, cooling the exhausting heat that felt as though the sunlight had embedded into her flesh.

Once she'd finished, he refilled the goblet again and returned it, but this time didn't command her to gulp it all down. Hands on his hips, he stared at her in an oddly appraising way.

"I can't decide if I like that costume. It's exotic but kind of bulky …"

She blinked, then gave him a swift once-over. "What about *your* outfit? Why are you dressed like a griffin? I didn't even recognize you …"

Except part of her *had* recognized him—the part that had been instantly, obsessively drawn to him. She brought the goblet to her lips, hoping the ice water might fend off her new blush.

"It wasn't my idea." Arching an eyebrow, he spread his arms. "How does it look? Miysis thinks I'm hot."

She spat out her mouthful of water. Hastily wiping her chin, she set the goblet on Miysis's empty chair. "He …" She cleared her throat. "He said that?"

"He didn't *say* it, but he was thinking it."

"How do you know?"

He smirked. "I'm an incubus."

"But he's …" She shook her head, too overwhelmed to fall down *that* rabbit hole. "It looks good on you."

Actually, "looks good" was an understatement of epic proportions. Lyre was already drop-dead gorgeous, but in the striking griffin garments, half his torso on display and each curve of muscle enhanced by the elaborate ink designs, with similar patterns encircling his forearms and turquoise accents beneath his amber eyes, he was beyond description. On Miysis, the outfit was exotic. On Lyre, it was *erotic*—fascinating, titillating, sinfully sexy.

"Ah," Lyre breathed. "So you like it."

She looked up and found dark eyes staring at her with deepening hunger. Her lungs locked, his allure stealing her breath.

Before she could recover, his hand slid into her hair and he leaned down.

His mouth closed over hers. The floor dropped out from under her and she had to grab his shoulders as she was swept away in the flood of burning heat that the touch of his lips ignited inside her.

He kissed her hard, mouth moving urgently against hers. He sank to his knees in front of the lounge and pulled her hard against his chest, still kissing her. She clamped her arms around his neck, her mind blank, her need for him all she knew. He held her even tighter, crushing her, but she didn't care.

In his kiss—in his touch—was a desperate edge. She felt it too. The urgent need to touch him, to kiss him, to meld with him after their separation. To feel, on every level and with every nerve in her body, that he was here, he was safe …

… he was hers.

Pulling back, he sucked in a deep breath, his eyes dark and pupils dilated. She panted, dizzy and clutching him. He brushed his fingers lightly across her jaw and over her lower lip, his touch soft ... slow ... intimate.

Her heart raced, feeling twice its normal size. Was she projecting or was there something about his touch that went beyond sensuality, went deeper than mere affection?

"I missed you." A catch marred his quiet murmur—a slight hesitation as if he was unsure of what to say ... or had never said those words before. Without giving her a chance to respond, he swept her into his arms and stood.

She yelped in surprise. "What are you doing?"

"You need to rest. Aside from that pretty flush in your cheeks, you're pale as the moon."

"I'm always pale."

"You're *extra* pale," he clarified as he carried her toward a wall of drapes and pushed through a gap. On the other side was a huge canopied bed, shaded by the heavy fabric. The temperature dropped noticeably.

When he made to set her down on the silk sheets, she clung to his shoulders. "Not like this! I'm covered in sand and dust."

"You can get new sheets."

He tipped her onto the bed. She tried to jump up again but he pushed her back.

"Don't make me tie you down," he threatened cheerfully. "I'd hate to waste my free pass on restraints unless we're *really* going to have fun."

"Free pass?" she spluttered, her face flushing yet again.

He smirked and vanished through the drapes, returning a moment later with the refilled goblet and pitcher. Exhausted, she didn't realize she'd closed her eyes until she felt a tug on her foot. Opening them blearily, she discovered Lyre sitting at the end of the bed, pulling her soft green boots off.

"I can do that," she mumbled.

"You can relax." He wiggled her other boot off and tossed it onto the floor. "You need to recoup some energy before your fancy dinner."

"Oh, right." She closed her eyes again. "Why can't I eat dinner with you instead?"

"You're a real emissary now. It's part of the job."

She groaned at the thought. "I need to get Miysis to stop calling me 'lady.' I'm not a—a—"

Her whole body went ice cold and she bolted upright so fast that Lyre sprang off the bed, ready to defend them from an unseen threat. Her breath came in a panicked wheeze. "He—he—he—"

"What's wrong?" Lyre's face appeared in front of hers. "What is it?"

"He—he called me Lady *Nereid*." She grabbed his arm. "How does he *know*? How did he find out? *No one* can know, especially not Ra!"

Inexplicably calm, Lyre sat beside her and, prying her fingers off his arm, took her hand in both of his. "You really don't know what was in that letter, do you?"

"No, but—"

"King Rouvin identified you, his official emissary, as a member of the Nereid family."

"He ... he did? Are you sure?"

"Miysis showed me the letter." Lyre squeezed her hand. "Your father didn't specify your exact rank or anything, but it looks pretty official. You're a Nereid for real now."

Emotions roiled through her, expanding until she couldn't breathe. She inhaled to speak—and burst into tears instead. Lyre wrapped his arms around her, and she pulled herself together as best she could.

Her father had named her a Nereid. It wasn't a secret anymore.

Lyre helped her lie back, his smile comforting. "Sleep, Clio. You've got a long evening ahead of you."

Even more exhausted than before, she let her eyes close. "Will you stay with me?"

"I'll be here." A note of amusement touched his voice. "And even if I'm not right here, my room is next door, so I won't be far."

She blindly slid her hand in the direction of his voice. His fingers closed around hers, warm and reassuring.

"Stay," she whispered. "I want you to stay with me."

She was already sliding into sleep, her thoughts fuzzy and disconnected, so when he answered, she wasn't sure if his soft, hopeless whisper was real or a shadow of a dream.

"I wish I could."

TWELVE

POLITICS gave her a headache. In the two years Clio had spent exiled on Earth, she'd forgotten about that aspect of palace life. Her dinner with Miysis Ra and a small horde of Aldrendahar's elite had left her almost as fatigued as crossing the desert had, but at least it was over.

She ambled tiredly, trying not to steal too many glances at her escort. Miysis kept his steps slow, showing no signs of impatience at her snail's pace. When she first met him, she'd been terrified of this powerful royal. Now she was less outright scared but about ten times more intimidated. And maybe just a bit awed.

The griffin prince was impeccably refined, aristocratic, and sophisticated. Without his almost undetectable help, which had included distracting the nobles from pestering her with questions, the dinner might have turned out to be several hours of humiliation for her.

"Did you enjoy your meal?" he asked, all smooth manners as he led her across the citadel's grand reception hall. A pair of griffin guards and a much shorter pair of her nymph guards followed at a distance.

"It was delicious." She would have complimented the dinner either way, but she didn't have to lie. The exotic fare had melted on her tongue. Their cuisine made human food seem like sawdust in comparison.

"I hope you were able to enjoy yourself." He smiled knowingly. "State dinners can be less than pleasant. As I understand it, you aren't accustomed to these functions yet, but you'll learn quickly."

"Hmm," she replied noncommittally. He had introduced her to the entire banquet as Lady Nereid, so her secret was as exposed as a puddle under the desert suns.

"I'm eager to learn more about you," he continued. "And a closer relationship with the Nereids, in general, would do both our families well, I think."

"Will that be possible?" She folded her hands together, squeezing her fingers. "After what Bastian has done?"

"I think it is, assuming we can rein in our respective parents from any drastic moves."

"King Rouvin isn't the type to …" She trailed off, realizing her mistake, then sighed tiredly. "You are being unfair, Prince Miysis."

"My apologies, Lady Nereid."

She huffed another sigh. Rouvin hadn't revealed her exact relationship to the Nereid family in his letter, but thanks to Miysis's sneaky remark, she'd just given it away. Lyre had warned her to be careful with the prince and she'd grown complacent. Miysis Ra was too easy to trust.

"I already suspected," he added as they reached the top of the sweeping marble staircase. "I tried to get it out of Lyre but he can be exceptionally evasive when he puts his mind to it."

A notch of tension released from her spine. Lyre had revealed sensitive information about Irida to Miysis, but he'd kept her most important secret.

"You two have a lot of camaraderie," she observed carefully.

"He has absolutely no respect for authority. I find it refreshing, though there are others here whose egos are more fragile." Miysis's bright yellow-green eyes flicked over her. "He must have been quite the handful at Chrysalis. How did his superiors react to his departure?"

This time she was paying attention and knew better than to answer. She stopped in the hallway and turned to the Ra prince, craning her neck to meet his eyes. "Please don't ask me about Lyre. If you want to know more, you'll have to ask him."

Miysis scanned her face. "Hmm."

"What?" she asked tersely.

"I figured you must have a backbone under that nymph passivity. Lyre wouldn't like you so much otherwise."

Her heart somersaulted under her ribs. Before she started blushing, she hastened back into motion. "Lyre is an incubus. He likes all women."

"Really?" Miysis followed half a step behind her. "When I sent two beautiful women to entertain him, he scarcely paid them any mind — to their immense disappointment."

"Is that so?" Why was Miysis telling her this? Time to change the subject. "Have you decided on your response to King Rouvin's letter yet? I can be ready to return to Irida with your reply at first light."

Miysis extended his stride to catch up with her. "I've already prepared my response. It will go by winged messenger tonight and arrive in Irida by sunrise."

When they reached her door, she cleared her throat. "Forgive my boldness, Your Highness, but may I ask how you've chosen to respond?"

The glowing crystal wall sconce behind him cast his features in shadow. "I have given King Rouvin permission to enter our borders and bid him to travel to Aldrendahar with all haste."

Her shoulders sagged with relief. "Thank you."

"I don't want a conflict with Irida any more than you do. We must move quickly to ally our kingdoms before Prince Bastian can strike again." He glanced down the corridor, his expression distant. "If King Rouvin departs in the morning, he'll arrive here the day after next."

Meaning two more days before their families could focus on finding and stopping Bastian. "What if he attacks again before that?"

"Preparations for the defense of Ilvanad and Shalla'isa are already under way," Miysis said, referring to the two other Ra cities Bastian had researched. Rouvin's letter had warned of his son's potential targets.

"Aldrendahar is the best defended city, isn't it?" she asked.

"It's the most defensible," he corrected. "Ilvanad and Shalla'isa are more exposed, larger, and richer, but deeper in our territory. It's difficult to say where Prince Bastian will attack, considering his forces are negligibly small."

Bastian's forces were small but the shadow weave made him powerful. Her lips quirked down. "Is there a ley line near here?"

"There's a ley line half a mile outside the walls. As the primary method of transportation in and out of Aldrendahar, it's quite well known." He stepped back and bowed. "I have matters to attend to, so I must bid you a pleasant night, my lady."

She quickly curtsied. "Thank you, Your Highness."

As he walked away, his wings tucked against his back, she slipped into her room and closed the door, lost in thought. With a ley line right outside the city, Bastian wouldn't dare unleash the shadow weave on Aldrendahar—or so she hoped. For that reason alone, Ilvanad and Shalla'isa were more appealing targets.

Soft light glowed from a wall sconce and heavy drapes were pulled across the gallery windows, while the curtains around her bed were open. The silk sheets were turned down and several sleep garments were folded on the foot of the bed, waiting for her to choose one. On the table, someone had left a platter with a new pitcher of ice water and a selection of sweets and snacks.

The room was more luxurious than anything in the Iridian palace, besides the royal suites, but she preferred the simplicity of nymph design. Griffins were a lot more ostentatious. She drifted around the room, skirting the tub. She now understood why it was there, but it still weirded her out. Bathtubs belonged in bathrooms or bathhouses.

The room's unfamiliarity scraped at her. Or was it the emptiness? She returned to the door and cracked it open. Flanking the threshold were two nymph guards, the others resting in the servant suite across the hall. Griffins were stationed at either end of the corridor, facing away from the guest rooms.

"Why don't you two take a break?" she suggested to her guards in a low voice. "You look exhausted."

They exchanged frowning looks. "Are you certain, Lady Clio?"

"Absolutely," she assured them. "Get some rest. I won't be far."

It was a testament to their exhaustion that they reluctantly crossed to the opposite door. "Someone else will be out in just a minute to take our place, my lady."

"All right," she agreed.

As soon as the door closed behind them, she slipped toward the neighboring room. Unwilling to knock and potentially catch the griffin guards' attention, she reached for the handle.

The fine hairs on her arm stood on end, a shivery warning passing over her skin.

She blinked her asper into focus. A lock spell webbed across the entire door, shimmering gold. It wasn't lethal but it wasn't a casual spell either. Short of blowing the door down, no griffins would be getting inside without permission.

She tapped a finger against the wood, disabling the weave, then silently turned the knob and slipped inside. Lyre's room was as dim as hers, illuminated by soft yellow light. The drapery in his room was closed, blocking the city view.

He sat cross-legged in the middle of the floor, wearing only loose-fitting pants, his bare torso decorated with elaborate ink designs. Scattered on either side of him were papers covered in his messy scrawl, writing utensils, measuring instruments, astrolabes, a compass, and other delicate tools.

In front of him was a circular sheet of steel two feet in diameter, polished until it shone like a mirror. Softly glowing golden lines spiraled across it, filling a bright outer circle near the edge.

His hands were raised in front of him and light danced across his fingers. He wove with a smooth cadence, a graceful rise and fall, the magic shimmering and sparkling as he added each delicate construct.

She carefully closed the door again, not allowing it to make a sound, and rekeyed his lock spell. He was wise to lock himself in. An interruption while he was weaving could range from annoying to outright destructive if his concentration broke at the wrong moment.

Silently, she sank down beside the door, back against the wall as she watched him. Eyes half closed, an unusual tranquility softening his features, he showed no signs of concentration or effort despite the complexity of the weave he was building strand by rune by sigil by shape. He didn't reference his notes. He didn't hesitate or stumble. His hands moved unerringly, the threads spinning from his fingers as he followed the perfect mental map he had created before he began.

She couldn't yet tell what he was weaving, the purpose of the spell. Her attention drifted from the magic to his face, to the way the golden light drifted across his features, highlighting his cheekbones, his jaw, his mouth. Her gaze wandered down, over his chest, his shoulders, the muscles in his arms flexing with each movement.

Watching him *weave*—this was what he was meant to do. In this moment, he was in perfect harmony with himself, and it was heart-wrenchingly beautiful in a way that had nothing to do with his appearance.

The flicker of light over his face fluctuated and his expression changed—a subtle creasing of his eyebrows. Her focus shot to his weave and from the incomprehensible tangle of lines and runes, shapes jumped out at her. She went cold as though she'd been doused in the nearby pitcher of ice water.

The shapes, the constructs—a web of death, woven from stunning golden magic.

The threads shuddered and twisted. Rhythm shattering, he snapped his hand out and plunged his fingers into the center of the weave. Threads tore and electric power surged up his arm as he drew the magic back into his body.

The weaving burst apart. His papers and tools went flying and he jerked back from the concussive discharge, swearing hoarsely.

Lurching up, she rushed toward him. "Lyre, are you okay?"

He jumped, his head whipping toward her. "Holy shit," he gasped, thumping a hand against his chest. "You almost gave me a heart attack."

"You shouldn't pull magic back in like that," she admonished, stepping over his scattered tools and crouching beside him. "Are you hurt?"

He lifted his hand. Angry red lines streaked up his forearm where the power had burned him. "It was that or let it explode. This is a lot less damage."

Hissing in sympathy, she took his arm and tugged him up. Guiding him over to the table, she pushed his burned hand into the pitcher of water.

He yelped. "Cold! It's cold!"

"That's the idea." She held his elbow so he couldn't pull his hand out. "How often do you do this to yourself?"

"In Chrysalis, I'd use shields most of the time." He shrugged one shoulder. "But here, I didn't want any big bangs that would draw attention. And Miysis probably wouldn't like it if I wrecked the room."

"What went wrong with the weaving?"

"Since you were watching, I'm hoping you can tell me."

"Um." She looked away, suddenly feeling the urge to examine the drapery. "I, uh … wasn't paying attention."

"You were waiting right there. What were you doing, sleeping?"

"I just zoned out, I guess." Fighting back a blush, she pulled his hand out of the water and steered him over to the lounge chair. "Sit down. I'm going to heal your arm."

"You don't need to—"

She shoved him down and sat beside him. Taking his chilled hand in both of hers, she sent a thread of healing magic under his skin.

"Clio—"

"Shh. I'm working."

He fell silent, and she quickly repaired the damaged skin and muscle where his magic, unstable from the weaving, had burned its way back to his core.

"There," she said on an exhale, her eyes focusing on the physical world again. Faint pink lines marked his skin where the angry burns had been minutes before. "How does it feel?"

"Hmm …"

Confused, she looked up to find his eyes had slid from her face, drifting downward, and by the time he reached her feet and started back up again, his amber irises had darkened to bronze.

"You look beautiful." His voice was a deep, husky croon.

She ducked her head self-consciously. Pampering guests was standard griffin hospitality, and before the state dinner, two lovely young women had arrived to prepare her. Clio's hair was elaborately braided and her eyes were lined with dark ink. A delicate *tapa* was draped over a silk chest wrap that tied on one side, leaving a strip of her stomach bare above layered skirts in violet and gray. The griffin women had debated over bodypainting, then decided to leave her naturally patterned nymph skin on display instead.

"What were you weaving?" she asked quickly, hoping to distract him. Not that she didn't like the way he was looking at her—or the hunger sparking in his eyes—but rather, she liked it too much. "I couldn't tell except that it … it looked …"

His lustful stare faded to bleakness as he glanced toward the steel sheet on the floor. "I can't hide here forever, and when I go back, I want to be prepared."

"Prepared for what?" she asked, an ominous shiver running over her.

"For my father."

She too looked at the weaving tools spread across the floor. A web of death. "Don't you already have combat spells you could use against him?"

"It'll take more than a regular battle weave to slow him down." The muscles of his forearm tightened under her hands. "Each Rysalis patriarch collects all the knowledge of his generation and compiles it for the next patriarch. My father has access to the combined genius of a thousand years of Rysalis weavers."

He turned dark eyes to hers. "You've got to understand, Clio. We're raised from the cradle to fight to be the best. We all want to surpass—and replace—our father someday. Lyceus survived seven older brothers, killed his own father, and has ruled the family for forty years."

"Forty?" she repeated in disbelief. "But he scarcely looks older than you."

"Incubi stop aging in their early twenties. We show few signs of age until our final five or six years."

Her eyes widened. "How old are you, then?"

"My early twenties."

"Oh."

"Lyceus ..." He pulled his hand away from hers, balling it into a fist. "After he became the family head, he killed his uncles so they couldn't assassinate him later. He killed every one of his brothers who challenged him, along with numerous cousins, and he killed his two eldest sons."

"I thought Andante was the eldest ..." she mumbled weakly.

"Andante is the eldest *surviving* son. The other two died before I was even born."

She shook her head. "How many sons has Lyceus *had*?"

"Twelve. Six surviving." Lyre was quiet for a moment. "So, you see the problem. My father has been killing master weavers since before I was born. He's the most powerful, the most skilled, and he has access to the accumulated knowledge of our entire bloodline. No one has ever defeated him."

"Do you think this new weaving you're making will kill him?"

"I don't know." He raked his hand through his hair. "I can't even weave it properly, so chances are it'll be useless anyway."

"I can help, if you want."

"If I can't weave something stable, your astral perception probably won't do us any good. I can't get it to hold. I'm not even sure if my theory is ..." His eyes went out of focus, turning to his mental schematic of the spell. "I have to weave the first half before I can weave the second, but the first half isn't stable by itself."

"What do you mean?"

"Symmetry," he murmured, drumming his fingers on his knee. "A spell that reflects itself, kind of like the linked trackers we've been using, but incapable of existing alone. The two halves are bound, dependent on each other. If I make it stable on its own, it won't function the way I need for ... but ..."

He puffed out a breath, his eyes focusing again. "It's impossible. Reed always said I have more vision than sense. Even if he was here, we still couldn't do it. The two sides have to be identical down to every strand and I don't know that I could produce a perfect reflection even if I watched myself in a damn ..."

He trailed off, his eyes going out of focus again.

She waited a moment then prompted, "A damn what?"

"A mirror," he breathed, his suddenly intense stare fixing on her. "A perfect reflection of my magic, just like a mirror. Like a *mimic*. Clio, how closely can you duplicate a complex weave?"

"I can make a perfect copy of the original, unless I'm rushing and screw it up."

"How close behind me could you mimic my weave?"

"A second or two?"

"It might be enough. You would have to mimic my aura too. Would our magic be indistinguishably identical? It might not ..." His excitement waned and his eyes darkened. "But I can't ask you to help me weave a death spell."

"Lyre, just tell me what you need me to do."

After one more searching look, he led her to the steel disc on the floor, glowing with its own weave. He returned to his spot and she sat across from him. Breathing deep, she focused her asper and her green aura shimmered to warm gold, identical to his.

He raised his hands into the air between them, poised above the steel disc. He didn't speak, but he didn't need to.

She raised her hands, hovering a few inches away from his, waiting with all her attention focused on him as she'd never focused before. No mistakes. If it went wrong, broken bones and a smoking hole in the floor would be the least of the damages they could expect.

Golden light sparked over his fingers, and he began to weave. Identical light spanned her fingers as she mimicked him.

His hands drifted in a slow rhythm, and she followed each gesture until they were moving in almost perfect unison. Sizzling magic spiraled out from their hands, identical shimmering gold, two mirror-image weaves forming side by side.

His fingers moved, hers dancing the same steps. She didn't have to think, her mind empty, her instincts tuned to the serene flow of the weave as he guided her through it. Time slipped away, and all she knew was the movement of his hands and hers, carried by the weaving rhythm.

THE BLOOD CURSE 119

Then he stopped. The intricate construct, two mirrored weaves bound together by their symmetry, hovered in the air between her and Lyre, their palms in the center of their respective creations. Magic sizzled against her skin—a warning of its deadly power.

Using his free hand, Lyre withdrew a small vial from his pocket and pulled the cork out with his teeth. Eyes fixed on the parallel weavings they had created, he upended the vial over the metal disc between them.

Silver liquid spilled onto it. The quicksilver didn't splash or splatter but pooled on the metal, spreading across the glowing weave already embedded in the steel. The liquid crept outward until it reached the weave's edge, where it stopped as though the line of magic was a physical barrier. The pristine surface reflected the spell above it, a perfect mirror.

Lyre's eyes met hers through the weave between them and he guided their creation down. It touched the quicksilver mirror and golden light flared. He pushed it into the liquid. The weaving melded with the quicksilver, and the runes and lines shifted within the solution, taking on a new form.

Her eyes widened as the true shape of the spell revealed itself to her asper.

When the shifting weave settled, Lyre set the empty vial in the center of the liquid pool and a spark of magic ran down the glass. The weaving in the disc brightened, then the quicksilver moved as though coming to life—climbing the sides of the vial and pouring itself into the container. Every single drop crawled back inside, leaving the metal disc perfectly clear.

As Lyre corked the container and slipped it back into his pocket, exhaustion hit Clio like an ocean wave. Letting her aura shift back to green, she groaned and stretched her stiff muscles. How long had they sat there weaving? A hollow ache in her head warned her that she'd depleted a significant amount of her magic reserves.

"It worked," he murmured. "It would have been impossible without you."

"I'm glad I could help." She hesitated. "Lyre, that weaving, it looked like ..."

"It isn't finished yet. That's just one part."

She considered prying for more information, but she was just too tired.

They picked themselves off the floor and collapsed wearily on the lounge. Lyre didn't seem motivated to clean up the mess left over from his weaving, so she decided not to worry about it either. She flopped back onto the pile of cushions. "What a night."

"Tell me about it. I'd already blown myself up a few times before you came in." He canted his head toward her. "How did your dinner go?"

"Well enough." She pulled a face at the memory. "More importantly, Miysis is giving Rouvin permission to come here. He's sending a messenger tonight."

"Good. Assuming they can sort things out, that should throw off Bastian and his grand plans in a big way."

"My father said … he's deposing Bastian." She peeked at Lyre, but he didn't look surprised by the news. "Petrina will become the crown princess."

"Rouvin doesn't have much choice. He can't overlook treason." He leaned back until he was lying across the foot of the daybed, his head hanging off the edge and eyes closed. "Will Petrina be excited to have her sister become a princess too?"

"I don't know. I think so?" She twisted her hands. "I haven't had a chance to think about the …"

"Repercussions" was the word that came to mind, which surprised her. For so long, she'd wanted nothing more than to be part of the Nereid family, but now that it had happened, she was more concerned than excited about what it meant for her. As nymph nobility, the anonymity she'd always enjoyed would be gone. Would she be expected to join their elite society and take on the duties of a princess?

"Clio?" Lyre asked as he sat up. "What's wrong?"

She realized how stiffly she was lying on the cushions. Pushing herself upright, she fidgeted absently with her braided hair. "I'm just not sure how to feel about … being a Nereid."

"Isn't this what you wanted?"

THE BLOOD CURSE 121

"Well, yes—I mean, I thought it was, but …" She tugged the tie out of her hair and started plucking the braid apart, just for something to do with her hands. "If Rouvin had asked me first, I'm not sure what I would have said."

His forehead creased in bewilderment. "You mean you might have turned him down?"

Being part of a family was all she'd wanted for years. She'd devoted herself to Bastian and Petrina, never questioning anything.

"It was the only thing I wanted," she whispered, "until I met you."

His eyes widened.

"Getting the KLOC to save you was the first time I made a real decision, a life-changing decision, that had nothing to do with the Nereids." She pushed her unbraided hair off her shoulders. "Since meeting you, I've realized a lot of things."

He went still, focusing on her with unexpected intensity. Without thinking, she touched his face, tracing the invisible tattoo that marked his cheek under his glamour.

"I always thought family and bloodlines were more valuable than anything else in the world, but now there are other things that matter more to me." She drew in a breath, a slight tremor betraying her fluttering heartbeat. "Like you. Especially you."

Something flashed in his eyes—a look almost like panic.

She stuttered, but she couldn't stop now. "Lyre, I don't know what the future will bring for either of us, but I—we can't just go our separate ways when this is over. We … I want to be with you."

He looked away from her, his jaw tightening and his expression indecipherable.

"You feel that way too, don't you?" she asked, a strange desperation rising in her when he said nothing. "Lyre, I—I love—"

He shot to his feet and took two lurching steps away from her.

"Don't say that to me." The words were flat, his back to her, his shoulders rigid.

Pain pierced her, deep and tearing. "But Lyre—"

"*Don't*," he growled, "say those words. Do you know how many women have said that to me? Cried it, screamed it, begged me to say it back? Those words are meaningless to incubi."

Her voice vanished, buried beneath a tide of anguish.

He didn't turn, keeping his back to her. "Whatever you feel, I can't reciprocate. *Incubi* can't. I'm sorry."

The silence was so heavy that the air felt like water in her lungs, the weight crushing her heart.

"I'm sorry," he repeated, his voice cracking. "I only wanted ..."

He wrenched out of his frozen stance. Without looking back, he strode across the room, disabled the lock spell, and vanished into the hallway. The door swung shut behind him, the clack of the latch shattering the quiet.

She sat unmoving on the lounge chair, staring at the door. Tears trickled down her cheeks.

For years, she hadn't pursued a single selfish desire besides having a family. Now, she'd finally found something she wanted, someone she could fight for, but he didn't want her.

Pressure built in her chest, crushing her lungs until she couldn't breathe. *I'm sorry. I only wanted ...* Whatever he wanted, it wasn't her love. He hadn't wanted to hear the words, but his refusal to listen didn't change how she felt.

"I love you," she whispered to the empty room.

The dam inside her broke and a sob tore through her lungs. She pulled a pillow into her arms, buried her face in it, and cried.

THIRTEEN

COWARD. He was a fucking coward.

He stormed up and down the length of an empty corridor lined with rows of arched windows, the farthest point from his room that he could get without leaving this floor. But he wished he could keep going. Keep running.

Coward. The word rang in his head. He should have looked at her. He should have had the guts to face her while he broke her heart, but seeing her face, her beautiful eyes filled with pain he had caused her … he hadn't been able to do it.

He paced the length of the hall. Why had he let this happen? He should have been more of an asshole or something. He should have … what? What could he have done? Women fell in love with incubi all the damn time, whether they were charming or horrible or pathetic. Didn't Clio know that incubi couldn't love?

Jerking to a stop, he closed his eyes. Love, no. But infatuation?

He wasn't an idiot. He *knew* he was infatuated with her. He cared about her, lusted for her, dreamed of her. He'd wanted her since the moment they met, and he only grew more obsessed the longer they were together.

But that's all it was. He wanted her because he couldn't have her. That's the way it always went for incubi. No matter how much they might want to stay with one woman, after a few days or weeks, they'd get bored, get distracted, and the next thing they knew, they were in bed with some other girl. He couldn't do that to Clio.

Pinching the bridge of his nose, he backed up to a pillar between windows and sank onto the floor. He'd already hurt her. He couldn't make it worse by pretending to love her for however long his interest lasted.

Once this was over, he'd disappear, just like he had with every woman he'd slept with ... every woman who'd ever claimed to love him.

Arms folded on his knees and head bowed, he didn't move from the corner, lost in dark thoughts as aching cold welled inside him. He knew the feeling well. Some incubi reveled in their transient encounters, but for others, loneliness was a constant companion, a hole they tried to fill with a parade of lovers to whom they could never remain faithful, even when they bothered to try.

Except now he realized how that cold ache had been less present these past weeks—since he met Clio.

Quiet scuffs sounded on the marble floor and he shot to his feet before identifying the sound. For the barest instant, he thought the feminine footsteps might belong to Clio, but the cadence was wrong.

A young woman with an armload of folded silk hummed softly as she ambled down the corridor. She spotted him standing beside the open-air window and jerked to a stop.

"Oh!" she gasped. "You startled me."

Belated recognition sparked and he forced himself to relax. She was one of the body artists who'd pampered him, but he couldn't remember her name.

"What are you doing out here at this hour?" she asked curiously, shifting her load to one arm.

He shrugged, aware of how suspicious he looked wandering the corridors in the middle of the night. He wasn't even dressed properly, having left his *tapa* somewhere in his suite. His shirtless state hadn't escaped her either, and her gaze drifted down to admire her ink handiwork displayed across his abdomen.

"I'm just stretching my legs," he answered nonchalantly. "Too restless to sleep."

"It's too beautiful a night for sleeping," she murmured as her eyes gradually climbed back up to his face. "Perhaps some company would help settle your spirit."

He forced himself to really look at her. Luxurious blond hair in two braids that hung down her shoulders, a curvaceous figure wrapped in teal- and violet-patterned silk, her green eyes bright and lined with dark ink to make them smolder. Feathered wings were tucked close to her back and her tail swished idly behind her.

She was lovely. Exotic. Obviously interested, ready and willing to fall under his power.

He hadn't taken a woman to bed since Clio had arrived in Asphodel. A long time for an incubus to remain celibate. His obsession with her had only grown in that time, and he could pin some of the blame on pent-up desire.

He should erase Clio from his mind and fill the chasm with something else—with some*one* else. A willing body, another faceless woman, was right here, waiting for him to offer what she wanted. Mutual exploitation. He would use her, and she would use him.

A dozen smooth replies to her invitation jumped to mind, from subtle to seductive to blush-inspiring and bold. He drew in a breath— but he couldn't say a single one.

He didn't want her. This beautiful, lush woman was offering herself to him, and he didn't want her. He had no desire to touch her, kiss her, undress her. He could have done it anyway, tested to see if the distraction would work, but even imagining it was unpleasant.

His hands shook and he clenched them into fists to hide it. With a wan smile, he turned away and leaned on the window parapet.

"It's been a long day." He spoke to the spectacular view of city lights. "I think I'll head to bed."

With a soft rustle, she joined him at the window, propping her bundle of fabric on the stone rail. He glanced at her, surprised by her sympathetic smile.

"You have the look of a man with a lot on his mind." She fidgeted with the folded silk. "I can listen, if you want to talk."

"I really am tired."

She laughed softly. "I wasn't aiming for an invitation to your bedroom. Two rejections from the most gorgeous daemon I've ever met is enough."

He grimaced.

"I'm offering an ear if you need it, that's all. You're far from home and isolated here in the citadel. That can't be easy."

He huffed out a breath. "It's not that bad."

"Mmm," she agreed noncommittally, staring out the window as though she had nothing better to do. A thousand warm lights flickered between the stone buildings, and a fair number of daemons moved through the streets, taking advantage of the cool night. Above, countless stars glowed in the velvety sky, not a cloud to be seen, and the planet radiated pale light across the dark dunes.

He wished she would go away. He'd prefer to return to his tormented brooding, thanks very much. He still had to figure out how to face Clio, how to explain that his infatuation was no more than stupid incubus instincts going into overdrive. Would she understand? Could she move past her feelings for him and …

… and what? And be his friend?

A choking sound—disgust and disbelief—rasped from his throat, and he rubbed a hand over his face with more force than necessary. What an inspiring new low he'd achieved.

"Could I have some space?" he growled abruptly.

"You know," the griffin girl replied, stubbornly unmoving, "when my betrothed got that sort of look, he always felt better after talking about it."

"You're *betrothed*?" He didn't bother to hide his sneer at her disloyalty.

"I was," she said simply. "He died."

He bit back a curse. "I'm sorry."

"Loving a soldier has its risks."

He remembered the griffins who'd died in the embassy and the raiders who'd died in the Brinford smugglers market, wondering how many of them had lovers, wives, children. It was easy to label enemies and forget they were anything more than obstacles and threats.

"What was it like?" The question was out of his mouth before he stopped to think.

"What?"

He considered dropping it, then plowed on. "Loving him. Being in love. What did it feel like?"

She looked contemplatively at the stars, sadness ghosting through her eyes. "You think about them constantly. You worry about them when they aren't with you. You miss them. When you're together, you can finally relax. You don't even realize how tense you are until they're back at your side." Smoothing her bundle of silk, she smiled wistfully. "It's like a part of your soul belongs to them. When they're near, you feel complete. When they're gone, you feel hollow inside."

He drew in a slow, steadying breath. "But how do you know you'll always feel that way? What if it changes?"

"We can never *really* know, can we?" Gathering the folded silk into her arms, she stepped back from the window. "But when you truly love someone, they keep that piece of your soul forever … even after they're gone."

With a final smile and a murmured farewell, she strolled away. He watched until she was out of sight, his mind churning. Infatuation. Obsession. Love. Where was the line between them?

Hollowness ached in his chest. *When they're near, you feel complete.*

He surged away from the windows. He barely saw the dark halls as he strode back toward his room. With the aid of a cloaking spell, he slipped past the griffin guards at the head of the corridor. A pair of nymphs stood in front of Clio's door and he couldn't hide from their asper, but they pointedly ignored him. Was Clio back in her room, or were they guarding an empty suite?

He stopped at his door. He could sense her somewhere on the other side and the hollowness in his chest faded.

Incubi couldn't fall in love. The fact was as immutable and steadfast as his power to seduce. Seduction without connection, lust without love, a thousand fleeting encounters without a single meaningful bond. That was the gift and the curse of incubi.

But if incubi couldn't fall in love, then what was *this*?

He pushed the door open. The room was dark, lit by a lone sconce, and the floor where he'd left his weaving tools was cleared of everything but the heavy steel disc. His tools were stacked on the desk, his notes in a neat pile.

Clio stood in front of the desk, staring at it, her arms hanging at her sides as though she'd been standing there for a while. At the sound of the door closing, she whirled around.

"Oh." She shrank at the sight of him, withdrawing to make herself a smaller target. "I'm sorry. I shouldn't have …"

He started forward, drawn to her as though caught in her gravity.

"I didn't mean to …" she mumbled incoherently. "I'll go back to my room."

She rushed forward, angling to sweep past him, but he stepped into her path. Halting, she fixed her gaze on the floor. Every second she refused to look at him hurt.

Motions slow, he reached for her face and gently cupped her cheek, tilting her head back. Her wide eyes met his, rimmed red from crying, her summer-sky irises darkened to ocean blue.

"I'm an idiot," he said hoarsely.

Her eyes went even wider and her lips parted, but she didn't speak. His harsh words from earlier still held her in silence, and maybe it was too late to take them back.

"I don't know," he whispered as he brought his other hand up to cradle her face in his palms, unwilling to let her bow her head because of him. "I don't know if I can be what you want me to be. I don't know if I'll just hurt you."

He leaned down until their foreheads touched, his eyes closing as he struggled to find the right words.

"All I know is that, right now, I'm obsessed with you. I want to be with you. I want to be beside you every damn minute."

She sucked in a quavering breath. He opened his eyes and leaned back just enough to bring her face into focus again.

"But I won't lie to you, Clio." His voice roughened. "As much as I'd love to be obsessed with you like this every day for the rest of my life, I don't know how long I'll feel this way."

Her eyes shone and a tear slipped down her cheek, catching on his fingers. She wrapped her hands around his wrists, staring up at him.

"I want to be with you," she breathed, the words trembling. "We can try, can't we?"

"But incubi never—"

She touched her fingers to his lips, silencing him. "You're more than your incubus nature, Lyre. Just like you're more than your family name. You've always been more, don't you see?"

Those words pierced him in a way he'd never felt before.

She slid her fingers from his lips to his cheek. "If this is what you want …" Her eyes met his, bright and blazing with inner fire. "If I'm what you want, then take me."

Take me.

His hands tightened on her cheeks.

Take me.

With those two words, she shattered his control. It didn't matter whether she'd meant them literally. He couldn't stop himself.

Ravenous hunger scorched his veins, but his lips met hers in a soft brush of skin on skin. Slowly, he pressed his mouth to hers, immersing his entire awareness in each sensation as though he'd never kissed her before.

That breathless pressure was back in his chest, squeezing his heart. He unhurriedly explored her lips until she parted them for his tongue. He tasted her anew, her face cradled gently in his hands, the touch as intimate as the kiss.

Her breathing quickened, her hands finding his bare chest with tentative touches. Urgency threaded through him, building under the surface, but he kissed her with slow passion, discovering every facet of her lips. His heart ached, his chest tight, his emotions electric. He'd had sex with women, had pleasured women, had used women. But he'd never made love to a woman. With every kiss, with every touch, he burned with the need to give her everything he had, to make her his in every way.

Angling his head, he deepened the kiss until she arched into him, and he swept her against his chest with one arm.

He wasn't thinking about seduction when his hands started roaming over her body. The hundreds of tricks he knew to arouse a female never entered his thoughts. He touched her for the pleasure of touching her, sliding his hands across her soft skin, tracing her curves beneath the silk garments. He kissed her because he wanted to, because he couldn't stop.

She melted against him and he shuffled them backward into the desk, then lifted her onto it while he stood between her knees. Now her face was level with his and he brought their mouths together again.

Each press of her lips felt new. Each flirting touch of her tongue was a first experience. The faceless women of his past—they didn't matter. They were nothing. They were forgotten.

There was only Clio.

When she ran out of breath and finally tore her lips free to suck in air, he shifted his mouth to her jaw. Her head tipped back, and he kissed slowly along her throat to her collarbone. Running his fingers down her sides to her waist, he pulled her against his hips. A soft moan slipped from her and she wrapped her legs around him, her skirt pushing up with the movement.

His hand found her bare leg, caressing smooth skin from her calf up to her lean thigh where nymph markings patterned her skin. Shivering beneath his touch, she stroked his chest with growing confidence.

He sought the clip on her *tapa*. Slipping the garment off, he tossed it aside, leaving only her chest wrap. His mouth drifted lower and his hand slid over the soft curves of her breasts, hidden beneath the silk band. As his fingers found her most sensitive spots, she gasped.

His hand on her thigh worked under her skirt and curled over her ass. He pulled her hips harder against him, needing to feel her heat, needing even more than that. The driving hunger he'd denied for weeks was raging through him. His fingers slid dexterously down the side of her top, plucking the ties apart, and he pulled it off her.

Leaning back, he took a moment to drink in the sight of her flushed cheeks and bright eyes, her swollen lips begging to be kissed. Fine green markings trailed over her shoulders and down her arms, slightly darker than her ivory skin. His eyes traced every delicious curve, the swell of her small breasts, her skirt hiked up and her bare legs wrapped around him.

Her blush deepened, and she self-consciously covered her bare chest.

He caught her wrists, gently forcing her arms away. "No," he murmured. "You're gorgeous. You're perfect."

He caught her mouth with his, kissing her deep and hard to erase her embarrassment. Sliding his lips down, he guided her hands to his hair to give her something to hold on to. Then he closed his mouth over her breast.

She arched into him with a gasp, clutching his hair and flinging the other hand out for balance. A cascade of weaving tools crashed to the floor. His notes were scattered across the marble, but he had no idea when they'd fallen and he didn't care.

His fingers slid over her bare skin, exploring every curve while he teased her with his lips and tongue. Her legs clamped tight around his hips and he rocked against her. She moaned between wild gasps. The sound stoked the fires of his lust and without thinking, he reeled in the aphrodesia that was slipping out of his control.

For so long, he'd fought how much he wanted her—because he'd been afraid. But after the succubus club, he should have realized he had nothing to fear. He wouldn't hurt her with aphrodesia any more than he would hurt her with a physical weapon.

What he felt for her was stronger than his hunger. Stronger than his instincts.

She clutched him like she was holding on for dear life. He teased her breasts until she was whimpering with need, then slipped his hand between her legs. She inhaled sharply.

He stroked her with careful, exploratory touches, his senses tuned to each minute reaction. When he found her rhythm, she moaned softly, her hips bucking with the motion of his fingers sliding across her.

"Lyre," she half gasped, half moaned.

He caught her mouth again, kissing her as she trembled. When she started to quake and gasp, he shifted his touch, slowing and softening.

"Not yet," he breathed against her lips as he withdrew his hand. "Not quite yet."

She sucked in a breath and pulled back, her hazy eyes full of reproach. "Why are you stopping?"

He plucked apart the tie of her skirt and pulled the fabric out from under her in one swift motion. She gasped as the fabric pooled on the floor at his feet.

"Oh, Clio," he purred. "I'm not stopping. I'm just getting started."

Her eyes widened and he couldn't help his low, husky laugh as he scooped her into his arms and carried her toward the waiting bed.

FOURTEEN

STRETCHING HER ARMS above her head, Clio indulged in a drawn-out yawn. She went limp again, sprawled beneath the silk sheets. The drapes were drawn most of the way around the canopied bed, allowing only a strip of sunlight to leak in.

Yawning again, she rolled onto her stomach and stretched her legs. Her muscles were sore, though not in an unpleasant way. She couldn't imagine an unpleasant feeling today. Contentment should be her middle name.

She wondered if all women felt like this after a night—or rather, two nights and an entire day—in bed with an incubus. Somehow, she doubted it.

I'd love to be obsessed with you like this every day for the rest of my life.

Her stomach swooped wildly at the memory of his words. It wasn't quite a confession of love, but she wasn't going to be picky. He didn't believe incubi could fall in love or stay in love, and maybe he was right. Maybe he would eventually get bored with her and move on. But she was willing to try—and she was unbearably relieved he was willing to try too.

With a final languorous stretch, she swung her legs off the bed and sat up. The red silk robe she'd attempted to don several times lay on the floor where Lyre had last discarded it. As she pulled it on, she wondered with a wry smile how long it would last this time. Now that he'd gotten her out of her clothes, Lyre was on a mission to keep her in a permanent state of nudity.

Tying the belt, she ambled out of the curtained bedroom. Warm light blazed across the space, the late afternoon suns glowing above the sandy horizon. Unexpected clouds dotted the desert sky.

Lyre sat at the desk, tapping a charcoal pencil against his chin as he stared at his notes. The moment she appeared, he turned toward her and his amber irises deepened to bronze. Her stomach fluttered with renewed acrobatics. He was insatiable.

Amazement washed through her. Despite all the warnings, all the fear, she had given herself to Lyre for her first time. In the moment, she hadn't remembered to check if he had his aphrodesia under control. But he hadn't lost control, hadn't hurt her, not even once.

After that, he had spent the night and the whole next day making up for lost time. It was all a euphoric blur of mind-blowing pleasure. His touch, his mouth, every new sensation, every explosive climax where all she could do was clutch him to her.

He turned on his chair as she approached, and the moment she was within reach, he pulled her onto his lap so she was straddling him. His warm hands slid up her thighs, then he was unknotting the belt of her robe.

"Lyre!" she exclaimed with a laugh. "I only just put it on."

"*Why* do you keep putting it on?" he complained, pulling the garment open. "You don't need it for warmth and it just gets in the way."

She didn't have a chance to answer before he drew her mouth to his. Her lips parted instantly and his tongue stroked hers. Liquid heat gathered low in her center. His hands slid up her sides and caressed her breasts.

It was an effort of will to tear her mouth away. "Lyre," she panted. "Maybe I could eat first?"

"Mmm." Unable to reach her mouth, he kissed her throat. "I suppose I could allow that."

"How magnanimous."

His hands curled over her backside and he pulled her down as he pushed his hips up. She gasped, thoughts of food evaporating from her head. Sliding her fingers into his hair, she guided his mouth down lower. His lips teased across her breast.

"I could eat later," she suggested breathlessly.

"I guess it depends how hungry you are."

He stood up, letting her slide down his half-naked body. Despite his newfound aversion to *her* clothes, he was wearing pants again, though that might have something to do with the food that kept arriving periodically. He probably didn't want to distract the maids.

Spinning her around, he pushed her down into his chair, then knelt between her knees. His scorching eyes caressed her body as he parted her robe again, and she had to fight a blush. He'd seen every inch of her already, but she couldn't help it.

He ran his hands up her thighs and back down, then guided her legs apart. Leaning into her, he trailed wet kisses down the center of her stomach, heading lower.

"Lyre," she gasped.

"Mmm." He hooked his arms under her knees, pushing them up so her feet were off the floor entirely. "Are you objecting?"

All she could do was grip the seat of the chair as his mouth moved even lower. It took her a moment to find her voice. "No, no objections."

He slid his lips along her sensitive inner thigh. "Aren't you hungry?"

"No."

"Mmm." His tongue flicked teasingly against her skin. "Well, if you're sure you—"

A rap on the door interrupted him. His head came up and he glanced across the room, then turned back to her.

"Should you answer that?" she asked reluctantly.

"Hell no."

The rap came again, louder this time. Annoyance flickering in his dark eyes, he released her legs and stood. She hurriedly covered herself and dove behind the bedroom curtain. Hidden from sight, she listened to the door handle clack.

Lyre muttered something, and a male voice answered. A moment passed, then the door shut again. Lyre's footsteps, almost silent, retraced his path to her. He stepped into the curtained room, pulled her close, and kissed her ravenously. She arched into him, arms sliding around his neck.

Pulling back, he sighed. "That message was for you. Rouvin and his entourage are expected at sundown."

Her face flushed. Considering she'd abandoned her room for upwards of thirty-six hours, she could assume Miysis—and her nymph guards—had deduced her location … along with what she'd been up to this whole time, locked in a bedroom with an incubus.

"You have about two hours to prepare," Lyre said. "I guess you're expected to join the welcoming committee."

"Oh, yes. I suppose I should."

He laughed at her reluctant tone, and the husky sound sent heat diving through her. She hooked her hands around the back of his neck and pulled his mouth down.

"I think," she breathed after thoroughly kissing him, "I can spare a few more minutes before I get ready."

"A few minutes," he agreed, that deep purr sliding back into his voice. Shivers ran across her skin. "Or maybe a bit longer than that."

This time when he untied her robe, she was the one to pull it off and throw it aside. He was right. It did just get in the way.

CLIO KEPT her eyes turned toward the horizon beyond the open city gates and hoped her dreamy state wasn't too obvious. Thoughts of Lyre spun through her head, and she had no ability whatsoever to focus. All she wanted to do was run back to his room.

Beside her, Miysis stood at attention with his hands behind his back and wings folded tight, his military background obvious. He looked as impressive as he had when she'd ridden into this plaza, his red and gold garments standing out even amongst the vibrant colors.

Unlike last time, this welcoming party was less threatening. There was still a plethora of soldiers, but they were in ceremonial dress, and the prince hadn't brought his opinaris to guard him. A line of nobles and city officials waited off to one side, and her troop of nymph soldiers waited on the other.

Long shadows stretched across the plaza as the sky gradually darkened. A sharp wind blew across them, tugging at the layers of fabric she wore, and the puffy white clouds from earlier in the afternoon had thickened, picking up the bright oranges of the sunset.

On the horizon, a cloud of dust was growing larger. She shifted her weight, her thoughts drifting back to the last two nights.

Miysis cleared his throat quietly. "Clio, may I step outside my rank for a moment?"

She blinked. Was he asking to speak plainly? "Yes, of course."

His yellow-green eyes flicked to her, his expression oddly neutral. "You've been thrust into a new role—a new life—in which you have little experience. Commoners, if you'll excuse the term, are accustomed to a certain degree of privacy in their lives, but that's a rare luxury for members of the nobility."

She nodded cautiously.

"You'll soon learn that nothing you do will remain a secret for long. I hope you will take this advice to heart: treat every decision, no matter how private, as something you may have to publicly defend later."

A blush crept into her cheeks. Miysis was referring to her spending two nights in Lyre's room, and she fought her embarrassment. She was wearing her nymph regalia again, but not the mask, meaning her blush was visible to everyone nearby.

Miysis casually scanned the plaza. "My guards and messengers will not repeat anything they saw or surmised, and I had your visitors turned away before reaching the guest hall, but—"

"Visitors?" she blurted. "What visitors?"

He gave her a sideways look. "Nobility flocks to nobility. They want to learn more about you, insinuate themselves into your circle, and uncover what advantages they can gain from your favor. They're unbearably curious about the mysterious new Nereid—and greedy, of course, but that applies to all nobles."

She pressed her lips together, letting that sink in.

"As I was saying, my people will not gossip—I have ensured that—and I've kept Aldrendahar's nobility away, but I advise you to speak to your guards as soon as you can."

"Speak to them?" she mumbled.

"Request—or demand—their discretion, otherwise they might bring their gossip straight to King Rouvin's attendants, and from there…" He gave a faint shrug. "Rumors are an unstoppable contagion."

Her jumping into bed with a daemon the moment she arrived in Aldrendahar was already unseemly, but her guards had seen Lyre. They knew he wasn't a nymph—or a griffin. Had they recognized him as an incubus?

"I appreciate your advice," she said weakly.

Miysis looked from her to the open gates, where the approaching dust cloud had manifested into thirty mounted daemons and three low carriages on runners pulled by teams of tachies.

"I would offer one more word of caution," he murmured, lowering his voice even more. "I don't know your intentions, but if you plan to take Lyre with you … know that with all eyes on the new Nereid princess, hiding him in Irida will be impossible."

At that moment, a soldier called a command and all the griffins in the plaza snapped to attention. With a deafening clatter, the king's entourage swept through the gates, and Clio had no chance to reply to Miysis's ominous warning.

FIFTEEN

AS THE TEAMS of tachies dragged the carriages into the plaza, the runners—made to slide over sand—screeched on the flagstones. Clio stood stiffly as the drivers pulled the beasts to a halt. The creatures tossed their heads in relief, long horns gleaming. The Iridian soldiers took their positions around the three carriages, and the driver of the centermost one opened the door.

King Rouvin of Irida stepped out, his slender body draped in layers of white, green, and blue. Four more nymphs, dressed similarly and wearing ceremonial masks, exited the other carriages.

Miysis moved forward to greet the king but Clio stayed where she was, her thoughts stuck on what the Ra prince had said.

He was right. Hiding Lyre would be impossible. *He* was temporarily hiding Lyre, but he commanded all the soldiers and citadel guards, so he could control what everyone knew about his mysterious guest. She didn't have that kind of power. She'd already raised dozens of awkward questions by allowing her guards to realize she was sleeping with an unknown daemon.

She hadn't thought beyond wanting to be with Lyre, but taking him back to Irida … was that too risky? Even if she crafted a new identity for him, there was no hiding the fact he was an incubus. If rumors of an incubus living in nymph territory reached Asphodel, Lyre's family would know exactly where to find him.

On top of that, a Nereid princess taking an *incubus* as her lover was a scandal that would eclipse even King Rouvin's secret affair with Clio's mother.

Snapping back to reality as Miysis and Rouvin approached her, she dropped into a respectful curtsey.

"I'm relieved you arrived safely." Rouvin clasped her hand affectionately. "And that you could deliver my missive so swiftly."

"I did my best," she murmured.

"Let us return to the citadel." Miysis glanced at the sky. "The weather is shifting and I expect we'll see a storm tonight."

"Is this the first storm of the season?" Rouvin asked conversationally as the two men started across the plaza. Clio followed, the four nymph advisors right behind her.

"It is, and it should be a phenomenal sight. It's been drier than usual this year, so I anticipate the storm will be especially violent."

They continued to discuss the weather as they crossed the city and entered the walled citadel. Clio chewed on her lower lip, unsure what she was supposed to do. As the two royals swept inside, she let Rouvin's four advisors draw ahead of her so she could follow their lead.

Skipping all further ceremony, Miysis led Rouvin straight to a private room on the ground level. Instead of chairs, leather benches circled a low, round table already bearing a selection of drinks, fruit, and other small snacks. Since Clio had positioned herself near the back of the group, she ended up sitting on the bench farthest from the royals—not that she was disappointed to be out of the limelight.

The nymph king and the griffin prince wasted no time in getting down to business. Rouvin launched into the actions he had already taken to find and stop Bastian, and revealed he'd publicly proclaimed to his court that Bastian was a traitor to the crown.

Miysis listened somberly until Rouvin was finished, then responded with his own efforts on tracking Bastian and preparing to defend the targeted Ra cities. Their discussion continued for nearly two hours, and Clio paid strict attention to every word. Reading between the lines, she gathered Miysis was eager for an immediate peace accord between Ra and Irida but he wasn't confident in his queen's support.

Thunder rolled in the distance as Miysis sipped his drink. "With your cooperation, Your Majesty, I think we can salvage this situation. Perhaps it can even strengthen the bond between our kingdoms."

"I would be relieved by such an outcome, Your Highness."

"In the future, I would love to introduce my youngest sister to your young daughter. They're close in age and might enjoy meeting."

"A fine suggestion," Rouvin agreed.

Miysis offered Rouvin a respectful bow. "Though Aldrendahar's councilors are eager to treat you to a welcoming feast, I'm sure your travels were tiring. A room is ready for you."

"Thank you. It was a long journey for these old bones."

Another growl of thunder sounded and Miysis glanced at the windows. "I expect, however, there will be a few lightning fetes tonight. You're more than welcome to join us."

"Lightning fetes?" Rouvin repeated with a chuckle. "Whatever is that?"

"We rarely pass up an excuse for a feast or a party," Miysis explained with a smile. "And, I'm afraid, the storm may make sleeping difficult. Instead, we indulge for the night and exercise profound laziness the following day."

"How charming. Perhaps I can join you after some rest."

With a farewell, the prince and his people exited, leaving Rouvin, Clio, and the four nymph advisors with a handful of officials eager to show them to their accommodations. The nymph advisors were taken to a different level, while the last official led Rouvin, with Clio and four of the king's bodyguards tagging along, past her room to the farthest door in the hall. Clearly, this was the level for the griffins' most important guests.

As the guards took up positions at the door and Rouvin entered to explore his suite, the official drew Clio a few paces away.

"Lady Nereid," he murmured in a low voice. "His Highness would like you to know that his … other *guest* has moved to a new room in a more private hall."

"Oh." She supposed that made sense, especially after the advice the prince had passed along to her. This corridor would be busy with advisors, officials, and guards for as long as Rouvin was here. "Where is his new room?"

"His Highness noted that discretion was of the utmost importance."

Her eyes narrowed but she didn't argue. If Rouvin was going to Miysis's lightning fete, then she would go as well. There she would find a private moment to badger the prince about where he'd hidden Lyre away.

The official gave her a swift bow and retreated down the hall. She hovered for a moment, wondering if she should return to her room, then turned back to the king's door, still hanging open. Passing between the guards, she peeked inside.

Rouvin was standing at the bank of open windows that formed one wall of the room. She tapped on the door to get his attention, and he waved her inside.

"It's quite lovely, isn't it? It's been many years since I've visited a Ra city." He glanced over as she prepared to curtsey again. "No, no need for that, my dear. Let us sit. I may not have walked, but riding in those sleighs is far from comfortable."

He sank down at the table and she poured them both goblets of ice water. At some point, she needed to ask Miysis where all this ice came from. Did he have a special team of daemons that spent all day traveling ley lines to bring back ice from a colder climate?

She sipped her water. "I'm glad you're here. It was an anxious wait."

"You've done an excellent job. And it certainly helps that the young Ra prince is so keen to pursue peace. I wouldn't have expected that from his reputation or his military rank."

"His reputation?" she repeated curiously.

Rouvin sampled a piece of fruit. "He's known among the nobility of other castes, ours included, as something of a snake charmer. He always gets his way, regardless of the opposition's stance—or strength."

"He hasn't seemed that ruthless to me."

"I think we are most fortunate that his goals are aligned with ours. He would be a formidable opponent otherwise."

"Prince Miysis has been very helpful," she murmured. "He's given me some good advice since I found out what you said in your letter … about me."

His pleasant expression sobering, Rouvin folded his hands on the table. "Clio, did your mother ever talk about me or how she and I met?"

"Not really." Clio shifted uncomfortably. "She did warn me about how falling in love makes people act foolishly, though."

Rouvin winced. "Your mother and I met only a few years after I had taken the throne. My marriage to the late queen was arranged, and our partnership was cordial but barren of meaningful affection. When Bastian was born, my wife devoted herself to motherhood to the exclusion of all else, including me."

Clio stared at him, the intimate revelation about his past surprising her.

"It was a difficult period. I was terribly lonely, and I would often retreat to my private garden for hours at a time." Rouvin looked out the window, his eyes distant. "It was there that I first met your mother; she was filling in for the usual gardener. It began innocently enough. She would hum while she worked, and I would sit and listen. Eventually, we started to talk. We grew close … inappropriately so."

Rouvin focused on Clio again. "I have no excuse for my unfaithfulness to my wife or my selfishness in putting Ariadne in such a reckless predicament. I can only say that she was the one person in the entire palace, perhaps in the entire kingdom, with whom I could truly be myself. I cared for her very deeply."

He drew in a slow, measured breath. "Almost a year after we met, she told me she was with child. I had hidden our affair, but how could I hide her pregnancy? I was terrified as only a young king can be when he foresees his downfall."

"In a panic, I turned to my most trusted advisor for help. I told him everything." He sat silently for a moment, head bowed and expression tight. "The next morning, Ariadne was gone. My advisor promised that she was safe, cared for, and most importantly, far from me."

Silence fell over the room, heavy with the ghosts of their shared past.

Rouvin smiled wearily. "It is astonishing, Clio, the lies we tell ourselves when the truth is too difficult to face. I convinced myself that Ariadne was better off without me, that she either hated me or had forgotten me, and that I should stay away. They were foolish, cowardly lies, but I repeated them until I believed them." His shoulders bowed. "I didn't learn of Ariadne's passing until the day you arrived with Bastian. I didn't know she had a daughter. I didn't know your name until Bastian introduced you."

Clio remembered that first terrifying meeting. Already overwhelmed by the journey through Irida and her first sight of the capital city, she'd then kneeled before a stone-faced king while Bastian explained who she was and how she would be living in the palace from now on.

Rouvin entwined his fingers together. "I am a stubborn old man and a prideful coward. There was my lost daughter, standing before me with frightened eyes—eyes just like Ariadne's. I should have welcomed you with open arms. Instead, I let shame and fear define my actions. I let you live in my home as a stranger instead of as my daughter.

"I was as cruel to you as I was to Ariadne when I abandoned her at her most vulnerable." His voice, barely a whisper, cracked. "I had learned nothing from my past mistakes."

Clio swallowed, her throat tight and her eyes stinging with unshed tears.

"But your courage has cast my weaknesses into sharp relief. Ariadne raised a far finer daughter than I have raised a son." He met her teary gaze. "It is time I righted the wrongs of the past as best I can."

Her hands trembled and she pressed them into her lap, blinking rapidly. "I don't know what to say."

"I expect my welcoming you into our family now is too little and far too late, but I will do whatever I can to repair the damage. Petrina can't wait for you to return." His faint smile was both rueful and sad. "I fear she is already preparing princess lessons for you."

"She's preparing what?" Clio mumbled, vaguely alarmed. She shook her head. "There are more important things to worry about right now ... like Bastian."

"Indeed," Rouvin agreed. "But anticipating your return is keeping her mind off her brother. To be honest, it is a comfort to me as well."

"But revealing that I'm your daughter ... it will reflect badly on you."

"It doesn't matter," he said simply. "You are my daughter, and all of Irida should be proud to have you as a Nereid. I will no longer hide the truth."

Her throat closed. Rising from her chair, she stepped over to her father and hugged him tightly. He returned the embrace, a hand pressed gently to her hair.

Withdrawing, she wiped away a tear and sank back into her seat. "Becoming part of the family has been my dream for years. I can't tell you how much this means to me, but ..."

Though he tensed, Rouvin waited patiently while she struggled with her thoughts.

"Becoming a Nereid princess is ... it's a new life. I'm not sure ... I'm not sure it's what I really want." The last few words came out in a stammering whisper. She could hardly believe she'd said them, but her perspective had changed so much in such a short time. A family wasn't the only thing she wanted anymore, and becoming a Nereid princess would mean losing Lyre.

Rouvin steepled his fingers. "You *are* a Nereid princess. I have already made that known in Irida. However, if this is not what you want, there are other options."

"I'm sorry," she whispered. "I just ... I don't know ..."

He reached across the table and touched her arm. "You don't have to decide anything this moment. It's a lot to take in."

She nodded weakly.

He rose to his feet. "It has been a long day for you, I'm sure. Why don't you rest?" Urging her to stand, he guided her to the door. "Shall I walk you to your room?"

"I'll be fine." She straightened and drew in a deep breath. "Thank you ... Father."

He pulled her into a brief but warm hug. "Sleep, child. The morning suns will bring clarity to your heart."

She hoped so, because her emotions were caught in a suffocating tangle. Walking between Rouvin's guards, she continued right past her suite door. Her chest ached from the effort it had taken to utter even a single doubt about the future her father was offering—a future that was everything she'd craved for so long.

There was only one person she wanted to see right now. One person she needed.

And she would find Lyre even if she had to turn the citadel upside down to do it.

SIXTEEN

"WHY ARE YOU upside down?"

Lyre tilted his head backward to bring the doorway into view. Miysis strolled inside, his eyebrows high above jewel-like chartreuse eyes.

"Do you ever knock?" Lyre shot back, not moving from his position on the lounge—lying on the seat, legs propped on the back cushion, head hanging off the edge as he held a sheet of paper in front of his face.

"You can learn all sorts of interesting things about people when you walk in on them," Miysis replied unapologetically.

"And no one can complain because you're a prince, huh?"

"One of my favorite perks." He stopped beside Lyre and looked down at him. "What *are* you doing?"

Lyre waved the paper. "Sometimes looking at something from a different angle helps me think."

"Couldn't you have just turned the paper upside down?"

"I'm not looking at the *paper* upside down. That would be useless."

Miysis shook his head. "I don't get it."

Lyre shrugged and pulled his legs off the back of the lounge chair. He'd *almost* figured out the next part of the mirror weaving Clio had helped him embed in the quicksilver, but the exact way to bind all the pieces together still eluded him.

Sitting up, he tossed the paper onto his stack of notes on the nearby table. "Why are you here? I thought you had a lightning thing to attend."

As though to emphasize his point, thunder cracked so loudly the porcelain vases in the corner rattled. The drapes of the much smaller window-wall of his new room were tied back to protect them from the erratic wind, and the sky beyond was unbroken black except for the occasional flash of light deep within the boiling clouds that covered the city.

His new accommodations weren't nearly as grand as his previous room, despite being on a higher level of the citadel. He was guessing this room was intended for a lady-in-waiting or a nobleman's valet—still nice, but much more utilitarian. The plush lounge chair looked like a recent addition pulled from some other room.

"I've been invited to about fifteen parties," Miysis answered as more thunder rumbled. "And I need to drop in on at least five so I don't mortally wound any noble feelings."

Lyre snorted. "The burdens of royal blood."

Miysis picked up a paper from Lyre's stack and glanced at it curiously. "What language is this? It looks like gibberish."

"It *is* gibberish—unless you know how to read it."

"You write in code?"

"A habit I started a long time ago to keep other weavers from stealing my work." He plucked the paper out of the prince's hand and dropped it back on the pile. "What brings you to my humble quarters while all those fragile noble feelings are waiting to be assuaged?"

"My room is about twenty yards down the hall, so it's not out of my way. I stopped to make sure you had everything you needed." He smirked. "And to assure you that the lovely Clio is in the middle of a deep heart-to-heart conversation with her father, so there's no need for you to wander the halls looking for her."

Lyre's mouth curved in an answering half smile to hide his instant alertness. He knew Clio's extended stay in his room hadn't gone unnoticed, but he couldn't begin to guess what Miysis might do with the information.

"So, you decided to keep me company instead?" he asked archly.

"That wasn't my plan."

Lyre let his voice slide into the deep purr that made most women blush. "You'd have way more fun with me than with those stuffy noblemen."

Miysis merely raised an eyebrow as though the innuendo had gone right over his head. "I don't doubt it, but duty calls. By the way, what does King Rouvin know about you?"

Lyre slouched back on the lounge, his gaze running over the prince from head to toe. He couldn't tell if Miysis was secretly interested in a romp with an incubus or just had an excellent poker face. Either way, Lyre's attempt to distract him from Clio-related topics hadn't worked.

"Rouvin knows I exist," he answered, "but we've never met and, unless Clio has told him, he doesn't know I'm here."

"I'll make sure not to mention you then." Miysis leaned against a marble pillar, his wings tucked behind him. "I suppose the Iridian king is also blissfully ignorant of the fact that his daughter spent the better part of her visit here locked in your room?"

Lyre raised his eyebrows innocently. "Like I said, I've never met the king. I have no idea what he knows or doesn't know."

The griffin's eyes sparkled mischievously. "I had been wondering if incubi's reputation for insatiable appetites was exaggerated, but I see my skepticism was misplaced." His expression sobered again. "Speaking of reputations, have you considered that you're treading on dangerous sands? King Rouvin isn't likely to approve of his daughter taking an Underworlder as a lover, let alone an incubus."

"I don't particularly care what he thinks."

"Your contempt for authority aside, that's a perilous attitude. He may not inspire terror like other monarchs, but he has enough power to make you disappear."

Lyre would have liked to reply that the nymph king would have a difficult time frightening him when he had the likes of Samael Hades—

to say nothing of Lyceus—hunting him already, but he merely shrugged.

His concerns shared, Miysis snapped his wings open and closed. "Well, at least you can cross 'illicit royal lover' off your bucket list."

Lyre blinked in surprise, then barked a laugh. "I guess I can."

"Clio may find future palace life stifling after her recent adventures. I doubt she'll find many daring lovers in Irida's capital."

Another of Miysis's searching observations. Lyre waved a hand as though it didn't matter to him at all, reinforcing his caste's promiscuous reputation.

"What about you, prince?" he purred enticingly, diverting the topic once again. "How many daring lovers have you encountered in the course of duty?"

Miysis smiled—a heated smile that caught Lyre off guard. Bracing his hand on the cushion beside Lyre's head, the griffin leaned down until their faces were close. "I've found a few here and there."

Lyre looked into those darkening green eyes and wondered who was playing who. Letting sensuousness slide into his body language, he touched a finger to the pattern inked on Miysis's stomach, then slowly traced the circular design.

The griffin didn't so much as twitch. Hmm. His poker face was damn good.

"I thought you were expected elsewhere," Lyre crooned softly.

"They can wait." Miysis leaned closer. "What if I've decided I want your company after all?"

Lyre pressed his palm flat against Miysis's stomach. "Only one problem," he purred. "You don't actually want me."

Surprise flickered in the prince's eyes.

"I'm not a truth-seer like you, but attraction and seduction are my primary weapons." He gave Miysis's muscled stomach a slight push. "And you, prince, have something else in mind besides a turn in my bed."

Miysis straightened and stepped back. Not a trace of embarrassment touched his features. "You're more cunning than I expected."

"Why, thank you." Lyre slung an arm over the back of the chair. "So, what are you really after?"

Miysis shrugged. "I wanted to know how serious you are about Clio. She has stars in her eyes for you."

"Why do you care if I break her heart? You barely know her."

The griffin sat on the edge of the lounge beside Lyre. "Her new life will be challenging enough without an affair with an incubus blackening her reputation on day one."

He didn't let the sick drop of his stomach show on his face. "That doesn't answer why you care."

Miysis looked up at the ceiling. "The honest truth? Prince Bastian has been impossible to deal with for years, but Clio is a blank slate. She has the potential to wield significant influence in Irida, and if I win her over early, it would give me a substantial advantage in maintaining our kingdoms' relations."

Huh. Lyre was pretty sure that was the first time Miysis had shared the full scope of his thoughts on anything—and the insight was both intriguing and worrying.

"You're more cunning than I thought as well," he murmured. Miysis had seen an opportunity with Clio and he'd gone after it from their first interaction. How much of his compassion was genuine and how much was ambition?

"I have no intention of betraying her trust," the prince added, his charming smile reappearing. "I would just prefer to cement it early."

Laughing quietly, Lyre shook his head. "You're not a bad guy, Miysis, but damn. You're a manipulative tyrant, you know that?"

"I object to the 'tyrant' part."

Snorting, Lyre pushed to his feet. He may have underestimated Miysis's capacity for calculated manipulations, but he didn't doubt his overall assessment of the prince. From what Lyre had seen, Miysis held himself to a high standard of personal integrity. He was genuinely charming and compassionate, even if he used that to his advantage.

He hoped the young Ra royal could hold on to that honor and integrity as he aged into his role. "Aren't you going to be late to your lightning parties?"

"I don't think I've ever heard so much derision in two words."

"Well, I mean, come on." Lyre gestured toward the dark window, where flickers of lightning illuminated the clouds. Thunder rolled almost nonstop, but it wasn't particularly loud or impressive. "I've seen more entertaining gusts of wind."

Miysis rose to his feet, arching his back and stretching his wings wide. "Your window is facing the wrong direction."

"Huh?"

"I'll show you. Come on."

Dubious, Lyre followed Miysis out into the grand corridor, lined with marble pillars and potted trees. The prince's bodyguards stood stone-faced by the wall and followed silently as Miysis led Lyre to a set of double doors. The prince carelessly shoved one door open and strode inside.

If Lyre's previous suite had been luxurious, he didn't know how to describe this apartment. Twenty-foot ceilings, a loft accessed by stairs with an elaborate golden balustrade, black-and-white marble floors, rich décor, wide-open space.

He gave up trying to take it all in and followed Miysis to the far end, where heavy drapes bucked in the wind. The prince pulled one open, and Lyre stepped up to the stone parapet, the arched windows offering a hundred-and-eighty-degree view of the city.

But it was the sky that commanded his attention.

Black clouds roiled for as far as he could see, and lightning ripped through them in a nonstop display. Sheets of white light blasted through the towering storm, and gargantuan bolts slammed into the dunes with a thousand thinner branches snaking in every direction. Dark mist streaked toward the ground where rain poured onto the distant sand, and powerful winds howled across the citadel tower, whipping at his clothes.

The constant roll of thunder now made sense. The electric explosion was ceaseless, engulfing the entire sky in a spectacular and terrifying demonstration of nature's power.

His jaw hung open. He'd never been afraid of thunderstorms before but he had the sudden urge to find a nice quiet basement and stay there until morning.

"It's moving this way," Miysis observed with no sign of concern. "The wind will worsen and it may rain over the city. We'll have to see."

"Your walls have giant holes," Lyre pointed out, waving at the floor-to-ceiling windows that made up the entire wall. The drapes on one side billowed, the other panel trying to tug free of Miysis's hold. "Won't the storm make a mess of things?"

"Servants are installing wall panels across the windows on the other floors. I asked them to do my room last. I enjoy the fresh air and I don't mind a little mess."

"Probably because you don't have to clean it."

"The lightning fetes are held in courtyards and on rooftops, and getting rained out is considered good luck for—"

Miysis broke off at the quiet clatter of something rolling across the floor. They both looked down as a sparkling gem tumbled to a stop at their feet. Green magic spun across the marble tiles, then the spell erupted in a crackling blaze.

Lyre leaped clear at the last moment, but Miysis crumpled beneath the wave of light, paralyzed. At the sight of the binding weave, shock rippled through Lyre, followed by fury. He recognized that spell.

He'd *invented* it.

SEVENTEEN

AS THE DRAPES whipped in the wind, lightning gleamed across steel. A daemon stood a few paces away, sword in hand and his reddish skin dark in the shadows. Horns curled above his head and a scaled tail swished behind him.

Lyre stood frozen, wondering where the hell the chimera had come from—then he spotted the three other chimeras and two nymphs waiting in the shadows. He dove for the floor, his hand stretched toward the binding weave. Touching the edge, he snapped it apart. It was his spell. He knew exactly how to break it.

Miysis jumped up and shouted something in another language—summoning his guards. The nearest chimera glanced between his two targets, then lifted his sword and sprang at Lyre.

Lyre spun a swift weave around his hands. Praying the chimera had nothing nasty coating his weapon, he caught the blade before it could cleave his skull open. The cold metal slammed down on his palms but his hasty shields held. He wrenched the sword out of the daemon's hands, flinging it away—and Miysis caught it out of the air. He slashed at the chimera and the daemon backpedaled, rejoining his comrades.

As Lyre scanned the gathered attackers, he bit back a curse. Chances were Miysis's guards wouldn't be coming to their rescue.

Miysis raised his stolen sword, his eyes darkening from green to black and a sizzle of yellow magic dancing up the blade. Lyre was already dropping glamour. Strength washing through his limbs, he plucked three throwing knives from the sheaths on his upper arm.

Thunder exploded above the city—and something else exploded *in* the city.

Visible from the windows, a plume of flames reared into the sky among the dark buildings. Torches and light spells along the citadel's parapet lit up as the guards reacted. A second magic-fueled explosion detonated at the other end of the citadel grounds, white-hot flames leaping upward.

Lyre darted a glance at Miysis, who returned the look with his teeth bared. Six against two—the daemons had probably intended to catch the prince alone. Having seen how Miysis could fight even exhausted and injured, Lyre figured their odds were decent.

The first three chimeras charged them.

Lyre dove into a roll, came up beside a chimera, and slashed with his knives. The daemon evaded, his sword cutting toward Lyre. He sprang back, activated the shield-piercing weave on his knife, and hurled it. The chimera tried to block with his sword but missed. The blade struck his throat—and bounced right off.

The knife clattered harmlessly to the floor and Lyre lurched back as two chimeras closed in on him. He didn't have his own shields up yet and had no time to activate them. Flipping a knife into each hand and activating their weaves, he thrust his fist toward the farther daemon. A swift blast of power threw the chimera off his feet.

Lyre turned on the remaining daemon. Ducking the sword, he slashed at the chimera's throat a second time, his blade scraping across the defensive shield.

It *should* have penetrated the barrier. His shield-piercing weaves could cut through most defensive spells—that's what he'd designed them to do. The only shields he'd ever encountered that he couldn't pierce in one hit were the advanced defensive weaves he and his brothers used.

He caught the chimera's sword with one shielded hand and jammed his knife into the daemon's throat for the third time. The fool, trusting his defenses, scarcely tried to evade it.

The blade sank into his throat. Lyre ripped it out, shoved the chimera aside, and twisted to meet the oncoming blade of the one he'd knocked down. He deflected the attack with his shielded hand, then threw another raw blast at the daemon's ankles. The chimera fell again, and Lyre slung a spell at the base of the nearby bookshelf. The bottom splintered and the heavy case tilted forward. It slammed down on top of the daemon.

Now Lyre knew what Bastian had been busy with the last few days. *Lyre's* binding spell. *Lyre's* defensive weaves. Bastian had stolen Lyre's spell chain during one of their encounters, and the piece-of-shit mimic had duplicated the best weaves to outfit his soldiers with. Each warrior carried gemstones equipped with some of the best protection a master weaver had to offer.

Teeth bared, Lyre whirled around. A dozen paces away, Miysis was fending off two chimeras at once, but they weren't aiming to kill him. The two petite blond nymphs stood farther back, and one was preparing another binding spell. They intended to capture the Ra prince alive.

Snarling, Lyre snapped a gem off his spell chain.

He activated the spell and threw it into the midst of Miysis's battle. It hit the floor and flashed. A ring of golden light whooshed outward and popped into the shape of a dome, trapping a nymph and chimera inside. The chimera smashed his weapon into the glowing barrier but it was as solid as a wall.

Lyre flung a blast into the other nymph's ankles. He knew the weak spots on his weaves—and how to attack them. As the nymph fell, Lyre pounced on the daemon's chest. He cast a swift binding over the soldier, right over the shield, and anchored him to the floor.

Not wasting the time to break the shield and kill the daemon, Lyre sprinted for Miysis, who was still battling the last chimera. Before he could reach them, Miysis slammed the chimera's weapon out of his hand, losing his own sword in the process. Unable to wound the shielded daemon, Miysis tackled him, driving the chimera into the floor and pinning him down.

Lyre leaped over and cast a binding spell on the chimera.

Miysis panted as he pressed a hand to the bleeding scratch on his arm. "What are they using for shields? I couldn't—"

The doors to the room blew open and another six daemons burst inside.

Miysis grabbed Lyre's arm and hauled him in the opposite direction—straight for the windows. As the griffin's wings unfurled, Lyre spun a binding weave across their hands and forearms, tying them together as they reached the rail. Miysis jumped onto it and leaped off.

In the moment before they dropped downward, Lyre glimpsed the city beneath them, lit by the electric black sky. The two explosions had multiplied. A dozen fires burned across the vista, half within the sprawling citadel grounds.

They plummeted twenty feet before Miysis snapped his wings out. Unlike Ash, the griffin had a better handle on flying with a passenger, and they arched away from the citadel, gliding in a fast descent toward the surrounding wall. The storm winds buffeted them, the turbulence terrifying with the ground so far below.

Orange light flashed.

"Watch out!" Lyre yelled as magic, thrown by a chimera hanging over the railing above, shot toward them.

Miysis banked hard. The spell whipped by, singeing the griffin's feathers.

Light flashed again and Lyre craned his neck back. All six chimeras were conjuring spells. Apparently deciding that taking Miysis alive was no longer a priority, they hurled a flurry of fiery magic.

Miysis folded his wings and they dove, evading the attacks—but the magic kept coming.

A violent gust of wind caught Miysis in mid-dive, flinging them off course. He overshot the citadel wall before laboriously bringing his flight under control again, fighting the wind. Lyre hung helplessly, hating every moment of his passenger status. They'd lost so much height that Miysis had to climb for the parapet, his wings beating hard.

Just as they reached the edge, moments from landing, the wall exploded.

A deluge of shattered stone hurled them back. As they plunged downward, Miysis got his wings open again and they careened past a tall building. The ground rushed closer.

Lyre had a split second to decide. Either they both crashed into the unyielding stone road, or Lyre gave Miysis a chance to recover his flight without a passenger's weight.

Teeth gritted, he snapped the spell binding him to Miysis and let go. As the dark street raced to meet him, he braced for impact.

ABSENTLY chewing on a fingernail, Clio ambled back toward her room. She'd checked everywhere, but Lyre wasn't on this level of the citadel anymore. How far had Miysis moved him? Would Lyre come find her?

She paused at a junction of halls and tugged at the oversized sleeves of her nymph ceremonial dress. Maybe she should have changed before wandering the corridors. This costume was so unwieldy and overdramatic—not that the griffins' preferred dress wasn't equally theatrical in its own way.

Sighing, she let her hands fall. She was so desperate to see Lyre that she was tempted to search other levels of the citadel, but finding him among the maze of corridors and rooms would be impossible. If she kept wandering around, she would run into guards and then she'd have to explain what she was up to.

Glumly, she passed a grand mezzanine with beautiful marble pillars supporting the overhang, potted trees and fine ceramics standing around their bases. A windowed corridor carried her back to the guest wing, the arched openings revealing the angry sky and flashing light of the storm. Thunder boomed, a deafening backdrop that covered the sound of her footsteps.

When she reached the posh guest corridor, her pace slowed. She didn't want to return to her empty room. Fidgeting with her sleeves again, she gazed across the stormy skies outside the arched windows.

Lights glowed everywhere in the city, from rooftop bonfires surrounded by "lightning fete" revelers to the glowing beacons of the city's tallest tower. She squinted at the cupola at its top, wondering what it would be like to stand that much closer to the storm.

A gust of wind blasted her in the face and she recoiled from the window. Perhaps that was enough desert storm for her. She turned toward the long stretch of deserted marble floor leading to her and Rouvin's rooms.

Her skin prickled. Where were Rouvin's guards? Had he left to join a lightning fete with Miysis?

She glanced around the empty junction. Weren't there usually griffin soldiers posted here? And where were *her* guards?

A spot on the white marble floor caught her eye—a streak of red near a narrow door, smeared as though someone had hastily wiped it up. The nervous weight in her stomach deepened into shivery apprehension.

Blinking her asper into focus, she cautiously approached the door. The scent of blood and death reached her nose. One hand poised to cast a spell, she twisted the handle and yanked the door open.

A storage room, filled with brooms, mops, and feather dusters. And, heaped on the floor in the middle, two griffins in uniform, blood drenching their feathered wings.

Before she could react to the sight of the murdered guards, a boom exploded through the city—but this time, it wasn't thunder.

Reeling away from the closet, she flew to the window and grabbed the railing. Orange fire surged above the buildings, belching black smoke toward the dark sky. Green threads of magic flickered among the flames.

Nymph magic. Bastian was here—and he was attacking the city.

Rouvin. She had to get to Rouvin. Whirling on her heel, she bolted down the corridor toward her father's room. He would know what to do. Skidding to a stop at his door, she reached for the handle.

Orange magic webbed the doorknob: a lock spell with a powerful kickback if anyone touched it. She recognized the tangerine hue of chimera magic.

She sucked in a breath, forcing herself to pause, to think. As dread twisted through her, she touched a weak spot in the weave and dissolved it. Instead of barging in, she carefully turned the handle and cracked the door open. A deep male voice that didn't belong to her father was rumbling in complaint.

"… boring as hell. Everyone else gets to have all the fun."

"*Someone* had to take babysitting duty," another voice replied, his scaled tail snapping back and forth. "Be proud the prince trusted us for this job."

A grunt answered him.

Holding her breath, Clio pushed the door open wider and stuck her head inside.

Six chimeras in dark clothing stood in a loose half circle. In front of them, Rouvin was bound to a chair, his chin resting on his chest, wrapped in a sleep spell. His bodyguards were slumped in a corner, unconscious beneath similar spells.

Babysitting duty. Bastian must have found out Rouvin was in Aldrendahar, so he'd sent a team of chimeras to keep the king out of the way. And Bastian had chosen chimeras for this job because he knew it would be impossible to convince nymph soldiers to attack their king.

She scanned the six daemons. Heavily armed and shielded with magic. Her eyes narrowed as she focused on the nearest chimera's defensive spells, embedded in lodestones on their belts. Why did that weave look so familiar? It was almost like …

Like Lyre's defensive weaves. An exact copy of his protective spells, one for magical defense and one for physical. Fury boiled in her blood. Bastian had stolen Lyre's spells and duplicated them for his soldiers!

Ducking back into the hallway, she detached the bulky sleeves of her outfit, then cast Lyre's most powerful cloaking spell on herself. They weren't the only ones who could draw on a master weaver's arsenal.

She eased the door open again and crept along the wall toward the corner where the chimeras had dumped Rouvin's four unconscious guards. Since the nymphs were wrapped in simple sleep spells, the chimeras must have been under orders to avoid killing them if possible.

No one glanced her way as the chimeras continued to gripe about all the excitement they were missing. Beneath the roll of thunder, cracks and detonations sounded with disturbing frequency.

Ducking into the shadowy corner, she touched the nearest guard and dissolved the sleep spell. His eyes flew open and she clamped a hand over his mouth.

"Don't move," she breathed in his ear. "Pretend you're still unconscious."

He sucked in a sharp breath, the air hissing past her fingers, then closed his eyes most of the way, keeping his body limp. She woke the next guard, giving him the same command to stay still and silent. To reach the other two, she had to kneel on the first one but he didn't react to her knees digging into his stomach.

She woke the last two, then slid into the shadows again.

"There are six chimeras," she whispered, hoping they could all hear her over the thunder, not daring to speak any louder. Her cloaking weave would only work if the chimeras weren't actively looking for an intruder. "They're protected by strong defensive weavings against magic and weapons."

She paused as one of the chimeras laughed at his comrade's joke, then continued. "I know how to break the shields, so if you watch me you should be able to do the same yourself."

All nymphs had astral perception, but without the mimic ability, they didn't have her instinctive talent for understanding magic—and seeing its weaknesses—but if she showed them how, they could break the weaves too. And she had no doubt these soldiers had the skill to learn the technique after a single demonstration—only the best of the best were given the honor of guarding the king's life. They'd never have been taken unaware the first time if the chimeras hadn't had master weaver spells to help them.

"I'll sneak around and distract them from the other side. Are you ready?"

Four slight nods. She slunk away, keeping to the shadows. Timing her steps to overlap with the chimeras' talking, she painstakingly circled around the room.

Crouched low, she lifted a full pitcher of water off the round table, its ice melted but the polished exterior slick with cold droplets, then crept farther until she was directly behind the chimeras. Beside her, the drapes that surrounded the bed rippled in the breeze.

She waited for the next thunderous boom, then slung the water across the marble floor. Setting the pitcher aside, she began two spells at once.

The problem with magic in a dark room: it glowed.

At the first flicker of green light, the six chimeras whirled toward her. The nearer two charged—and slipped on the slick floor. One daemon fell while the second flailed wildly for balance. She flung her first spell—a whip of force that struck their legs, taking the flailing chimera and another one down.

Then she snapped out her second spell. The blade of power sliced across the top of the drapes and the sharp breeze blew them over the chimeras. They batted furiously at the tumbling fabric or leaped aside to stay clear, distracted only for a few seconds.

And in those seconds, the four nymph guards launched at the chimeras from behind.

Eight daemons clashed in a frenzy of gleaming weapons and flashing magic. Clio danced out of the way as the first chimera she'd downed lunged from under the drapes and grabbed her arm. She slipped on the wet marble and fell backward, but the chimera fell too, landing on top of her and crushing the air from her lungs.

Wheezing, she slapped a hand to his side. She didn't need to reexamine the weaving to learn how to break it; she'd found its weakness back in Asphodel when she'd faced Madrigal. She shredded the physical defense ward, then grabbed the nearby water pitcher. Not bothering with a spell, she smashed it into the side of his head.

He jerked back and she scooted out from under him. Two chimeras were already down and the others were battling the four nymphs, while the unconscious king sat in the middle, blades flashing dangerously close.

She sprang at the back of the nearest chimera. He spotted her and tried to dodge away but his nymph opponent threw a flare spell in his face—harmless, but the chimera flinched. It was just enough of a pause for her to shove a hand against the chimera's back. This time, she didn't break the physical defense weave. She broke his magical defense one.

The nymph guard saw the shield fail, and green light blazed over his sword. The chimera was about to find this opponent a lot tougher to handle.

Clio left the nymph to it and raced for the next chimera. The moment he was distracted, she darted in and broke his magical defense weave. He whipped around to face her—and the nymph behind him conjured a glowing green spear and sank it into the daemon's back.

She went for the next chimera. His tail snapped out, striking her legs, and she hit the floor before she knew what had happened. The chimera cast a wall of orange flames at his opponents, then spun his sword down toward Clio.

A nymph guard burst through the flames. His curved saber, the blade glowing, caught the chimera's heavier sword, and at the same time, he jammed his fist into the daemon's side. Light flashed and the chimera's shield dissolved.

Baring his teeth, the chimera tackled the nymph guard. They went down in a jumble of limbs, then the nymph rolled free, his spelled blade spinning, and he drove it into the chimera's shoulder.

Clio grabbed the injured chimera and spun a binding spell over him. "Help the others!"

The nymph rushed toward his companions while she finished the binding. Still fighting to breathe after her hard fall, she jumped to her feet.

The last chimera collapsed, caught between two spells. The nymph nearest to Clio turned to the chimera she'd bound, and before she realized what he intended, he thrust his sword down into the helpless daemon's chest. She backed away, her stomach twisting. No mercy for traitors.

One nymph guard lay unmoving with a puddle of blood slowly spreading beneath him. His sword was still embedded in his opponent's torso.

Clio stumbled to Rouvin and touched his chest. A spark of magic dissolved the sleep spell, and his eyes flew open. He jerked upright and she hurriedly broke the binding spells.

Rouvin's face paled as he scanned the bloody scene. When he saw his fallen guard, grief flashed in his eyes but he didn't let the emotion touch his expression. Of his remaining protectors, one had hastened to defend the door, while the other performed a fast healing on an ugly slice in his comrade's leg.

"Clio," Rouvin whispered hoarsely. "Is Bastian here?"

"Maybe." She swallowed hard. "Those chimeras mentioned 'the prince' and I saw—"

A roaring detonation rattled the room, followed by another roll of thunder. The wind whipped through the windows, blowing the torn bedroom drapes across the floor. Rouvin pushed to his feet and strode to the open arches. Clio followed, her legs weak from fading adrenaline and growing dread. Together with her father, she looked across the city.

Fires burned everywhere, the flames reaching for the orange-tinted sky where lightning raged. Flames ran along the citadel walls and chunks were missing from the stone parapets.

"I thought he would choose an easier target," Rouvin said bleakly. "But he chose the best-defended town to show his strength."

"He can't use the KLOC here." She pressed her hands against the stone rail. "There's a ley line only half a mile away."

"I wish I could say he's not that reckless, but I don't know anymore."

His two guards approached, the third still covering the door. "Your Majesty, what do you want to do?"

"You should stay here," Clio said. "Your other guards must be nearby—I bet the chimeras incapacitated them too. If you can wake them up, you'll be well protected. I'll find Miysis and—"

"You need to find Bastian," Rouvin interrupted. "Clio, he must be stopped. The damage he's inflicted could be irreparable." He glanced at the soldier who had perished protecting him. "Some damage already cannot be reversed."

"But ... where is he?" She turned to the violent city vista, ravaged by fires on the ground with the storm threatening from above. Chaos reigned, dark shadows darting in every direction as Aldrendahar's inhabitants fled the attacks.

As she looked across the destruction, she knew Bastian was there somewhere. He wouldn't let this important phase of his plan unfold without him. Her gaze darted from fire to fire but the darkness and distance were enough to defeat even her asper. Bastian could be anywhere.

In the city's center, the shadow of its tallest tower rose above everything—the narrow watchtower whose guiding lights had blazed brightly through the storm when she'd last looked out at the vista.

But now the tower was dark, its lights extinguished.

Her hands tightened on the stone railing. The watchtower was in the center of Aldrendahar, a strategic point from which the city's guardians could spot any danger—or from which an enemy could oversee their invasion.

She pushed back from the window. "I'll find him."

Rouvin nodded, not questioning her sudden determination. "Be careful."

"You as well." She glanced at his two guards, catching their eyes, then added, "Stay here. If I see Miysis or his soldiers, I'll tell them where you are."

The guards nodded, their dark eyes alert and simmering with protective fury.

She rushed across the room. As she reached the door, the third guard held out a hand to stop her. He pulled off a belt and reached around her to buckle it over her hips. She looked down at the two long, lightweight daggers.

"You should be armed with more than magic," he said quietly. "Just in case."

"Thank you," she murmured. "Protect the king."

"With my life."

Hoping it wouldn't come to that, she sprinted away from the room. The halls sped by. As she dashed down the grand staircase and into the sprawling main level foyer, the statues of griffin matrons stared down at her disapprovingly.

The reception hall wasn't empty like the guest wing. Griffins were streaming in from outside as they sought shelter, some panicking or injured, others attempting to direct the new arrivals. Soldiers and citadel guards were controlling the chaos as best they could.

Slowing so she didn't crash into anyone, Clio wove through the refugees. She passed women, children, and teenagers dressed for the lightning fetes, their fancy outfits charred or torn. Beside a pillar, one of the body artists who'd dressed Clio for the state dinner was crouched over a teenager with blood coating her arm and half her wing feathers bent the wrong way.

Clio's throat tightened. These daemons weren't soldiers. They weren't warriors. They were regular civilians who'd just wanted to enjoy a special night in their harsh desert town.

Something close to loathing bubbled up in her as she flew through the citadel's front doors past more injured and frightened griffins. Many daemons had no combat training, only survival instincts, and those instincts did little good when the enemy was attacking from the shadows. What else could they do but flee?

As she ran down the steps, she corrected her assumption. Fleeing might have been the reaction for some, but for every daemon who sought shelter in the citadel, two more were outside. And they weren't terrified.

They were enraged.

She slapped a hand to her chest and reinforced her cloaking spell, unsure if the griffins might target her. Some clustered in snarling groups while others perched on rooftops or coasted on the rough winds, carrying weapons or ready to fight with nothing but magic and fists.

Had Bastian anticipated that griffins, a caste inherently more aggressive than nymphs, would react with violence instead of fear?

When she saw the citadel gates were open, she sighed in relief. Twenty griffin soldiers and a dozen civilians guarded it, but they were allowing a flood of injured and frightened daemons into the fortified citadel walls. Keeping to the shadows, Clio darted past them and out into the street. If the soldiers saw her, they didn't care about a lone daemon fleeing in the wrong direction.

She cut into an alley, heading toward the watchtower. As she sped through the streets, she passed magic-fueled fires from the detonations she'd heard. Green and orange magic splayed across the ground, glowing in her asper, and frustrated griffins tried to extinguish the flames while others circled the areas as though hoping the culprits would return to the scene.

As she neared the watchtower, the streets emptied. No fires burned here, reinforcing her guess on where to search. Bastian wouldn't want to draw attention to his location. Slowing to a careful jog, she passed a small bazaar with wooden stalls, miraculously unburned, then ducked down a narrow street between buildings.

Ahead, the alley opened into a wide square, and at the farthest end, the narrow watchtower rose high. Lush palm trees formed a circle around a crystalline spring in the square's center, the bench-like edges of the pool carved from marble.

In the shadow of the tower, green and orange auras were huddled together. A large ring of glowing green, filled with runes, had been drawn across the ground beneath them. She scanned the spell from across the square, squinting to make out the details, then blinked her asper away. Without it to show her the magic, she saw nothing but deep shadows that the lightning failed to illuminate.

An illusion spell. She hadn't seen this exact weaving before, but she'd seen—and used—a similar invention of Lyre's to evade archers during her escape from the bastille in Asphodel.

Blinking back her asper, she counted the daemon auras. Thirty soldiers, and as she watched, two more appeared from inside the tower. One of those green auras was Bastian. She was sure of it.

She backed out of sight, hoping none of the nymphs had spotted her aura. What now? She couldn't take on thirty soldiers alone. She couldn't even approach without being seen.

Squeezing her eyes shut, she calmed her frantic thoughts. The constant flash and flicker of lightning blazed through her eyelids, and the cacophony of thunder and shouting, interspersed with fiery detonations, continued ceaselessly.

With a crackling rumble, the sky opened. Torrential rain hit the city, pouring from the raging heavens. It drenched Clio in seconds, the cool wind cutting like ice.

She squinted through the downpour. She couldn't fight this alone, but she was in the middle of an abandoned neighborhood and with the storm and rain, no one would find her. She needed help and she needed it now, before Bastian could flee or move on to the next phase of his plan—whatever that was.

She slipped her hand into her pocket. Her numb fingers found the smooth edges of a gem and she pulled it out. It glittered under the rippling lightning.

The signal spell Lyre had given her before she'd left for Irida. One ally was better than none, and if she was lucky, he would bring help with him.

With a deep breath, she triggered the spell and prayed he was still carrying his.

EIGHTEEN

A NONE-TOO-GENTLE SLAP across the face woke Lyre. His eyes flew open and he groaned at the pain throbbing through his head, shoulder, and left leg.

Miysis's blurry face hovered over him. "Finally! I was about to leave you here."

Lyre cautiously lifted his head. Pain shot through his neck and shoulder but the injury—just bruising, he hoped—didn't impede his movement. Miysis pulled him into a sitting position and Lyre's vision blurred even worse before finally focusing.

They were at the edge of a wrecked market booth, and he assumed the fabric awning and the wooden table underneath had broken his fall.

"You didn't split your skull," Miysis said as he unceremoniously hauled Lyre to his feet. "You cracked the bones in your left leg but I already healed it."

"Thanks," Lyre grunted, testing the injured limb. Pain shot through his calf muscles. Accelerated healing on the battlefield wasn't all that thorough.

"I hope your head is still working," the prince growled as he dragged Lyre into motion, ignoring his limp. "Tell me what you know about the spells those daemons were using."

"They're Chrysalis spells," he answered, furious all over again at the reminder. "Bastian stole them from me and I'd say he's been putting his mimic ability to good use since then."

Miysis swore as he stopped at a junction of narrow streets. Thunder cracked every ten seconds and lightning rippled through the clouds, the increasing wind cool and humid. Beneath the roar of the weather, shouts and frightened cries filled the city.

"Finding my men in this storm is going to be hell, and the wind is too strong for sustained flight." Miysis glanced at Lyre, his normally bright eyes black with anger. "Can you walk on your own?"

Miysis didn't wait for an answer before letting him go and striding forward. Lyre trotted after him, evaluating the wobbly weakness in his left leg. His head and shoulder ached too but not as badly. He would get Clio to check him over for other injuries—as soon as he found her. He glanced at the dark shape of the citadel and hoped she was safe.

He and Miysis jogged through the streets, angling back toward the citadel. Still out of glamour—no sense in weakening himself just to spare Miysis any discomfort—he activated his defensive weaves and pulled his bow off his shoulder.

Miysis glanced at him. "How useful will that be in this wind?"

"Short range will be fine."

The prince grunted and picked up the pace. They rounded a corner and Lyre's senses sizzled from oncoming magic. Ten feet away, a green gem rolled across the ground, sparkling brightly.

He grabbed Miysis, shoved him down, and cast a bubble shield. The gemstone detonated into a fireball, blasting a hole in the flagstones and tearing chunks off nearby stone buildings. The flames surged upward, heat rippling off them. At their base, a green tinge was the only indicator that a spell fueled the inferno.

Lyre sprang up, scouring the darkness for a sign of whoever had thrown that gem. Miysis joined him, weaponless but ready to fight.

A hint of movement on his left.

Lyre snapped his hand out, a flare spell igniting in a blinding flash. The chimera reeled back, his cloaking spell losing its effectiveness now that Lyre had spotted him—but he didn't spot the second daemon until a blade hit him.

It deflected off his defensive weaves, and Miysis cast a glowing yellow spell, but the magic sloughed off the chimera's identical shields. Dropping low, Lyre swept his bow into the daemon's ankles, knocking him off his feet.

As Lyre snatched an arrow from his quiver, a third attacker slammed into his back. His left leg gave out and he pitched forward, landing on his stomach with his bow caught under him. The daemon jumped on his back, pinning him to the ground. The other two chimeras rushed Miysis, their blades reflecting the nearby flames.

A piercing shriek shattered Lyre's eardrums. A pale shape burst from the dark clouds of smoke, huge wings spread wide.

The opinari swept over Miysis's head and slammed both chimeras into the flagstones. Grabbing a daemon's head in its beak, the beast wrenched sideways. The chimera's neck broke with a stomach-turning crack, audible even over the thunder.

With furious shouts, six griffin soldiers dropped out of the sky from the same direction as the opinari, long-handled halberds at the ready.

The daemon pinning Lyre jumped to his feet and bolted away. Rolling onto his back, Lyre slapped his arrow onto his bow and fired at the fleeing nymph. It didn't pierce his shield, but the binding spell in the arrowhead surged around his legs.

Lyre rolled to his feet as a blood-curdling scream erupted. The opinari had caught the last chimera, and it turned out that with enough pressure, even a master weaver's shields would give out. The creature's hooked beak sank into the chimera's chest, snapping ribs.

The griffin soldiers gathered around Miysis, waiting silently while one answered the prince's barked questions about troop locations and enemy numbers.

Lyre glanced at the nymph he'd captured. If it had been one of his brothers, he wouldn't have trusted a binding spell to hold for more than ten seconds. But despite his master-weaver-quality shields, this guy wasn't a master weaver. The binding held.

"Lyre."

He turned to Miysis, who stood with his soldiers arrayed around him, waiting for orders. The opinari—Rushi from the stable, his white fur stained with scarlet splatters—hovered behind his master.

"How do my men break those shields?" the prince demanded.

Lyre grimaced bitterly. "There's no easy way to penetrate the shields. They're designed to be unbreakable."

"*You* know how to break them."

"Yes."

Something dark and cold gathered in Miysis's eyes. "Did you create the original spells?"

If he lied, Miysis would know. "Yes."

The prince analyzed him as though seeing him for the first time, but frustration quickly replaced his arctic stare. "Give me *something*, Lyre. How do we fight them? We can't rely on opinaris. There aren't enough of them and they can't hear my commands in this weather."

Lyre wished he could pull a shield-breaking miracle spell off his chain and save the day. He was a fool for letting his weaves fall into enemy hands—not that any enemy besides a mimic could have duplicated them.

"Cut the head off the snake," he said harshly. "Ignore the explosions. Ignore the two- or three-man teams. Go for their commander."

Miysis's eyes gleamed malevolently. "But where is he?"

The sky rumbled and rain plunged out of the clouds like an overturned bucket, transforming the street into a shallow river in moments. The magic-fueled fire hissed and spat but kept burning.

In the next instant, a jarring pulse vibrated in Lyre's aching skull— the signal spell. He spun around, facing away from the citadel and toward the city streets. Dead ahead, the thin silhouette of the watchtower rose above everything else.

Clio had activated her signal spell. She was calling him. But what the hell was she doing out *there*?

As rain ran down his face, his lips pulled back from his teeth in a cold smile.

"I think," he told Miysis, "we may have already found him."

AFTER MIYSIS sent half his soldiers off to locate reinforcements, he, Lyre, three griffin warriors, and the opinari raced deeper into the city. Lyre led the way, following the pulse of the signal spell. The streets grew quieter, and with the spell thudding in his aching skull, he ducked down a narrow alley.

Clio appeared from the darkness as she disabled her cloaking spell. Rain had plastered her hair to her head, and her white and green nymph regalia was drenched. She was still gorgeous and despite everything, he had to resist the urge to pull her into his arms.

Her eyes locked on his, intense and magnetic, then flicked to Miysis.

"You brought help," she remarked as he crouched beside her.

"And more is coming." Unable to resist, he brushed his fingers across the back of her hand, needing the physical contact. "What've we got?"

"About thirty daemons," she reported promptly. "Half nymphs, half chimeras. There may be more in the watchtower. They're hiding behind a shadow illusion, and from what I can tell, most of them are protected by your defensive weavings."

Lyre frowned, trying to remember what other weavings had been attached to the chain Bastian had stolen. "He might have some other nasty surprises waiting, depending on what he's duplicated from my spell set."

"From this distance, it's difficult to make out details," she apologized.

"The defensive weaves will be the biggest problem." He rubbed the water off his face, but the pouring rain immediately drenched his skin again. Turning, he found Miysis crouched behind him, listening intently. "How good are your soldiers?"

"Very good."

"Good enough to hit an enemy three times in the same spot without getting killed?"

Miysis looked at his men and raised an eyebrow questioningly.

"We'll make it happen," a griffin answered.

"Okay." Lyre exhaled. "We might be able to make this work."

"There are thirty of them," Clio protested, gesturing helplessly at their small band. "And only six of us."

Miysis smiled bleakly. "Not for long."

Exactly on cue, shadows glided out of the darkness. Miysis's other soldiers had returned, bringing with them another twenty griffins and two more armored opinaris. They gathered silently, bristling wings and black, bloodthirsty stares. These warriors were hungry for vengeance.

Bastian was a fool. Griffins were not a caste he could frighten into submission.

"Give me your weapons," Lyre said to the nearest two soldiers.

They handed over their halberds and he passed one to Clio. She gripped the long handle gingerly.

"Ready?" he asked her as he placed a hand on the blade. "I can't go slow this time."

She laid her hand on the curved steel as well. "I can keep up."

As Miysis looked between them, a confused crease in his brow, Lyre began to weave. Golden light spiraled over the blade, and beside him, Clio's green magic coated her weapon. He wove the shield-piercing weave over the steel, imbued it with power, and activated it.

He handed the weapon back to its owner, the blade shimmering faint gold, and Clio returned her copy.

"With that weave on your blade, hitting the same spot repeatedly will break the enemy's shield," he told them. "Three hits usually does it, but if you hit harder than I can, maybe less. Each time you make contact, you'll use up the weave's power, so don't miss."

They nodded, and Lyre gestured at the next two griffins. They handed over their weapons and he again passed one to Clio. Miysis hovered beside him, his frown deepening, but he didn't ask the question Lyre knew he wanted to voice. Did Lyre and Clio have enough magic between them to arm over twenty griffins with the shield-piercing weave?

They didn't have a choice. They had to, otherwise Miysis's force would be at a dangerous disadvantage.

He and Clio wove the next pair, and Miysis had two more weapons ready. Again, they wove the spells. And again. And again. His head throbbed, the ache growing worse as he depleted his magic, but he focused on the blades Miysis kept handing him until he'd lost count.

Finally, he handed off a heavy sword and there were no more weapons waiting. Exhaustion buzzed along his nerves and he slumped back against a wall, breathing hard. Miysis caught his elbow and eased him down. He realized Clio was already sitting in the mud, her face haggard and pale.

"Rest for a minute," Miysis told them before turning to his men and launching into a strategy discussion.

Closing his eyes, he slipped a hand into his pocket and dug his fingers into his pouch of diamond lodestones, but only one had any reserves left. He'd drained the others during his spellcrafting efforts over the last few days. Damn, that had been shortsighted.

Since it was all he had, he drew on the power in the lodestone. Hot magic flooded his aching body and he breathed easier.

"Are you okay?" he asked Clio. She didn't look as tired as he felt, but nymphs had larger magic reserves than incubi did—and she hadn't spent several days weaving nonstop like an idiot.

"I'm fine." She glanced at the griffins. "Will this be enough?"

"It'll have to be."

As his men formed into squads, Miysis stepped away from them and glanced over Lyre. "Where do you plan to wait?"

"Wait?" he repeated as he climbed to his feet. "I'm not—"

"You're not coming with us," the prince said, his commanding tone brooking no argument. "You're exhausted and your leg gave out in that last fight. You're a liability in close combat."

Lyre bit back a curse, unable to deny it. "I still have my bow."

"In this weather?" Miysis considered it, then nodded. "Jaspar will take you up onto a rooftop. Stay there and make sure you don't hit any of my men."

That was probably all Lyre was good for right now. "Clio—"

"I'm going with Miysis," she said before either he or the prince could say anything different. "If Bastian has any more nasty surprises in store, they might need my help."

His throat tightened. Too dangerous. She was good with magic and she handled herself well in a fight, but she wasn't trained for this kind of combat. He pulled his spell chain off his neck and lowered it over her head. Her eyes widened as his defensive weavings settled around her.

"You need it more than I do," he said hoarsely. "Be careful."

She nodded, her eyes bright and shimmering. "You too."

He could say nothing more—not with a bunch of flinty-eyed warriors watching them—so he let Miysis pass him off to another griffin. The heavily muscled soldier drew Lyre down the alley, and he glanced back one more time as Clio took a position on Miysis's right flank.

Pushing his fear for her out of his mind, he focused on what was coming: the battle that would decide Aldrendahar's fate.

NINETEEN

LYRE FOLLOWED Jaspar through a maze of alleys, then into a building. They climbed pitch-black steps and came out on a rooftop that overlooked the square. Deep shadows coiled at the base of the watchtower.

Below, Miysis, Clio, and a third of his men had advanced into the square, circling the spring in the center. How long until Bastian launched an attack from within that shadow illusion? Clio was the only one who might have any idea what was happening beneath the blanket of shadows.

Going down on one knee as the water-laden wind howled around him, Lyre pulled an arrow from his quiver, the steel point blank of any weavings. Eyes closing halfway, he wove a swift spell through the metal. Illusions were easy to break if you knew how they'd been woven—and since he'd invented that weaving, he knew exactly how.

Shrugging his bow off his shoulder, he nocked the arrow and let it fly. The bolt whipped across the square, hit the ground just inside the shadow illusion, and flashed bright gold.

The illusion dissolved in a whirl of fading shadows.

"Nice," Jaspar complimented. He put a foot on the rooftop ledge. "I'm off."

Lyre nodded as he pulled another arrow from his quiver and nocked it. The griffin soldier jumped off the edge, wings spread to slow his drop to the flagstones. In the square, the first group of chimeras charged toward Miysis and his men. The griffins leaped to meet the enemy soldiers, and Clio ducked out of the way as the two forces clashed.

Lyre activated the spell and the arrowhead lit up. Aiming for a cluster of Bastian's men yet to join the fight, he fired the bolt. It struck the ground in the middle of the group and a circle of golden light flashed outward. The ground inside the circle shattered. As stone burst in every direction, the daemons collapsed in the unstable rubble beneath their feet.

From their hidden location in a nearby alley, another third of Miysis's force charged into the square and descended on the nymphs and chimeras flailing in the rubble. Two opinaris bowled over daemons, catching helpless victims in their huge beaks.

Lyre ran his fingers across his arrows. Most were spelled for battle against regularly shielded daemons, but he had a few options. He slipped a bolt from the quiver.

As another group of Bastian's soldiers surged forward, Lyre activated the arrow and loosed it. The bolt arced upward then dropped toward the troop. Twenty feet from the ground, it exploded like fireworks and a hundred fiery orbs plunged down.

The blobs of magical fire stuck to the daemons' shields. They faltered, batting frantically at the flames. Not lethal, but excessively distracting.

As the daemons flailed at the sticky fire, Miysis's third team appeared from the other side of the watchtower, completing the trap that pinned Bastian's forces against the structure, leaving them no room to retreat.

Lyre scanned the chaos, searching for the nymph prince, but he was too far to make out details through the rain. Miysis was easy to pick out as he expertly drove a borrowed halberd into a chimera's chest.

THE BLOOD CURSE   181

Clio darted among the warriors, her nymph agility surprising Lyre all over again. He was too used to her being clumsy.

She whirled between battling daemons, and with deft touches, she destroyed their defensive weaves. A trio of griffins had attached themselves to her—one guarding her, the other two falling on the enemies she exposed. Relieved she was safe, he again surveyed the fight—and his stomach sank.

It wasn't enough.

Though even in numbers, Bastian's soldiers only needed to land one hit to critically wound a griffin, while the griffins had to strike the same spot multiple times to take down a single warrior. The nymphs were fast and deadly with their magic, and the chimeras were powerful and almost as fast. They worked in pairs, lethal in combination, and the griffins fell one by one.

Lyre lifted his bow, arrow nocked. As the light of magic and flames flashed brighter, Bastian was illuminated. Guarded by four warriors, he waited at the tower's base, the griffins unable to reach him.

Lyre drew the bowstring back but the wind gusted worse than before, and he knew he couldn't make the shot. The two sides had mixed, enemies and allies tangled together, and he might take out griffins with his arrow.

Cut the head off the snake. That was the plan, and he had to make sure it happened.

Jaw clenched, he turned away from the ledge and ran back to the stairs. If the griffins were overrun, Aldrendahar would fall—all because of Lyre's magic.

This. This was why Chrysalis was so rich, why Hades was so powerful, why master weavers were so sought after. This was why Bastian had invested years into molding Clio to his will so he could send her to Asphodel to steal Chrysalis's spellwork.

The right magic could turn a battle. The right magic could win a war.

He reached ground level and careened outside, his leg aching but the limp almost gone. Slinging his bow over his shoulder, he dug into his pocket and pulled out his pouch of spells. Pausing in the shadows, he sorted them at speed, then selected the set he needed. Unfinished, unstable, and might blow up in his face, but it was all he had that could possibly work.

Gems clenched in his fist, he charged into the square. Furious shouts and pained cries rose over the roar of the storm. He dodged warriors as he cut toward the center, homing in on Miysis. Off to his left, Clio and her small team of griffins had been pushed to the fringe of the battle, defending against three chimeras and a nymph.

He couldn't stop to help her. Ramming a nymph off his feet with one shoulder, Lyre dove into the circle of griffins around Miysis as the prince slammed the butt of his halberd into a chimera. Another griffin threw the daemon backward.

"What the hell are you doing?" Miysis shouted, rain plastering his blond hair to his face.

Wheezing, Lyre skidded to a stop beside the prince and faced the tower. On the other side of a dozen battling daemons, Bastian stood safe.

Lyre drew himself up. "Are you ready to fight the snake?"

Miysis's eyes widened.

"If he pulls out a clock, don't let him use it," Lyre added before placing a gemstone between his teeth.

He held one stone in each hand, extending them so the three formed a triangle. Eyes narrowing in concentration, he activated the one in his left hand. A crackling line of magic shot to the gem in his right hand and he activated that phase of the weave. A double line of light shot for the gem in his teeth, and power vibrated his skull as they connected. He activated the third gemstone.

A triple beam of power shot to the first gem, forming a triangle. Golden light burst through the center, filling it with lines and runes. The power continued to shoot from gem to gem, growing in force with each pass. His muscles strained, fighting to hold the gems in place as he waited for the right moment.

Building. Building. The golden blaze eclipsed even the lightning above.

He triggered the final phase of the spell.

The force spinning through the three gems rerouted to the center of the triangle and blasted outward in a shrieking beam of power. It crashed through every daemon in its path, hurling them into the air with bone-breaking force. With a sizzling shriek, it hit the base of the tower and tore right through the stone.

Then the three gems shattered and the backlash slammed into Lyre. He hit the ground, unable to breathe, but it didn't matter.

The blast had cleared a path, and Miysis didn't hesitate. He launched into the opening, three griffins on his heels, and raced toward Bastian. The nymph bastard had dodged Lyre's blast, but his protectors hadn't been as quick and only two were still on their feet.

Despite the ferocity of Lyre's spell, the battle continued. He rolled painfully onto his side, his ribs screaming. Feet surged all around, splashing in the puddles. He had to get up before they trampled him. He had to move.

He tried to rise but the pain locked his lungs. A pair of boots stopped nearby and he jerked his head up. A chimera stood over him, sword raised for a killing strike.

The daemon stumbled forward, then dropped to his knees. Clio appeared behind him, clutching a long dagger—its blade coated in the chimera's blood. Her face was white but her eyes were black, her teeth bared. She mercilessly shoved the chimera over and knelt beside Lyre, already casting a bubble shield over them. She pressed her hand to his chest.

"You cracked your ribs *again*!" she growled. "Couldn't you tell that spell was unstable?"

He stared at her. That was the sexiest growl he'd ever heard.

Not waiting for his answer, she sent a hot wave of healing magic rushing into his chest. Healing bones took more time than they had, so he assumed she was adding extra support to keep his ribs in one piece. The pain diminished, and the moment he could breathe again, he pushed upright, his gaze flashing past her.

Miysis had reached Bastian. A griffin soldier had fallen and the other two were battling Bastian's protectors, leaving the two leaders to face each other. Prince against prince.

Miysis's halberd whirled in his hands, wings arching off his back. Bastian darted side to side, unable to retreat with the tower behind him. Defensive weavings shimmered over his body and magic flashed down the lightweight saber he wielded.

Miysis didn't hesitate, didn't falter. He drove in hard, his magic burning across his body. His shields were strong and fast, holding against Bastian's spells, and he was stronger, more fit, and a hell of a lot angrier.

His halberd struck Bastian high on the left arm and bounced off the weaves. Bastian whipped out a spell but it burst on Miysis's swift spot-shield—a battle-fast barrier, small and tough for deflecting single attacks. Spinning, Miysis dropped low and used the butt of his halberd to sweep Bastian's legs out. The nymph fell and launched up again in almost the same motion, but Miysis's halberd swung around and hit Bastian's left arm a second time.

Lurching back, Bastian tried to grab the chains around his neck, desperate for something more powerful—but he didn't have time. Lyre could see it. There was a very good reason that he and his brothers, despite wielding some of the deadliest magic in the three realms, were well trained in several forms of physical combat.

Never depend on magic alone. It could be fast or it could be powerful, but it was rarely both. And fast, weak magic wouldn't be enough to defeat Miysis.

Before Bastian could select the right gem, Miysis's halberd came down on his arm for a third time. Blood splashed from the wound.

Beside Lyre, Clio tensed. Conflicted anguish twisted her face and her mouth moved in a whisper Lyre couldn't hear, but he read the shape of the words on her lips.

"His shields are gone."

Miysis's strike hadn't just cut a hole in Bastian's defensive weaves. The griffin had damaged the shield to the point of failure, and that meant his next strike would kill.

Wounded and shocked, Bastian staggered. Miysis drew the halberd back and a hush fell, muting the battles and the storm.

Miysis lunged forward, blade aimed at the nymph's heart—just as a nearby griffin battling a chimera stumbled backward. And Bastian, with no time to cast a spell, grabbed the griffin's wing and pulled the off-balance warrior into Miysis's path.

THE BLOOD CURSE 185

Sliding on the wet flagstones, Miysis pulled his blade away in a desperate attempt to abort his attack, but it was too late. He slammed into his own man, blade catching the griffin's unprotected side and cutting deep. The warrior crumpled, his blood gushing across the flagstones.

For an instant, Miysis stood frozen in horror.

Bastian blasted Miysis's halberd out of his hands. The force threw the griffin prince back and he landed on one knee.

Blade flashing, Bastian plunged his saber into Miysis.

TWENTY

HALFWAY ACROSS the square, Lyre could only watch as Bastian shoved his saber into Miysis's chest, digging the point in between his ribs. With one twist of his blade, the nymph could kill Miysis.

"Griffins!" he yelled, using magic to amplify his voice over the storm. "Stop or your prince dies!"

The clash of weapons stalled as griffins across the square disengaged from their opponents and turned to see their prince on his knees, the enemy blade in his flesh.

"Lay down your weapons," Bastian ordered.

The griffins hesitated. No one moved. Lyre didn't so much as twitch, Clio crouched beside him with horror etched across her face.

"Surrender or he dies!" Bastian shouted furiously.

"Kill me," Miysis snarled, chin raised despite the sword between his ribs, cutting the wound wider with each shift of Bastian's hand. "You fight like a coward, and you should kill me like a coward."

"Put down your weapons!" Bastian ordered again, pushing his sword in deeper. Miysis clenched his jaw, the tendons in his neck standing out sharply, but he didn't make a sound.

The griffin soldiers stood silently, weapons in hand, waiting.

Bastian hesitated, at a loss for what to do. Baring his teeth, he looked down at the Ra prince, blood streaking his chest.

"What will this solve, Bastian?"

The unfamiliar voice floated across the square, rising above the sound of the storm. Bastian's head snapped around.

From the shadows near the watchtower, an older nymph stepped over the rubble of the hole Lyre had blasted in the tower's base. A team of nymphs in the uniform of the royal guard followed him. A silent ripple of movement passed through every nymph and chimera in the square.

The newly arrived nymph made a small gesture. His royal guards stopped, hanging back, as he slowly approached Bastian.

"Will slaughtering their unarmed prince strike fear into the griffins' hearts?" King Rouvin asked his son. "Or will it forge their hatred into even greater strength? Will murdering Miysis impress your power upon the Ra queen, or show her your cowardice?"

"Cowardice?" Bastian spat. He'd dropped his amplification spell, but his snarl carried over the wind anyway. "How dare you call *me* a coward. *You* are the spineless puppet who's catered to their every demand since you took the throne!"

He gestured violently at the city, jerking the sword in Miysis's chest. The griffin's shoulders slumped, his head falling forward for the first time.

"What can you call *this* except cowardice?" Bastian ranted. "The nymph king, racing to a Ra city the moment their prince snapped his fingers, desperate to beg their forgiveness!"

The bubble shield surrounding Lyre and Clio flickered out. As Bastian snarled at Rouvin, Clio slipped into motion, creeping between unmoving soldiers toward her father and brother. Lyre half rose but dared not step closer. Bastian saw him as a threat, but maybe, just maybe, he wouldn't notice Clio.

"I am here to salvage peace as best I can," Rouvin said calmly. "Can you not understand why?"

"You should have stayed out of my way, old man." Bastian looked down at the sagging griffin caught on his blade. "I've already won. I'll kill their prince, raze their most fortified border city, and ensure their queen knows exactly what she's dealing with. And I'll do it again, and again, until we're free of their control."

"No, Bastian," Rouvin said sadly, drifting closer. "You'll kill their prince, enrage the populace of this city, and watch them slaughter your men even if they must fight to the last man, woman, and child. You'll enrage their queen, and she will bring the entire might of her kingdom down on *our* people."

"She won't attack us. I have a weapon she can't—"

Green light flashed in Rouvin's hand. His lightning-swift cast hit Bastian, knocking him backward. His saber pulled free from Miysis's chest.

Clio launched from between two oblivious chimeras. Her blast hit Bastian in the hand, tearing the saber out of his grip. As Rouvin stepped in front of Miysis, Clio dove to the griffin's side, pushing him up with her shoulder as he collapsed. She pressed a hand to his chest, healing magic sparking under her fingers.

With a furious shout, Bastian snapped his arm up, a spell taking form. Rouvin stepped forward, his counterspell dissolving Bastian's the moment it left his hand. They faced each other in the downpour, green magic racing over their arms.

"Stop this, Bastian," Rouvin pleaded. "Surrender before any more die."

Bastian hesitated, fiery green light flickering over his hands. He stared at his father, only his father, then slowly lowered his arms. "I'm not done. I may lose your respect, and I may lose my family, and I may lose my throne, but I will not stop until I have freed Irida from Ra's shadow."

"Bastian." Rouvin's voice cracked with sorrow.

The nymph prince stepped back, his face pale and lips pressed tight. "Everything I am doing, I do for our people, even if you can't see it yet."

He turned away from his father, his hand rising to issue a command to his men.

With a crack that shattered the air itself, a blazing lightning bolt sprang from the sky and struck the top of the tower. The impact shuddered through the earth, driving half the daemons in the square to their knees.

The top of the tower collapsed.

Massive fragments of rock tumbled toward the flagstones where Clio supported Miysis, Rouvin in front of them, and Bastian standing several long steps away.

There was only a single moment to act.

In the instant before the deadly barrage struck the earth, Bastian leaped toward safety. In that same instant, Rouvin's hands came up. His spell hit Clio and Miysis, hurling them away from the tower.

Rock smashed into the square. Shards ricocheted in every direction, whipping into daemons and smashing into the flagstones. Debris clattered violently, but Lyre scarcely noticed it as he ran for Clio, sprawled beside Miysis.

A howl rose above the subsiding fury of falling stone, a tormented cry of denial. Unaware of the blood running down his face from a cut on his scalp, Bastian staggered toward the heap of rock.

"*No!*" he shouted hoarsely.

Clio raised her head as Lyre skidded to a stop beside her and Miysis.

"Father!" Bastian grabbed his hair with both hands as though he might rip it out. "Father!"

His voice cracked and broke, and he fell to his knees. Rouvin's bodyguards, who'd obediently waited by the tower while he confronted his son, dug desperately in the rubble, their faces contorted in silent horror.

Clio's mouth opened, confusion twisting into disbelief. "Father?" she whispered.

A deep, booming *crack* shuddered through the tower. A fissure snaked up its side, racing from the rough hole in the bottom to the shattered top. Stone creaked ominously and the entire structure quaked.

With an earsplitting roar, the watchtower began to topple.

Lyre grabbed the chain around Clio's neck. As the other daemons fled on foot or by wing, he triggered a dome shield. It flashed out, solidifying around him, her, and Miysis just before the weight of the tower slammed down on them.

He instinctively ducked as rock battered the barrier. The glowing runes vibrated ominously, but the shield held. Rock tumbled past them, going on and on until silence finally fell. A pile of debris was heaped against one side of the barrier.

Clio stiffened. Lyre twisted around and spotted a shimmer of green light—Bastian dispelling his own dome shield, copied from Lyre's stolen chain. Rock collapsed into the gap and the prince struggled free. He looked at Clio and Lyre, his face haggard.

Then he turned and fled into the rain and dust.

Before Lyre even knew what she was doing, Clio dispelled his shield. She raced into the maze of rubble—pursuing the vanishing shadow of her half-brother.

One hand pressed to his ribs, Lyre sprang after her. He'd already lost sight of Bastian in the darkness, but Clio's asper wasn't as limited. She ran without hesitation, and Lyre sprinted in her wake. Glancing back, he caught a glimpse of Miysis among the rocky debris as an opinari landed beside him, wings arched protectively over its master.

Leaving the prince to his fate, Lyre focused on Clio as she chased her brother into the howling storm.

TWENTY-ONE

THE LAST TIME Clio had felt this kind of pain had been the night her mother died. She'd spent three days watching the vibrant nymph wither away before finally passing in her sleep, and it had ripped Clio's heart from her body.

Somehow, this hurt even worse.

Her father was dead, and with him had died the budding new relationship between them and all the potential it had contained. With him had died an entire future she'd only glimpsed.

She was alone. Her mother was dead. Her father was dead. And her brother was a foul traitor in every sense of the word.

Except she wasn't alone. As dark buildings and fiery destruction flashed past, Lyre followed right behind her. He was here. He was with her. He would stay with her. And he would help her stop Bastian.

She charged after her brother, his aura glowing brightly in her asper. He cut through an alley and into a wide street where griffins were clustered, confusion and chaos still gripping the city in its icy talons as the storm raged above. Nonstop lightning ripped through the clouds.

Bastian whipped past the frantic and furious griffins without slowing. As she followed, a griffin turned on her and grabbed her arm, but Lyre was there, slamming a magic-assisted blow into her assailant's chest. She and Lyre shot forward again.

They raced through the city but no matter how hard Clio pushed herself, she couldn't close the gap. Bastian was drawing ahead, fresh where she and Lyre were exhausted and drained. Aldrendahar's outer wall loomed, the massive gates open.

The wind buffeted her and her lungs burned. As Bastian flew across the plaza toward the desert beyond, she conjured a spell and flung it. It fizzled out short of reaching him and she clenched her jaw as he vanished through the arched opening.

She and Lyre sprinted onto the desert sand. Outside the protective city walls, the screaming wind tripled in force, driving rain into their faces. They sloshed through the wet mire, their progress slowed even more.

In the darkness ahead of Bastian's glowing aura, a rippling wall of bluish-green light flickered through the downpour. The ley line. They'd never close the gap in time.

"Clio!" Lyre shouted, coming to a sudden halt. "Help me."

Sliding in the mud, she whirled around as he yanked his bow off his shoulder and plucked an arrow from his quiver.

"I can't see him." Lyre lifted his bow. "Help me aim!"

Springing to his side, she rose as high on her tiptoes as she could and stretched her arm over his shoulder to point at Bastian's fleeing aura—only fifteen paces from the ley line.

Lyre sighted down her arm as he drew the string back with a grunt of pain. He activated the arrow's spell—but he didn't fire.

Ten paces from the line.

"Come on," Lyre snarled, holding the bow at full draw, a tremor in his arm.

Five paces.

"Lyre!" she cried over the howl of the wind.

Four paces.

Bastian stretched a hand toward the waiting line.

Three paces.

The wind shifted, whipping against their backs—and Lyre fired the arrow. It flew straight and true, pushed by the wind.

Golden light flared and Bastian fell.

Clio and Lyre dashed forward again, the ley line rippling taller as they drew near. Bastian was sprawled on his stomach, feet away from the line, Lyre's arrow sticking out of his thigh and a binding spell wrapping him from head to toe. He convulsed under the weave, fighting to free himself as Clio slid wildly down a shallow dune toward the line.

Green magic flared around Bastian, and the binding spell unraveled. He lurched to his feet, clutching his leg.

No! He couldn't reach the line!

Clio threw herself at him, her hand outstretched. As he dove into the rippling light, her grasping fingers caught his elbow.

Rushing power flooded her senses and she spun protective magic around herself. Bastian leaped into the emptiness between worlds, and as he dragged her into the Void, she felt Lyre snatch her other hand.

The world turned to screaming, silent nothingness.

CLIO TUMBLED out of the ley line, and her ears rang in the sudden quiet after the roaring storm. The hazy orange light of a sunrise lit the scrubby trees and withered bushes that surrounded the ley line, and Earth's air, stale and dead after the rich, magic-infused atmosphere of the Overworld, filled her nose.

As Bastian collapsed to his knees, she staggered and fell too, still holding his arm. Lyre pitched out of the line last, crashing into them, and they all crumpled to the ground in a tangle of limbs.

Tearing free, Bastian crawled back toward the ley line, but Lyre was already half up again. He kicked Bastian away from his only escape route.

Clio pushed to her feet, her entire body shaking. Raising her hands, she didn't even cast a spell. She just hurled an uncontrolled blast of magic into her brother's chest.

He slammed down on his back and the arrow in his leg snapped in half. Hissing in pain, he rolled over and struggled to his feet, blood running from a cut on his scalp. He flung a binding spell.

She slashed her hand through the air, dispelling it before it touched her.

"Get out of my way!" Bastian yelled.

"No!" Her fingers balled into fists. "Father is dead!"

"Don't talk about him!" Green light rippled up Bastian's arms. "He's *my* father, not yours."

He hurled another spell and she flicked it away. Battling Bastian before had seemed impossible, his spells swift and unstoppable, but now his magic was slow and easy to counter. She didn't know if he'd grown sluggish or if she'd gotten faster.

"You left him to die," she shouted, tears burning her eyes.

"He died saving *you*!" Bastian conjured a trio of glowing discs but she blasted them apart before he could throw them. His hands clenched and he shook with rage—and grief.

She fixed her glare on him, fury and torment twisting together. "Everything that's happened falls on you. All the people who've died—Father—nymphs—chimeras—griffins. How many have you killed? And what have you achieved? Nothing!"

"I'm freeing Irida from—"

"You're a stupid, arrogant fool!" she screamed over him. "How can you be so blind? You're not freeing Irida from anything! You're dragging us into a war we can't win! What will happen to Irida, with no king and no prince?"

For the first time in her memory, doubt shadowed her brother's eyes.

"You've doomed us," she said hoarsely. "For nothing but pride, you've engineered our destruction. The only thing you can do to save Irida is surrender to Ra."

"No," Bastian whispered. Then, more forcefully, "No." He thrust his hand into his tunic and pulled out the KLOC. The gemstones glittered on the silver gears. "I have the ultimate weapon. With this, I can bring Ra to their knees." He raised it triumphantly. "With this, I can—"

An arrow tore through Bastian's hand. The clock flew from his grip and thudded in the dirt a few feet away.

Clio turned to find Lyre lurking in the shadows of a tree where he'd been silently watching. He drew another arrow from his quiver, laid it on the bow, and looked at her—waiting for her to make the next move.

She faced Bastian again. "Surrender. If you give yourself over, Irida will be safe."

"Never," he hissed. "Never! You're no better than Father, worshipping the ground the Ras walk on."

Deep, arctic sorrow settled over her, dousing the fiery rage. Tears spilled down her cheeks. "How can you say that? Father gave his life to protect Irida. If Miysis had died, nothing would have stopped Ra from destroying our kingdom. Not even the shadow weave."

Bastian's jaw tightened, the veins standing out in his cheeks. Blood-smeared, drenched, and bitterly furious, he was no longer the composed, handsome prince she'd always admired.

"Surrender, Bastian," she commanded one more time.

His shoulders slumped, his fury evaporating as grief twisted his face. A tear slipped down his cheek and, shocked, she wondered if regret had finally overcome his pride.

Bastian jerked forward. He stumbled a step, fell to his knees, then collapsed, revealing the feathered shaft of the arrow rising from his back.

She couldn't move, her mind blank and body frozen.

"Clio …" he whispered, blood running from his mouth. His hand slid weakly across the dirt toward her, shaking from the effort. Then the light in his eyes dimmed and his shoulders slumped, a final breath wheezing from his lungs.

Woodenly, she turned to Lyre, but his bow was only half raised, the arrow still nocked in place. His eyes were wide, staring at Bastian like he didn't understand what had happened.

The realization that the arrow hadn't come from Lyre's direction hit her at the same moment his eyes focused on a spot behind her. He whipped his bow up and fired the arrow in one swift move.

A bowstring twanged somewhere behind her.

An arrow flashed past her shoulder, sliced through Lyre's bowstring, and embedded in his forearm. Golden magic blazed from the arrowhead.

He dropped like a marionette with cut strings and hit the ground screaming. The sound tore through her shock, and as he writhed in agony, she launched toward him.

Something slammed into her back, throwing her off her feet. She landed on her hands and knees as the broken shards of an arrow flew past her—shattered on impact with her shields. Lyre's chain of spells hung from her neck, his defensive weaves protecting her instead of him.

He was still screaming, his voice hoarse and cracking.

She whipped around, magic already forming over her hands as she faced the two approaching daemons.

And then the aphrodesia hit her.

Her knees thudded back into the dirt, her legs painfully weak. Ravenous need seared her flesh and lit her bones on fire. She trembled from head to toe, blood boiling, throat closing, heart racing so fast pain shot through her chest.

Desperately, she clung to the sound of Lyre's tormented cries, anchoring herself to his pain before the aphrodesia washed away her will. Worse. So much worse. Overwhelming, irresistible. The pounding, scorching desire obliterated every thought from her head.

Her fragile protection against aphrodesia was gone, and it was all she could do to cling to awareness as the waves of blinding heat kept building.

Madrigal stopped in front of her. She knew it was him, she could smell his citrus-spice scent, but she didn't look up, staring at his legs to avoid his magnetic eyes. If she looked into his eyes, she would be lost.

The second incubus passed Bastian's unmoving body and leaned down. She glimpsed his gleaming amber eyes, a dark tattoo on each cheek—one that matched Lyre's, and a different one on the opposite side of his perfect face. Lyceus's hand disappeared into the short grass, and when he straightened, he held the clock.

Ignoring everything else, he ran his fingers over the gears in a minute examination. Clio tried to summon magic, to form a spell, but all her body would do was tremble, her hands quaking too badly to cast anything.

Lyre's cries grew weaker, his beautiful voice breaking.

"Madrigal," Lyceus murmured without looking up from the clock, his harmonic tones shuddering through her like poisoned honey. "Lift your weave before he dies."

"Wasn't that the idea?" Madrigal slung his bow over his shoulder. "We came here to kill him."

"Not this moment. Lift your weave."

With an irritated grunt, Madrigal stepped around Clio. His feet crunched on the dry grass, then a pulse of magic. Lyre went silent.

Gathering herself, Clio launched to her feet.

"Naughty nymph." Madrigal's hypnotic voice rolled over her. "*On your knees.*"

Power rippled through the words and she fell back to the ground. She ached, shook, burned. Madrigal reappeared in front of her and crouched. She desperately fixed her stare on his jaw before his eyes captured her.

"What a disappointment, little princess," he crooned. "I was looking forward to breaking you."

She clenched her jaw, fighting the waves of aphrodesia rolling off him. In her asper, the golden haze around his body was thick enough to choke.

"Still a hint of that innocence, though." He stroked her cheek and burning warmth spread across her skin in the wake of his fingers. "I can have *some* fun."

"Is Lyre conscious?" Lyceus interrupted, glancing up from his analysis of the clock.

"Difficult to say at this point." Madrigal shrugged. "A shock spell should bring him around."

"Wake him up."

"Behave yourself, little princess," Madrigal whispered. "But if you want to run, I'll enjoy chasing you."

With a silky, cruel laugh, he returned to Lyre and dragged him from the trees, dumping him a few feet away from Clio. Lyre's eyes were half open but unfocused, and if not for the harsh rasp of his breath, she would have thought he was dead.

Madrigal pondered his brother, then kicked him in the ribs.

Lyre cried out, his eyes bulging as he clutched his side with one arm, the other impaled by an arrow. His ribs were cracked and that kick had likely done more damage.

"Oh?" Madrigal laughed. "In bad shape already, are you, brother?"

"Control yourself," Lyceus snapped. "I want him coherent."

"Why? He won't have anything useful to say."

As he walked over to Lyre, Lyceus tossed the clock to Madrigal. "Can you replicate this?"

Madrigal turned the device over in his hands. "What *is* this?"

"That is what he will tell me." He used his boot to push his half-conscious son onto his back. "Lyre."

Lyre panted for air, eyes squeezed shut and face contorted in pain, still gripping his chest as though holding himself together.

"*Lyre.*"

The power of the aphrodesia in Lyceus's voice struck Clio with more force than the howling winds of the desert storm they'd escaped. Lyre went rigid, every muscle in his body tensing. Then he slumped to the ground as though all his pain had vanished — or he couldn't feel it anymore. His eyes opened, hazy and blank.

Lyceus held his hand out to Madrigal, who returned the clock. The Rysalis patriarch crouched beside Lyre and took hold of his chin, forcing their eyes to meet. Lyre's eyes darkened to black, going even more out of focus.

"Lyre, tell me what this is."

Clio gasped when Madrigal grabbed her arm. He dragged her away from Lyceus and his helpless, enthralled son.

"Shall we find some privacy, love?" Madrigal crooned. "I don't particularly care to watch them."

Whimpering, she fought his hold but her entire body was quaking. She suspected he could have taken full control of her will at any point, but he was enjoying her pitiful resistance.

"I've never liked that," the incubus continued conversationally as he hauled Clio into the trees. "Our father using aphrodesia on us is …

well, you probably don't know that it's an absolute rule that incubi never use aphrodesia on other incubi."

He threw Clio to the ground. She landed on her back and he straddled her thighs, pinning her in place. "Our father has never had a problem with it, for some reason."

He trailed off, and in the absence of his purring tones, the power-laden rumble of Lyceus's voice drifted through the silent trees.

"I suppose it worked though," Madrigal continued, a slight rush in his words. "Trained us to never lie to him."

He glanced over his shoulder then quickly refocused on Clio. He didn't want to hear what Lyceus was doing to Lyre, she realized fuzzily. He was talking to cover the sound of the interrogation.

"I'm glad this little side trip is over." He leaned down to capture her eyes, but she looked away, breathing fast. "I thought we would have to wait *weeks* for Lyre to come through a Brinford ley line and trigger one of the signal traps we set."

He touched the chain around her neck and the defensive weaves shielding her body dissolved. His hand trailed down, dragging over her breast and across her belly. She writhed, desperate for his touch while also hating it.

Fight him. She needed to fight him. How did she fight him?

"Mmm," Madrigal crooned. "That fire in your eyes. Delicious. Did you fight Lyre too, or did you spread your legs for him like a proper whore?"

Baring her teeth, she pulled together her shredded thoughts, focused her asper on his swirling aura, and mimicked it.

He recoiled, then grabbed her by the throat, cutting off her air. "You didn't think that would work on me twice, did you?" he hissed. "I did my research after the last time. A *mimic*. Impressive ability, but not enough."

Still sitting on her legs, he dragged her up and crushed his lips to hers. She shrieked against his mouth but if his aphrodesia had been powerful before, now it was as intense as the sun. Her magic and concentration evaporated from the heat raging through her veins. Her mind emptied and her body took over—her hands grabbing at his shoulders, her mouth opening for him.

Through the trees, a cacophony of shouts erupted—voices that didn't belong to Lyceus or Lyre.

Swearing, Madrigal let go of her and jumped up. With a flick of his hand, he cast a binding spell over her, then raced into the trees. She hit the ground again, the spell trapping her arms and legs.

The moment he was out of sight, her awareness returned. She gasped, then gagged, spitting his taste out of her mouth.

The soft rush of the ley line gliding along her senses stuttered like a stone thrown into a stream—the sensation of a daemon coming or going through the line. The sudden chaos through the trees increased. Strange voices bellowed, then a burst of magic.

She struggled against the binding. Her body ached and burned, her muscles twitching, her heart still racing out of control like she had a deathly fever.

Sucking in a breath, she brought her asper into focus and craned her neck to examine the binding spell. She channeled a rough surge of magic over her body and a sloppy tangle of threads broke.

She clambered to her feet, breathing hard. Her legs shook but she pushed into the undergrowth. As she approached the tiny clearing, her foot caught on something that clattered against a nearby tree trunk.

Lyre's bow, the string cut. Grabbing it, she peered through the foliage.

Madrigal and Lyceus stood side by side. The latter held the front of Lyre's shirt, and he hung limply in his father's grip, head rolled back. Madrigal had his bow raised, an arrow aimed at their new adversaries.

A dozen daemons spanned the space in front of the ley line—nymphs and chimeras in dark clothing, soaking wet, splattered with blood and orange mud from the desert. Bastian's men. But Bastian was dead, sprawled on the ground with his blond braid gleaming in the morning sun, an arrow protruding from his back.

This spot must be Bastian's rendezvous point. His soldiers, escaped from Aldrendahar, had arrived—only to find their prince slain.

One chimera was already down with an arrow in his throat, and the others had formed up, battle ready. With another blip in the line, two more nymphs came through. They took in the situation in a single shocked sweep of their asper, then jumped into position with their comrades. Every one of them was wrapped in master-weaver defensive shields.

This development didn't appear to concern Lyceus. Still holding Lyre by the shirtfront, he raised his other hand, fingers spread wide. Light flashed out from his palm and formed a golden circle filled with runes and markings.

Clio's mouth hung open. He hadn't woven that circle. He hadn't activated a gemstone weaving. The spell had just *appeared*.

Hovering in front of his hand, the circle rotated and the runes changed color—glowing red, green, blue, purple, orange. As power crackled through it like electricity, the whole circle and all the markings in it flashed to bluish white.

Bolts of pure lightning ripped out of the spell circle and launched at the Iridian soldiers. Half of them leaped frantically away. The other half trusted their shields to protect them.

Eight daemons crumpled to the ground, their bodies burnt and smoking, flesh ripped open.

Clio braced her hand on a nearby tree for support. Was that even *magic*? She'd never seen anything like it. Even with her asper, she had no idea how the spell worked. It had blasted through the duplicates of Lyre's defensive weavings like they weren't even there.

The terrified Iridian soldiers backpedaled, some of them angling toward the ley line. Smirking, Madrigal lifted his bow and loosed an arrow. It struck the ground beside the chimera nearest the ley line. A beam of golden light burst from the arrowhead and slammed the five closest daemons away from the line.

Over a dozen of Irida's elite soldiers, protected with advanced shields, would be slaughtered by two master weavers.

Her hand rose to her throat, fingers closing over Lyre's chain. She lifted it, checking the remaining gemstones for something, *anything*, that might save them.

In the clearing, Madrigal pulled another arrow.

She pinched a ruby between her finger and thumb. An illusion spell. But of what? No way to know, but if Lyre was carrying it on his main spell chain, it had to be intended for dire circumstances.

With furious bellows, the remaining soldiers raised their swords and charged the two incubi. Clio snapped the ruby off, activated the spell, and threw it into the clearing.

Light flashed, startling Madrigal and causing Lyceus to look over. A web of magic shot across the ground, racing beneath the feet of every daemon and casting a wash of golden light over them.

Another flash, and suddenly there were forty daemons in the clearing instead of ten.

The illusion had created doppelgangers. As the nymphs and chimeras recoiled from their illusory doubles, the fakes mimicked their movements. The chaotic tangle of daemons and illusions was dizzying.

Gripping Lyre's bow, she threw herself into the mayhem.

With everything cast in a golden hue, the duplicates and the originals all looked alike. But not to her—and not to the other four nymphs. They scarcely hesitated before turning on Lyceus and Madrigal. Their lookalikes charged too.

Clio rushed in behind the distracted incubi, a spell already forming in her hand—but not an attack. She skidded onto her knees beside Lyre and used her cast to cut through his shirt just below Lyceus's hand. Lyre fell from his father's grip and hit the ground with a wide-eyed gasp.

Lyceus's head jerked around, his amber eyes darkening. Crouched beside him, Clio swung Lyre's bow as hard as she could—smashing it into Lyceus's ankles, the weakest point in the master-weaver shield.

Lyceus pitched sideways, falling into Madrigal.

Clio grabbed Lyre's uninjured arm to haul him up, but he was already stumbling to his feet. Clutching each other, they bolted toward the ley line. Clio led the way, cutting through the illusions while dodging the real daemons. The ley line loomed only a few yards ahead.

Agony exploded in her shoulder. She crashed to the ground and before she even realized she'd been hit, Lyre had grabbed the arrow and ripped it out. He threw it away as the spell activated, the whirl of golden magic snaking harmlessly across the dirt instead of her flesh.

Sagging from the pain, she twisted around. As Madrigal shot down another nymph to clear a path, Lyceus strode toward her and Lyre, his hand rising, fingers spread for another cast.

Lyre reached over his shoulder, snatched a black-fletched arrow out of his quiver, and closed his bloody hand around the arrowhead. Red light shone between his fingers. Teeth bared, he threw the bolt.

It landed point first in the ground halfway between them and Lyceus. The incubus stopped, his attention fixing on the arrow.

The eerie red glow pulsed once.

Lyre clamped his arms around Clio.

It pulsed again.

He launched to his feet, pulling her with him.

It pulsed a third time.

Lyre threw them into the ley line, and the moment before they fell into the Void, the arrow exploded—a screaming eruption that turned the whole world crimson.

TWENTY-TWO

PULLING HER LEGS closer to her chest, Clio buried her face in her knees. She wanted to cry but she didn't have the energy. She was supposed to be keeping watch but she just didn't care anymore. She had nothing left.

Leaning against the stained brick wall beside her, Lyre was in an almost identical position—knees drawn up, arms folded on top, head pillowed on his arms. Asleep, or close to it. She'd told him she would keep watch. If he'd known she was too tired, he would have tried to stay awake.

He needed rest more than she did. Whatever state she might be in, it was nothing compared to the sick emptiness that had haunted his eyes since they'd escaped his father. He looked like his soul had been ripped out of him.

She scarcely remembered their desperate leap through the ley line or the exhausting trek into the city afterward. They hadn't dared to linger, not even to heal their wounds. With the "signal traps" Lyceus and Madrigal had set around the Brinford ley lines, they'd had to run for it and hope the incubi pair were too busy butchering Bastian's soldiers to follow immediately.

She and Lyre still weren't safe. There were ways, mundane and magical, to track a daemon's movements and she had no idea which ones Lyceus might know or employ. They shouldn't have stopped at all, but they'd gotten lost in the unfamiliar industrial district. Too weary to keep going, they'd hidden away in an abandoned factory.

Forcing her head up, she propped her chin on her arms and squinted to bring her asper into focus. Not even a glimmer of magic. She relaxed her vision again, saving the last dregs of her strength.

Maybe they should have gone back to the Overworld. She wasn't sure why Lyre had jumped them to a different Brinford ley line. Maybe he hadn't had time to think and he still perceived the Overworld as too dangerous.

Or maybe he'd known exactly what he was doing. Returning to Aldrendahar meant heading back into the storm, and who knew what the situation in the city was like. The safer option would have been returning to Irida, but that was just too much to face.

A shudder rolled through her body and she gasped back the sob climbing up her throat. She had to keep her composure. Jaw clenched, she scrutinized the dim interior of the factory, full of rusting machinery and conveyor belts, distracting herself with questions about what had been manufactured here and why it had been abandoned. Patches of sunlight moved slowly across the floor as the minutes turned to hours, and her eyelids grew heavier and heavier …

She jerked upright with a silent gasp. The factory interior was pitch black, the machinery no more than hulking shadows. Where had the sun gone? Had she fallen asleep?

Scarcely breathing, she blinked her asper into focus and scanned the cavernous room, straining her senses. The only magic in sight was Lyre's glowing aura. He lifted his head, scouring the building just like her. Her skin prickled, chilly unease sliding along her nerves.

A soft skittering sound, then large golden eyes appeared above a conveyor belt. Trilling quietly, the small dragonet hopped onto the conveyor, her dark body almost invisible.

Light bloomed—a tiny spot glowing above a gloved hand.

Face covered in a wrap, decked in weapons, Ash stood beside his dragonet. Clio's breath escaped her lungs in a rush, and she sagged forward, chin thumping on her knees. Even a small dose of adrenaline had left her weak.

The draconian glided around the conveyor and sank into a crouch in front of her and Lyre. He studied her from head to toe, then gave Lyre the same thorough appraisal. When they'd last parted, Bastian had been escaping with the KLOC while two incubi closed in on the Ra embassy. She cringed, waiting for his inevitable barrage of angry questions.

Ash pulled his wrap off his face, leaving it to hang around his neck. "How bad is it?"

The question was quiet, no anger in his voice. Not quite sympathetic, but there was understanding in those dark eyes—the empathy of someone who'd been at rock bottom and knew what it felt like.

"Bad," Lyre whispered, his voice so hoarse it was almost unrecognizable.

"Bastian?" Ash prompted when neither of them said anything more.

Clio swallowed painfully. "He's dead."

"And the KLOC?"

Another long pause.

"Lyceus has it." Lyre's gaze shuttered, that hollow look intensifying. "He may or may not know how to use it. I don't … I don't remember what I told him."

Clio's heart constricted and she wanted to wrap him in her arms until the life returned to his amber eyes.

Ash's stare flicked between them. "What else?"

She steeled herself to speak the words, as though it wouldn't become real until she said it. "Bastian attacked Aldrendahar, in Ra territory. He … the King of Irida was there, and …"

"The Iridian king is dead too," Lyre finished for her.

Ash absorbed that information in silence. It probably didn't matter to him. He only cared about keeping the shadow weave away from Hades.

"Well," the draconian finally said. "The second worst daemon possible now has the KLOC. But *Samael* doesn't have it, so there's that."

Lyre snorted without amusement. "If that's your idea of good news, it's pretty weak."

"From what I can tell, Lyceus has been keeping information about your 'secret spell' to himself. No reason to assume he'll change tactics now." Ash rose to his feet. "Our target has shifted, but the goal is still the same. And Lyceus will be easier to find."

"You can't be serious," Lyre protested. "Going up against *Lyceus* to get the KLOC? You have no idea what that means."

"It's that or wait until Samael finds out about it." Ash held out his hand to Lyre. "Suck it up, incubus."

Lyre's jaw flexed. He grabbed Ash's hand and the draconian pulled him up, then steadied him when he swayed. Their eyes met and Ash's blazed with a look Clio remembered well—a steely challenge, daring her to give in, to give up.

"He may have won," Ash said, "but you haven't lost. Not until you stop fighting."

Clio looked away, pretending she hadn't heard the quiet but fierce words not meant for her ears. After a long silence, Lyre stepped toward her. She looked up to see his hand extended, his other arm pressed against his ribs. Dried blood stained his clothes and skin, but she'd removed the arrow from his forearm and healed the injury after arriving at the factory. He'd done his best to patch up her arrow wound as well.

"Let's go, Clio," he murmured.

She took his hand, her fingers curling tightly around his, but she pushed up from the floor before he could pull her. Wobbling on exhausted legs, she looked between him and the draconian. Ash's eyes unyielding, Lyre's exhausted but not quite as haunted as before.

Lyceus, one of two daemons they'd been desperate to keep the KLOC away from, now had the weapon. She had no idea how they would reclaim the shadow weave from the head of Chrysalis and patriarch of the deadliest weaver family in the Underworld.

But they were going to try anyway.

"POWERFUL MEN are predictable," Ash said, all business as he shut the door of his bachelor suite. The space was too barren for him to live there, and Clio suspected it was a hideout more than an actual home.

Lyre moved stiffly to the wooden chair and sat, one arm wrapped around his side. She collapsed onto the mattress, her legs aching and her shoulder burning. Leaping off Ash, Zwi hopped on top of the kitchen cabinets and folded her wings, surveying the room.

"They follow patterns and routines," Ash continued as he pulled off his heaviest sword and strode to a stack of boxes in the corner. "Bastian was difficult to track because he was well outside his regular patterns, but Lyceus doesn't want to draw attention to himself."

He unearthed a handful of clothes and tossed them to Lyre. The draconian paused for a moment, frowning at Clio, then turned an even deeper frown on his stash of supplies. After a moment, he pulled out a black t-shirt and flipped it toward her.

She picked it up. Clean, but about five times her size. It was probably a loose fit on the muscular draconian.

"All I've got. I'll bring something back for you." He headed into the kitchen—three whole steps over the tiny floor space. "Once we figure out where Lyceus is and what routine he's following, we can plan our next move."

As Ash pulled a few cans and boxed food from the barren cupboards, Lyre shifted uncomfortably in his chair.

"Ash, I don't think you're getting this. Lyceus is the single deadliest daemon in the three realms. There is *literally* no one more skilled or powerful in magic than him."

"No one is invincible. Everyone has weaknesses." The draconian flipped an old knife into his hand and jammed the blade into the top of a can. "I'm an assassin, incubus. I know a lot of ways to kill someone without cutting them open."

"If you're thinking of poisoning him or something ..." Lyre frowned. "That'll be difficult to pull off."

"I'll worry about that part. What I need from you is insight."

"Insight?"

"Into Lyceus," Ash clarified impatiently. He pulled out the hot plate and dropped the cans on top of it. "When hunting, you don't wander around the woods at random. You study the trails and go where your prey is likely to appear. The more you can tell me about his behavior, the more time it'll save me."

"I don't know his routines. I barely know him at all."

"Anything is better than nothing. The faster we move, the better our chances of catching him off guard." The draconian dumped two boxes into a pot and poured an arbitrary amount of water into it. "If we take too long, he might start experimenting with the KLOC."

Lyre nodded with a distracted air as Ash braced the pot over the sink then flicked his fingers, lighting an ebony fire under it. *In* the sink. Clio stared.

"Uh ..." Lyre nodded toward the pot. "Isn't that bad for the sink?"

Ash gave the incubus an expressionless stare that clearly said, "As if I care."

Lyre cleared his throat. "Okay, what do you want to know about Lyceus?"

"Where is he most likely to go?"

"He's either still here, searching for me, or he's gone back to Chrysalis."

Leaning against the wall, Clio shivered at the memory of Chrysalis's sterile white corridors, harsh and bright to hide the darkness the building housed.

In the middle of rubbing his hand through his hair, Lyre lifted his head. "Unless ..."

Clio looked at him sharply.

"Unless Lyceus doesn't want to take the KLOC into Asphodel," Lyre muttered, his eyes losing focus. "If he plans to keep it secret, he might have taken it to the Ivory Tower."

"The what?" Clio asked blankly.

Lyre looked at Ash, even more grim. "In Kokytos."

Clio huffed, annoyed at his vagueness. "*Where*?"

"Koh-*kigh*-tus," Lyre repeated more slowly. "It's a city in the Underworld. A city-state, actually, independent from the surrounding territories."

"That doesn't sound so bad," she suggested cautiously.

"Kokytos is composed entirely of the corrupt, illicit, criminal, crooked, and nefarious. The worst of the Underworld, all packed into one lawless haven."

"I don't mind it." Ash poked a spoon into the steaming contents of the pot. "No one pretends to be anything else. It's refreshing."

"I suppose you'd fit right in, wouldn't you?"

"Why would Lyceus go there?" Clio asked Lyre.

"The family keeps our repository of knowledge in a location independent of Hades." He drummed his fingers on his knee. "In Kokytos, the best protection in the Underworld is up for sale, if your budget is big enough. The Ivory Tower is part of a sort of fortress in the middle of the city where the richest, nastiest daemons have set up their refuges. Crime lords, gang leaders, war criminals ..."

"And some infamous mercenaries," Ash added as he dispelled his sink fire with a wave. He dished a soupy mixture into two bowls, and judging from the smell, it was supposed to be oatmeal. But when he poured beans on top and handed her a dish, she doubted her assessment. It didn't *look* like oatmeal.

Ash passed the other portion to Lyre, then dug into whatever was left in the pot. Jumping onto his shoulder, Zwi investigated his meal.

Clio halfheartedly poked the mixture with her bent spoon.

"If you don't like it," Ash said around a mouthful, "starve."

Lyre was already shoveling the food down so fast he probably couldn't even taste it. Sighing, Clio scooped a spoonful into her mouth. It was hot. That was the only good thing about it.

Swallowing with effort, she reluctantly reloaded her spoon. "Next time, can I cook?"

Ash shrugged and kept eating.

While she slowly forced down the meal—disgusting as it tasted, it was hot and filling and her body needed it—Ash questioned Lyre about Lyceus's habits in Chrysalis and the Rysalis setup in Kokytos. Finishing his portion with some help from Zwi, the draconian tossed the pot into the scorched sink and grabbed his huge sword. He swung it over his shoulder and buckled the baldric.

"Give me your lodestones," he said to Lyre, extending his hand. "I'll charge them while I'm out."

Lyre paused with his spoon poised above his almost empty bowl. "How are *you* going to charge lodestones?"

"The same way I charge mine all the damn time. Shut up and hand them over."

Setting his bowl on the floor, Lyre stripped off several bracelets and added them to his pouch of diamond lodestones. Ash pocketed it, then turned to Clio.

"And yours?"

"I, uh, don't have any. I've never had the need for one before ... all this."

"You have a need for them now." Ash returned to his stack of boxes, dug around, then held out three large shards of pink corundum. "Channel some magic through these."

She took the stones with a frown.

"They won't be easy to use, but it's better than nothing," Lyre added. "Lodestones take weeks to properly attune."

Blowing her hair away from her face, she flooded magic through each stone, then handed them back. Ash slipped them into his pocket, indifferent about giving her three expensive lodestones, second in value only to diamonds.

"I'll be gone for a while." He headed for the door. "A day at least, two if I have to scout Kokytos as well as Asphodel. Be ready to go when I return."

As he pulled the door open, Lyre straightened in his seat. "Ash."

The draconian looked back.

"Thanks ... for everything."

Ash's eyes darkened, his expression hard. "Don't turn this arrangement into something it isn't, incubus. If you don't start being useful, I'll kill you myself."

The door snapped shut behind him and Clio shivered. Her appetite gone, she set her bowl on the empty chair beside the mattress.

"Maybe," she mumbled hesitantly, "we should be more careful with Ash. Trusting him seems ... risky."

"Hmm?" Bowl in hand, Lyre eased off his chair and crossed to the sink. "If he was still seriously planning to kill me, he wouldn't make threats. He'd just do it."

She frowned worriedly as he rinsed his bowl out, then filled the empty pot with water to soak. He retrieved her bowl and rinsed it out too.

"Do you really think we can get the KLOC back from Lyceus?" she asked.

Lyre stared into the sink. "I don't know. If it was just me, no. But with you and Ash … maybe."

"I won't be much use." Her shoulders slumped. "I'm not a warrior like you or Ash."

Shutting off the tap, he crossed to the mattress and crouched, putting their faces on the same level. The ruby at the end of the braid hanging alongside his face glittered, and the family mark on his cheekbone looked even darker than usual against his pale complexion. With so little magic left, his true face wasn't quite as hypnotizing as usual—but still breathtakingly stunning.

"Clio, without you, we wouldn't have a chance."

Her breath caught.

"I could probably get through Chrysalis but if we have to break into the Ivory Tower? Ash and I wouldn't make it ten steps without you to spot the traps and get through the wards. Ash and I will worry about the fighting stuff. You do what you do best." A tired smile curved his lips and he brushed his fingers across her cheek. "How can you say you're not much use when I'd be dead twenty times over if not for you?"

Tears stung her eyes. "I couldn't save my father, though."

His thumb stroked her cheek. "There was nothing you could have done, Clio. He made his choice."

The anguish she'd buried deep down was pushing through the stubborn walls she'd erected around it. What would happen to Irida? She tried not to think about it, but she couldn't stop the thoughts from popping into her head—the royal council's reaction, the city in mourning, the uncertainty and fear that would spread through the kingdom.

And hardest to stop were thoughts of Petrina, alone in the palace, her father and brother dead. Her entire family, gone in a single night.

With a shuddering breath, Clio focused on the amber eyes in front of her. Sliding one hand into Lyre's hair, she pulled his mouth to hers. His kiss was soft, gentle, and too soon he pulled back.

She tightened her hand in his hair, stopping his retreat. "Lyre, make me forget."

His brow furrowed. "What?"

"Make me forget everything, just for a little while?" She pulled his face down again until their lips were touching. "I don't want to think about anything but you."

He hesitated, then his mouth closed over hers. This time, his kiss was slow and deep and consuming. She held his head in place, never wanting the kiss to end. His hands slid gently over her, avoiding her sore shoulder.

Still kissing her, he guided her back onto the mattress. Heat gathered deep inside her, warming the chill that had clung to her limbs since the drenching desert storm. Her fingers trailed down his neck and across his collarbones, his skin smooth and warm.

Her breath caught with a sudden realization, and she opened her eyes. He raised his head, eyes darkened to bronze, his hot stare questioning.

"What is it?" he asked, a hint of mesmerizing harmonics leaking into his voice.

She touched his cheekbone where the family mark stood out against his skin, then traced one ear to its point. His real face. His real body, with no glamour disguising him.

She pulled his mouth back to hers, renewed desire igniting through her. She wanted to touch and kiss and discover him all over again.

Sensing the change in her, he growled softly, a hungry sound. Pushing her back into the mattress, he slid his hands over her and found the fabric belt of her outfit. As he pulled it apart, she tugged at his shirt, unable to figure out the ties on the unfamiliar style.

He sat up and stripped it off in one move. Pressing both hands to his chest, she stroked hard muscle. Dried blood streaked his skin, but she didn't care. Judging by the fire in his eyes, he didn't care either that she was smudged with dirt and blood. He lowered himself down, pulled her mouth back to his, and did exactly as she'd asked—and more.

She forgot about everything but him. She thought of nothing but him. She felt nothing but him. His touch, his kiss, his heat, his body, his strength. His fire consumed her, burning deeper and deeper until there was no room inside her for sorrow or fear.

They eventually found their way to the shower, where he distracted her all over again beneath the pounding water, heated by a spell he'd added to the showerhead. Clean, satiated, and so relaxed she could barely stand, she stayed under the water to soak a little longer.

After another luxurious ten minutes in the cramped shower, she dried off with a threadbare towel and pulled on the oversized shirt Ash had left her. It fell halfway down her thighs.

When she drifted out of the bathroom, planning to join Lyre in bed for a long nap in his arms, she instead found him sitting on the floor, facing the kitchen chair. Perched on the seat was the vial of glowing quicksilver—the mirror spell she had helped him create.

Lyre stared at it, his eyes strangely out of focus. Slowly, he raised his hand, tracing an unfathomable shape in the air as his lips moved soundlessly. Her stomach dropped, apprehension diving through her, but she had no idea why.

"Lyre?" she murmured.

He blinked, his gaze snapping to her, but almost immediately, his stare returned to the vial. He put one finger on the cork.

"I figured it out," he whispered. "I know how to make it work."

She said nothing, wondering why his words failed to trigger the expected rush of exhilaration or triumph. Instead, an even icier wave of dread spiraled through her core.

TWENTY~THREE

INHALING SLOWLY, Clio tasted the air.

She hadn't thought she would ever return. After her disastrous first visit, she'd been utterly content with the idea that it had also been her *last* visit. How wrong she'd been.

Back again. In the Underworld.

Tilting her head, she squinted at the overcast sky. Heavy clouds blocked any glimpse of the suns or the massive planet, and the earth beneath was dim and gloomy, almost like twilight—though, according to Ash, it was midmorning.

As if summoned by the thought, the draconian joined her on the boardwalk where she waited. He was in full warrior gear—all black, armored vest, protective bracers, heavy belts holding weapons and gear, the hilt of his giant sword jutting above his shoulder, and a wrap covering the lower half of his face. Zwi clung to his other shoulder, head swiveling on her graceful neck.

Behind him, Lyre was adjusting his own gear and Clio couldn't help but stare even though she'd already gotten a good look at his new attire—several extended good looks, if she was honest.

His black, sleeveless shirt was a heavy, leather-like texture that offered some protection against attacks. Throwing knives were strapped to his upper arms, and his quiver, restocked and bristling with arrows, was belted over his shoulder. His restrung bow hung from a clip on the quiver, and an armguard covered his left arm, an archery glove on his right hand. Sets of knives were belted at his waist and around one thigh.

His deep hood was pulled up, and a black scarf was slung around his neck, one end trailing behind him. As he stopped beside her and Ash, he tugged it over his mouth and nose, loosely hiding his face. His amber eyes gleamed from the shadows of the hood.

It took effort to tear her gaze away from him and focus on Ash. "Are you *sure* we want to walk in there dressed like this?"

She plucked at her shirt in emphasis. Her outfit was similar to Lyre's, but her fitted top ran down her arms and cinched tight at her throat, leaving only her face and hands bare. Tight black pants, boots that were uncomfortable and heavy, and belted around her waist was the pair of daggers given to her by Rouvin's bodyguard in Aldrendahar. Her hair was braided into a tight bun and a scarf hung around her neck, but no one here would recognize *her* face.

Under her left sleeve, strapped to her forearm, was one more weapon: a small throwing knife Lyre had given her, hidden out of sight. "Just in case," he had said.

"Yes," Ash answered shortly.

"But—"

"You'll see why." He started along the rickety boardwalk.

She followed with a doubtful frown, Lyre trailing after her. The ground was a muddy tangle of marshland, with patches of tall plants interspersing still pools, their surfaces covered in green scum. Insects buzzed across the foul water, and the reek of rotting vegetation hung in the air, a palpable cloud.

If not for the boardwalk, they would have come out of the ley line right into the mud, but she had to wonder how much longer the planks would last. They creaked alarmingly, the wood crumbling underfoot. Ash didn't seem to notice as he led them up dilapidated stairs that climbed a small, steep hill.

Puffing, she reached the crest and stopped, squinting across the landscape before her.

The boardwalk continued down again, stretching another two hundred yards across marshes that grew increasingly waterlogged before the river absorbed them. The wide band of water was the largest she'd ever seen, stretching almost two miles across.

The dull gray expanse of liquid was broken only by a series of jutting rock formations—and built upon them was a city.

"Kokytos." Lyre sighed. "I still can't decide if this is better or worse than Asphodel."

Clio suppressed a shiver. When Ash had finally returned from his reconnaissance in the Underworld, she'd already known what he would say—where Lyceus had disappeared with the secret shadow weave.

The city was built vertically, its horizontal sprawl limited by the size of the rocky islands. From this distance, she could see no rhyme or reason to the shapes and structures—no common theme, no matching architecture, not even visible streets or pathways. The only consistency was that most of the city seemed to be constructed of wood—probably gathered from the forest barely visible beyond the river's far bank.

Rising from the centermost island were three stone towers. They were completely different: one was black and ponderous, with aggressive bulwarks; one was narrow and elegant, constructed of shimmery gray stone, and one was deceptively simple, a featureless white cylinder broken only by narrow windows evenly spaced along its levels.

The Ivory Tower. The haphazard wooden structures of the surrounding city looked dirty and pathetic around it.

Ash lifted Zwi off his shoulder and threw her into the air. Her small wings snapped open and she sped toward the river, a speck of black that shrank as she drew ahead.

"Let's move," he said, leading them down a ramp. "We don't want to hang around near—"

The power of the ley line, flowing serenely behind them, stuttered. Ash glanced back, eyes narrowing.

With a clatter of talons, the new arrival from the ley line appeared on the hilltop. The daemon paused at the sight of them, then continued down. Clio didn't even breathe as he stalked past her.

His steps slowed. He stopped and looked back.

Forcing herself to inhale, she lifted her chin in a silent challenge—anything to deny the fear shivering through her. He wore a bone-white skull with a protruding beak over his face, the empty eye sockets full of shadows, and a collection of bizarre, frightening skulls hung from his belt. His fingers flexed—each one ending in a long talon.

Silent on the rotting boardwalk, Lyre stepped to her side, the deep hood pulled forward to hide his face.

"Problem?" he crooned at the daemon.

A shift of movement on her other side, and Ash appeared. He said nothing, but the threat was obvious.

The daemon glanced between them, his bird-skull mask bobbing, then he shrugged and resumed his odd, clattering walk—his gait warped by the shape of his legs. His feet looked like a hawk's instead of a human's.

"I was afraid of this," Ash muttered irritably. He glanced over her head at Lyre. "She has 'prey' written all over her."

"We could give her more weapons?" Lyre suggested dubiously.

"Won't help. The problem is her body language."

When they both frowned at her, she scowled back self-consciously. "What do you want me to do, strut around spitting like an angry cat?"

"That might help," Ash said seriously.

"You can look tough when you want to," Lyre added. "You're actually kind of scary when you shade."

Her scowl deepened. "I can't just shade on command."

Lyre and Ash exchanged another look.

"What?" she demanded.

With a slight shake of his head, Ash continued onward and Lyre fell into step behind her. A little ways ahead, the beak-mask daemon was bobbing toward the river. The boardwalk ended abruptly at the edge of the marsh, where a small, rectangular barge was moored to a post.

Beak-face hopped onto the barge and strode to the far end, and Ash jumped from the boardwalk to the grimy barge deck with equal ease. Clio hesitated, then leaped. The barge shifted in the current and she stumbled on landing, but Ash casually caught her elbow, the movement smooth enough that Beak-face didn't notice.

Lyre jumped on last. As they all stood there, doing nothing, Clio looked around in confusion. Kokytos was almost a mile away across murky, rippling water, and the barge had no guide ropes, poles, or paddles. In fact, she realized, it wasn't even moored to the dock. It was just … floating in place despite the current, tied to nothing.

Just as she was about to whisper a question to Lyre, a splash broke the quiet.

Something surged out of the river. Black, webbed hands grabbed the edge of the barge, and a humanoid torso rose out of the water, leaning on the edge. The daemon smiled at them, his dark hair dripping wet. His hands were black and shiny, with the darkness fading to gleaming scarlet farther up his arms. A pointed dorsal fin with red spines rose off his back.

"Welcome aboard," he drawled in a wet, slurring voice. His eyes were red and black to match his scales—black pupils, everything else cherry red. "Show your payment before you put it in the box."

Beak-face had already pulled out a handful of silver coins. He held them out to the water daemon, then dropped them through a slot in the top of a small steel box bolted to the deck. Ash stepped forward, a coin pouch in his hands. He counted out some plats, displayed them for the daemon, then added them to the box.

"Good, good," the daemon slurred. "Anyone else coming?"

"No," Ash answered.

"Where to?"

"Main island."

Without a word, the daemon pushed off the edge and dove back into the river. As he went under, a black-scaled body ending in a broad fish tail flipped out of the water before vanishing after him.

The barge lurched away from the boardwalk. Clio grabbed Lyre's arm for balance, staring at the spot where the black- and red-scaled barge master had vanished.

As the boat drifted mysteriously across the river, she craned her neck back to take in the three towers. From a distance, she hadn't realized how tall the city was—tangles of structures on top of structures, linked with rope bridges and crooked, zigzagging catwalks. They drew even closer until the city blotted out half the sky, the island piled with buildings.

The barge slid past a small island into a channel between rocky outcroppings. The river current, deceptively sluggish, revealed its true power as the ripples grew more pronounced and the heavy barge rocked sickeningly. But it held to its course, running beneath a multitude of rope bridges stretching between islands.

The largest island reared out of the water ahead, the current pushing them toward it. It didn't stretch as high as the Iridian capital, but it was so densely packed with wooden buildings that she couldn't see the stone beneath.

Gliding to a low dock, the barge bumped into the thick posts. No sooner did it make contact than Beak-face jumped off. Ash followed, and Lyre nudged her forward. She tried to look confident and graceful as she sprang onto the dock. Her nymph form would have helped, but dropping glamour was not something she wanted to do in this city.

With a faint splash, the finned daemon popped his head out of the water, checking the dock for any returning passengers. Seeing her watching him, he grinned to reveal lines of pointed teeth.

Shivering, she started to turn around.

"Hey!"

Lyre's snarl came out of nowhere, and his bow snapped down, the wood cracking against Beak-face's hand. She sprang back, shocked to find the daemon right there, reaching for her.

Clutching his taloned fingers, Beak-face hopped away, hissing. His head swung toward her and a long, thin tongue snaked out of his mouth from beneath the bone mask. She jerked back another step — and her heel slipped on the dock's edge. She pitched backward.

A hand thumped on her butt and shoved her forward again.

"Careful, careful," the water daemon slurred as she stumbled onto solid footing. His red eyes fixed on Beak-face. "No trouble on the dock, yes?"

Beak-face hissed again and his skull mask turned to Lyre. He said something in a sibilant language she'd never heard before, then he turned and clattered along the dock and up a steep flight of stairs, the skulls on his belt clacking together.

"What did he say?" she whispered faintly. She expected Lyre or Ash to answer, but a different voice spoke first.

"Ahhhh," the water daemon drawled. "Not for lady ears, those words. But a good warning, yes? Tasty morsels are eaten swiftly in hungry places like this."

Cackling with what could have been amusement or malice, he pushed away from the dock and vanished beneath the surface.

Pulling Clio toward the stairs, Lyre shot an irritated glare at the water. "I bet *he'd* make a 'tasty morsel.'"

"Grilled on an open fire," Ash agreed, taking the lead again.

"Served over lemon rice." Noticing her horrified stare, Lyre snickered. "Kidding, Clio. We don't eat daemons."

"Some daemons eat other daemons," Ash pointed out tonelessly as he climbed the steps.

"Let's not get into that."

"The water daemon wasn't as freaky as Beak-face," she mumbled.

"The *ekek* was just curious," Ash said. "The water daemon is the one who'd eat you without a second thought, if he didn't have his barge to worry about."

She resisted the urge to look back at the water. "I see."

At the top of the stairs, Ash stopped and looked down at her. "I can smell your fear. That means other daemons can smell it too. Toughen up, or I'm taking you back to the ley line."

Alarm shot through her. "No. I'm *not* going back."

"If you smell like fear, every predator who crosses your path will hunt you."

And that would put Lyre and Ash at risk protecting her. Her shoulders wilted, but she forced them straight again. "I won't be afraid."

Ash's forehead crinkled skeptically.

"She'll be fine," Lyre said. "She'll be too busy tripping everywhere to be afraid."

She bristled. "Excuse me?"

"Don't play dumb." He rolled his eyes. "We all know you can't walk twenty steps through a new location without falling down."

"What? That's not—"

"How many times have you almost fallen since we got here?" He prodded her up the steps again. "You're graceful as a cat in the night *out* of glamour, but in glamour, you flop around like a fish out of water."

"I *what?*" She tried to turn on him but he pushed her to the top of the stairs. Growling angrily, she stomped after Ash. The towering wooden structures closed over them, buildings and walkways stacked on top of each other as high as she could see. Some paths were alarmingly narrow, but Ash seemed to be following a main route.

They moved through the twisting catwalks and across bridges that made her stomach plunge. Though the dock area had been mostly empty, Ash was leading them deeper into Kokytos. And it was no longer deserted.

Daemons moved through the streets, and glamour—which most daemons used in Asphodel—was a rarity. The walkways and bridges were so narrow that avoiding the other residents was impossible.

A painfully thin, boyish daemon with skin so white it had the bluish tinge of ice drifted past them without issue, not even glancing their way as his huge, solid blue eyes stared without blinking. But halfway across a bridge, they met a seven-foot-tall beast with a thick mane and gray-blue fur, walking on two stocky legs and massive paws.

The beast couldn't fit past Ash, and the draconian faced off with the creature, the wooden planks creaking under their weight. Clio clutched the rope railing.

"Out of the way," the beast growled, the words mangled by his bear-like muzzle.

Instead of answering, Ash settled his hand on the hilt of his sword.

Her hand tightened on the rope. Wouldn't it be better to yield to the huge furred monstrosity?

"You know, this bridge reminds me of Irida," Lyre whispered in her ear, leaning in from behind her. "Have you ever fallen off a boardwalk there?"

"Shut *up!*" she hissed under her breath.

"I was just wondering," he replied, all innocence. "Don't you think it'd be fun to keep a tally of your wipeouts?"

She gritted her teeth and focused on Ash's confrontation, but she must have missed something, because the furred beast was awkwardly backing down the bridge as Ash advanced, menace oozing from him with each step.

With the beast out of their way, they continued on. She kept her eyes on Ash's back as much as possible, but that didn't stop her from spotting creatures that would haunt her nightmares. Thankfully, they soon came out on a wider street, the wooden planks thunking hollowly underfoot, and Ash didn't have to challenge anyone else for the right of way.

Flimsy doors and tarnished windows lined the thoroughfare, nothing labeled with a sign or address, but daemons were coming in and out as though the buildings were open businesses. A humid miasma that smelled vaguely of rotting fish hung over the island.

Just as she wondered how Ash could possibly navigate this maze, he came to an intersection and stopped, glancing one way then the other. Was he lost?

The thud of hooves interrupted her anxious wondering. A daemon strode past, his naked upper body human, but his lower body that of a horse—four legs and all. Except it wasn't quite a horse body, because it was plated with shining black scales the size of her outstretched hand.

Deciding on a direction, Ash swung left and headed down a narrower street. Once again, he ended up challenging various daemons to get out of his way, winning every time without having to draw a weapon. Only once did he give ground, suddenly stepping to the side of the street. Clio hastily followed his lead, Lyre shadowing her.

A woman glided sedately down the center of the wooden path—and every daemon cleared the way for her. She didn't look at anyone, her pale eyes gazing straight ahead. Sprouting from the sides of her skull was a pair of magnificent antlers, woven with living vines that hung almost to the ground. Her long green hair and flowing dress trailed after her, and she seemed to float more than walk.

After she had passed, Ash cut back onto a wider street and Clio breathed a sigh of relief. She again focused on his back, ignoring the intermittent flow of daemons.

A shadow moved in her peripheral vision, and she glanced around Ash. Ahead on the street, a dark figure moved toward them. The creature drifted with a sort of directionless languor, cloaked in black with ragged strips of ghostly fabric hanging from his body. Curved horns adorned his forehead and a shaggy mess of dark hair was tangled across his face, hiding his eyes.

Her nerves prickled as the dark daemon drew closer. He came level with Ash—and stopped.

"Son of dragons." The singsong voice was soft and light, at complete odds with his nightmarish mien. "Blood of the blood."

"Keep walking, wraith," Ash said, his voice quiet but edged with steel.

"Seek your fate in my shadows." The daemon lifted his arms, his flesh black as night. Then the tatters of his cloak shifted—except it wasn't a cloak. Ragged feathers fluttered as he spread dark wings. "I will lay your future bare, Ashtaroth."

"Not interested."

The wraith smiled—a maniacal upturning of his lips, his eyes still hidden. "Perhaps another time, then."

His wings pulled in again, resuming their camouflage as a tattered cloak, and he drifted into motion. Clio didn't move as his pale face, the only break in his dark form, turned to her. Three short black horns protruded from his forehead between the larger two, almost invisible in his tangled hair. That same deranged smile pulled at his mouth, but he said nothing to her as he glided past.

Ash waited until the wraith was a safe distance away before speaking. "I can smell her fear again."

"Yeah, well," Lyre muttered. "Riling her up is more difficult when I'm freaked out too. What the hell *was* that thing?"

"A wraith," Ash said with an unhelpful shrug. "We're almost there. Come on."

"What about what he said to you?" Lyre asked, taking Clio's arm as he hurried after Ash. "What he called you?"

"Everything a wraith says is nonsensical garbage."

Lyre pressed his lips together, and when he glanced at Clio, she saw her own questions reflected in his eyes.

She didn't have time to wonder about the encounter, because Ash finally selected a building from among the endless blank doors and swept inside. Gulping down her nerves, she followed him in. This was it.

TWENTY~FOUR

OR THIS WASN'T it at all. As a sickly-sweet food smell almost as foul as the stagnant water odor hit her, Ash passed the bar and tables, cutting straight through the restaurant and out the back door.

They came out into a crooked, narrow path between buildings, barely wide enough for two people to squeeze past each other. Luckily, there was no one else in sight. He strode swiftly down the rows of back entrances, then stopped at one on the opposite side of the alley to the restaurant they'd cut through.

Pulling his face wrap down, he knocked twice on the door. A moment later, it opened a crack.

"You're late," a voice hissed from within. "Did you bring the incubus?"

"He's here."

The door swung wide. Ash vanished into the dark interior, and Clio cautiously followed. Inside, there wasn't much to see—just a dusty backroom stacked with wooden crates.

The daemon muttering to Ash had huge furred ears, pierced with multiple gold and silver hoops, and his feet ended in cloven hooves.

He tugged absently at his apron as he scrutinized Lyre, ears perked forward.

"Thirty minutes. That's it. Make him change first." The daemon gestured at a stack of white fabric waiting on a crate. "If he's caught, I don't know any of you."

"Of course," Ash agreed. He handed the daemon a small pouch that clanked with coins. "Where is she?"

"In the private dining hall. I'll have the boys step out in five minutes." The daemon thudded toward a curtained doorway. "Don't make me regret this, draconian."

"We'll be done and gone in half an hour."

Grunting, the daemon pushed through the curtain and vanished.

"Uh." Lyre arched his eyebrows at Ash. "You told me I'd be charming a female informant, but I think you left out key details."

Ash pointed at the folded white garments. "Hurry up and change."

With an annoyed grumble, Lyre investigated the clothing, then sighed and started unbuckling weapons.

"Your mark is the assistant to the head of a top security group," Ash explained in a low voice. "They're employed by the most exclusive daemon families in the city, including some in the Ivory Tower."

"Is there anything in particular I'm supposed to get out of this woman?" Lyre stripped down to his undershorts and shook out a pair of white leather pants. He started to yank them on and almost fell over. "Damn, these are tight."

"Everything you can learn about the Ivory Tower," Ash answered. "I can't get much out of anyone about its security, and if I ask too many questions, someone will notice."

Frowning, Clio picked up another piece of the white outfit—an incomprehensible contraption of white leather straps. "What *is* this? How is it supposed to go on? *Where* does it go on?"

Lyre finished squeezing into the skintight pants and buckled the belt. It clung scandalously low on his hips. "What the hell have you volunteered me for, Ash?"

The draconian plucked the leather straps from her hands. "Clio, check in the main room to see how he's supposed to wear this." He turned to Lyre. "Your mark is a banshee. She's been working for …"

His low voice grew inaudible, his rundown of the banshee target lost as Clio stepped through the curtained doorway. On the other side was a grungy industrial kitchen where half a dozen daemons worked over sizzling pans and magical fires. The cloven-hoofed daemon who'd let them in was yelling at another guy, a puddle of pink sauce staining the floor between them.

No one looked at her, so she quickly crossed to a pair of swinging doors and cracked one open.

The room beyond couldn't have been more different from the grubby kitchen. Polished wood floors gleamed, the timber pillars rimmed with tasteful gold accents. Soft white curtains partitioned the space into a series of small, private rooms. Waiters—at least, she thought they were waiters—breezed between the rooms, carrying trays of drinks or food.

And every single one was an incubus.

They wore identical uniforms, and the weird leather thing Lyre was supposed to put on wrapped around their shoulders and crisscrossed their toned chests. They were all in glamour, and with the matching outfits, they looked like a bunch of identical twins.

Tittering laughter erupted from a curtained room near Clio. An incubus backed out, a tray of empty drinks balanced easily on one hand, and blew a kiss back into the room. More giggles answered. As he turned, letting the curtain fall again, his sultry smile vanished, and he rolled his eyes at a passing coworker. The other incubus mimed gagging, then pulled a smile onto his face before slipping through a different curtain.

Clio retreated to the backroom. Lyre was holding the strap thing as he listened to Ash's history on the banshee.

"What is this place?" she blurted as soon as she was through the curtain. "An incubus restaurant?"

"A ladies' club," Ash corrected.

"Oh." Lyre snorted. "An incubus whorehouse, then. Lovely. Thanks, Ash. Really appreciate the heads up."

"I didn't want to listen to you whine about it the whole way here." Ash shrugged and gestured to Clio. "Can you put that on him?"

Shooting the draconian an annoyed look, she took the leather straps, turned them around, and helped Lyre into them. As she buckled the straps over his chest, she noted her tension level must be off the charts, because Lyre's mouthwatering near-nakedness wasn't distracting her.

Well, wasn't distracting her *much.*

"There," she said, stepping back. "You look just like the incubus clones out there."

He rolled his eyes. "Incubi don't look *that* alike."

"Yes, you do," Ash said. "And we're counting on most daemons not being able to tell incubi apart. The banshee always takes the room in the corner to your right. You have twenty-five minutes."

Lyre drew in a deep breath, the inflexible leather pressing against his shoulders and chest. Clio watched, fascinated, as he straightened and relaxed, a new fluidity imbuing his body language. An invisible mask slid over him, his shrewd intelligence disappearing behind a charmingly seductive smile, a mischievous sparkle in his bright amber eyes.

This playful, harmless version of the deadly master weaver gave her a teasing wink, then sauntered past Ash without a hint of self-consciousness and disappeared through the curtain. It fluttered into place behind him, and she puffed out a breath.

"Disconcerting," Ash muttered, frowning at the curtain.

"Huh?"

He waved vaguely in Lyre's direction.

She tilted her head thoughtfully. "I think it works because it's not entirely an act. That's one side of his personality. He just makes the other side … disappear somehow. Do you think he's always had that ability, or if he taught himself how to do it?"

"No idea," Ash grunted. "Either way, it's a useful talent."

"I don't think you could do it," she told him dryly.

He snorted. "Not even going to try."

"Ash …" Her humor faded. "Are you sure we can do this?"

His dark, stormy eyes slid over her, making her shiver. "I'm not sure about anything."

Dread doused her veins, leaving her cold all over. "Is this a suicide mission?"

"Maybe. Maybe not. We won't know until we make the attempt." He shrugged, seemingly unconcerned by the prospect of likely death. "I need to check on something. Wait here and stay out of sight. I won't be long."

Pulling his wrap over his face, he slipped out the door, leaving her alone. Fidgeting nervously, she glanced at the curtained threshold. She wouldn't have much warning if someone came in. Collecting Lyre's weapons and clothes, she stuffed them behind a stack of crates, then crouched in the shadows and cast a cloaking spell over herself.

The minutes crawled by as she waited, wondering how Lyre's banshee questioning was going. How far would he have to go to seduce information out of the woman? Would she realize he wasn't one of the incubi who worked here?

An incubi whorehouse, Lyre had called it. If that was an accurate description, the restaurant couldn't be the entire business. He'd told her before that many incubi monetized their sex appeal. If he hadn't been born into a spell weaver family, would Lyre have ended up in a place like this?

"I don't care!" someone shouted from the kitchen. "Save your excuses and go get some more!"

The curtain jerked open and a short daemon with neon-pink hair stormed through, her face twisted with anger. Clio froze in her corner, not daring to move as the daemon stalked to a stack of crates and opened the top one, muttering under her breath.

Not finding what she was looking for, the daemon moved on to the next stack, working her way closer to Clio's hiding spot. If the woman got too close, Clio's cloaking spell would fail. There was nowhere else to hide, and the door to the alley was closed.

Stay out of sight. Ash had been clear.

When the daemon stuck her head in a crate, Clio darted out of her spot and ducked into the kitchen. She'd intended to hide in a cupboard nook, but the moment she came through the curtain, the cloven-hooved daemon almost fell over her.

Snarling in annoyance, he shoved her out of his way. She stumbled backward, and when the other cooks turned to look, she dove for the nearest escape—the double doors into the restaurant.

She froze two steps into the large room, no idea what to do next. She definitely didn't want to disturb Lyre and the banshee. Squaring her shoulders, she strode purposefully toward the front doors. Two incubi flicked curious stares at her—why wasn't the cloaking spell working on them?—but they didn't stop her.

Breezing past the host, she stepped into the entryway, set back from the street. She'd circle around and come in the rear entrance again. It couldn't be that difficult to find a way into the alley, could it? She zipped out into the street, took a few steps, and saw that a heavy fog had rolled over Kokytos. A white haze blanketed the far end of the street—but that wasn't what set her heart pounding.

The street was empty. Silent. Tension hung in the air, thick and palpable.

Then hands grabbed her.

She was yanked into a narrow crevice between the incubi club and the next building. Twisting to see who held her, she half-expected Ash—but instead, she came nose to skull with Beak-face, the creepy daemon from the barge.

She tried to jerk away, preparing to cast a defensive spell, but his grip on her shoulders tightened, talons threatening to break her skin.

"*Shhh,*" he hissed. His skull mask bobbed as he nodded toward the street.

Her stomach flipped with nerves but she took a chance and looked around. Only when she blinked her asper into focus did she see it—the auras of the daemons in the street. Every one was tucked into shadowy corners and doorways, still and silent.

As she looked back at Beak-face's ugly brown aura, she spotted the gleam of a deep purple aura behind him. Another daemon was lounging in the gap—tall and fit, his long black hair tied back, his dark clothes interspersed with light armor, and several weapons hanging from his belt.

He arched an eyebrow above vibrant amethyst eyes and held a finger to his lips. Fighting to ignore the ekek's taloned hands holding her shoulders, she peeked into the street again. Some sort of procession was moving slowly closer, but she couldn't make out any details through the fog.

"What is it?" she whispered.

Beak-face squeezed her shoulders and croaked something in an unintelligible language. The violet-eyed daemon shifted closer.

"New here?" he asked her in a rich, rumbling voice.

She reluctantly nodded, seeing no point in pretending otherwise. She shrugged her shoulders, hoping Beak-face would let her go, but he tightened his grip again.

The violet-eyed daemon leaned against the wall beside her and folded his arms. "One of the queens of Kokytos has deigned to descend from the palace. If you get in her way, you'll be mincemeat before you can blink twice."

"The palace?" Clio repeated in confusion.

"One of the towers." He shrugged. "The Ivory, I think?"

The ekek rattled off something else incomprehensible. The other daemon listened, then replied in the same language.

"She's taking her sweet time," the daemon added, directing the quiet words at Clio. "I think they stopped for something and we're all stuck waiting until she moves again."

Squinting into the fog, Clio tried to lean forward to get a better look but the ekek yanked her deeper into the shadows.

She jerked her arms. "Let me go."

Beak-face didn't move.

The other daemon said something in the ekek's language. Beak-face hissed angrily and the daemon spoke again with more emphasis. Growling softly, the ekek released her. She rolled her shoulders and inched forward, uncomfortable with him behind her but unwilling to turn her back on the street—or leave the dark nook. If all the nearby daemons thought it was too risky to be in the street with the "queen" on her way, Clio would follow their example.

"Do you know him?" she asked the violet-eyed daemon, who was still leaning against the wall beside her and the ekek. The space was barely wide enough for the three of them.

"Nope. Do you?"

"We came in on the barge together."

The daemon arched his eyebrows again. "Interesting coincidence that you both ended up on the same street."

"Yeah," she muttered darkly.

Behind her, Beak-face poked at her hair, tugging gently on the bun like he'd never seen one before. The procession was moving again, shadowy figures drawing closer. Two nondescript daemons in glamour and wearing black came first, followed by four creatures—heavyset lizard men with snake faces and scaled bodies—carrying a canopied litter on their shoulders.

As they passed Clio's hiding spot, the faint breeze lifted the curtains of the litter, revealing the woman sitting inside. Large fin-like appendages framed her face, and waves of turquoise hair flowed over her shoulders, decorated with fine gold chains. Her pale skin was flawless, and a turquoise stripe ran down her forehead and over her nose. Then the litter passed, and the small procession continued down the street.

"Where is she going?" Clio asked.

"Who knows? Probably to the ley line. Her type doesn't leave the towers for many other reasons."

"Why does—"

With a sharp tug, the ekek pulled her bun apart. Her braid tumbled loose and he lifted it under the beak of his mask, inhaling loudly.

The other daemon snorted. "Barbarian. Don't you have *any* manners?"

The ekek croaked a long string of noises.

"Whatever he said," Clio growled through gritted teeth, "could you tell him to let go before I blast him right off the island?"

The daemon smirked, humor lightening his eyes. "He said you smell of faraway places he's never visited."

The ekek sniffed her hair again, then hissed something else.

"He asks where you come from, and also if he can taste you."

"How thoughtful of him to *ask* this time." She grabbed her hair and yanked it out of his hand, then whirled on the ekek. "No, you may not *taste* me."

The violet-eyed daemon repeated that in the other language. The ekek growled unhappily.

"Tell him to stop following me as well."

He arched his eyebrows.

"Please," she added belatedly.

Mouth quirked in a half smile, he turned to the ekek and spoke again. Beak-face hissed something back.

"He says he followed you because someone is going to eat you soon and he will never find out why you smell so interesting."

She blinked and looked at the ekek. He hooked a talon under the beak of his skull mask and lifted it enough for the light to catch on iridescent jade eyes with slitted pupils—and the matching third eye in the center of his forehead, surrounded by dark markings with the texture of bone.

In a sudden movement, he snapped the mask into place and sprang backward. An instant later, Ash dropped off a nearby rooftop and landed behind her, his hand on the hilt of his sword.

"Making friends?" he muttered to her.

"Kind of."

The violet-eyed daemon sidestepped out of the crevice and into the street, caution replacing his earlier good humor. "Draconian."

"Daeva."

The tall daemon took another step away from Ash and his relaxed demeanor returned. He flashed a brief smile. "Daring choice in companions, pretty lady. Don't get eaten."

Turning, he walked off, and she was surprised to see that his hair, tied into a thin ponytail, fell well past his waist. When she glanced back into the crevice, the ekek was already gone.

Ash shook his head. "Can you stay out of trouble *at all*?"

"I had to bail on my hiding spot because someone came in." She twisted her hair back into a bun and tied it into place. "The ekek must have followed us."

"I know. Zwi was keeping an eye on him, but she lost his trail. Evasive rat."

Clio gave the draconian a look. "Is that what you went to check on? Looking for the ekek?"

He nodded. "Where did the daeva come from?"

"He was already there, waiting out the tower 'queen.'"

Grunting, Ash started forward and Clio hurried to keep up. The violet-eyed daemon had vanished in the fog.

"Hey, wait." Her head snapped up. "The guy was a *daeva*? As in the same caste as that skeevy warlord from Samael's party you killed?"

She shuddered at the memory of Suhul, the grossly obese warlord who'd been overly fascinated with her before making the mistake of trying to touch Ash in a show of superiority.

Ash swung into a gap between buildings. The moment she stepped into the shadows after him, he whipped around and grabbed the front of her shirt, shoving her in front of him.

"Keep your voice down," he hissed. "And don't talk about Samael here—or anywhere. If you run your mouth off about *anything* you saw in Asphodel, I'll permanently silence you."

Her blood chilled. That threat, unlike the one he'd directed at Lyre a couple days ago, rang with vicious intent.

"I'm sorry," she whispered. "I won't say anything else."

He took a step away from her, his eyes lightening from black to storm-cloud gray. "That warlord didn't die. Lost a few fingers, though."

"So Suhul and that daemon are both daevas?" she asked as Ash continued down the alley. "They're *completely* different."

"That daemon is a better representative of the caste. Their warlord is a pig and none of them like him."

They came to the door of the ladies' club and Ash reached for the handle. Before he could touch it, the door flew open and Lyre fell out, still dressed in the white waiter "uniform" and his arms full of his clothes and weapons. Shouts burst from the building's interior.

"There you are!" Lyre blurted, wild-eyed. "Time to go."

"What happened?" Ash barked.

Clio was still gawking when Lyre launched down the alley, leaving her and Ash to rush after him.

"Some women react poorly to rejection," Lyre explained breathlessly. "Especially when they've paid a lot of money to not be rejected."

"You blew your cover by *rejecting* her?" Ash snapped.

They fled down several alleys before Lyre skidded to a stop and whirled on Ash, still clutching his belongings.

"I'll dress up in stupid costumes," the incubus snarled with unexpected temper, "and I'll pretend to be a paid whore, and I'll even let a crucial informant pinch and paw at me." He thrust an accusatory finger at Ash. "But I will *not* allow that nasty old hag's tongue anywhere near me, not even to save the damn world!"

Ash blinked.

Scowling blackly, Lyre shoved his armload at Ash, then pulled a dagger from the pile and cut his leather-strap top off. "Next time, *you* can do the nasty stuff and *I'll* kill people."

Ash blinked again, seemingly at a loss for words. Lyre continued to mutter angrily as he dragged the pants off and redressed in his black outfit. Clio stood a few steps away, her hand pressed over her mouth to hide her smile. Even with most of his face covered, Ash looked off-balance for the first time she could remember, a wrinkle between his dark eyebrows.

"Was she that disgusting?" he ventured, sounding a lot less like a hardened mercenary than usual. He normally seemed years older than Clio, but she was pretty sure he was actually a little younger.

"Worse," Lyre growled. "Whatever you're imagining as 'disgusting,' make it about ten times more revolting."

The draconian winced as though he had pictured it, and the mental image had hurt. "I never saw her myself."

Lyre slung his quiver over his shoulder and buckled it. "Be glad you didn't." His anger faded and he smirked. "It's fine, Ash. Hardly the most scarring thing I've ever done. And"—his smile sharpened predatorily—"the banshee was a *goldmine* of information."

Ash straightened, all business again. "Did you get what we need?"

"I think so."

"Good." He started forward. "Then it's time for phase two of the plan."

TWENTY~FIVE

LYRE BREATHED DEEP, letting the rotting water stench of the city wash the odor of sickly perfume from his airways. Damn. He considered himself a professional in seduction—he could fake interest in almost anyone—but *that* had been a challenge.

At least the brothel was well behind them. Ash once again led the way as they crossed the island to a nicer neighborhood. The three towers of Kokytos leaned over them, lurking in his peripheral vision no matter which way he turned. Soon, they would test their luck on the most impossible infiltration he'd ever heard of.

Clio followed behind Ash, her scarf wrapped around her head and face like a shawl so only her eyes were visible. He watched her hips sway with each step, smiling to himself. He didn't need to antagonize her anymore. She'd found her confidence again and fear no longer laced her scent as she gazed around with curiosity and only a hint of wariness. She was tougher than she realized.

He glanced at the cylindrical Ivory Tower one more time, then put it out of his mind before *he* started giving off the wrong signals. He could quietly panic about the impossibility of their mission later.

The street they followed hung on the island's outer edge, a flimsy rail all that prevented a tumble off the brink. Below, more catwalks and bridges ran along the buildings before the gray water took over.

"Keep your mouths shut for this," Ash warned as they approached a door. "I don't want anyone guessing who you are. Especially you," he added to Lyre.

Lyre tugged his hood lower and made sure his scarf was covering as much of his face as possible. "My lips are sealed."

The new establishment was far more to Lyre's liking than the last. Dim interior, rough wooden tables, a bar at the back, and a big fire pit in the center that vented out the peaked ceiling, giving the room a pervasive but pleasant wood-smoke scent. Beneath that, the aroma of simmering broth made his stomach rumble.

Ash wound between the tables, heading straight for the back corner. At a table tucked almost out of sight, two daemons were already seated, empty bowls and plates in front of them. Ash dropped into a seat, then used his foot to push the second chair out for Clio. Dragging a nearby chair closer, Lyre sat and casually slung his arm over the back.

The two draconians at the table watched the new arrivals with cold, pale blue eyes.

They resembled Ash only superficially. Similar black clothes and heavy weapons. Their shoulder-length hair was tied back, the black waves shimmering in the firelight. The two draconians were identical except that one had a scar cutting diagonally across his left eye, the eyelid twisted and permanently closed.

"Ezran," Ash murmured in greeting, pulling his wrap down around his neck. "Eliya."

"Ash," the one-eyed draconian replied, his deep, sepulchral voice making Lyre's bones itch. "This better be good."

The other draconian reclined in his chair, his pale eyes scrutinizing Ash. "Why are you even here? Aren't you on a contract?"

"I have a job for you two," Ash said, ignoring the questions. "A one-night bang and burn."

The one-eyed guy snorted. "We're not taking jobs from *you*."

"Besides, we're already on assignment, which you damn well know."

"Fine." Ash shrugged. "Go back to whatever boring shit you were doing."

The two draconians stared him down, and Lyre didn't envy Ash being on the receiving end. They were taller than him, broader in the shoulders and heavy with hard muscle. The real difference was in their faces though—the lines around their mouths, the stiffness of their jaws, and the hollow emptiness in their expressions.

With a snarl, one of them waved his hand. "Tell us the job, then."

"Not unless you agree to take it." Ash reached into his pocket, then flicked something small toward the daemons. "Four of those for payment."

The one-eyed guy caught it and held it up between his finger and thumb. The large, rough-cut diamond sparkled prettily in the firelight, and Lyre suppressed a wistful sigh. Losing half his best lodestones was a blow, but he hadn't been able to refuse when Ash had asked him to donate the "fee."

The twins examined the diamond, then their stares turned to Lyre and Clio.

"Your clients paying for this?" one growled.

"Do you want the job?" Ash replied.

"We don't even know what it is."

Ash leaned back, saying nothing. The draconian pair glowered at him.

The one-eyed guy closed his fist around the diamond. "Fine. Payment up front."

"Half now, half on completion."

"Bastard." He folded his arms. "What's the job?"

"Attack the Black Tower."

"*What?*" the one-eyed guy barked. "You can't be fucking serious."

The other draconian shook his head irately. "If this is your idea of humor—"

"Attack the Black Tower," Ash repeated. "Don't enter it. As loud and flashy as possible, but strictly black ops. No one sees you and you leave nothing that could link the attack to draconians. Thirty minutes of noise, then you disappear."

The twins exchanged a long look. "You want a half-hour distraction outside the tower?"

Ash nodded.

The one-eyed guy thought about it. "You're not insisting on zero casualties, are you?"

"Hell no. But I'll throw in one more diamond if you make the attack look like another caste is behind it."

"Humph," the other one grunted. "Harpies, then. Those buzzards will take any job. Imitating their attack style won't be difficult."

The one-eyed draconian grinned—a bloodthirsty expression that sent a cold prickle down Lyre's neck. "This could be fun."

"Be ready by two hours into the eclipse," Ash instructed. "But wait for my dragonet's signal to start."

"Wait, this is *today*? Fuck me." The draconian shoved back from the table. "You're a prick, Ash."

His twin stood as well. "Where's the rest of the down payment?"

Ash tossed them another diamond. The one-eyed draconian pocketed it, then leaned into Ash's face.

"Leave the rest of the payment in escrow, as usual." He smirked evilly. "Just in case you get your cocky ass killed while we're handling your distraction."

Firelight gleamed across steel. Ash suddenly held a narrow-bladed knife, the point aimed under the daemon's chin. The older draconian backed up with more haste than nonchalance.

Ash spun the knife and it disappeared under his armguard. "Do the job, Eliya, and I'll pay you."

The other brother joined Eliya and the pair strode away without a backward glance, disappearing through the door. Silence fell over the table.

"Um," Clio eventually mumbled.

"Wait here." Ash pushed his chair back and headed in the opposite direction of the draconian twins, approaching the daemon behind the bar.

Clio let out a long exhale. "Are all draconians like that?"

Lyre wasn't sure, but when it came to the draconians who called Samael "master," he doubted many had cheerful dispositions. He'd bet the twins were trapped in Hades's employ as much as Ash was, though Lyre had no idea how Samael was keeping any of these powerful warriors under his control.

Waving at Lyre and Clio to follow, Ash led them through a side door, across a back room, and down a narrow flight of stairs. At the bottom was a cellar illuminated only by the light leaking through the floorboards above. Preserves filled the shelves along the walls, with extra chairs and crates stacked in the corners.

"The barkeep is allowing us to spend the day here." Ash went to the shelves, fished around for a minute, then pulled out a stack of blankets. "He's decently trustworthy and I paid him well, so it should be safe enough."

As he dropped the blankets on a crate, Lyre pulled a chair off the stack and set it in the corner for Clio. She sank down gratefully, pulling her scarf off. Her creamy skin looked milk-white in the darkness.

"So," Lyre prompted Ash. "The *Black* Tower?"

"Attacking one tower is insane enough. No one will expect simultaneous attacks on two towers. Hold on."

The draconian headed back up the stairs. Sighing, Lyre sat on the floor and leaned back against a crate. He and Clio waited silently until Ash returned, balancing three bowls of steaming stew. He handed them out, then crouched on his haunches, bowl in one hand and spoon in the other.

"Stealth will only get us so far," he continued as though there had been no break in their conversation. "I expect we'll get caught, and when that happens, I want as much confusion and chaos as possible to cover our movements. If Ezran and Eliya attack the Black Tower, the Ivory Tower guards will be less likely to expect an infiltration of *their* building, and when it happens, they'll be thrown off."

Lyre blew on a spoonful of stew, then stuck it in his mouth. It scalded his tongue, but damn, it was good. He could see why draconians frequented this tavern.

"Even using the banshee's information," Lyre said after a few bites, "we'll have a hell of a time with or without distractions. Just getting in the front doors undetected is probably impossible. There's only one way in or out, and after that, we'll still need to make it through the tower."

"Let me guess," Ash said. "Lyceus owns the top floor."

"Actually, the second to the top. I guess he was too stingy to outbid the siren queen."

"Queen?" Clio lowered her spoon. "What does a siren look like?"

Lyre frowned at the question, and Ash answered instead.

"Pale skin, big fins in place of ears, blue-green hair, and" —he drew a line from his forehead down his nose— "a big blue stripe in the middle of their faces. I've heard they have wing-like fins that fold against their backs, but their clothes cover it up."

Clio frowned at her bowl, a wrinkle between her brows and that sharp churning look in her eyes that she got when she was thinking fast. Ash started to ask something but Lyre gestured at him to wait.

Finally, she looked up. "What if we *could* make it through the tower without getting caught?"

"What are you thinking?" Lyre asked.

"If there's only one way in, then we'll need a disguise." She smiled conspiratorially. "And I know the perfect one that will get us right to the top."

FROWNING, Lyre tilted the metal disc one way, then the other. Touching a finger to its center, he added another glowing gold thread to the weave. Back in Chrysalis, this was about the point when he would have indulged in some creative and heartfelt profanity, but he needed to keep quiet.

Clio was curled on her side, a blanket wrapped around her, head resting on his thigh. It didn't look like a comfortable way to sleep, but she was snoring softly so who was he to judge.

Returning his attention to the makeshift weaving apparatus, he let out a frustrated breath. She had too much faith in his ability. Illusions were his favorite spells to weave, but they were projects he devoted *weeks* to, not hours.

And, to add to the challenge, he didn't know exactly what the illusion should look like. Clio had described the siren queen and even helped him with a sketch, but it wasn't the same as seeing the daemon for himself. He'd seen sirens before but not recently.

The plan was good, assuming Lyre could pull off the illusion. Ash was currently investigating the siren queen's departure to confirm she had left the city. Assuming she wouldn't be back soon, Clio would take her place—an illusion spell, a queenly costume, and Lyre and Ash posing as bodyguards.

It was the best plan they had, and there were still a million ways it could go wrong.

Setting the half-finished illusion down, he slipped his hand into his pocket and withdrew the quicksilver vial. Golden magic shimmered within the metallic liquid. It was finished. Everything was ready. But he wasn't sure he could use it. Even if he could make it work, he wasn't sure he *dared* to use it.

His trip ward on the top cellar door pinged in his head and he quickly slipped the vial back into his pocket. The door clacked, then Ash glided down the stairs and into the cellar, his dragonet riding on his shoulder and a large bundle of fabric under his arm.

"The siren queen is gone," he said without preamble. "I couldn't find out anything about when she's supposed to return, but considering the entourage she took with her, I'd say at least half a cycle."

"We've got enough time, then."

Ash dumped the clothing bundle on a crate, and Zwi leaped onto the nearby shelves, her tail swishing. "How's the illusion?"

"Slow going but I'll get it done in time—I think."

"Good." Ash paced the length of the room, brimming with restless energy. "The eclipse starts in three hours. We need to be at the tower two hours after that."

"And then we'll find out if we're as smart as we think we are or considerably more stupid."

Ash grunted in agreement. As he paced across the room again, Lyre brushed two fingers over Clio's forehead, casting a light sleep spell. No point in letting Ash's edginess disrupt her rest.

"Do you trust those draconians?" Lyre slouched tiredly against the wall. "Will they do the job?"

"I don't *trust* them, but they'll do it." Ash twitched one shoulder in a shrug. "They're reliable when it counts."

"You should have warned them about incubi. They probably won't run into any of my relatives, but it's always better to be on guard."

Ash's mouth twisted.

"You'll need to be careful too," he added. "Keep five feet away if they're in glamour, ten feet if they're out."

"*You* caught me because I wasn't expecting it. That won't happen again."

Lyre's eyes narrowed. "It could easily happen again. Just because you know you can be enthralled doesn't grant you special immunity."

"I'll ram a sword in them before they can mess with me," Ash snapped impatiently. "I'm more concerned about Lyceus's magic."

Easing Clio's head off his lap, Lyre rose to his feet. Sliding his hands into his pockets, he watched Ash pace.

"His reputation is formidable," the draconian continued. "How do you plan to handle him?"

"I don't think you understand, Ash."

He stopped pacing and frowned at Lyre. "Understand what?"

"You're used to being the strongest daemon in the room," Lyre said, his voice slow and lazy. "You're used to blasting your way through any obstacle with that magic-incinerating black fire."

"Dragon fire," Ash corrected, his frown deepening. "What the hell are you going on about?"

Lyre pushed away from the wall, drifting closer. "It's easy to underestimate subtler magic. When I used aphrodesia on you, that was full bore—everything I had because I needed to stop you from 'ramming a sword in me,' as you so delicately put it."

"And you only succeeded because I was right on top of you and I wasn't expecting it," Ash growled in annoyance. "I won't put myself in that position again."

"Oh, I know," Lyre purred, moving even closer. "But maybe next time you won't be thinking about avoiding it."

Ash stepped backward without seeming to realize that he was retreating.

Lyre advanced. "Aphrodesia isn't just blasting an enemy and leaving them frozen and slack-jawed. That's like saying you can only use your magic to blow shit up and nothing in between."

"I don't know what ..." Ash trailed off as he withdrew another step. His back bumped into the wall.

"Aphrodesia works best in low, subtle doses," Lyre crooned. "It can be used to charm, to placate, to confuse, to disarm ... or even to make you very ... *very* ... suggestible."

He leaned in, bringing his face within inches of Ash's.

"What do you think, Ash?" he whispered. "Do you want me to touch you?"

The draconian's eyes widened but he didn't move. Lyre pressed both hands to Ash's stomach and he jumped at the contact. But, trapped against the wall, he had nowhere to retreat. Lyre slid his hands slowly upward, dragging Ash's shirt up.

"What do you think?" he purred softly. "Do you want me to kiss you?"

Ash's breath caught. His eyes flashed to black and he jerked his hands up to throw Lyre off, but Lyre had already slid away, out of reach.

"I'll take that as a 'no,'" Lyre remarked in a normal tone. "But that's okay, because I still had plenty of time to weave a spell or two while you were distracted."

Ash stiffened and looked down as though expecting to see a weaving stamped on his chest.

Lyre rolled his shoulders to relieve the tension as he locked down his aphrodesia again. "Relax. I didn't actually weave anything."

Ash growled, a low, vicious sound. "Fuck with me again, incubus, and I'll—"

"Grow up, Ash," Lyre interrupted calmly. "You know perfectly well that was a demonstration so you quit dismissing a dangerous power just because you find it distasteful."

The draconian's jaw clenched.

"Do you get it *now*? Unless you plan to murder every incubus within ten seconds of encountering him, you need to be on guard against our power."

Ash stood rigid for a long moment, then flexed his shoulders. "Point taken."

Lyre sat beside Clio and arched an eyebrow at the draconian. "At least you didn't blush. Most men blush when I offer to kiss them."

Ash blinked—and the faintest red tinged his cheeks. Lyre looked away, deciding to be merciful and not point it out.

Huffing out a breath, Ash resumed pacing. Lyre watched him, recognizing the draconian's relentless energy for what it was: nerves. He wouldn't say Ash was *afraid*—the draconian seemed incapable of real fear—but he was nervous as hell about their plans for the eclipse.

"Aren't you tired?" Lyre asked, picking up his illusion spell. "When did you last sleep?"

Ash paused, his eyes scrunching in thought, then he resumed pacing without answering. So, he'd gone long enough without proper rest that he didn't want to admit it. And judging by his tireless pacing, he didn't plan to take advantage of this final chance to recuperate. Sighing, Lyre allowed a few tendrils of aphrodesia to uncoil around him again.

After letting the seduction magic simmer in the room for a few minutes, he glanced up. "Would you sit already, Ash?"

"I'm fine."

"I can't work with you distracting me. Just sit down for five minutes."

Ash hesitated but didn't come over. Lyre let another whisper of aphrodesia saturate the air. Just enough to take the draconian's nervous edge off. He would never know.

Lyre lifted the paper with his and Clio's siren sketch. "Come look at this."

"Why?"

"Get over here, damn it."

Reluctantly, Ash stalked over and leaned over to peer at the paper. Grabbing his arm, Lyre yanked him down. Ash sat with a thump, growling, but Lyre shoved the paper in his face before he could get up again.

"Do siren head fins have four or five spines?" he asked.

"I don't know."

"Try to remember."

Ash squinted at the paper. "Five, I think. This looks right."

"Okay, good. Now just sit there for a few minutes so I can work on this in peace."

Ash grumbled something nasty under his breath, then leaned back against the wall with one arm resting on his upraised knee. Lyre prodded the weaving again. After a moment, Zwi hopped down from the shelves, slunk over, and curled up between her master's feet.

Feeling Ash's attention on him, Lyre began talking about his work, using as many technical terms as possible. Gradually, he let his voice sink into a soothing croon, adding a little aphrodesia for good measure. Ash's head drooped forward, his eyes drifting closed as he listened.

As Lyre described the geometric variables of thread construction, weight settled against his shoulder. Ash had slipped sideways to lean against Lyre's side, his breathing slow and even. Finally.

In the draconian's face, relaxed in sleep, Lyre saw traces of the boy he'd first encountered three years ago. It was easy to forget Ash was four or five years younger than him. The draconian's upbringing in Asphodel had matured him too quickly, and like Lyre, he was alone in a dangerous world with no allies, no one he trusted.

Young, but already a veteran warrior. Headstrong, but cunning and capable. Fearless, but wary and mistrustful.

Lyre briefly closed his eyes, a wry smile on his lips. How surprising it was to realize he'd come to trust the draconian mercenary. The only two people in the three realms he could trust with his life were in this room, both fast asleep.

He let his head fall back, resting it against the hard wall. Unless he was very much mistaken, he'd somehow earned Ash's trust too. Otherwise, the leery draconian would never have come so close scarcely five minutes after Lyre had enthralled him.

Sentimental smile fading, Lyre lifted the illusion weaving and got back to work.

TWENTY~SIX

"I CHANGED MY MIND," Clio whispered urgently. "This is a bad plan. A terrible one. We should do something else."

"Stay in character," Ash growled.

"How?" she hissed back. She didn't know the character she was portraying!

Lyre and Ash walked ahead of her, leading the way to the looming Ivory Tower. Its sister towers, the steely gray one and the pitch black one, rose behind it, the latter almost invisible against the inky darkness of the sky.

The Ivory Tower's pale exterior, so majestic and daunting from a distance, was dull and grimy up close, though that didn't diminish her feeling of intimidation. According to their informant, it had twenty-five levels, but the colossal cylinder looked even taller.

Twenty-five levels and the Rysalis family owned the one just below the penthouse. That meant she, Lyre, and Ash had to pass twenty-three floors of the most dangerous daemon criminals in the Underworld to get to Lyceus and the KLOC on the twenty-fourth.

But first they had to get through the front doors, and Clio rather doubted they would make it that far.

Lyre had worked his weaving magic with his usual brilliance. *He* wasn't satisfied with the siren illusion that cloaked her, but Ash had said it was fine. To passersby, she was a regal, stern-faced siren, face framed by delicate fins, her cold turquoise eyes staring straight ahead. Her hair fell down her back in waves, tinted to the same blue-green shade.

Her clothes weren't an illusion at all. Creating illusory fabric that would flow across the ground hadn't been possible with the time limit, so Ash had found an outfit for her. The flowing dress shimmered like delicate fish scales, trailing on the ground behind her.

Judging by the reactions of the daemons they passed in the streets, it was a convincing disguise. But as for whether it would fool anyone in the tower, she was about to find out.

A few broad steps led up to the wide entryway. Beastly guards in matching armor were positioned nearby, but they would only move if someone who obviously didn't belong tried to enter. *Most* daemons weren't stupid enough to walk in through the front doors.

Clio lifted her chin and concentrated on keeping her gait slow and gliding. Dressed in black like the siren queen's guards, Lyre and Ash strode ahead of her with flawless confidence, their weapons hidden under glamour.

As they passed through the threshold, the ashen stone steps changed to shining white marble. The entrance hall, a huge, barren rectangle of glistening marble with paired colonnades along each side, rose to a ceiling twenty feet above their heads. The smooth walls were broken by three access points—a large archway at the far end, and two closed wooden doors off to the sides.

Twenty guards, ten on each side, stood at perfect attention, one positioned in front of each marble column. Unlike the rest of Kokytos's inhabitants, they were all in glamour, creating an eerily uniform look.

Clio blinked her asper into focus. A ward spanned the archway, so complex it triggered an instant headache. Its golden threads glowed with the reddish tinge of blood magic.

This ward was the tower's first security feature and it would stop most infiltrators dead—literally. Designed by Chrysalis, it was keyed to the blood of every daemon permitted inside the tower, from the lords and ladies down to the lowliest security agent.

Clio kept her walk slow and sedate as she rapidly scanned the ward for a weakness. In front of her, Lyre and Ash closed in on the deadly spell. If either of them touched it, they would die—painfully, judging by the weave's constructs. She had to find the "off" trigger before they reached it.

The guards watched her pass, but she didn't have to worry about them noticing something off about her expression. The illusory siren face was static, its eyes fixed straight ahead, its expression locked into a strict mask.

She inspected the ward with growing urgency. Where was the trigger? She couldn't see any weaknesses in the design, but there *had* to be a way to disable it. Coming up to the archway, Lyre and Ash stepped aside to let her go first. She glided between them, panic cutting into her lungs. Would they fail here, at the very first obstacle?

As she took her final step, her toes inches from the glowing barrier, she scanned it one more time. There!

Pretending to stumble on her skirt, she pressed a hand to the marble archway. A spark of magic fired deep into the weaving's heart quieted the ward and its threads went dark.

She walked beneath the arch, and Lyre and Ash followed without hesitation.

Guards lined the columns of another identical grand hall. The only difference was two slim desks carved of matching marble, facing each other with another archway beyond them. Several daemons in tower livery stood watchfully behind the desks.

As she paced forward, now in the lead, her panic levels rose again. The daemons at the desks looked like helpful receptionists, but they were as much a part of the security as the burly guards.

Residents of the tower—or their attendants—were required to check in and out, no matter how brief their excursion. Choking back her nerves, she continued as though she had no reason to stop.

"Lady Mare," a receptionist—if the sleek, dangerous-looking daemon could be called that—greeted her. "We weren't expecting you until the next cycle."

Clio kept walking. The illusion's facial expression couldn't change, and she dared not speak when she had no idea what the siren queen sounded like—or even what language to use.

Instead, Lyre responded in an unfamiliar, guttural accent. "An interruption of plans. Did you not receive word?"

"We haven't heard anything about—"

"We sent a message *hours* ago," he snapped.

"As I said, we didn't receive—"

"Your disorganization is not my concern." He swept past the desk after Clio.

The daemon cleared his throat. "Lady Mare, if I could trouble you to—"

Clio didn't look back but she heard Lyre stop.

"Do you remember *nothing* of our message?" he hissed in a low tone. "We warned you not to bother her."

"But we didn't—"

"The lady is not pleased and I suggest you figure out the issue with your schedule on your own."

"I'm afraid that is not possible. Without confirmation from Lady Mare, I can't allow—"

With her heart pounding, Clio turned around. The daemon wouldn't let them pass on Lyre's word alone, but Clio couldn't speak without giving them away. As she faced the desk, she focused on Ash in her peripheral vision. His dark aura rippled over his body like midnight flames.

She brought the essence of his black power into her mind and body. Rich, intoxicating magic shivered in her veins. Holding on to her newly draconian aura, she looked at the daemon behind the desk and lifted her chin imperiously.

The daemon shrank back, his face paling and eyes darkening with a shadow of fear. He opened his mouth but couldn't find his voice.

Lyre made a dismissive gesture with one hand. "I'll send someone down to sort it out once the lady is settled."

"That … that would be appreciated."

Clio turned back toward the archway, aware of how the other daemons in the room had gone rigid with the shivery dread inspired by a draconian's presence. Pausing as though waiting for Lyre, she casually touched the marble. The second ward went dark. Unless another daemon examined it, they would have no idea the weaves weren't functioning.

The three of them passed through the archway and into a curving hall. Letting go of Ash's aura, Clio breathed a relieved sigh.

"I can't believe that worked," she whispered, picking up her pace.

"Me neither." Lyre pinched the bridge of his nose. "That guy is way too committed to his job."

They followed the curving hall until they reached a third archway—this one leading into a staircase.

"Here we go," Lyre muttered.

Clio disarmed the ward and cautiously placed her foot on the first step. The Ivory Tower didn't rely on magical defense alone. The building was its own defense. On the outside, it bore only thin slits for windows, too narrow for a person to squeeze through even if they flew to the top without being spotted.

On the inside, it contained three spiral staircases, connected on each level by an interior corridor that followed the same circular shape as the tower. All three staircases rose the full length of the tower—but not all were equal. There was only one route to the top level, and it required using certain staircases on certain levels. Lyre had gotten the proper order from their informant and all three of them had memorized it, but any mistake would likely be fatal.

"Main floor to third floor on jade," she whispered, her eyes following the green inlay that ran through the center of each stair.

They ascended the spiral steps to the first landing. Black marble inlaid in the floor formed an unfamiliar symbol that she assumed was a number.

She glanced around cautiously. According to their source, the circular main corridor on each level that connected the three stairways was regularly patrolled. Seeing no one, she crossed the corridor and continued upward. They reached the second landing, continued past it, then stopped on the next one.

Lyre glanced at the symbol on the landing. "Third floor."

"Three to seven on azure." Clio glanced both ways. "Which way is azure?"

"Left," Ash said. "Going clockwise, it's jade, azure, scarlet."

She headed left, keeping her walk swift but not too fast. The wide corridor was pristine white marble, interspersed with pillars and light crystals. Every inch of the walls was embedded with spells of varying purposes. Another archway held a ward she had to disable, and shortly after, they passed a broad, polished wood door that likely led into one of the tower suites.

When the next staircase came into sight, a troop of guards marched onto the landing.

Clio didn't flinch and kept walking. The guards, identical to the ones on the main level, stepped aside for her and her two protectors. She swept up the next staircase and hoped no one had noticed her racing heartbeat.

They ascended four long flights, each step adorned with a blue stripe, then circled to the jade stairs again. Exiting on the eleventh floor, Clio gulped air, her legs burning. Dropping glamour would have helped, but she couldn't do that here—not unless things got really bad.

They looped around to the scarlet stairs, passing another squad of guards that moved aside for her. Either the siren queen was so feared that no one dared to question her, or the security wasn't as tight as rumors suggested. Then again, how could they have anticipated an Overworld mimic who could disarm all their wards? Sneaking through the building without her disguise would have been near impossible. There was nowhere to hide in the brightly lit marble corridors, and every step echoed loudly. Not even Ash could move in silence.

But their plan was working and she allowed herself the tiniest hope that maybe they could do this.

They followed the scarlet stairs up to the fifteenth level. Clio stepped into another boring white corridor, identical to all the others.

"Fifteen to eighteen on the azure stairs," Lyre murmured. "Head right."

Another warded archway barely slowed them down, and they approached the azure stairs.

From within the spiral staircase, a small creature jumped down into the corridor. It looked like a cross between a cat and a fox, with all its features exaggerated—ridiculously huge ears, a petite muzzle, long legs, and a giant bushy tail. Its spotted teal fur drifted around it, immune to gravity.

It fixed huge eyes on Clio, Lyre, and Ash. It had no pupils or irises—just pure white eyes.

With graceful hops, two more fox-cats joined the first. All three of them stared at Clio and the guys, motionless except for their gently floating fur.

"Ah, shit," Lyre muttered. "*Pards.*"

She assumed "pard" was the creatures' name but she didn't get a chance to ask.

"*Illusion magic.*" The three small beasts spoke in perfect unison, their shrill animal voices almost unintelligible. "*Foreign magic. Deception. Intruders.*"

Clio's blood went cold. Lyre and Ash launched ahead of her, already shimmering out of glamour—but not fast enough.

Glowing spots of light manifested in front of the three pards' foreheads. The orbs spun, expanding—then shot at Clio, Lyre, and Ash.

The center orb smashed into Clio's chest, blasting her off her feet. As Lyre went down beside her, she hit the floor on her back, wheezing painfully. Ash skidded from the impact but, with his tail snapping for balance, he kept on his feet and drew the two short swords strapped to his thighs.

Ignoring the panic his daemon form triggered, Clio jumped up. Her illusion spell had disintegrated.

On his feet again too, Lyre activated his defensive weaves and pulled an arrow. As the pards surrounded Ash, Lyre drew the bowstring and fired.

The pard's body rippled, going semitransparent. The arrow flashed right through it without slowing, hit the floor, and ricocheted into the air. It flipped end over end, then hit the marble wall. Magic pulsed through the wards, then the entire corridor lit with crimson light.

Lyre lowered his bow. "Oops."

"Fucking *genius*," Ash snarled as he swiped his sword at a pard. The creature leaped clear with absurd agility.

Running to the wall, Clio pressed her hand to it. The ward—and the red light—went dark, but it was too late to undo the damage.

"I—can't—hit—these!" Ash growled, finally catching a pard with his sword, only for it to turn semitransparent. His blade passed right through. "Damn it!"

The three pards leaped into the center of the corridor, shoulder to shoulder. White magic sparked again, but instead of three separate orbs, they conjured one huge one. Wind rushed through the hall as the sphere spun.

Shifting both swords into one hand, Ash conjured a handful of black fire. He hurled it as the pards launched their attack and the two forces collided in midair. Power exploded outward, almost throwing Clio off her feet again. The pards tumbled across the floor and launched up, unharmed.

Then Lyre's arrow hit them, skewering two on the same shaft.

The third one screamed, the sound piercing Clio's ears like knives. It bolted away but Lyre already had a second arrow nocked. It struck the pard in the back and the creature slid across the floor, leaving a streak of blood in its wake.

Stepping over to Ash, Lyre slapped a hand against the chain around the draconian's neck and activated two of the three gems. Defensive weaves whooshed over Ash's body.

"I made you shield spells, damn it. Use them."

Since her disguise was ruined, Clio dropped glamour. The siren dress vanished, replaced by her black outfit—swapped with her nymph clothes, since skirts weren't appropriate for a deadly infiltration mission. She touched the chain hidden under her shirt and activated her own defensive weaves.

Ash's head tilted. "I hear daemons coming. At least a dozen."

"We'll outrun them." Lyre's hypnotic incubus voice caressed her skin. "No more sneaking around. Just race for the top."

Ash nodded and took a step—then a dull boom rocked the tower. The floor trembled.

"Wha—" Lyre began.

Shouts erupted from the direction of the scarlet stairs, then another crashing boom from somewhere outside the tower.

"Ah." Ash pulled his wings tight against his back. "Eliya and Ezran have started their diversion."

Clio's eyes widened as another tremor shook the floor. How powerful were their attacks that they were making *this* tower tremble too?

"Let's go," Ash said.

Clio took the center position as Ash charged up the azure stairs, his tail snapping side to side. With each breath, she had to fight the dread his daemon form caused. Lyre kept to the rear, bow in hand and an arrow nocked.

They made it to the eighteenth floor, then ran for the jade stairs. Halfway there, a squad of guards blocked their path. Clio braced herself to fight but Lyre and Ash shot ahead of her. Protected by master-weaver shields, Ash charged in more carelessly than usual, his huge sword coated in black fire and cleaving through their adversaries.

Lyre picked off three daemons with arrows, then tossed his bow to her, pulled two long knives that glowed with weaves, and dove in after Ash. The guards were not easy opponents but Ash and Lyre cut through them, the screams of the dying shattering the haunting silence of the tower.

The moment the last one fell, Lyre yelled at her to hurry. Joining them, she passed Lyre his bow, wishing she could do more, but the guys had been clear. She was supposed to stay back in the fights. They couldn't risk losing her asper.

She disarmed another ward, then they were racing up the jade steps to the twentieth level. Ash whipped out of the spiral stairway, then lurched to a stop. Clio skidded into his back.

Waiting in the corridor was a lone daemon. His skin and hair were the same shade of grayish alabaster, his eyes the pale red of an albino. A thick, shiny white rope was coiled around his neck and over his shoulders.

He swayed from foot to foot, then lifted two curved blades. In response, Ash sheathed his large sword and pulled out his twin short swords.

Lips stretching wide, the daemon hissed loudly. The rope around his neck slid sinuously, then a diamond-shaped head emerged. The snake's tongue flicked out.

Lyre yelped in surprise and his bow clattered to the floor. He fell to his knees with a massive white snake coiling rapidly over him.

As he grabbed at a scaly loop constricting around his neck, Clio took a running step toward him—then a cool weight dropped onto her back. The impact knocked her onto her knees but she jumped up in a panic as the slippery coils of the snake wound around her shoulders.

The snake daemon launched at Ash. The draconian met the charge in a clash of blades, throwing his assailant back, but he had no chance to help Lyre or Clio before the daemon darted in again, his movements as quick as the striking snakes he commanded.

With her free hand, Clio dug her fingers into the snake's side and cast a sleep spell. The reptile went limp, its heavy body slipping off her. She turned toward Lyre—and found herself face to face with an even larger snake.

She instinctively cast a shield. The reptile struck, its huge fangs scraping the barrier in a splatter of purple venom—and her weave dissolved like threads dipped in acid.

The spell burst apart and the reptile spun around her legs. Losing her balance, she fell. The moment she landed on the floor, the snake coiled its body over her. She writhed, but the harder she struggled, the tighter the snake constricted.

Too far to help, Ash fought the agile snake master. The daemon was quicker than a nymph, his darting movements forcing Ash to retreat.

The draconian parried a swift strike then cast a wide band of black flames. Diving beneath the fire, the snake master flung a magic attack. Ash stumbled, his tail whipping to the side for balance. The daemon lunged in, blades flashing, but Ash jumped back with a snap of his wings. His blade caught the daemon's sword and flung it away.

From around the daemon's shoulders, the white snake shot out, mouth gaping. It bit Ash's arm, its fangs sinking right through his shields.

TWENTY~SEVEN

LYRE HAD DESIGNED his defensive shields to counteract most attacks—but not something like this. Death-by-giant-snake hadn't even occurred to him.

The reptile squeezed tighter and tighter around his shield weaves— built to deflect impacts, not prevent compression. He desperately held back the coil around his neck, fighting the reptile's overwhelming strength. Nearby, Clio was down with another snake wrapped around her.

He needed a free hand to cast a spell, but no matter how hard he pulled, he couldn't shift the snake off his neck long enough to weave something. Pain built in his chest and his bones creaked under the pressure. He couldn't breathe.

A flash of black fire. Farther down the corridor, Ash stumbled. The naga daemon—slithery little bastard—attacked with his blades and the draconian countered, knocking a sword away with impressive speed.

But he wasn't fast enough to evade the striking snake.

The venomous fangs pierced Ash's arm just above his armguard. His sword whipped down again, lopping the reptile's head off too late. The naga laughed triumphantly.

Ash spun his blade in his hand, then slashed the point across the inner crook of his own elbow. Blood gushed down his arm.

The naga's eyes bugged out in disbelief, but his shock didn't last long. He sprang at Ash, who caught the enemy blade with his own, ignoring his bleeding arm—but whether he'd successfully purged the poison from his bloodstream or not, he wouldn't last long with that wound.

Lyre let go of the slippery coil around his neck. It snapped tight, crushing his throat as he grabbed his spell chain and pinched a gem between his fingers. This was going to suck.

He activated the spell and a huge golden circle spun out, encompassing Lyre, Clio, Ash, and the naga. Electric power surged through the circle—and everyone in it.

Pitching forward, Lyre landed on his face with his muscles convulsing. The snake writhed, its constricting loops going slack. Still trembling from the shock, he pulled a throwing knife from the sheath on his upper arm and jammed it into the base of the reptile's skull.

Hoping Clio could handle the last snake, Lyre spun toward Ash and the naga. The daemon was scrambling to his feet, but Ash was still down, blood spattered around him like a macabre painting.

Lyre hurled his knife. Ducking it, the naga lifted his weapon.

Then a thick blade burst through his chest.

Ash hadn't wasted time drawing a throwing knife—he'd thrown his whole damn sword. Before Lyre could recover from the surprise, Clio flew past him, already reaching for Ash as he slumped over.

"Shit!" Lyre hissed, racing over to them. He wrapped his hands around the draconian's arm just above the elbow and squeezed to slow the blood flow. "Hang on, Ash."

Clio pressed her hands to his chest. "There's venom in his blood. I think he stopped most of it, but I don't know how to purge poisons."

"Don't worry about the venom," Ash rasped. "Draconians are resistant. Just stop the bleeding."

"Right." Clio moved her hands to his wound, her eyes closing as she focused on her healing magic.

Crouched beside them, Lyre kept a tight grip on Ash's arm so he wouldn't lose any more blood. Dead snakes littered the corridor and silence had fallen, except for the irregular booms of Eliya and Ezran's explosions outside.

Then heavy footsteps vibrated the floor, drawing closer.

At the farthest end of the curving corridor, a mass of multicolored scales and muscles surged into view. Was this the reptile floor or something? Each one was seven feet of solid muscle, with tough scaled hides and crushing lizard jaws. They carried staves and pikes, half of the weapons topped with giant spelled crystals.

Already on his feet, Lyre stepped in front of the other two. Ash was scarcely holding on to consciousness and Clio couldn't defend herself and heal Ash at the same time. Lyre was on his own.

He pulled three arrows, the fletching pinched between his fingers. Drakes were physical fighters with even less magic than the average incubus. Their weapons were spelled and their hides were magic-resistant, but that was it. Lyre had a chance.

His first arrow struck the lead drake's chest and only sank about an inch into his flesh. The daemon's stride didn't falter—then magic flashed up the arrow shaft. The bolt exploded, blasting the drake's chest open. It collapsed mid-step, but the others didn't slow.

Lyre was already firing the second and third arrows. They struck two drakes and detonated.

He pulled three more arrows and shot them in seconds. A blast of needle-like barbs sent two drakes crashing to the floor. A crackling paralysis spell ripped through another. A third one howled when blades of power erupted from his chest.

Lyre pulled three more arrows, but they were close. Time and space were running out. Nock, draw, loose. Nock, draw, loose. As drakes fell, the survivors' fury increased until they were bellowing in rage as they bore down on him.

Time was up. Lyre tossed his bow behind him, snapped a gem off his spell chain, and dropped it at his feet. Then he leaped into the oncoming horde.

Behind him, the gem he'd dropped flashed into a shimmering barrier that would slow any drakes that tried to reach Clio and Ash—but he needn't have bothered. The beasts wanted him dead first.

He ducked a swinging staff and clapped his wrists together. The gemstones in his bracelets clacked and their shared spell sparked to life. A ribbon of glowing light stretched between his hands.

Before he had a chance to use it, a huge hand tipped with claws slammed him off his feet. His defensive weaves absorbed most of the blow, but the impact jarred him from head to foot. He rolled and came up, hands spread with the ribbon of magic stretched between them.

He darted into the drakes' midst. They bumped into each other as he ducked under their arms, a golden ribbon trailing after him. Barely evading a grasping hand and a swinging pike, he dove between a drake's legs and popped up behind the beast, magic spinning from his hands.

Whirling through the group one more time, he skittered backward, aching from the glancing blows he hadn't quite dodged. His back hit the wall and the drakes surrounded him. He was trapped.

Raising his hands, he clapped his wrist together a second time.

The second phase of the weaving triggered and power surged down the golden ribbon—now tangled through the group of drakes. The entire line blazed.

In uncanny unison, all six drakes crumpled to the floor.

Breathing hard, Lyre returned to his barrier spell and dissolved it. Clio was bent over Ash's arm, but the draconian was staring at him.

"What?" Lyre asked.

Ash just shook his head.

Clio lifted her hands from the draconian's arm. "I've healed the wound but there's still venom in his system."

"My body will burn it off," Ash grunted, sitting up.

Lyre helped him to his feet. The draconian wobbled unsteadily, panting for air, then straightened. Showing no hesitation despite the gore, Clio yanked his sword out of the dead naga and passed it to him.

Ash sheathed it and his other blade. "We need to keep moving."

Lyre took point, trusting Clio to keep an eye on the draconian. They jogged to the scarlet stairs and started up. Clio raced behind him, Ash trailing at the back.

Lyre crossed a landing and continued up, his thoughts racing ahead to the twenty-fourth floor. His foot came down on the next step—and the stone sank beneath his weight. A popping sound ricocheted through the stairwell.

The stairs beneath him collapsed.

He leaped backward as they fell. Clio reached for him—but the steps beneath her gave way too. They plummeted, their hands meeting in midair, his fingers closing tight around her wrists.

They came to a jarring stop as fast as they'd fallen. Clio let out a strangled cry as his weight jerked her arms. She hung upside down, Lyre dangling from her wrists, nothing but pitch darkness below them.

Sprawled on his stomach at the edge of the gap, Ash clutched Clio's ankle.

"Ash," Lyre gasped. "Pull us up."

The draconian pulled, but his recently healed arm shook and Clio's ankle slipped a few inches in his grip. His talons dug into her flesh and Clio gasped, her face red from the blood rushing to her head.

"Shit." Lyre squeezed Clio's wrists. "Should I try to climb up?"

"If you jostle her, I'll drop you both," Ash snarled. "Just wait."

"Wait? For *what*?"

Ash snarled again. "Just shut up and hold on!"

Lyre clung to Clio, breathing fast with his feet dangling over inky nothingness. What could they *possibly* be waiting for? Ash to have a sudden surge of strength? Was the draconian even thinking straight or was he delirious from the venom?

Ash's arms trembled visibly from the strain of holding two people after suffering injuries and being poisoned. Lyre met Clio's eyes and saw his terror reflected in her dark stare. Was this how they died?

"Lyre," she whispered. "I know you didn't want me to say it, but I—"

"*No*," Ash snarled. "Spare me the final declarations of love. *Fuck*."

"We have nothing better to do," Lyre snapped furiously. "Since we're just hanging here prior to imminent death, we might as well—"

The words died on his tongue as a huge black shape appeared above Ash—giant wings, scaled body, and glowing golden eyes. The dragon rumbled quietly, then stretched her long neck down and took a mouthful of Clio's clothing. With massive strength, the dragon lifted

Clio from the abyss, drawing Lyre up with her. Once he was in reach, Ash pulled him onto the steps as well.

Lyre slumped on solid ground, shaking from adrenaline. The dragon, filling half the corridor, rumbled again as she backed away. Black flames burst over her body then shrank, and when they dissipated, Zwi was back to her usual cat-sized form.

"Thanks, Zwi," Clio panted.

The dragonet trilled importantly, then chattered sternly at Ash. He scowled at her. With another chirp, she took off on dark wings and soared back down the stairs.

"Where is she going?" Lyre asked.

Ash heaved himself to his feet. "Getting back into position."

Lyre staggered up, then offered a hand to Clio. Together, they retreated to the previous landing.

"Damn," he muttered. "That was my fault. I forgot it switches after the twentieth floor."

"Each level uses a different staircase now." Clio turned left. "Jade, azure, then jade again. Three more."

"Let's go."

Lyre let Clio take the lead. He kept at Ash's side, glad to see the draconian was moving easier. His immunity to poisons was one hell of an impressive trait.

Thankfully, the corridor was empty. Between Clio disabling every ward they came across and the draconian twins' impressive ruckus outside, the Ivory Tower's security either didn't realize they'd been infiltrated or hadn't caught up yet.

At the jade staircase, they sped to the twenty-second floor, then sprinted along the corridor to the azure staircase. Clio led the charge up that one and onto the landing of the twenty-third level. One more to go.

They rushed through another echoing white corridor, heading toward the jade stairs. One more level and they would have accomplished the impossible.

"Stop," Ash hissed.

Lyre and Clio slid to a halt. He scanned the corridor for whatever danger Ash sensed, but he couldn't see anything but white marble walls and a single closed door. Ash stood motionless except for the swiveling of his head, his nostrils flaring and his eyes black.

"I can smell you," the draconian growled.

A quiet giggle echoed through the hall, then a daemon was suddenly standing in the center of the corridor as though he'd been there all along.

Not just any daemon. A familiar daemon.

Ragged feathers hung around his dark body and trailed on the floor, his mess of black hair hiding his eyes. Two large horns sprouted from the sides of his skull and three smaller ones protruded from his forehead.

The wraith smiled delightedly at Ash, exposing sharp fangs.

"Blackfire," he sang in a high, raspy voice. "The halls taste of your blood."

"What are *you* doing here?" Ash barked.

The wraith fluttered his dark hands, long fingers tapering to wickedly sharp claws. "I offered, did I not? Your fate I divined, but you would not wait."

"What are you doing here?" Ash repeated, his voice dropping into a dangerous snarl.

The wraith's maniacal smile widened. "Too late to change your path now. The crossroads lie behind you, passed by unseen, fate's hand unknown." He tilted his face up to peer through his shaggy hair and the light caught on pupilless eyes that swirled with shifting streaks of red and silver. "Upon this road, death awaits you on all sides."

Ash reached over his shoulder and drew his broadsword. "Lyre, take Clio and keep going."

"But Ash—"

"Go!"

Lyre shot an agonized look at the draconian, then grabbed Clio's arm and sprinted down the corridor. The wraith's mad laughter rang out, echoing across the shining marble.

With Clio's hand clutched in his, Lyre raced up the final flight of stairs and onto the twenty-fourth landing. The Rysalis floor. He hoped Ash had recovered enough to battle the wraith, but now—now it was *his* next battle he needed to worry about.

TWENTY~EIGHT

CLIO STOPPED at the wide door, its steel handle gleaming in the light of the spell crystals. The corridor was empty except for her and Lyre. The booming ruckus outside—Eliya and Ezran's distraction—had gone quiet.

She couldn't hear anything from the level below either, and she didn't know if that was good or bad. She wished they hadn't left Ash to fight the wraith alone.

With Lyre standing rigidly beside her, she stretched her hand toward the door. The ward darkened under her fingers, disarmed by a single spark of her magic. All the magic in this tower—web after ward after trap after alarm—would have stopped anyone but a mimic. Even Lyre, who could probably have broken through the wards, wouldn't have been fast enough.

No intruder should have ever made it this far. Gulping down her twisting stomach, she pushed the door open.

The change from white marble to warm granite took her by surprise. A round vestibule with carved pillars and elaborate buttresses welcomed visitors. She cautiously stepped inside and turned to the open archway.

She wasn't sure what she'd expected, but not this.

The spacious room was constructed entirely of speckled brown stone, and an obsidian inlay in the floor formed a symbol matching the one on Lyre's cheekbone. The high ceilings arched into domes, and sconces in the walls held, not harsh light spells, but oil lamps that gave off a soft, flickering glow.

Cabinets and shelves lined the walls, filled with stacks of everything imaginable—papers, books, spells, weapons, weaving tools, and random trinkets that might have been souvenirs from across the Underworld. Worktables with chairs or stools were scattered around, some empty, some buried in half-finished work. On one side, the room rose several steps to a platform beside the vertical, slit-like windows. Cozy furniture was arranged around a low table where a book sat open as though waiting for someone's return.

Under different circumstances, she would have been delighted to explore those cabinets or sit by the windows with a book and a cup of tea. The room was used, lived in, comfortably worn—far different from the stark white halls of Chrysalis. Which was the better representation of the Rysalis family? Lyre's workroom had been similar to this—a cluttered, welcoming mess.

Opposite the windows, an archway led into another room. Lyre moved silently toward it, pausing at the threshold, but the protective ward was already dark and inactive.

The antechamber beyond was constructed of the same granite, but it was empty of furniture. On one wall, another archway offered a glimpse of an expansive library. A third doorway led into a dim hallway. And the final wall also held a door, but a very different one.

The circular vault entrance was set in a colossal stone slab, and it was so heavily spelled that it glowed even without her asper. Layers upon layers of weavings crisscrossed the stone door, and the anchor lines of the weave had been physically carved into it. She belatedly realized why the Rysalis level was all granite—it was a significantly harder stone than marble and would hold, and deflect, magic far better.

"If he's stashed the KLOC anywhere," Lyre whispered, "I'm betting it's in there."

She nodded. "Should we check the rest of the level first?"

"It'll be all storage and living quarters. This is where the best magic and the secret records are kept."

Stepping up to the vault, she began a careful study. "This is the most complex weaving I've ever seen. There are elements to this that I can't ... I'm not sure they make sense, even with asper."

"Don't rush," he encouraged her. "Take your time."

But they didn't *have* a lot of time. She leaned closer, squinting as a headache built behind her eyes. So many layers full of tricks and traps and backup weaves to take over if the main ones failed. There had to be a method to disarm it, but the way it was embedded into the carved stone made it seem as permanent—and unbreakable—as the granite itself.

"Blood magic," she whispered, finally finding the right constructs. "It's keyed to someone's blood, but there's something strange about it. It's linked to one person but not ... a specific person?"

"How does *that* work?" Lyre muttered, shifting his grip on his bow.

A purring incubus voice that didn't belong to Lyre responded.

"It's probably too sophisticated for you to grasp, brother."

At the end of the corridor, Madrigal stepped into sight—his bow already drawn. The string twanged as he released it, the deadly arrow shooting for Lyre's chest.

Lyre snatched the arrow out of the air, flipped it onto his bow, and fired it back. Madrigal sprang aside and the arrow shattered against the wall behind him.

"To put it simply," the incubus went on, ignoring the near-deadly interruption, "the ward is keyed to the blood of the Rysalis patriarch. Only our father can open that vault, and if he dies, the power to enter it will pass automatically to his heir—meaning Andante."

Lyre pulled an arrow from his quiver.

"You have a lot of brothers to kill if you plan to open that door," Madrigal concluded with a smirk as he also drew another bolt. "Not even a mimic can get through the ward."

He flipped his arrow onto his bow, drew back, and fired in a single swift motion. Lyre snapped his string back and released. The two arrows collided in midair, shattering into splinters.

Madrigal advanced toward the antechamber, shouldering his bow as he came. Protective shields shimmered over his body and he was loaded with weavings—gemstones hanging from his neck, his wrists, his belt. He stopped in the threshold and turned darkening amber eyes to Clio.

She looked away, ignoring the heat rising through her body. He was out of glamour and she felt the irresistible pull—but Lyre was also out of glamour, and his allure was even stronger.

"I'm curious." Madrigal's smirk grew patronizing. "What exactly did you plan to do once you got up here? Or do you just enjoy suffering?"

"Well," Lyre said, "for starters, I plan to kill you."

"I'd like to see you try." With a laugh, Madrigal pulled a handful of gemstones from his pocket and tossed them across the floor.

They burst into golden flares, but Lyre cast a ripple of magic that hit the four gems and sent them flying. Two hit the vault door and burst into dust. Two triggered harmlessly as they ricocheted off the walls. The third ruptured into spiraling wires that launched at Clio and Lyre. She flung both hands out and cut through the threads. The spell died.

As Madrigal pulled another gem, Lyre launched forward, Clio right behind him.

Madrigal activated his gem and pitched it at Lyre. A binding spell whipped out, but Clio grabbed the back of Lyre's shirt, her magic rushing over him. He leaped through the dissipating glow and slammed into his brother. They tumbled across the floor, then Madrigal broke free, a cast flaring across his fingers.

Clio's hands came up, mimicking him. As he cast his spell, she flung her copy over Lyre's head. The magic collided, the explosion throwing Lyre and Madrigal back even with their defensive weaves.

Lyre rolled to his feet as golden threads spiraled through his fingers. Madrigal started a counterspell.

Conjuring a dart of magic, Clio flung it into Madrigal, interrupting his cast, and Lyre threw a sizzling binding that shackled his brother's arms and legs. The incubus wobbled, then caught a gem hanging from his bracelet. Light flared and the binding burst apart.

No longer smirking, Madrigal whipped another gem into the floor. Power blasted from the stone, hurling Clio and Lyre in opposite directions. She slammed into the wall only a few feet from the lethal vault door and her protective weaves shuddered, threatening to fail.

In the center of the room, Madrigal whirled on Lyre, hands raised for another cast.

Still gasping on the floor, Clio mimicked him. She lobbed the spell at Madrigal's back as he threw his in Lyre's face. Lyre crumpled with a pained cry, and Madrigal fell too, shouting in surprise as much as pain.

Both incubi surged to their feet and began to cast again, but this time, Clio didn't mimic Madrigal. She mimicked Lyre.

Magic coiled across his fingers, and she followed him so closely they were moving in almost perfect unison. It didn't feel like she was copying him so much as he was guiding her hands along with his own. She didn't think. She just wove.

Madrigal threw a desperate counter at Lyre's weave—a moment before Clio's copy hit him in the back. He went down a second time, tangled in a binding. As he writhed helplessly, Lyre pulled his last spelled throwing knife from the sheath on his upper arm.

A silent, shuddering vibration rippled through the vault door. A rainbow of colors shimmered across the weaves, then the threads flashed to crimson. The vault door slid outward, then rose as though drawn toward the ceiling by invisible pulleys.

Standing in the round threshold, Lyceus surveyed the antechamber with cold amber eyes.

Lyre scarcely hesitated. Arm snapping back, he flung the knife at his father.

Lyceus didn't move. A spell circle appeared and the knife hit it— sticking in place as though it had sunk into clay instead of a glowing weave. A weave Lyceus hadn't cast. *Summoned* was the only word she could think of to describe the way the magic had instantly materialized, called into existence by his thoughts alone.

The Rysalis patriarch pointed at Lyre's feet. With a golden flash, another spell circle appeared on the floor beneath Lyre. Colors swirled across the threads, then it flared white—and bolts of lightning arched upward, forming a sizzling cage with Lyre in its center.

Madrigal squirmed and the binding around him snapped apart. He rose hastily to his feet, face contorted in embarrassed fury.

"Can you handle the nymph on your own?" Lyceus asked flatly.

Madrigal's face flushed. "Of course I can."

"Then get her out of my sight." He stepped over the circular threshold into the antechamber and the vault door glided back into place, sealing shut. "And stay out of the way."

As Madrigal turned to Clio, a spell sparking over his fingers, she raised her hand. Enough time for one last cast.

Lyceus's magic was incomprehensible to her, but even if she didn't understand how the weavings worked, she knew how spell circles worked.

In the same moment Madrigal flung his spell at her, she whipped her cast at the electric cage around Lyre. Her magic hit the circle and cut through the outer ring. Power burst outward, electricity arcing toward the ceiling and scorching the floor.

Then Madrigal's cast hit her chest and everything went dark.

THE ELECTRIC CAGE exploded. Lyre skidded across the floor, limbs convulsing and vision blurring. With a gasp, he lurched half upright.

Clio had collapsed, taken down by Madrigal's spell—a cast she could have countered, but she'd freed Lyre instead. Grabbing a handful of her long hair, Madrigal glanced back at Lyre, a triumphant leer twisting his lips. He dragged her out of the antechamber.

Madrigal didn't plan to kill Clio—not immediately, anyway—and she would have to defeat him on her own. Lyre couldn't help her.

He turned to his father, taking measure of the head of the family with a glance. The daemon who'd sired him was a stranger. He was the powerful family leader, the distant and unknowable god who distributed orders and determined punishments. He was the man who judged his sons' worth and decided whether they lived or died.

In an instant, Lyre's bow was in his hand and an arrow in the other. He nocked and fired.

A spell circle appeared in front of Lyceus, this one slightly different than the last. Instead of catching the bolt, it deflected it. The broken shaft skittered across the granite.

Jaw clenched, Lyre pulled three arrows with three variations of his best shield-piercing weaves. He shot them in rapid succession.

Two more spell circles materialized, blocking Lyre's arrows as though they weren't spelled at all. Wood splinters flew across the room. Lyre reached over his shoulder a third time, fingers brushing across his dwindling arrows for a spell that might break through that defense.

Lyceus finally moved—a careless flick of his hand.

Lyre didn't even see the cast. His bow was torn out of his grip and slid into the far corner of the antechamber. Pain shot through his ring and pinky fingers—broken by the impact.

"Enough," Lyceus said. "You have always been persistent to the point of senselessness."

Lyre gritted his teeth and reached for his spell chain. Lyceus made another small gesture and his three shield circles doubled to six. They drifted around him, ready to snap into place no matter which direction an attack came from.

"But your stubbornness is a strength as well," his father added unexpectedly. "Without it, you wouldn't continually persevere long past where others have given up. What many would consider impossible, you have achieved—and you've done it over and over again."

Lyre paused with a gem between his fingers, a strange tightness rising in his chest. His father had never, not even once, said something positive about his most disappointing son.

"The shadow weave is brilliant," Lyceus murmured. "The construction of the clock is ingenious. You have surpassed my expectations."

Lyre couldn't move. This was all wrong. He'd mentally prepared for every variation of a confrontation with his father—except this one.

"There is a reason I've tolerated your petty defiance and *secret* rebellions." A faint, mocking smile curved Lyceus's perfect lips, identical to Lyre's. "And a reason I wouldn't allow your older brothers to kill you."

He made a slow gesture and his spell circles spun faster. "Your weavings aren't limited by rules and conventions. You are my only son with the capacity to master the most difficult techniques documented in that vault. With another five or ten seasons of experience, and with your rebellious phase behind you, I expected you to kill your brothers and take Andante's place as my heir."

Lyre slowly lowered his hand to his side. "You ... did?"

"Tell me, Lyre." Lyceus's eyes gleamed. "What was it like to weave a spell from within the Void?"

His whole body went cold, every muscle tensing until it hurt.

"I can't fathom how you arrived at the idea. Embedding the very essence of the Void, of *nothingness*, into the weave—it is a truly catastrophic magic you have created."

"It's not ..." Lyre shook his head slightly, unable to form an intelligent response. "I made it to clear lodestones."

Lyceus smiled indulgently. "I would like to know more about its development." He raised a hand toward his son. "Share your invention with me, Lyre, and I will share my magic with you. A fair trade, don't you think?"

Lyre stared blankly at his father's offered hand, then looked into those amber eyes that, during their last encounter, had burned with devastating aphrodesia as he'd strangled Lyre's mind into submission.

"If you want to know about the shadow weave," Lyre said, "then you'll have to coerce every single word from my lips before you kill me."

Lyre flicked his wrist, casting the gem in his hand across the floor. It flared with golden light, then glowing spears launched out of it, streaking for Lyceus.

His father's spell circles snapped in front of him and the spears bounced harmlessly off.

Lyceus sighed impatiently. "Stubborn to the last. Very well. I offered to share my magic with you—so allow me to demonstrate."

The shield circles spun behind him as he raised his hand, fingers spread. A two-foot-wide spell circle manifested in front of his palm, geometrical lines forming an intricate shape filled with ancient runes Lyre had never seen before. The golden threads shimmered in a wave of colors, then turned to reddish orange.

Fireballs burst from the circle. Lyre cast a bubble shield as they shot across the room and into the barrier—which disintegrated under the barrage. His defensive weaves fell apart just as easily, and pain scorched his skin as he staggered back, his clothes burning.

Lyceus flicked his fingers and the circle reformed into a new arrangement of lines and runes that flashed to pale blue. An arctic wind whipped ice shards across Lyre. His back hit the wall, the fires extinguished but a hundred bleeding cuts scored across his body.

Gasping, he snapped a spell off his chain. Before Lyceus could summon another circle, Lyre activated his best dome shield and dropped the gem onto the floor. A glowing web spread across the granite, then the dome rushed over him. He sagged, sucking in air as he tried to come up with a plan.

"Fire and ice are easy enough," Lyceus remarked. "Perhaps this will impress you."

He tilted his head and another spell circle appeared—directly beneath Lyre's feet *inside* his dome shield. The twisted, unfamiliar runes shimmered from gold to murky brown.

The granite floor turned to liquid. Lyre sank up to his knees and his gem was absorbed, the dome weave tearing apart. The fluid stone surged up his body, encasing him. Though it flowed like water, it was hard as rock against his limbs and he couldn't shift as it compressed his chest and climbed over his shoulders. He gasped a shallow breath as the stone crawled up his throat and cold pressure slid over his jaw.

Lyceus snapped his fingers and the granite sloughed off Lyre's body, simultaneously pushing him out of the pool before returning to its normal state. He collapsed onto his knees, panting. Terror shivered along his nerves from the sickening realization that he didn't understand this magic at all and had no idea how to fight it.

He staggered to his feet anyway, but he didn't know what spell to use—what weaving he would waste.

His father summoned a crackling yellow circle. A spinning ball of electricity smashed into Lyre and he slammed into the floor, convulsing again.

Lyceus summoned another one. And another. The spells lined up in front of him, crackling spheres forming in each circle.

With no time for anything else, Lyre cast a bubble shield. The first electric orb smashed it apart, and the second and third hit him in the chest one after another. He skidded across the floor and hit the wall in the antechamber's corner.

Hacking for air as his diaphragm seized, Lyre struggled to rise. Not yet. He couldn't give up yet. He lifted his head—and saw his bow a foot away. Grabbing it, he lurched onto his knees and reached for an arrow, ignoring the pain in his broken fingers.

Lyceus slashed his hand through the air.

Lyre's bow shattered. The splintered wood fell from his hands and clattered to the granite in pieces. On his knees, his best weapon destroyed, he looked up into his father's eyes and knew there was no way he could win.

But then, he had never intended to win this fight.

TWENTY-NINE

CLIO'S EYES flew open. The first thing she saw was Madrigal's smile.

His aphrodesia hit her an instant later and she arched up from the floor as heat sizzled along every nerve in her body. He touched a fingertip to her heaving chest and traced it between her breasts, dragging at her shirt.

"It sounds like my father is just about done toying with Lyre, so I figured we could have some fun," he purred, the layered harmonics of his voice throbbing with power. "What do you think, my love?"

She bared her teeth. "Don't call me that."

"What? 'My love'?" He leaned down, getting in her face. She closed her eyes before she got lost in the dark amber. "Oh, but you *are* my love tonight, Clio. And some other woman will be my love tomorrow. Shall I call you my darling instead? My dearest? My sweetheart?"

He laughed huskily and she clenched her jaw harder. When he was being teasing or seductive, Lyre used similar pet names—but hearing them from Madrigal's mouth, she realized Lyre didn't call her those names anymore.

As Madrigal slid his hand back up her belly, she balled her hand into a fist and swung it blindly upward.

Her knuckles met his defensive weaves with a painful crunch that jarred all the way down her arm. Even though her strike hadn't hurt him, Madrigal recoiled and she slapped her hand to his lower abdomen. With a slice of magic, she disabled his defensive weaves.

His fist swung down and slammed into her cheek. Black spots danced in her vision.

"Stubborn little princess," he sneered, his voice beautiful but his tone ugly. He grabbed her jaw and pulled her face up. "Look at me."

She squeezed her eyes shut again.

"Look at me."

Power flooded his hypnotic words and her eyes opened against her will. She met his black stare and her mind crumbled under the sweeping aphrodesia. Fire tore through her body, lighting every nerve on fire, and she *needed* so badly it eclipsed the urge to breathe.

Somewhere beyond the arched doorway, something exploded.

The sound jolted through the boiling heat in her veins, and as she stared into Madrigal's black eyes, she had a sudden vision of Lyre's mouth pressed to a succubus's plump lips—her flesh between his teeth, her blood running down his chin. Even deeply caught in aphrodesia, he had fought back.

A strange new pain rose through her—this one ice-cold and burning. With slow, dreamy movements, she reached up until her hands found Madrigal's face. She slid her fingers across his jaw, and his luscious, inviting mouth turned up in a satisfied smirk.

She wanted his mouth. She wanted it on her lips, on her skin. She wanted—and she loathed him for it.

Her fingers pressed to his cheek and green light flashed. Her swift weave spun across his mouth and jaw, sealing them shut.

He flinched back with a muffled snarl, his hands flying to his face. She shoved both fists into his chest and unleashed a blast of power. He flew backward.

She lunged to her feet. Desire raged through her, a poison in her blood—heart racing, lungs heaving, perspiration beading her overheated skin—but fierce aggression boiled up from inside her. If her pair of long daggers hadn't been missing from her belt, removed by Madrigal, she would have stabbed him.

As Madrigal grabbed at his face, she blasted him again. He pitched over backward, his head smacking into the granite floor.

"Do you remember that spell?" she asked as she began another cast. "You used it on Lyre once."

A memory as clear as her asper—in Chrysalis's lowest level, Lyre hanging by his arms from a chain as Madrigal silenced him with a weave. Now Madrigal was the one who'd been silenced. Without his voice, he could still pump her full of aphrodesia—but he'd lost the ability to command her.

As long as he didn't get a chance to break the weave.

She flung her next cast—another copy of his magic. The pain spell he'd used on Lyre in the antechamber hit him and he crumpled with a strangled groan. As her fingers danced, forming a new weave, he thrust his hand out.

The shapeless power blasted her in the chest and she almost crumpled, her defensive weaves long gone. Madrigal shot to his feet, his eyes black and face twisted with rage.

She stretched her arms out, fingers curled into claws. She felt no fear, only icy rage for this daemon who thought he could control her, who looked at her and saw only a victim. The burn of his aphrodesia, the tremble of her limbs, and the parched hunger for his touch only made her more furious.

Green magic spilled across her fingers as she wove two spells simultaneously.

Teeth bared, Madrigal hurled an attack. She shielded and counterattacked, but he flicked her spell out of the air. More magic flowed from her fingertips, spells she'd learned from Lyre, from other weavers, from watching Ash. She cast again and again, and Madrigal faltered under the onslaught, defending against her with no time to attack—and whenever he did, she mimicked it.

Faster and faster—not powerful magic, but magic swifter than he could follow. He just couldn't keep up.

With a garbled noise, he launched a wide band of power that forced her to shield, then he charged in right behind the attack. He drove her to the floor and his weight came down on top of her, crushing the air from her lungs. Grabbing her by the throat, fingers squeezing, he pulled her face toward his, his blazing black eyes calling to her.

She blindly grabbed for his neck. Her fingers closed around a gem on his spell chain and she activated it.

Power burst from the stone, then a dome shield similar to Lyre's formed over the two of them. Madrigal's mouth twisted into a laughing sneer as he shot a cold wave of magic into her flesh.

Her other hand pulled away from the hidden sheath in her sleeve, and she rammed a short blade into Madrigal's side.

His eyes bulged. She blasted him off her and into the side of the barrier. Tearing her black scarf from around her neck, she jumped on his chest, shoved the scarf over his face to protect herself from his alluring eyes, and pressed the point of her knife to his unprotected throat. He went still.

She sucked in air, rage and triumph blazing through her. She had beaten him in magic, and now she'd beaten him without it.

Golden light blazed out of the archway from the antechamber where Lyre and Lyceus were fighting. Her head whipped around, her heart leaping into her throat. Crackling power rippled out of the room.

The antechamber exploded in a lethal deluge of shattered granite walls.

"GIVE UP, LYRE," his father ordered.

Stumbling to his feet, Lyre braced one hand on the wall. Every muscle hurt. Every bone hurt. He squinted, his lungs aching with each breath.

"No," he said hoarsely.

"You never had a chance." Lyceus raised his hand and six more spell circles appeared. "You can't defeat me."

Lyre pulled two long daggers from the sheaths on his thigh, the blades shimmering with weaves. "Quit hiding behind your magic and fight me."

"Hiding?" Lyceus's eyebrows rose mockingly. "I wouldn't call this *hiding*. But if you insist."

He flicked his fingers and the spell circles faded. Two new ones appeared, wreathing his wrist and his opposite arm. Blades of shining blue ice sprouted from his right fist and left elbow, leaving his other hand free for casting.

Gripping the hilts of his daggers, Lyre cautiously advanced. Lyceus was humoring him. Toying with him. He could have killed his son a dozen times over.

But he didn't want to *kill* Lyre. Lyceus wanted to break him—to crush his spirit so he would surrender. So he would willingly reveal how he'd created the shadow weave. Aphrodesia wouldn't be effective for an interrogation on complex weaving techniques.

Lyceus wanted Lyre to surrender and tell him everything. Then, promises or not, Lyceus would kill him.

Daggers in hand, Lyre threw himself at his father. Catching a steel edge on his ice weapon, Lyceus whipped his second crystalline blade around and almost gored Lyre. Shielding wouldn't protect him against his father's magic.

Lyre jerked back, feigned left, then struck low. His dagger arched toward Lyceus's thigh—then a spell circle appeared and his blade sank into it and stuck in place. He tried to tear it free and lost his grip on the hilt.

Lyceus's ice blade raked across Lyre's chest. As he staggered backward, his father lunged at him, and Lyre frantically countered with his remaining dagger. Lyceus slashed again. The first ice blade missed but the second sliced across Lyre's thigh. His leg buckled and he almost fell.

"This is pointless." Lyceus flicked his fingers.

Another spell circle appeared, manifesting around Lyre's chest and locking his body in place. His right arm, hand clutching his dagger, was trapped in the spell too.

Lyceus stepped closer, scanned his son thoughtfully, then rammed an ice blade into Lyre's stomach. The crystalline weapon slid into his flesh and every muscle in his body went rigid from the blinding pain.

Pushing the blade deeper, Lyceus studied Lyre's contorted face. "It will take several agonizing hours for you to bleed out. Perhaps you'll reconsider your refusal in that time."

Gasping, Lyre grabbed the ice blade with his free hand. The frigid crystal burned his skin, but he gripped it tighter as his senses focused on the magic within. Bizarre, unfamiliar, but all magic had rules. All magic had structure—structure that could be broken.

Lyceus pulled the blade out of his body.

As the ice slid through Lyre's grasp, his fingers bit into the blade. Just before it left his hand, he flooded power deep into its core and golden magic rippled up the crystal.

The ice burst apart.

Shards sprayed Lyre and Lyceus, tearing their clothes and cutting their exposed skin. Lyceus flinched as a razor-sharp piece sliced across his cheek, and the binding circle around Lyre vanished. Blood splattered on the floor.

Stepping back, Lyceus turned his hand over to inspect the damage—dozens of thin cuts that leaked blood. Superficial wounds. Not even enough to slow him down.

"Mildly impressive, Lyre, but irritating."

Lyre sank to his knees, the dagger falling from his hand and clattering on the granite. He pressed an arm against his middle as he stared at his splattered blood—with a few droplets of Lyceus's blood mixed in.

"Finally," he whispered hoarsely.

Lyceus paused, confused and maybe curious. He made no move when Lyre reached into his pocket, then extended the small vial. The liquid silver within shone with golden light and the faintest shimmer of red.

"Blood magic?" Lyceus asked. "Not even that can pierce my defense."

Lyre looked up at his father, cold hate giving him courage. "That's just it. This … doesn't have to."

With a spark of magic, he shattered the vial. The quicksilver splashed across the floor, mixing with the blood already smeared on the granite.

Lyre's blood. And his father's blood.

The quicksilver glowed incandescent and threads snaked out from the liquid. The spell raced across the floor, seeking its targets. It touched Lyre and Lyceus at the same time, and in beautiful, perfect symmetry, the magic coiled over father and son in a web of interconnected lines, embedding into their flesh.

"What—" Lyceus gasped. His face hardened. "Binding us with blood?"

Lyre pressed his arm to his bleeding stomach. The magic in the spell pulsed, power building through the weaves.

"If I harm you now, I'll inflict the same damage on myself. Do you think that will save you?" Lyceus sneered, his face crisscrossed with the golden lines of the spell. "This weave will protect you only for as long as it takes me to purge it."

"The purpose of the weave isn't to protect *me*." Lyre smiled coldly. "It's to kill *you*."

As the crackling energy gained intensity, Lyre stretched his weave-marked hand toward the glowing floor. Horrified comprehension flashed in Lyceus's eyes.

Lyre pressed his palm into the quicksilver puddle—and the spell surged across his fingers. The tangle of golden lines wrapped in and over his hand turned crimson. A few steps away, the same red glow appeared on Lyceus's hand.

The ruby tinge leeched through the golden weave like a spreading infection, climbing their arms. In perfect unison, the blood curse flowed into their veins, father and son bound to the same fate.

As the mirrored weave darkened to throbbing crimson, as arctic claws closed around their chests, as death's chilling touch found their hearts, Lyre met his father's eyes with grim triumph.

The weave pulsed red one final time—and the two lives held in the blood curse's embrace extinguished.

THIRTY

ASH HELD perfectly still, his senses straining. Giggling laughter echoed through the corridor.

His nostrils flared as he inhaled the scents permeating the air. Blood—his, mostly—and the unpleasantly sweet odor of his opponent. He could sense the emptiness of the corridor.

Then something shifted.

He pivoted, wings flaring as he thrust his sword into nothing. With a flutter of feathers, the wraith appeared, slipping away from his blade like a fish gliding through river currents. The daemon cackled insanely, flashing pointed teeth, and his hair shifted to reveal his eyes—no pupils, just red and silver light swirling like a bizarre galaxy contained in his skull.

The daemon's ragged black wings spread wide, filling half the corridor. "Ashtaroth," he chanted. "I will tell your fortunes if you would but listen."

"'Death awaits,'" Ash mocked. "How could I forget?"

He lunged, swinging his blade. The wraith melted away as though gravity had no hold on him, then disappeared. Ash went still again, trying to sense his location.

"How indeed," the wraith chimed delightedly, his high voice echoing off the marble. "You will forget that which should never be forgotten. A moment to come, lost in the next."

Unable to sense the daemon unless he moved, Ash had already wasted too much time going in circles while the wraith taunted him. Ash snarled silently. He was done with this bullshit.

The wraith giggled. "A summons in the nothing, a whisper beyond the light. When the ever-night comes, will you fall upon its blade, dragon lord?"

Flipping his sword in his hand, Ash drove the point into the marble. Ebony flames shot down the blade, met the floor, and exploded in a spiral. The corridor turned to searing black fire, charring the polished stone walls.

The flames died, and hovering above the floor in a spherical shield of rippling red and silver power was the wraith, unharmed. He laughed, his tattered wings spread but not flapping. How the daemon was floating like that, Ash didn't know. And he didn't care.

He snapped his wings down as he sprang for the shield. His flame-coated sword cut right through it, and this time, when the wraith slid clear of his blade, he slammed the bony top of his wing into the daemon's face.

Head snapping back, the wraith dropped like a rock. Ash landed and thrust his sword at the fallen daemon. As the wraith evaded with uncanny agility, Ash flicked his wrist. The blade hidden in a sheath under his forearm sprang into his hand, and he slashed it across the wraith's belly.

The steel passed through the darkness of the daemon's torso, but whether it had connected with flesh, Ash had no idea.

Gliding backward, the wraith lifted a dark hand, his strange eyes swirling. "Our time is up, Ashtaroth."

Not knowing what attack was coming, Ash grabbed the gem around his neck and activated the third spell Lyre had made for him.

The golden barrier formed around him an instant before the wraith's cast struck. A tornado of red and silver blades ripped across the barrier. Teeth gritted, Ash waited for the shield to fail and the blades to tear into him, but the weaving held.

The daemon's spell died away, revealing the empty corridor. Ash disabled the barrier like Lyre had taught him and focused on his senses—the usual ones and his preternatural ones.

The wraith was gone for good.

He sheathed his sword, giving his arm a break. Exhaustion shivered in his muscles and feverish pain throbbed in his bones from the snake venom, but he ignored both as he tapped into the lodestones hidden in his bracers. Power flooded through him, replenishing his reserves.

He'd taken too long. He had to get to the next level—and he didn't give a shit about going unnoticed anymore.

He pointed his fist at the ceiling. Magic sizzled through him, building in his arm, then he snapped his fingers open. The blast struck the marble and the ceiling collapsed into the corridor in a wave of shattered marble and white dust.

Launching into the haze, Ash sprang upward with a beat of his wings. He didn't need to see—he could sense the opening. Just as he could sense the electric vibrations of lethal magic building in the air.

He shot through the hole into the twenty-fourth-level corridor and half leaped, half flew toward the intensifying power. A broad door beckoned, and he hoped the wards were disabled. Hitting it full force, he slammed the door open and wheeled into the room beyond. In a single glance, he took in everything.

Clio, straddling an incubus's chest with a dagger at his throat, both of them encased in a dome shield.

In the next room, framed by the archway, Lyre. On his knees, a hand pressed to the floor, a tangled gold weaving wrapped over and through his body. The Rysalis patriarch stood a few feet away, an identical weaving coiled around him.

Crimson light flared over their hands and raced up their arms in perfect unison. Surging across their shoulders, the blood magic spread over the golden webbing on their chests. The red light consumed the entire weave—

—and the antechamber exploded.

The detonation ripped the walls apart. Ash leaped for the nearest shelter—Clio and Madrigal's dome shield. He ducked behind it as chunks of granite hurled past, followed by a wall of fire that disintegrated the dome.

The antechamber walls were gone. The library was in flames. Only the vault, with its granite front and circular door, remained intact, scorched but otherwise undamaged.

In the center of the room, Lyre and Lyceus lay unmoving. The blood-red weave that had covered their bodies was gone, and fires burned across the floor as though the room had been splashed in oil.

Golden light blazed and Clio flew backward, hitting the floor with a yelp. Not noticing Ash, Madrigal sprinted into the antechamber.

Ash followed more slowly, unconcerned by the fire as he scanned the downed incubi. Crouching beside his father, Madrigal pressed a hand to Lyceus's chest, checking for signs of life.

"*How,*" the incubus snarled. "How could *Lyre* have …"

Ash crossed to Lyre and dropped onto his haunches. The incubus's half-open eyes stared, empty. Dead. Ash touched Lyre's throat, waiting for a pulse. Nothing.

Madrigal turned around, then startled backward at the sight of Ash. Fear bloomed in his scent, pupils dilating from adrenaline. "You! Where did you come from?"

Ash lifted his fingers from Lyre's lifeless neck and gestured. "Hunting Samael's contract." He rose to his feet. "Dead is dead, even if I didn't get to kill him myself."

Hissing, Madrigal stormed over and roughly grabbed Lyre by the throat. Ash felt the thrum of magic as Madrigal checked that his brother was properly dead. He let the body fall back to the floor.

"Crazy bastard. I thought Dulcet was the insane one." Covering his mouth and nose with his arm as smoke hazed the air, Madrigal looked at Lyceus. "I can't believe he killed himself just to kill our father. How the hell did he do it?"

"Who cares?" Ash intoned. He canted his head. "I need to report back. Are you coming?"

"Am I—what?"

"You probably can't hear it, but daemons are approaching—half the tower is about to pile onto this level." He snapped his wings open and closed. "I'm leaving the fast way."

As Madrigal frowned, Ash headed across the room. He didn't look for Clio—didn't risk drawing attention to her. With the shock of his father's death, Madrigal had forgotten about everything else. Ash could smell her nearby, but smoke was rapidly overwhelming all other scents. It billowed from the library and half the main room was on fire too, the bookshelves consumed by flames and the shelves collapsing.

Ash stopped before the sitting area, the narrow windows reflecting the firelight. He extended his hand, summoned another wave of power, and unleashed the blast. The windows exploded into a gaping hole.

He stepped up to the new exit.

"Wait," Madrigal snapped. "I'm coming. The faster I can get my brothers back here ..."

Trailing off into mutters, he darted into the vestibule and slammed the door shut. Magic sizzled as he engaged the wards, then he joined Ash.

Ash pulled the incubus in front of him. "If you squirm, I'll drop you."

Madrigal grumbled something under his breath. As Ash pushed the incubus up to the hole, he glanced back once, but the smoke was too thick to see anything more than the dark shadows where Lyre and his father had fallen. Magic-fueled flames spread implacably across the floor, and in a few hours, when Madrigal returned with his brothers, there would be nothing left but ashes.

But that didn't matter, because Madrigal had witnessed the two daemons' deaths first. And Ash would ensure he reported both deaths to the Rysalis family—and to Samael.

Taking hold of the incubus, he sprang into the cool night air and swept away from the burning tower.

THIRTY~ONE

HER LUNGS HURT.

Clio huddled in the corner, her scarf wrapped around her nose and mouth as smoke displaced the air. She counted in her head, silently chanting each second as it passed.

Carrying Madrigal, Ash leaped through the hole in the outer wall, his terrifying wings lit by the fire before he vanished into the darkness. The moment they were gone, she burst from her hiding spot. Leaping through the scorching flames, she rushed into the antechamber and fell to her knees beside Lyre.

His dead eyes stared blankly, his skin white and body so still, marred by dozens of bloody cuts. Her eyes darted to the hole in his lower abdomen, stained crimson but no longer bleeding. To bleed, his heart needed to beat.

Two hundred and forty-three seconds since he had fallen. Just over four minutes.

She fumbled at her throat and snapped a gemstone off her chain. Tearing Lyre's shirt open, she laid the gem on his chest, then used a granite shard to cut the pad of her thumb. Blood welled and a single drop fell onto the stone.

Touching the bloodied gem, she activated the spell. Green light, tinged with red, flared across his chest. She laid her hand over the gem and focused her asper into his body.

Deep inside him, a minute weave in her green magic slept. So tiny, so buried, that Madrigal hadn't sensed it. She'd spent hours practicing the spell under Lyre's direction, hours perfecting it before she'd woven it into his body. He hadn't been able to demonstrate the complete spell for her, so she'd had to learn the hard way.

She channeled a spark into the slumbering weave. It flared brightly, linking with the spell in the gemstone, and both weaves turned red. A pulse of magic rippled through Lyre's body.

His chest heaved under her hand.

Tears of relief spilled down her cheeks. He gasped desperately, eyes rolling back. Sucking in another breath, he started to cough. She pulled his scarf over his nose and mouth to filter the smoke.

"Hold on, Lyre," she whispered, not sure if he could hear her over the roaring flames.

She pushed to her feet and rushed to Lyceus's fallen body. In *his* chest, there was no pre-woven spell to revive him. He was well and truly dead, his life snuffed out by the blood curse she and Lyre had woven together.

If Dulcet were alive, she might have thanked him for showing them how to kill Lyre—and how to bring him back again.

She wormed her hand into Lyceus's inner shirt pocket and pulled out Lyre's KLOC and its key, the shadow weave glowing so brightly she'd seen it through the fabric. Tucking it into her pocket, she snapped the last gemstone off her chain and set it on Lyceus's chest. A touch of magic activated the weave.

As she backed away, the gem erupted in a wave of searing white fire. Lyceus's body vanished under the devouring flames. When the Rysalis family returned, there would be nothing but ashes left—both bodies, they would believe, consumed in the inferno.

Racing back to Lyre, she drew his arm over her shoulders and helped him to his feet. He pressed a hand to the wound in his stomach, his face deathly pale. Taking shallow breaths of the smoky air, she pulled him out of the antechamber and into the main room.

Beneath the roar of flames, a different sound rose—shouting voices. The ward on the main entrance flickered and flashed as something hit the door. Daemons were coming, Ash had said before he left. How many were out there, filling the corridor and trying to get in? Would the ward hold against them?

She guided Lyre past the vestibule and flame-engulfed bookshelves to the raised sitting area where fresh air gusted in through the shattered wall. As Lyre sank weakly to the floor, she leaned into the gap, scanning the black sky. It was empty.

"They're coming," Lyre said hoarsely.

Another slam against the door, then an explosion shook the wall. A burning bookshelf collapsed in a burst of sparks. The daemons outside couldn't break through the ward so they were breaking down the wall instead.

She put her back to the hole and sank down, sick terror gathering in her chest. Sucking in the deepest breath she could manage, she put her hand into her pocket.

"Get into glamour, Lyre," she whispered.

He stared at her like he might argue, his eyes exhausted and shadowed by pain, but instead, his form shimmered. The dark tattoo on his cheek vanished as he slipped into his human form.

She pulled glamour over her nymph form, then, shoulder to shoulder with Lyre, she inserted the key into the back of the clock and wound it. With the key still inside the device, she looked up at him, her heart racing. They could use glamour to protect the weavings they carried in their daemon forms, but they could protect nothing else from the devastation of the shadow weave.

He put his hand over hers and pulled the key out.

The gears turned, the second hand whirling around the clock face. She watched the seconds tick down, her pulse hammering. Finding Lyre's hand, she clutched it, their fingers entwined so tightly it hurt.

The vestibule wall exploded inward. Hunks of rock tumbled across the floor, scattering flames, and six hulking daemons poured inside. Security guards, furious and eager to punish whoever had infiltrated their tower.

She squeezed Lyre's hand tighter as the clock counted down.

Ten. Nine. Eight. Seven.

The enraged daemons spotted her and Lyre. They surged into motion.

Six. Five. Four.

The first two reached the stairs to the raised sitting area.

Three. Two.

The lead daemon swung his pike around, bringing the point to hover in front of Lyre's face.

One.

The shadow weave erupted from the clock. For an instant that lasted an eternity, it engulfed her in icy power that pulled her body apart at the same time it sucked every particle of her being into her center like a black hole had spawned in place of her heart.

Then it ripped out of her, an expanding bubble that passed through every solid material—the granite floor, the daemons standing on it—then raced down twenty-four floors of the tower to the rocky ground beneath. She couldn't see it, but she could feel it gathering strength and speed as it consumed the magic of every daemon on the island, every spell, every ward.

With a boom like a tidal wave, the shadow weave hit the surrounding river and the water absorbed its power.

Quiet fell again. Clio slumped beside Lyre, her glamour gone and her body screaming with exhaustion. With a shaking hand, she reached for the three lodestones Ash had charged for her, protected from the shadow weave by her glamour. The minuscule delay between the shadow weave's touch and losing glamour—thereby exposing the lodestones—had been enough to spare them.

Power flooded her body, hot magic that rushed to fill the void the shadow weave had left.

Beside her, Lyre shuddered as golden light shimmered over him—his aura revitalized as he too drained the lodestones he'd saved for this possibility. He straightened, glancing across the collapsed and groaning troop of daemons that had been about to kill them. A couple of the toughest ones were trying to push up from the floor, trembling from shock.

A quiet chirp behind her. Clio turned.

Zwi perched on the broken wall. The dragonet tilted her head and trilled at them, unharmed by the shadow weave.

"You're here," she gasped in relief.

The dragonet hopped inside and black flames whooshed over her small body, expanding rapidly. When they dissipated, the large dragon spread her wings, holding them out of the way.

Clio helped Lyre mount, then grabbed the dragon's mane and hauled herself onto her back. As Zwi took a lumbering step toward the gap in the wall, Lyre slipped a gemstone from his pocket. Light flashed and he flicked it over his shoulder.

Zwi took three running steps, then sprang through the hole. As she sped away in a fast glide, cool air rushed over Clio, whisking away the stench of smoke. Clutching the dragon's mane, she glanced back.

Golden light blazed from the breach in the pristine white tower, then roaring flames gushed out of it.

She faced forward, grateful for Lyre's arms around her. The city below was eerily silent, no sound or movement. She focused ahead on the dark silhouette of the shore, refusing to look back at the flames leaping from the twenty-fourth level. The daemons in the tower room were dead. No one could know survivors had escaped the burning wreckage.

Lyre Rysalis, master weaver of Chrysalis, was dead, and soon his family and all of Hades would know.

ZWI SWEPT downward. The dark ground rushed to meet them with more speed than Clio would have liked before the dragon flared her wings. Zwi met the ground in a rolling trot to absorb the last of her momentum.

The instant the dragon stopped, Lyre slid off with a shaky exhale. As she hopped down after him, she remembered he didn't like heights.

They'd landed near a hill, the ley line waiting on the other side. Patting Zwi on the shoulder, Clio looked across the river where a faint orange glow marked the Ivory Tower's top.

"So, you made it."

Choking back a scream, she whipped around. Ash stood a few paces away, back in glamour. He seemed unharmed—or at least no more harmed than when she'd last healed him. In a flare of black fire, Zwi shrank down to dragonet size and sprang onto his shoulder.

He scanned Lyre from head to toe, taking in the countless cuts scoring his limbs. "Alive again?"

"Mostly." Lyre glanced around the dark, marshy hillside. "Where's Madrigal?"

Ash jerked his thumb over his shoulder, pointing toward the ley line. "Unconscious. *Spelled* unconscious," he added at Lyre's worried look. "I'll wake him up in Asphodel so he can report immediately."

"Good." Lyre arched an eyebrow. "So, the only three people who know I didn't die are right here."

"Three might be too many."

Lyre shrugged. "I think I can trust you two."

Surprise flickered in Ash's eyes, then the faintest smile curved his lips, gone so fast Clio wasn't sure if she'd imagined it. "Get lost, incubus, and stay that way."

With no more farewell than that, he walked off. His dragonet looked over her shoulder and trilled sadly, then they both disappeared into the inky darkness.

Glancing at Kokytos, Lyre sighed. "Well, that *almost* went to plan."

"It could have been a lot worse," she murmured.

"It would have been, if not for you. Your weave worked perfectly."

She stepped closer and touched his cheek with gentle fingers. Then she smiled teasingly. "You defeated your father. Does that make *you* the deadliest weaver in the three realms now?"

He laughed, then pressed a hand to his punctured gut, wincing. "No, I don't think it does."

She wrapped her arm around his waist. "As soon as we're out of the Underworld, I'll heal your wounds."

Shadows gathered in his eyes. "Where are we going next?"

She looked toward the unseen ley line as sharp sorrow awakened in her chest, compressing her lungs.

"Irida," she whispered. "It's time to go home."

THIRTY-TWO

FOR THE SECOND TIME, Clio sat at the head of the table in the royal council room. Beside her, in Rouvin's former seat, Petrina held her chin high as though trying to stretch a little taller. The huge table and heavy chair made her diminutive frame seem even more frail.

"After careful consideration," the oldest of the royal advisors announced, "the council has determined a regent is required to rule in Princess Petrina's stead until she comes of age in her twenty-first year."

Clio let her gaze move slowly across the twelve advisors. The four who had gone to Aldrendahar with Rouvin, and who had returned with his body, had the palest faces.

"It is the duty of the council to elect a suitable regent," the elderly advisor continued. "We will vote based on nominations made by the councilors."

"I nominate Councilor Philemon," a nymph said immediately. "He has served on the council for over forty years and loyally supported King Rouvin, may his spirit rest peacefully, and his father before him."

Several advisors nodded in solemn support. Clio kept her expression neutral as Philemon, the second eldest of the councilors, raised one hand in gracious thanks.

Under the table, small fingers closed around Clio's, squeezing tightly. Petrina straightened even more, somehow lifting her chin another inch. Her blue eyes were bright despite the dark circles bruising the pale skin underneath them.

"I nominate Princess Clio Nereid as regent," she declared in a ringing voice.

Clio's hand tightened convulsively around Petrina's. Silence pressed down on the room as the advisors glanced at one another, nervousness vibrating between them.

Philemon coughed delicately. "Your Highness, I must advise caution. Lady Clio's unusual heritage could be used as a claim upon the throne. Assigning her power as a regent—"

"King Rouvin's will was clear," another advisor interrupted. "And *Princess* Clio has accepted his determination that Princess Petrina's right to the throne takes precedence."

"Be that as it may—"

"I'm not withdrawing my nomination," Petrina cut in firmly. "Princess Clio is the best possible regent and the only one I'll support."

The eldest nymph cleared his throat. "Princess Petrina, the decision does fall upon the council. However, we will take your preference into consideration."

Clio's stomach clenched sickeningly. She and Petrina didn't look at each other as the advisors discussed Clio's credentials—which, aside from a tentative rapport with Miysis Ra, were none—versus Philemon's. No other candidates were suggested.

"Let us vote, then," the elderly nymph stated. "All those—"

"One moment," Petrina interrupted. "Since Councilor Philemon's been nominated, he can't vote, can he?"

"Ah," the old advisor murmured. "A pertinent observation. Councilor Philemon?"

The nymph glanced around the table. "I will abstain."

"Very well. The vote, then. All in favor of Princess Clio Nereid assuming regency of the throne?"

A heartbeat passed where no one moved.

In almost perfect unison, all four advisors who'd accompanied Rouvin to Aldrendahar placed their hands, palms down, on the tabletop. The nymph who had defended Clio also placed his hand on the wood. Five votes supporting Clio, while six advisors sat motionless.

Philemon smiled faintly.

Then the elderly councilor stretched out a wrinkled hand and placed it on the table. "Majority vote in favor of Clio Nereid."

Under the table, Petrina squeezed Clio's hand so hard her fingers ached. She gripped just as tightly, fighting to stay calm.

"Princess Clio." The councilor turned to her. "Do you accept the position of regent, ruler of Irida in Princess Petrina's stead, for the next ten years until she takes the throne upon her twenty-first year?"

Clio looked from face to solemn face: the elderly leader of the council waiting patiently for her answer; Philemon with his expression frozen in a stony stare; the four councilors who'd witnessed the battle in Aldrendahar watching her expectantly.

Finally, she looked at Petrina. The girl's eyes blazed with triumph above hollow cheeks, her complexion too pale even for an ivory-skinned nymph. But beneath her exhilaration, vulnerability lurked — the shadows of doubt and fear.

Clio took Petrina's hand in both of hers, holding the girl's cold fingers tightly.

"Princess Clio," the elderly councilor prompted, his voice quiet and grave. "Do you accept?"

Whichever choice she made, it would change her life forever. Whichever path she chose, her heart would suffer.

But, deep in her soul, she knew there was only one answer she could give.

CAREFULLY CLOSING the door to the council room, Clio pressed her back against the wood, eyes squeezed shut. She concentrated on breathing, on controlling the panic bubbling up inside her. It was done. There was no going back.

She pushed away from the door. Her steps grew faster and faster as she sped through the palace halls, her dark brown skirts fluttering around her legs. The council meeting had immediately followed Rouvin's parting ceremony, and Clio still wore the colors of mourning—deep browns to match the earth that welcomed the deceased back into the cycle of death and rebirth.

The palace guards straightened as she swept past, a reaction she wasn't used to. No one had paid much attention to her when she'd been a lady-in-waiting.

She passed through courtyards and verandas, heading toward the farthest wing of the palace: the rarely used northeast tower. A familiar pair of nymphs stood in front of the tower door—two of Rouvin's bodyguards, now without a king to protect. Petrina had her own devoted guardians, so upon Clio's return to Irida, they had offered their services to *her* instead.

She nodded to them as she slipped through the door. Her steps echoing on the tiles, she crossed the main hall and out into the courtyard on the far side.

The garden was overgrown, but the wildness was more beautiful to her than manicured squares. She pushed aside the hanging branches of a willow-like tree and walked toward the stone parapet that marked the courtyard's edge.

Beyond it, the mountainside dropped away. The view of the capital spreading across the slope below was spectacular, but nothing compared to the miles of forested wilderness dotted with towns, villages, and farms. Far to the west, the sprawling peaks of the Kyo Kawa mountains were a shadow against the clear blue sky.

Lyre leaned against the railing, both elbows braced on the stone. After three days of rest, his complexion had returned to its usual bronze tan, the color brought out even more by his dark red garments. He wore a chimera-style outfit—a sleeveless jerkin belted in the front and fitted, leather pants and boots.

At her approach, he turned. She didn't slow, walking right into his arms and pressing her face into his chest. His arms closed around her.

"Lyre," she whispered, her voice cracking.

He ran his hand down her hair. "How did it go?"

"The parting ceremony was lovely," she answered, knowing that wasn't what he was asking about. "The entire city came to say goodbye."

"I could see the crowds from up here."

She glanced toward the open meadow in the valley where thousands of nymphs had gathered to pay their respects to the fallen king. A tear slipped down her cheek and she quickly brushed it away.

"What about the council meeting?" Lyre asked.

She pulled herself tighter against him, terrified to let go.

"We were right that they would elect a regent," she whispered. She and Lyre had discussed every possibility over the last three days. "They voted … and … they chose me."

She started to shake and he crushed her to his chest. The feeling — being held in his arms, his warmth, his cherry scent — pushed her over the edge and a sob shuddered through her.

"Clio," he whispered.

"I accepted," she wept. "I'm so sorry, Lyre. I couldn't leave Petrina alone. She needs me."

He slid a hand into her hair, holding her as she cried.

"The only other candidate was Philemon," she explained desperately, fighting to control her sobbing so she could speak. "He would have controlled everything and never let Petrina make a single decision. He's extremely traditional and he might have —"

"I know," Lyre murmured. "Clio, I understand."

She sucked in a trembling breath. He cupped her cheek, his thumb rubbing away a trail of tears.

"I knew if they offered you the regency, you would take it." He leaned down, his mouth brushing across her lips, then her tear-streaked cheek. "You aren't the type of woman who could abandon her sister and her kingdom. You would never be happy skulking around Earth with me while Petrina was alone, her entire family lost."

"Stay here with me, then."

Pain tightened his face as he looked away. Fresh tears slid down her cheeks.

He couldn't stay here, and they both knew it.

Before Aldrendahar and Kokytos, maybe Lyre could have hidden away in a remote corner of Irida. But not anymore. A single rumor could ruin everything. If Hades, and therefore Chrysalis, heard of an incubus connected to the nymph territory, they would jump to one conclusion: the deceased master weaver who'd fled Asphodel with a nymph wasn't dead after all.

Clio, as Irida's regent, would have eyes on her constantly—not just nymphs and chimeras, but dignitaries, emissaries, and rulers from across the Overworld. No matter where Lyre was or how far he fled, if she went near him, she would bring all that attention with her. Seeing him at all would mean risking his life.

Lyre rested his cheek against the top of her head, his arms tight around her.

"I can't stay here," he murmured. "We knew all along I couldn't. Incubi stand out wherever we go, and the only way I can disappear for good is to become just like them. Just one more anonymous, skirt-chasing incubus. That means going where there are other incubi."

She pulled back sharply. "You don't mean that horrible ladies club in Kokytos, do you?"

He let out a surprised laugh. "No, I don't plan to go anywhere near Kokytos. I don't plan to go back to the Underworld at all."

"I want to be with you."

"You belong here, Clio. You need to be here."

Vise-like pain crushed her heart. "But if you leave, we won't … we'll never …"

"Never?" He caught her chin, tilting her face up to his. "*Never* is a very long time."

His mouth closed over hers, soft but urgent. She kissed him desperately, her arms clamping around his neck.

"You don't have to go yet, do you?" she asked, her eyes stinging with the threat of more tears.

"No," he whispered, pulling her lips back to his. "I don't have to leave yet."

THIRTY~THREE

PERCHED ON A ROCK with the late afternoon sunlight warming her face, Clio nibbled on a piece of cheese. A basket sat beside her, fruits and nuts waiting to be sampled. The large lunch it had originally carried was long gone.

Beams of golden light streaked through the trees, making the red and orange foliage glow. Leaves fluttered down to join their fallen comrades or landed on the rippling pond, the current churning from the short, tiered waterfall on its far side. The crystalline liquid sparkled, reflecting the green light of fireflies dancing above it.

A splash shattered the ripples and scattered the fireflies as Lyre stood up. Water ran from his hair and trailed down his bare torso, following every delicious line of his body, hard muscles sheathed in golden-tan skin. Standing in the waist-deep water, he scrubbed both hands through his hair.

Popping the last bite of cheese in her mouth, she wondered if he'd intentionally mussed his hair in the sexiest way possible, or if it was a fluke. Either way, she silently enjoyed the view as he splashed more water over his arms. He looked perfectly clean to her, but if he wanted to keep up the show, she wasn't going to complain.

As though reading her thoughts, his amber eyes flicked to her. "I can't believe you did that."

"Did what?" she asked innocently.

"You should have warned me."

"I thought it was obvious."

"*Obvious* that the harmless-looking shrub would explode into a cloud of pollen at the slightest disturbance?"

She gave a dainty shrug, her chin still resting on her hand. "I told you not to touch anything in Overworld forests."

His eyes narrowed. She smiled at him, fighting to suppress a laugh. If she'd realized he was about to walk into the shrub, she *would* have warned him. But she hadn't noticed his doomed trajectory any more than he had, because he'd been sliding his hand up her skirt as he told her in a deep, hypnotic purr about what he planned to do next.

"You should have been paying attention to where you were going," she added unhelpfully. He scowled, but despite the ominous expression, his eyes sparkled.

He raised his hand and crooked a finger. "Come here."

"Uh-uh. I don't need to wash a garden's worth of pollen out of *my* hair."

His eyes darkened and power threaded into his voice. "*Clio.*"

She arched her eyebrows, pretending to be unaffected even as luscious heat spilled through her. "Using aphrodesia on me? That's cheating."

"I would never do such a thing."

Stifling a giggle, she gave him a stern look. "Aphrodesia is entirely inappropriate."

"What I'm going to do once you're in here with me—*that* will be inappropriate."

Her whole body flushed in anticipation and she had to work to keep her breathless excitement hidden. She fluttered her fingers at the water lapping just below the rock where she sat. "But I'm not getting in."

"No?" Magic sparked over his fingers.

"Lyre—" she began warningly.

The glowing golden rope looped around her waist and he yanked it. She flew off the rock and plunged into the cool water.

Popping up again, her clothes drenched, she spluttered. "I can't believe you—"

He reached her in three strides through the water, swept her against his bare chest, and kissed her. She melted against him, heat diving through her as his tongue slipped between her lips.

When she was so breathless she could barely stand, he finally lifted his head. "You were saying?"

"My clothes are wet."

"Good thing you don't need clothes."

His mouth closed over hers again as his hands found the ties of her shirt, laced in the back. In moments, his dexterous fingers were pulling it over her head. Her skirt disappeared just as quickly.

An hour later, the sky blazed orange, the setting suns already out of sight below the tree line. She lay tucked against Lyre's side on their picnic blanket, blissfully relaxed as he trailed his hand up and down her bare back. Eyes half closed, she ran her fingers through his hair as leaves fluttered down from the overhanging branches.

Summer had faded into autumn over the weeks since they'd returned from Kokytos. She had spent most of that time in the Iridian palace, busily preparing for her new role as regent by day and sneaking into Lyre's sequestered tower by night.

Their time together had slipped by too quickly, full of moonlight walks through the gardens and along remote mountain paths behind the tower, hilarious shared meals where she'd bring him the strangest Overworld foods she could find in the capital, and passionate nights where they would make love, catch their breath, then start all over again. They had been the best weeks of her life.

And now they were over.

Tomorrow was Petrina's coronation, to be immediately followed by Clio's official appointment as regent. Lyre shouldn't have stayed this long. Irida's neighbors and allies from across the Overworld were already flooding into the capital to witness the coronation—nobility and royalty from dozens of castes. Miysis, two of his sisters, and an assembly of griffin nobles were arriving first thing in the morning.

Tomorrow, everything would change for her. She would become the new ruler of Irida, and she would be Petrina's shield against the ambitions of others while also easing the princess into her future role. Clio could feel the weight of responsibility settling over her. A few months ago, she would have been petrified at the prospect of ruling Irida, but after everything she'd been through, she felt determination more than anxiety. She was prepared to face the coming challenges, but not excited—not when it meant losing Lyre.

Their last day together. She'd tried so hard not to think about it.

That morning, before dawn had touched the sky, she'd collected supplies and together, she and Lyre had snuck out of the city and into the countryside. She'd led him into the wild forests, and they'd explored game trails and discovered streams and waterfalls as they meandered west.

Now the suns were setting, the day over. Half a mile west, at the edge of the forest, was a ley line—the spot where Lyre would leave the Overworld and never return.

Before she knew it, hot tears were streaking down her cheeks.

"Clio …" Lyre whispered, his voice almost soundless.

"I'm sorry," she choked. "I didn't mean to cry."

He ran his hand down her back. The cooling breeze washed over her bare skin and she pulled the blanket around them as she tilted her head up. His amber eyes lingered on her face as though memorizing her features.

She touched his cheek where his family mark was hidden beneath glamour. "Lyre, I don't want this to be the end for us. This *can't* be the end."

He let out a slow breath, his chest rising and falling under her arm. "As much as I don't want to, I have to leave."

"I know." She pressed her hand against his face. "When Petrina turns twenty-one, I'll step down as regent. I won't be a public figure anymore."

His eyebrows furrowed.

"Ten years," she said. "In ten years, when my regency is over, maybe things will be different. What if by then you don't have to hide so carefully? What if by then I can leave Irida?"

"Do you *want* to leave Irida?" he asked doubtfully. "Living on Earth won't be easy."

"Ten years, Lyre. So much can change. I don't want this goodbye to be forever." Pushing up on her elbow, she leaned over him, her hair falling like curtains around her face. "I know it's a long time, but I can wait."

"Wait?" He shook his head. "You're right, it's a long time. People change."

Was he worried that he would change, or that she would?

"Can't we try again?" she whispered. "When I'm free from the regency, let's find each other."

He touched her lips, tracing their shape. "What if our feelings change?"

"What if they don't?"

Scorching intensity gathered in his stare. "You want to meet again in ten years? No matter what happens between then and now?"

"No matter what. We'll find each other again—and we'll figure out a way to be together. We'll make it work."

"Are you sure?"

She leaned down and pressed her mouth hard to his. He kissed her back, deep and intense.

"Do you promise, Lyre?" she asked breathlessly. "Do you promise to come back to me in ten years?"

Something fierce hardened his features, an unyielding determination she'd only glimpsed in him a few times.

"I promise." He captured her wrist and pressed her hand to the center of his chest. "My heart is yours. No other woman has touched it, and no one but you ever will."

Her hand trembled, his heartbeat thudding under her palm. She knew what he was saying. He was an incubus; ten years of celibacy was impossible for him. Even if he could do it, it would be unjustifiable torture.

But though he couldn't save his body for her, he would save his heart. That was his promise.

She looked into his mesmerizing amber eyes. "My heart is yours. Forever."

The amber darkened, then his lips were crushing hers. He rolled on top of her, his hands in her hair, holding their mouths together. Her hands slid over him with equal urgency, committing every inch of him to memory—memories that would have to last her a decade.

Until that distant day, this was their last time together. Love and grief twisted with urgency, and she couldn't breathe for the emotions constricting her lungs. Need more intense, more painful, more soul-searing than anything his aphrodesia could inflict burned through her.

As the last of the sunlight faded into murky twilight, as the forest turned azure with the glow of awakening night flora, they made love one last time beneath the trees.

With darkness settling over the forest, she and Lyre redressed and collected their things. Hands entwined, the silence between them heavy with the weight of their hearts, they walked through the luminescent flowers until the trees gave way to an open glade.

Rising from the tall grass, the ley line danced and rippled in waves of blue and green light. The soft power rushed across her senses as she and Lyre stopped a few long steps from the line. She tightened her hand on his, chin held high as she determinedly blinked back tears.

He turned to her. "Ten years from now, on the autumn solstice, I'll be here."

"I'll be waiting."

Cupping her face, he brought his mouth to hers. Slowly he kissed her, each press of his lips so intense she wouldn't have been surprised if he was weaving a spell to bind their souls together across the realms.

Finally, he raised his head. His thumb brushed across her lower lip as he let his hands fall. Her skin felt so cold in the absence of his touch.

"Be safe, Lyre," she whispered. "Take care of yourself."

"You too, Clio."

She touched a hand to her chest, over her heart. "In ten years."

"In ten years," he whispered.

When he walked away, she trembled with the need to reach for him, her hands clenched at her sides. Reaching the ley line, he turned and stepped backward into the green and blue light. His eyes met hers.

He brought his hand up and touched his heart, mirroring her gesture. Then the rush of earthly power stuttered.

Between one instant and the next, he was gone.

A tremor tore through her, but she straightened her spine. Turning, she looked east toward the glittering stars and glowing face of the planet. Beneath those stars, the Iridian palace was perched upon its mountainside. For the next ten years, she would devote herself to Petrina and her kingdom.

After that, on the autumn solstice ten years from this day, she would wait right here for the moment Lyre returned to her.

THIRTY~FOUR

ONE PERK of being an incubus was supposed to be an immunity to heartbreak. Lyre still didn't know how that had gone wrong for him.

He rubbed his hands together, then blew on them, his breath puffing white in the cold air. Soft white flakes drifted from the sky, twirling toward the snow-dusted ground. Heavy darkness lay over the abandoned park, broken only by a flickering pair of lampposts.

A couple weeks out of the Overworld and he was still moping. Then again, he didn't have much to celebrate. But beneath the unpleasant gloom was a hot spark of hope. He would cling to Clio's promise through however many shitty days, weeks, and months awaited him.

Ten years wasn't that long compared to a lifetime.

In a decade, his family should have well and truly forgotten about him, and once Clio was out of the spotlight as regent, maybe it would be safe for her and Lyre to find their own little corner of the realms where his past couldn't reach them. Maybe. He could hope. He was going to hope.

He blew on his hands again, wishing he could stomp his feet to ward off the cold. But making noise would defeat the purpose of standing in the deep shadows beneath the trees as he watched the little circle of empty pavement with a single rickety wrought-iron bench.

From what he'd carefully gleaned, the bounty on his head had been dismissed and most of the mercenaries who'd flocked to the city to hunt him had dispersed again. It was almost pleasantly quiet, and he was getting better at the whole anonymity thing.

He'd had a lot of practice pretending to be something he wasn't. In Chrysalis, he'd encouraged his brothers to see him as careless and flippant, a sloppy smartass who didn't care about anything. A few tweaks to that persona and he could easily fit into the role of a harmless flirt, rolling about the city with no purpose, picking up jobs here and there while hitting on every pair of pretty legs that passed by.

To the rest of the world, he would become an average incubus with average abilities. But first, he had one more loose end to take care of.

As he rubbed his chilled hands together again, a shadow slipped out of the trees. The daemon, wrapped in a warm coat with the hood pulled up, stopped near the bench and surveyed the spot.

Lyre stepped into the circle of light emanating from the lampposts. The daemon turned to him, and as he tilted his head up, the orange glow caught on jewel-like green eyes.

"I wasn't sure you'd come," Lyre said.

Miysis pushed his hood back a bit, revealing glamour-short blond hair, cropped close to his head. "How could I resist an invitation from a dead man?"

Lyre arched an eyebrow in question.

"When I inquired about your fate," Miysis explained, "the esteemed Regent of Irida informed me that you perished in a confrontation with Chrysalis weavers. Then she handed me your letter and gave me the sort of look that promised extreme and long-lasting punishment if I screwed up." The griffin rubbed one gloved hand over his jaw. "What especially intrigued me was that, when she said you'd died, she wasn't lying."

"The incubus weaver who was running around Aldrendahar casting spells and blowing shit up did die. He's gone for good."

"Is that so? Who are you, then?"

"Someone else."

Miysis's expression smoothed into his unreadable princely countenance. "I see."

"If another griffin asks you what happened to that incubus, what will you say?"

"I'll tell them the only thing I know: Clio said he died and she was speaking the truth."

Lyre nodded, managing not to flinch at Clio's name.

"So, weaver whom I've never met, why did you summon me here?"

"I have a proposal for you."

"What might that be?" Miysis asked, almost wary.

Lyre concealed his nervousness. He didn't like this idea one bit, but he was at his limit. Broke, homeless, and straight up lacking in any resources or connections, he wouldn't last through the winter without taking drastic steps.

"A dead man can't sell his skills to just anyone." He waited a beat for Miysis to catch his meaning. "Would you be interested in the services of a Chrysalis-quality spell weaver?"

The griffin's eyes widened in disbelief. "What exactly are you offering?"

"I'm open to the possibility of making myself semi-regularly available to take commissions … at something of a discount compared to the usual rates."

Miysis rocked back on his heels as he no doubt ran through the many possibilities.

"Caveats," Lyre added. "I won't weave anything designed to kill, maim, torture, etcetera. I can refuse to weave anything I don't want to weave."

Miysis nodded thoughtfully, well aware that Lyre's arsenal was impressive even without those sorts of weaves. "On one condition. You will weave *only* for me. You'll take no other paying clients, though obviously you can make and give away whatever magic you please."

Lyre frowned. "That's extremely limiting."

Miysis's lips curved into a cool smile and his eyes gleamed with sharp cunning that sent a chill through Lyre.

"I have more than enough work to keep you busy, if busy is what you want to be. I don't know what Chrysalis charges for custom work, but I'll pay to ensure you remain committed to my commissions alone."

And by doing that, he would ensure none of Lyre's weavings ended up in the hands of Ra enemies or political opponents.

"This arrangement will exist entirely between you and me," Lyre said. "No one else can know about it. If we encounter each other outside our planned meetings—"

"We don't know each other and have never met." Miysis's eyes darkened to the color of a twilight forest. "I can't be known to associate with an Underworld weaver, especially one from Chrysalis. Depending on the circumstances, that could mean I would have to act against you—or kill you."

Well, at least the prince was honest. "Noted."

"It would be safer if you stayed clear of me otherwise."

"That shouldn't be difficult." Lyre extended his hand. "Do we have an agreement?"

Miysis grasped his hand and shook it.

Lyre stuck his frozen fingers in his coat pockets. "I'll see what I can come up with for how we'll communicate and arrange meetings."

The prince nodded. "Speaking of communication, I'll request my first commission now."

Lyre's eyebrows shot up. That was fast.

"I need spells for coordinating teams over long distances … discreetly."

"In what context, exactly?"

Miysis glanced around the empty park as though expecting to find spies hanging from the tree branches. "I'm searching for something … but some of my people are entrenched in such a way that they can't report to me and I can't track their movements."

"Hmm. I already have a spell set that might work, but I'll see if I can tweak it to be less conspicuous."

"Excellent." Miysis reached into his coat pocket and withdrew a pouch. "This is all I have on me, so consider it a down payment."

Lyre accepted the bag and peeked inside. Controlling his expression, he slipped it into his pocket. With one "down payment," his money woes were taken care of for, oh, the next six months at least.

Relieved he wouldn't starve, he arranged to meet with Miysis in three months. After that, they would probably connect only once or twice a year—just often enough to swap completed work for new commissions.

Plans made, Miysis pulled his hood up again. "By the way, I heard an interesting rumor—a very expensive one obtained from an exclusive Underworld informant."

"Oh?"

Green eyes gleamed from the shadows of his hood. "A couple months ago, the head of Chrysalis was killed—by his own son, apparently." A moment of silence. "The son died too, or so I heard."

Lyre raised an eyebrow. "Sounds terribly tragic."

"Terribly." Miysis smiled, pulled the collar of his coat up to block the wind, and walked off into the swirling snow.

Rolling his tense shoulders, Lyre watched him go. Damn. Well, keeping secrets from the griffin prince probably wouldn't have worked in the long run anyway. He weighed the pouch of coins in his pocket, his thoughts shifting to other matters.

Miysis had mentioned Clio, but he hadn't said how she was doing. Lyre hadn't asked, and he hoped she wouldn't come up in future conversations with the griffin. Ten years. He would never survive that long if he dwelled on her all the time. He needed to bury her deep in his thoughts, along with the rest of his past, and he would only think of her when he needed a reminder of what he was fighting for.

He watched the snow melting on the pavement. His financial problems were solved, but he still needed to figure out the rest—where to live, how to survive as a nobody, how to move around the city unnoticed. He didn't know how to do any of that.

Funny thing, though. He happened to know someone who was well versed in surviving on the outskirts of society. And Lyre just so happened to be borrowing that particular daemon's dingy apartment while he was otherwise homeless.

He hummed a quiet, thoughtful note. Hands in his pockets, he walked out of the park. Snow swirled quietly, muffling sound as he made his way through the downtown streets. Giving the Ra embassy a wide berth, he headed along a street that would take him to the neglected apartment complex.

A flutter of sound in the muted night.

Wings flapping, a small dragon swept out of the snowy darkness and landed on Lyre's shoulder. He blinked in surprise as she folded her wings and trilled a quiet greeting. Her tail swished, thumping against his back.

Arctic panic slammed into him. Lyre managed not to stagger, keeping his pace steady. With a deep *whoosh* of displaced air, huge dragon wings swept wide as the draconian dropped out of the sky.

His wings shimmered out of existence as he landed lightly beside Lyre and fell into step without missing a beat. Lyre kept moving, their strides perfectly matched.

"You messed with my wards," Ash said without even a greeting first, as though only days had passed since they'd last spoken.

"Your wards were terrible. I replaced them."

"I can't get into *my* apartment."

"I wasn't expecting you back so soon." Lyre shrugged, accidentally dislodging Zwi. She chattered in annoyance as she hopped onto her master's shoulder instead. "You weren't using the place, so ..."

"I don't care if you use it, but get rid of the damn wards."

"I have a better idea. I'll just teach you my wards."

Ash's stride faltered slightly.

"Yours suck," Lyre added, in case the draconian had missed it the first time.

Scowling, Ash brushed his snow-dusted hair from his face. "I don't want your help, incubus."

"Consider it a trade. You let me crash in your apartment, and I'll upgrade your weaving skills."

When Ash didn't argue, Lyre quashed a smile. Though the draconian was under Samael's command and could only visit Earth while on assignment, he and Lyre could learn a lot from each other. A mutual exchange of skills—and, for Lyre at least, an occasional friendly face among the masses of strangers he could never trust.

Well, *almost* friendly. Close enough.

As they passed beneath a glowing streetlamp, the only light source on the block, Ash slowed to a stop. "Did you destroy it?"

"Destroy what?"

The draconian's stare turned steely.

Lyre smirked. Passing Ash, he ambled a few more steps down the street. "I took care of it."

He turned to find Ash hadn't moved, the crease between his dark eyebrows cast into sharp relief by the light above. The shadow weave's fate wasn't something Lyre intended to discuss with anyone. Along with the method of its creation, the secret would die with him.

"Before any weaving lessons," he said seriously, slipping his hands into his pockets, "I think there's something else we should figure out."

Ash's frown deepened. "What's that?"

Lyre glanced at the snowy sky and sighed. "One of us should probably learn to cook."

A snorting laugh escaped Ash, his eyes flashing to a pale gray Lyre hadn't seen before. The draconian's smile was brief but genuine, and Lyre grinned in response. The gloomy weight in his chest eased a little.

Ash started forward and Lyre fell into step beside him. Together, they strode into the night, leaving the lonely glow of the streetlamp behind.

LYRE & ASH'S ADVENTURES CONTINUE IN
THE STEEL & STONE SERIES

LYRE & CLIO'S STORY CONTINUES IN
THE BLACKFIRE SERIES

THE BLOOD CURSE

BONUS EPILOGUE

Want more of Lyre and Clio? Join them five years later in the bonus epilogue.

Download your copy at
www.annettemarie.ca/bloodcurse-bonus

ABOUT THE AUTHOR

Annette Marie is the author of YA urban fantasy series *Steel & Stone*, its prequel trilogy *Spell Weaver*, and romantic fantasy trilogy *Red Winter*.

Her first love is fantasy, but fast-paced adventures, bold heroines, and tantalizing forbidden romances are her guilty pleasures. She proudly admits she has a thing for dragons, and her editor has politely inquired as to whether she intends to include them in every book.

Annette lives in the frozen winter wasteland of Alberta, Canada (okay, it's not quite that bad) and shares her life with her husband and their furry minion of darkness—sorry, cat—Caesar. When not writing, she can be found elbow-deep in one art project or another while blissfully ignoring all adult responsibilities.

Find out more at www.annettemare.ca

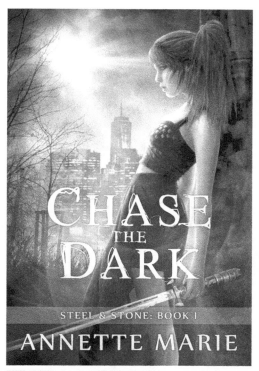

 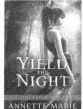   

THE STEEL & STONE SERIES

Five years after the Spell Weaver trilogy, the story continues ...

The first rule for an apprentice Consul is *don't trust daemons*. But when Piper is framed for the theft of the Sahar Stone, she ends up with two troublesome daemons as her only allies: Lyre, a hotter-than-hell incubus who isn't as harmless as he seems, and Ash, a draconian mercenary with a seriously bad reputation. Trusting them might be her biggest mistake yet.

www.annettemarie.ca/steelandstone

To save her world, Piper will need Ash's strength, Lyre's cunning, and Clio's magic ... but even that might not be enough.

Ten years ago, Clio and Lyre fought to protect the realms in *Spell Weaver*. Five years ago, Piper and Ash battled the evil of Hades in *Steel & Stone*.

Now, the story continues in an all-new series that will bring Piper, Ash, Lyre, and Clio together for the first time.

BLACKFIRE

Sequel to Spell Weaver and Steel & Stone

www.annettemarie.ca/blackfire

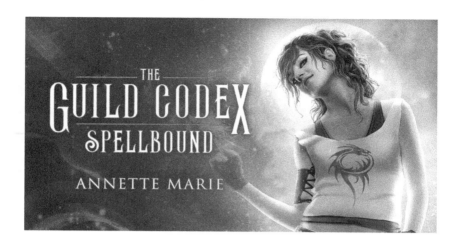

A new urban fantasy series by Annette Marie

Meet Tori.

She's feisty. She's broke. She has a bit of an issue with running her mouth off. And she just landed a job at the local magic guild.

Problem is, she's also 100% human. Oops.

THE GUILD CODEX: SPELLBOUND
Coming Fall 2018

www.annettemarie.ca/guildcodex

THE RED WINTER TRILOGY

A destiny written by the gods. A fate forged in lies.

In this exotic, enchanting fantasy, Emi Kimura's life as a mortal will soon end, and her new existence as the host of a goddess will begin. But when she discovers that her long-awaited fate is not what she was led to believe, she makes a dangerous bargain with a *yokai*—a spirit of the earth and an enemy of the goddess she will soon host—to find the truth. As her final days as a mortal approach, she must choose whether to bow to duty … or fight for her life.

"Red Winter completely immerses readers in a beautiful world mined from the richly fertile and varied landscape of Japanese myths and mythos." – Flylef Reviews

"Vivid, beautiful characters that ripped my heart out at times … and a fantasy world that has enough realistic touches to be relatable." – Red Hot Books

"It was a thrill to go on these adventures with all these amazing characters and fantastical creatures and learn more about the world." – Linsey Reads

www.annettemarie.ca/redwinter

CPSIA information can be obtained
at www.ICGtesting.com
Printed in the USA
LVHW091737251019
635356LV00002B/315/P